CW01072649

*To Pat am
with Best h
from Te*

July 2008.

Crinkles Academy for Wizards

by

Edward Grieves Dunn

**Grosvenor House
Publishing Limited**

This book is published by
Grosvenor House Publishing Ltd
28-30 High Street, Guildford, Surrey, GU1 3HY.
www.grosvenorhousepublishing.co.uk

The characters and events in this book are fictitious.
Any similarity to real persons, living or dead,
is coincidental and not intended by the author.

A CIP record for this book
is available from the British Library

ISBN 978-1-906210-98-4

Dedication

*This book is dedicated to the
Memory of Maria Dunn.*

1943-1997

*Who made the lives of all those
who met her the happier for it.*

*It is also dedicated to
Children everywhere who are seriously ill in Hospital
or at Home, and to those dear Children
who have neither a Hospital nor a Home to go to.*

*This book may make no money, but if it does,
the author's share will now and
forever be donated to help seriously ill Children.*

*Initially this will be donated
to Children's Leukaemia Research.*

Prologue

"Jenny run faster!! Run faster!! They're going to catch us."

"I can't." Panted Jenny, "I can hardly breath and the pains in my chest and legs are getting worse, I've got to stop."

"No!! No!! Don't stop, try to run faster Jenny, Try!!" Gasped David.

"You get away David and find some help."

"I'm not leaving you."

"You must!! Go on bring help."

David reluctantly increased his speed he could barely get any air into his lungs and his legs felt like lead.

He glanced back over his shoulder. Jenny had stopped running and the two men had nearly caught up to her. David looked forward wondering which direction to go in, there was a street junction up ahead crowded with people. If the two men stopped when they reached Jenny that would give him time to reach the people at the junction and run amongst them, he would be lost from view and hopefully give them the slip and it would give him time to try and sort out in his mind what to do next.

He glanced again over his shoulder and was dismayed to see that only one man had stopped to grab Jenny, the other one had ran straight on past her and was gaining on David. Turning his head back David ran slap bang into a lady.

"S—-sorry." He stuttered, and regaining his balance he was about to dart off once again but the lady was holding on to him.

David struggled as violently as he could in an attempt to break free.

"Let me go! Let me go!" He cried.

But she held him in a grip of steel.

"Oh I think not." She said in a soft friendly voice.

David stopped struggling and looked up into her face, it was not soft or friendly, his blood turned to ice. It was the most frightening face he had ever seen.

The alarm clock on the small cabinet next to David's bed went off, startled he jumped up in bed, it was 7a.m. He wasn't sure where he was, a cold sweat swept over him, looking around he tried to get his bearings, he sighed with relief as he recognised the dorm and the other boys whose alarms were going off now, some sat up in bed stretching and a couple of boys were already out of bed.

This is real, isn't it? Yes this is real, I must have been dreaming thought David.

During the mid morning break David told me about his dream and how with only slight variations he had the same dream nearly every night. I told him I would mention it to the Headmaster at the first opportunity.

At lunchtime I was able to talk to the Head and he suggested we all gathered in his study as early as possible after the Evening meal.

It was my job to inform everyone and at 7.30p.m David, Jenny, Smithers, Miss. Millthrop and myself Brian had all gathered in the Headmasters (Dr.Phillpotts) study.

The Head welcomed us all and asked David to describe his reoccurring nightmare. When David had finished we all sat quiet for a while then the Head told us that for some time he had intended having a get together.

He felt that because so much had happened to so many people in such a short length of time that some things disappeared into the corners of our minds, and in the future may reappear, disjointed and muddled up in dreams and nightmares.

Although I agree with what the Head said, I couldn't help wondering was there another explanation, was it an insight into the future? There was this feeling in my bones that everything had become too normal, too quiet too soon.

It was as though nothing had happened, but of course it had and only a few days ago, I couldn't help thinking about what may happen next.

The Head went on to tell us that having thought over many times in the past few days the recent incredible events that had involved all of us and Crinkles, that after a great deal of consideration he felt the best solution was that we meet twice a week in his study after our evening meal. This would enable each of us to tell the others what they had experienced. It was crucial he felt that this was done in the correct order the events had taken place so that a complete picture could be built up, and very little if anything of importance would be left out.

We all agreed, and so here is the story of Crinkles Academy for Wizards. From the start of the adventures through to the return of David, Jenny and the Head from New York, as told by those of us who met on so many evenings in the Head's cosy study.

Contents

CHAPTER ONE

Crinkles Academy

Who would have thought that Crinkles Academy 'Held The Most Powerful Secret On Earth'.

Dusty, quiet, peaceful Crinkles, nothing ever happens at Crinkles, well for centuries nothing ever happened until the Summer Term when David and Jenny joined the School.

May I introduce myself and say "Hello". My name is Brian. I'm the School caretaker come handyman and the job of story-teller has been given to me. I can be easily confused and often forget names, so I've always thought that a story should begin at the beginning, and so does the Headmaster, so blame him that we don't jump straight in at exciting bits.

You see we don't want you to be just a reader of a story. We want you to feel that you're a pupil at Crinkles and that you also took part in the adventures.

So to feel and understand what it was, and is like to be a pupil at Crinkles we're going right back to the old days.

Crinkles Academy is the oldest Wizard School in England in fact in the whole World. It's a large dilapidated detached house standing on the original site of the first Wizard School and was rebuilt over 300 years ago.

When first built it stood in a quiet leafy lane in the middle of rolling fields miles and miles from anywhere.

Over the years Villages sprang up here and there then one by one joined together until they became a Town, which in turn grew and grew until it became a City.

As time passed the City spread and almost engulfed the old house, it stands in what is left of its once beautiful grounds, now it's surrounded by houses, there's a Supermarket just up the road a large modern Comprehensive School nearby and a dubious Second Hand Car Salesroom opposite.

The trees around the house do offer some protection from these modern intrusions, but one can quite easily see into the grounds from the top deck of the number 33 double-decker bus which passes the school every 20 minutes from 7.30a.m to 10.30p.m at night.

You could quite well have passed Crinkles every day and never suspected it was anything other than an 'Ordinary very Old Large House' that had been 'Converted into a School.'

Why should you? There was so little magic practised there that it was virtually just 'Another School.'

The Magic side of it had become that poor that the combined talents of all the Wizards could not stop a tap dripping. In the end Mr. Henderson the local plumber did the trick.

It was an undisputed fact that nothing exciting happened at Crinkles, no one could remember anything exciting in living memory. The Headmaster Dr. Philpotts, a tall, thin, dignified looking man with grey hair and dark thick rimmed glasses, always dressed in a dark grey suit, and wearing an old black Headmaster's gown could be seen wandering around the School on most days smiling and patting the odd pupil's head.

The only words anyone ever heard him pronounce clearly were, "Don't run child." or "Not so noisy please." He would appear at every Friday morning assembly and mumble a few words that no one could hear or understand then nod to the pupils and shamble off back to his study.

Older pupils would tell the new ones that he went there to study 'Mysterious Mystic Arts' when in fact they knew that he just dozed all day in his big high backed winged leather chair.

His assistant, Miss. Melissa Millthrop actually runs the place (well in a fashion). She appears forceful, full of energy

2

and enthusiastic. But in reality she gets so engrossed in minor problems that she achieves nothing other than increase the general chaos. You can hear distinctly every word she says, the problem is she never stops. She talks constantly, never use one word when you can use ten should be her motto.

She is large, very formidable, has dark hair and a round serious looking face that can occasionally break out into a very pleasant smile. She always wears a dark green tweed jacket and skirt, and she either wears the same clothes all the time or has a wardrobe full of identical jackets and skirts, no one is sure which.

She usually wears a cream or white blouse with a string of white pearls. First year pupils are kidded that they're not pearls but the teeth of misbehaved children that she has pulled out herself.

Now as all first year pupils are sent to her if they feel ill, and she decides if they need to see Matron, this story about her necklace has a strange effect. Once they realise they have to go and see Miss. Millthrop they all appear to achieve remarkable recoveries.

She wears black flat brogue type shoes with a steel tip on the sole and heel, fortunately for misbehaving pupils this makes her sound like a platoon of paratroopers approaching.

When she's in a hurry, which she always is, it's best to keep well out of her way as she strides out forcing anyone with her to almost run, her robe flowing behind her looks like a huge billowing black sail, her voice sounding remarkably similar to a fog horn, and her feet thudding into the ground almost cause minor Earth tremors.

"You child what are you doing?" Her voice would boom out. If you were with her at the time looking around you wouldn't see any child.

"Yes! Yes! You! Come here this instant!" Sure enough a child would appear. She had an eagle eye and could detect the slightest movement at a hundred yards, the younger pupils are terrified of her but the older ones rather like her, at least she is a bit of a character not too bad really, whereas the Head, well, he may as well not be there he just sort of quietly floats by.

As for the other Master's, they aren't much better than the Head! There are four pleasant but very quiet lady teachers, in their defence perhaps they are afraid of Miss. Millthrop and have decided best to stay tucked away.

The male Masters certainly believe in keeping their heads down below the trench top when Millthrop's about. Although on one occasion I did hear an incredibly heated argument between Mr Brownly the Physics Master and Miss. Millthrop.

A crowd had gathered and I was determined to find out what it was all about. This had to be something of great importance to the School as I'd never seen Brownly so annoyed, in fact I had never seen him annoyed before.

You always saw him wondering around with a number of books stuffed under his arm, you always expected him to drop one he carried that many, and usually a rolled up newspaper, although that was to swat any pupil who was acting up a bit. Apparently he would smack you lightly with the newspaper and say: "There boy!" (even if it was a girl). "Your brain has just been in contact with more knowledge and information than it has been all week."

I drew closer and heard Millthrop screaming. "Do you really know how much this extravagance is costing the School? Do you? Do you? And how long has it been going on for? Tell me that!"

Brownly's face was bright red and he was shouting at the top of his voice. "I don't have to stand for this! Who do you think you are?"

Just then the Headmaster appeared. "Tut, Tut. We can't have this now, can we? I think a spot of tea is called for in my study."

Both Millthrop's and Brownly's faces took on a very strange expression when he mentioned tea and they fell silent. "Follow me." said the Head turning away with a smile on his face and softly chuckling.

I found out later that the argument had all been about the number of tea bags Brownly was using, he apparently likes very strong tea and they had ran out of tea bags that morning in the Staff Common Room when Millthrop had wanted to make herself a pot of tea.

She enquired as to why there were no tea bags when a full box had been opened only last week and was told it was due to Mr. Brownly's insistence on really strong tea. When she later spotted him in the quadrangle she couldn't resist confronting him. Apart from this one outburst Brownly is just like all the other male Masters who appear to be wrapped up in their own private worlds, most of them seem ancient to the pupils and I must admit some of them seem ancient to me.

The uninspired Masters meant that Crinkles was a disaster, not only does it not produce any Wizards of quality, in reality it doesn't produce any Wizards. All lessons are the same as in a perfectly normal school (if such a thing exists): Maths; English; History; Geography; Physics and Woodwork, etc.

Unfortunately the School is not even good at teaching normal subjects so year in year out pupils leave without having achieved any real qualifications. Quite a few of the boys became joiners, as Mr. Graeme's woodwork class is the best-taught subject in the School.

You would never in a thousand years have suspected anyone from the Old School could have become a Wizard.

The biggest success story in recent years was Heckinwicker, who after leaving Crinkles became a motor mechanic at a small local garage and now owns and runs the garage directly opposite the School, 'Heck's Super Auto Deals'.

There was some excitement last Easter Term when a new young Master Miss. Hudson joined the School to teach Maths and at the start of the Summer Term when Mr. Scorn joined to teach English.

All the boys thought that Miss. Hudson (Cecilia) was gorgeous. She is pretty and compared to the other lady teachers who are a lot older she is gorgeous. All the girls thought Mr. Scorn (Ian) was a real heart - throb and for weeks the girls watched every move they made sensing romance in the air (or in reality hoping that romance was in the air).

However by the end of the Summer Term it was evident to even the most romantic girl in the School that neither Miss. Hudson nor Mr. Scorn had shown any interest what so ever in each other.

The School building is in very poor shape, we have quite a few leaks in the roof and plenty of draftee poor fitting windows. It has a permanent, damp, musty sort of smell which after a while you don't notice. Most of the rooms have wood panelling in dark mahogany, I hate to think what it was like in the old days when there were only candles, it's very dingy now even with electric lights.

It has long stone floored corridors, with the odd gloomy picture hung here and there of past Headmaster's or country scenes that depict grey miserable misty days, you would find it hard to discover more miserable pictures anywhere. What seems like endless flights of stone stairs and all sorts of nooks and crannies, numerous attics and cellars, or as the older pupils like to call them, 'cells', to frighten the youngsters.

At the back of the School is a large old stone built stables which still has the steel tethering rings on the inside and on the outside of one of the walls. The wooden stalls having been removed years ago it is now used as a shed for storing gardening gear and other odds and ends, but the steel rings lend themselves marvellously to tales of terror and torture. I'm sure that really helps new pupils especially the borders to quickly settle in.

I have no doubt there are tall stories told in the dormitories at night after lights out that encouraged many new pupils to write and ask their parents could they come back home – immediately!

Truthfully it's really gloomy and a bit of a creepy place to any new comers, but you would soon feel the current of laughter and happiness that runs through the Old School when it is full of pupils at term time.

Matron is very abrupt but with a soft heart and will do anything for one of her patients.

The Cook is brilliant, cheerful, honest to a fault, and can make even the glummest new pupils face cheer up with the best food you've ever tasted. She has two assistants and a couple of younger women give her a hand in the kitchen, set tables, wash up and do all the other behind the scenes jobs that have to be done on a daily basis.

There are four cheerful friendly cleaners come maids who also help out in the kitchen from time to time. Harry the old gardener and his young assistant Eric who is 65. (Harry always says young Eric will make a good gardener one of these days). They look after the School grounds, Harry keeps the large lawn at the front and the smaller one at the back immaculate with very pretty flowerbeds outside the Schools Main Entrance.

Eric looks after all the trees and is forever trimming and cutting back, he loves a good bonfire and so do all the pupils so he gets on very well with them, whereas poor Harry always trying to protect his lawn and flowerbeds wages a constant battle with football kicking pupils.

All three of us try to maintain the drive, and the walls that are ten foot high and run around the entire School. We also do a bit of pointing, gutter repairs and gutter cleaning. Of all the many outside jobs we have to do the one we hate is cleaning all the small windows, there's hundreds of them and no sooner do we finish then you have to start again.

As I mentioned earlier my name's Brian, I'm the Caretaker come odd job man at Crinkles. I'm the one who tries to keep the old place going single-handedly on the inside as far as maintenance and repair work is concerned, though Harry and Eric also help me to clean all those small windows on the inside.

I was on holiday when the leaky tap problem appeared otherwise I would have been the one to fix it, without the aid of Magic, as unfortunately I can't do any Magic.

I wish I could do Magic, Oh how I wish I could, I'd sort that Traffic Warden out at the end of the street and just think what I could do for my little 'Local Football Club'. Every traffic light would always be on green for me and there would always be a parking space whenever I needed one. Ah well, anyone can dream.

However, things were about to change at Crinkles Academy, amongst the new first year pupils to start in the Summer Term was David, full of confidence and actually interested in and practising Magic, with brilliant presentation flair but unfortunately he has a very, very poor memory.

Without fail he would mess up all but the simplest of spells, at the last minute he would forget the final words and guess the spells ending with disastrous results.

On the other hand Jenny, who had joined the School at the same time is a fantastic spell maker who knows a lot of spells and is always word perfect. Unfortunately she has no confidence and is terribly shy. Her spells never worked because she mumbled the words and as even you and I know, not only must the words for a spell be correct they must be spoken boldly, forcefully, and clearly if the spell is to work. Neither of them were advanced enough to do thought spells.

The amazing thing about David and Jenny is the fact that they want to do any Magic at all. You see none of the other children in the School seem to want to, the children's Parents and Grandparents had all been pupils at the School, but generation after generation had done less and less Magic until most could do none at all.

Is that the time? And I've still got to buy my lottery tickets! I have this feeling one day I will win! Now if I could just get the help of some of these Wizards in choosing the numbers, but there's fat chance of that I reckon. Maybe I'd be luckier doing the pools!

Let me see now, Newcastle against Chelsea now that should be a good game a draw I reckon. Arsenal against Tottenham, Arsenal should win that one I think. Watford against Manchester United., now then let me see Manchester should romp it but I've got a feeling it will be a draw. Blackburn Rovers at home against Fulham what do you think? Oh, I'm forgetting you can't tell me, can you! Pity! Well I had better press on, the pool's collector will be here soon and you never know, this may be my lucky week.

CHAPTER TWO

The School Concert

It was near the end of the Summer Term when Miss. Hudson the new Maths teacher had the idea of an end of term Concert with mixed entertainment.

Her suggestion however was met with very little enthusiasm from anyone. Not to be beaten she used a type of Magic that all of us can have. Namely: enthusiasm, determination, drive and energy.

Miss. Hudson cudgelled, pleaded, and prodded everyone into action and surprise, surprise, bit by bit everyone warmed to the idea and soon invitations were sent out to the parents inviting them to the concert.

Perhaps someone sprinkled acceptance dust onto the invitations but I doubt it, I don't think that anyone has made a dust spell for centuries, although just out of eyesight there seems to be centuries of dust about the place.

Miss. Hudson (Cecilia) was very pleased at first at the response from the invitations that had been sent out, every post brought fresh acceptances along with requests for more tickets. This is an example of a typical reply:

Dear Miss. Hudson,

We are very pleased to accept your kind invitation to the School Concert and thank you for the four tickets you have enclosed.

Our Billy's favourite Aunty, Aunt Matilda, would just love to come along to the concert, if you could possibly arrange for say another 3 tickets we would be very grateful.

Yours Faithfully,

Mr. and Mrs. Hodgson (Billy's Mam and Dad)

How big is his Aunt Matilda? Thought Cecilia, as she read the letter, if she needs three seats!

Almost every other acceptance was requesting more tickets.

Later that day she happened to be in the dining room when in came Billy Hodgson. "Billy." Cecilia called out, he turned and she added, "Have you got a minute?"

"Eh! Yes Miss." He replied and walked towards her wondering what on earth he could have done wrong.

"Billy, have you got a favourite Aunt?"

"No Miss."

"Do you have a least favourite Aunt?"

"Yes Miss." Billy couldn't understand why she was asking all these silly questions.

"What's her name Billy?"

"Aunt Matilda."

"Why is she your least favourite Aunt?" asked Cecilia.

"Because she never gives me any pocket money when she calls round, she's always on about my hair, it's too long then it's too short, or she doesn't think I've washed my face because it looks so scruffy, at Christmas she buys me socks or hankies and…."

"That's enough Billy, thank you." One minute he didn't want to speak the next you couldn't stop him.

Billy rejoined his friends who couldn't wait to find out what it was all about. Cecilia had left Billy Hodgson very confused for the rest of the day, he decided he would keep an eye out for her in the future and keep well out of her way as she might want to know about his Uncles next.

Cecilia had no shortage of helpers when it came to making some scenery, painting a backdrop, fiddling with lighting or the sound system. An army of people loved to arrange or rearrange the seating in the hall or helping with refreshments. Everyone was full of enthusiasm for all but one item, the item where she needed the most help, namely the rehearsals or the lack of them.

The initial enthusiasm Cecilia had was beginning to fade and panic was starting to set in.

Oh why did I suggest it she kept thinking to herself, the more acceptances that kept coming in the more desperate and despondent she became.

What had seemed like a great idea now appeared to be the most stupid idea she had ever had. Cecilia had discovered what a few of her colleagues already knew, and what many of the others had suspected, namely that the children at Crinkles had absolutely no talent as far as any form of entertainment was concerned.

Some of the children were to recite poems written by them, the poems were so poor that it was now to be children reciting poems that other people had written. However the children who spoke reasonably clearly seemed unable to get beyond seven or eight words before forgetting the lines or producing original lines that the author wouldn't have been very pleased about.

The handful that could almost remember a complete poem without feeling the need to alter the words spoke so softly they couldn't be heard. No matter how hard Cecilia tried they insisted on reciting the poems to their feet, and so poetry was abandoned.

The magician, George Potts, was so slow and so obvious that it was embarrassing. When he said his next trick was dangerous and produced three large knives which he had collected from the kitchen, Cecilia felt for his own personal safety and the safety of everyone else she had to call a halt, so that was the magician out.

Now Kathleen Green was said to be a very fine pianist. After hearing 3 pieces from Kathleen's supposedly extensive repertoire, Cecilia could take no more and could only conclude that the person who had claimed Kathleen to be a very good pianist either took enjoyment from watching a large number of people suffering unnecessarily, or was completely deaf.

The piano recital was crossed off.

Cecilia's list was now down to individual singers, group singers and the choir to try and save the day, her worst nightmare was about to begin.

Endless arguments erupted on what songs should be selected, everyone had a favourite but unfortunately nobody had the same favourite.

There were many cries of: "Oh! Everyone will like this one." But nobody ever did.

Finally some sort of selection was made and serious rehearsing started. First Cecilia decided to select the soloists, the auditioning for the soloists sent Cecilia's morale plummeting down to depths never before reached.

Those who couldn't sing thought they could and insisted on singing no matter how bad they were.

Strangely they all appeared to have a large number of friends who cheered and clapped and some took it too far and even shouted for more. Oh how Cecilia would have loved to kick some backsides, she would stand trying to smile and offer encouragement, she had to keep repeating in her mind (don't shout Cecilia, don't shout, keep cool).

"That wasn't too bad Mary can you try it again please, try and project your voice so that everyone will be able to hear you, are you ready? Good, away you go."

"No Mary! They are the wrong words. You do know the right words Mary you've sung it five times already. All right! All right! Now don't cry." Cecilia sighed. "Keep cool Cecilia, keep cool!" she mumbled to herself.

"I think that's enough for this evening children same time tomorrow, thank you everyone."

If only I didn't have to say those three words, 'Same time tomorrow'. Thought Cecilia, I've got to go through all of this tomorrow and the next day and the next.

Cecilia went straight up to her own room, as she couldn't face the Common Room. All that….

"How's it going then?" or "Sounded a bit better tonight." With the emphasis on 'bit'! Or they would start to discuss nervous breakdowns: "I knew a teacher who had a nervous breakdown during rehearsals." Or someone would chip in with something like "I thought most nervous break-downs took place after a show when the reality sets in."

Some of the comments were intended to give some encouragement - they didn't, others only as a bit of fun - it wasn't.

Tonight she wanted to be on her own and was sitting in her room having a cup of tea when there was a knock on the door, she opened it and there stood Ian.

"Hello." He said, "Missed you tonight can I come in." Cecilia stood to one side to let him in.

"Mmmm, I see teas up." Said Ian "Any left in the pot?"

"Yes." Replied Cecilia "I've just made it, it's almost full." She left and came back with a cup, saucer and plate. "Will I pour?" she asked.

"Yes please, white with one sugar."

"Help yourself to some biscuits Ian."

"I certainly will." They both sat munching biscuits and drinking tea.

Cecilia was surprised that she felt so pleased that Ian had missed her in the Common Room and had taken the trouble to call round.

"Did it not go too well tonight?" Ian asked.

"It was a complete disaster Ian." Then she suddenly burst into tears, Cecilia was sobbing her heart out.

Ian felt a little embarrassed, he sat for a while wondering what to do, and was about to say thank you for the tea and get up and go, but to his surprise he put his tea cup down and crossed over to Cecilia and put his arm around her. She didn't seem to mind, or perhaps she wasn't even aware of it.

"It will be better tomorrow, you'll see." He said to comfort her. But unfortunately it wasn't any better it was worse.

The concert date was approaching rapidly and it was time to try and get the choir licked into shape, if one bad singer grates on your nerves imagine what a whole choir of bad singers can do.

Why, oh why, is it 'the poorer the singer the louder they sing'. Cecilia could not even hear the few reasonable singers and she was standing in front of them! What chance would anyone in the audience have of hearing them?

"Let's start again!" Called out Cecilia, and they tried again and again but no matter how many times they tried it didn't seem to improve.

Cecilia had noticed that Ian had started to sit in the hall all alone during rehearsals, surrounded by row after row of empty seats. The novelty having worn off some time ago the singers were no longer getting any support from their friends and everyone else avoided the rehearsals completely. So now it was row after row of empty seats. If only that was what we would be singing to thought Cecilia, rows and rows of empty seats! But soon they would be full, full of people expecting a concert.

She glanced in Ian's direction did she see him wincing? She wouldn't be surprised if he had, she was!

The last week of rehearsals flew over, if there was any improvement Cecilia could not detect it. She had just finished the final rehearsal and the following day was the actual Concert, the only thing that kept Cecilia going was the thought that this time tomorrow it would be all over for better or worse.

But how was she going to face all her colleagues? She just didn't know.

Ian had come up on stage and was smiling, trying his best to portray confidence.

"What do you think Ian?" Cecilia asked hopefully.

"Oh, I think you'll find it's a lot better on the actual night. It usually is." and gave Cecilia another big smile as he gathered up her music and escorted her out of the hall.

I had started to sweep the stage and thought to myself, 'I hope so Ian but I doubt it'.

As though poor Cecilia didn't have enough problems, three of the better singers, Lisa Gray, Catherine Jones and Paul White, had, in my opinion, been deliberately trying to ruin the group and the choir singing.

I've had them marked down as a bunch of troublemakers for some time. Nothing serious could be attributed to them, but numerous minor incidents of misbehaviour usually by what appeared to be by other pupils I felt sure was instigated by them.

They hid their tracks carefully, and manipulated other pupils usually the younger ones very successfully. This was due to the younger pupils admiration of the three troublemakers who oozed confidence and had many of the teachers eating out of the palm of their hands, that of course made them appear more important than other pupils their age. Or the manipulation was a result of fear of being ridiculed by them or bullied, sometimes both.

When the evening of the concert arrived, every parent, brother, sister, grandparent, niece, cousin and what have you turned up.

I doubt the old place had ever seen so many people gathered in the School Hall before. I think so many people had turned up because this was the first time the School had ever given a concert and of course to see their little darlings perform.

The Head welcomed everyone and hoped that they would enjoy the show, bearing in mind all the hard work the children had put into it under the enthusiastic and careful guidance of Miss. Cecilia Hudson.

There was tremendous applause and Cecilia wished she was anywhere but here, even a visit to the Dentists seemed preferable. She smiled and thanked the Headmaster and then said:

"Let the show begin."

As the show progressed poor Cecilia was looking increasingly miserable. It was quite obvious that far too little rehearsing had taken place, add to that some stage fright and well to be truthful it was really awful.

Quite a few of the faces in the audience had turned from loving smiles when their children came on stage, to frowns, and then to embarrassment. Behind the scenes backstage there were a lot of tears.

David was standing next to Jenny waiting to take part in the 'Grand Finale'.

Jenny, in a surprisingly loud voice, said. "I could have made everyone perform perfectly." She was not talking to anyone in particular just talking out loud to herself.

Having heard this David nudged her and whispered. "What do you mean?"

"What do you mean, what do I mean?" Mumbled Jenny.

"Well you said you could have made everyone perform perfectly."

"With a spell of course!" said Jenny, annoyed that she had been overheard.

"A spell!" David almost yelled.

"Sssh. Not so loud. Yes a spell, we are supposed to be a Wizards School aren't we?" Replied Jenny.

"Do you know a spell that would do it then?" Asked David excitedly.

"Well of course I do!"

"Then why not do it?" Asked David.

"I can't."

"You can't? Why not?"

"I'm too afraid."

"Afraid it won't work?"

"No of course not, I know it will work! I'm just afraid."

"Well I'm not! Tell me the words and I'll do it."

"No! It wouldn't be right."

"Mmmm," Said David.

They both stood in the wings waiting with everyone else to go on stage for the 'Grand Finale'.

Joan and Joyce, two second-year girls were singing a duet. It was terrible! Both were out of tune out of time and standing as though frozen to the spot.

David had a peek through the curtains at the audience and nudged Jenny towards the gap. The audience looked as though they had all received the biggest phone bill of their lives or arrived on holiday to find their hotel was an assortment of porta-cabins in the middle of the local waste tip.

David looked at Jenny.

"We've got to do something." He said. "Whatever we do even if it went wrong it couldn't be any worse than this."

"Yes we've got to do something." Agreed Jenny.

Joan and Joyce had finished, they stood there rooted to the spot. The audience sat in total silence, then a lone member of the audience started to clap and fortunately a few others joined in.

Cecilia ushered Joan and Joyce off the stage, whispering "Well-done girls."

Walking to the centre of the stage Cecilia summing up all her strength and courage thanked the audience for attending and for their enthusiasm, and she especially thanked all of those who had taken part on stage and behind the scenes.

She paused, but there was no applause. In fact she noticed some movement starting to take place amongst the audience, people wanting to make a quick get away, no doubt hoping to beat the rush for home and who could blame them.

"So," Cecilia said enthusiastically and as loudly as she could. "We now come to the 'Grand Finale' a short melody of assorted songs performed by all of the 'School's Pupils'."

Without a doubt you could feel a silent groan ripple throughout the assembled audience. Cecilia stayed centre stage whilst the rest of the staff ushered on stage all the pupils who sullenly trudged into position, forming three large semi-circles.

There was a few seconds of silence apart from a little shuffling into place on stage and some crinkling noises from some of the audience who were desperately searching pockets hoping to find one last sweet to give some comfort from the ordeal about to start.

Those who had intended to make an early get away had thought better of it deciding to stay until the bitter end, if the others could take it, so could they, albeit reluctantly.

"Ladies and Gentlemen, Boys and Girls, the 'Grand Finale'." proclaimed Cecilia.

But even her voice now sounded dismal.

She then turned to the children, "Right children, let's do the best we can." She said softly.

David and Jenny had slipped to the back of the group and waited until Miss. Hudson had raised her arms.

This was going to be harder than they had first thought. It was essential that each line of singers heard the Magic Spell, this meant repeating it to each of the three rows separately and clearly enough for the intended row to hear but not the others in case the odd word of the spell was not heard or heard incorrectly.

As Cecilia looked around to see if everyone was ready, David spoke the Magic that Jenny was whispering in his ear to the back row holding his wand horizontally in front of him.

As soon as he'd finished but before Cecilia could start the singing Jenny started to cough loudly.

Cecilia still held her arms aloft and the spell was repeated for the second row. David still had to put the spell on the third row, but by now Cecilia was looking annoyed at this constant coughing by Jenny just as she was about to start, and the audience were becoming very restless.

"Jenny!" Said Cecilia. "I'm afraid you will have to leave the stage."

"No! No! Miss. Hudson I'll be alright!"

"Right then, let's get started," Said Cecilia, and without any more delays she did.

David and Jenny had managed to put a spell on all but the front row.

The front row was terrible it drowned out all the rest, it seemed as though the bad singers were determined that only they would be heard.

It was so bad that Cecilia stopped the singing, she could not put the audience through this torture, they had already endured more than enough.

"Why have we stopped Miss?" Whispered Jenny.

"We can't go on Jenny we're that bad." Replied Cecilia.

"Just one more time Miss! Please! Just one more time!" Begged Jenny

Something in the urgent pleading of Jenny's voice made Cecilia decide to try again. "Once more children a fresh start! Are we ready?" Cecilia started to raise her hands and David repeated the spell for the front row of the chorus only just in time.

David felt exhausted, "This Magic takes more out of you than you think it would," he mumbled looking at Jenny who also looked tired and drawn.

David had been surprised that none of the pupils seemed to notice him putting the spell on them, he had expected someone to ask what he was up to, but there had been no response from anyone. They all had a strange glazed look on their faces, perhaps the realisation of how bad they were and having to go through it all again singing the final selection of songs had totally mesmerized them. One thing was for certain he couldn't have managed a fourth row.

All of the pupils at Crinkles were singing, and how they sang, and with each new song the singing got better, and better.

The audience were beaming at each other. Mothers and Fathers, Uncles and Aunts, Grandads and Grandmas, were flushed with pride at their little darlings singing so well, and even Brothers and Sisters in the audience had to admit it was good.

All the Masters sighed with relief. The day had been saved. Cecilia conducted with great enthusiasm carried along on a tidal wave of pure blissful singing.

Only two people thought it all a little odd at that moment in time. Mr. Scorn eyed David and Jenny suspiciously and noted that they were not singing, he had also noticed them moving between the rows of singers. The other person was the Head-master who stood with an amused look on his face. He had doubts when he gave permission for Miss. Hudson to give the concert, and was as relieved as all the other staff that disaster had been averted.

When the last song ended the audience gave a standing ovation and insisted on an encore, so with Cecilia once more conducting with great gusto the pupils enthusiastically sang all the songs a second time. The singing was even better, the Old School Hall had never seen such a happy cheerful evening before.

It had all been a huge success. How very clever of Miss. Hudson and her colleagues to get the children to pretend that they couldn't sing, and so all the parents, relatives and friends departed in good humour, beaming, smiling and congratulating everyone as they left the School Hall.

David and Jenny had no idea at the time how long it would take the spell to wear off, perhaps it never would. The follow-ing day many of the pupils wandered around the School singing their heads off.

Some asked Miss. Hudson when they could do it again, but Cecilia had the sense to quit when she was ahead and although she told them we shall have to wait and see, she knew that she had no intention of ever doing a School Concert again.

Some pupils talked about forming groups, others about going solo, and others about bringing out a record. It was driv-ing David and Jenny crackers, thank goodness they would be breaking up for the Summer Holidays the next day.

It was strange that over the Summer Holidays none of the children's parents seemed to notice that gradually their children didn't appear to be able to sing as well as they had at the concert.

On the following day everyone was departing for the Holi-days, excited about all of the fun that lay ahead and the great freedom the Summer Holidays would bring. No more stuffy lessons for six weeks!

David and Jenny had not talked since the concert, they still felt worn out as well as a little guilty about using Magic to make the concert a success and so had avoided each other.

David was standing outside on the steps of the Schools Main Entrance with some of his friends when Jenny passed him on her way to her parent's car with her cases. She smiled at him but for some reason that David didn't understand he found himself scowling at her and saying loudly: "I wish the School didn't allow girls in!"

"Dead right!" agreed Mason, also in a loud voice. Mason was a first year pupil who David couldn't stand. Mason was one of those people who would agree with anything anyone said and if he did have a personal opinion on anything no one was ever aware of it.

David tried to avoid him and hadn't realised he was standing so close. David now had a horrible sinking feeling in his stomach why had he said that? Why had he given Jenny such an awful look? If he was really truthful he did know why, he had been trying to show off in front of his friends and now he bitterly regretted it, as he really liked Jenny. What had made matters even worse was David's friends starting to laugh after Mason had agreed with David's remarks.

Jenny had heard what David said and although she felt hurt and puzzled she ignored him. Her Mum helped Jenny put her cases in the boot, she climbed into the car without looking back, but once inside looked through the rear window and saw David looking in her direction and still scowling.

'Big headed pig', she thought. 'At least I won't have to see him for weeks and weeks!' not realising David's scowl was in annoyance with himself.

David watched the car drive away, why was I so stupid that I did that? He thought. Jenny's okay really, he was beginning to feel really miserable, what a great start I've made to the holidays.

"Here are your folks David." Called out one of his friends.

David picked his cases up. "See you all after the Holidays, have a great time!" He shouted above all the voices around him. As he made his way down the steps towards his parent's car all he could think about was why had he been so nasty and mean to Jenny.

Jenny's Mam was driving through the School gates now and had been chattering away nineteen-to-the-dozen, but Jenny had not heard a word. She was too busy thinking about what David had said about girls and the look he had given her.

"Are you listening to me?" Asked Jenny's Mam. "I've been telling you all about our plans for the Holidays and I don't think you've taken a bit of notice. Well, as I said, your cousins Daphinia and Peter Michael are staying with us for a couple of weeks, it will be such fun you'll love it."

'Love it!' thought Jenny, 'Like I love toothache!'

CHAPTER THREE

The Summer Holidays

The School Holidays were almost half over and David was munching through his third slice of toast. It was Saturday so everyone was down for breakfast.

His younger sister was kicking his foot under the table.

"Can I come with you?" She asked for the tenth time.

"No you can't! Anyway, I'm not going anywhere."

"I bet you are, you just don't want me to come." She scowled at him and continued to kick his foot. David looked at her and thought, 'Oh! How I would like to turn you into a toad.'

"Mam." He said.

"Yes dear?" She replied.

"Did you have Magic Lessons when you were at Crinkles Academy?"

"Magic Lessons, no I can't remember having any but I think your Dad did."

"Did what?" asked his Dad.

"Have Magic Lessons at School?" explained David excitedly.

"Mmm." said his Dad. "Yes we did, we were taught by old, Urmmm, what's his name, I can see him now he's been retired for years of course, years and years we all liked old what's his name."

"Can you still do some of the Magic Dad?"

His sister had stopped kicking his foot and was listening intently, but David's Mam seemed totally uninterested busying herself about the kitchen.

"I dare say I could," replied his Dad. "But I'm not sure where my Wand is, haven't seen it for years."

"Do you know where Dad's Wand is Mam?" asked David.

"I've no idea David it could be anywhere! He's got his tools scattered everywhere around the house, your Dad never puts anything back after he's used it and you're exactly the same! Just look at your bedroom!"

David's Dad buried his head in his newspaper, he knew David's Mam would rattle on now for what would seem like hours on her favourite subject - how untidy everybody was.

David decided to venture one more question,

"Dad."

His Dad looked over the top of his paper with a look that said this had better be short.

"Dad." David repeated. "Why don't you do any Magic?"

"Don't need Magic anymore. No one does. The Non-Wizards are so clever now Magic is not needed, it wasn't all that effective anyway as I remember, it usually created more problems than it solved, best to leave it alone."

Up went his Dad's newspaper that meant no more questions. David got up from the table and walked over to his Mam who was ironing.

"Do you like ironing Mam?" David asked.

"What a silly question to ask! You know I don't!"

"Then why not use Magic to iron the clothes?"

"Because I don't know any Magic that would iron clothes and don't bother asking your Dad, because even if he said he did I wouldn't trust him."

"But it could save you lots of work Mam!"

"David. Your Aunty Gertrude years and years ago decided she would use Magic to hang her washing out in the garden. Out went shirts, towels, along with the rest of the washing and also the pegs all heading towards the washing line. Unfortunately they didn't stop and none of them were ever seen again.

A couple of weeks later after talking things over with your Dad and your Uncle Jack, she decided to try again. This time she had the embarrassing situation of trying to explain to neighbours how her washing came to be hanging on their lines, she never tried that again and anyway, I'm quite happy with my lovely steam iron thank you."

It didn't surprise David that his Aunty Gertrude couldn't get a spell right. She was usually under the influence of sherry, all taken for medicinal purposes of course.

"Mam. Where do you think Dad's Wand might be?"

"Oh! I don't know David, I don't even know where mine is, although your Dad's is probably in the garage amongst all the old junk he stores there, no wonder we can't get the car in!"

Right thought David, the garage! It might just be there. He slipped away leaving his Mum ironing and talking about the rubbish in the garage, and his dad engrossed in his newspaper. His younger sister had been listening to every word and David had not noticed how sheepish she looked.

Off to the garage went David to start on the 'Mammoth Task' if it was anywhere in the garage it would be in one of the many assorted boxes at the back, but there were mountains of stuff he would have to move to get at them.

His younger sister had gone up to her bedroom that was full of cuddly toys. She went to a set of drawers near the window and opened the top one, pushing the pile of notepads, pens, pencils, rulers, old birthday cards and hair clips towards the back.

She picked up two Wands and looked at them, then she put them back in the drawer and covered them again. She went downstairs and out into the garden to the garage, David had already covered some of the drive and the front lawn with boxes, bicycles, all sorts of weird and wonderful odds and ends, as well as the usual dozens of half used tins of paint and old hard paint brushes that almost everyone seems to collect.

His sister stood watching him for a while.

"Can I help?" She asked.

"No you can't! Go away!" replied David.

She follows me everywhere thought David, I'll almost be glad to go back to Crinkles Academy. Strange how I always miss Crinkles when I'm at Home, and Home when I'm at Crinkles.

David started to think about all the things he misses when he's at Crinkles. I miss my Mam and Dad of course, and strangely, occasionally my sister. I miss my two best friends Christopher and his brother Michael. Christopher's a great football player and my Dad often tells him: "Remember Christopher, you don't sign for any football team before seeing me I'm going to be your manager one day." Then he laughs away to himself and always adds, "You're going to make me very rich."

I play with Michael on his computer all kinds of games but he's better than me and always wins. We both have a huge collection of football stickers that we swap with our friends.

Sometimes their Dad takes us fishing. I once caught a 4-pound 2 ounce Cod using a bright orange plastic octopus, that fish was 20 inches long, it struggled that much before I landed it I thought I had caught a whale and I was really a little disappointed when I saw the size of it.

Since then though I have only caught two fish and they are getting smaller, a 1 pound and 2 ounce Whiting, 11 3/4 inches long and a 9-ounce Flounder, 10 3/4 inches long.

I really miss our cats Sophie and Ben. Sophie is an elegant tortoiseshell, she is really beautiful and she likes to sit on top of anything you leave lying about especially if it's new, for example magazines, a book, wrapping paper, clothes, in fact just about anything. Hence Mam is always complaining about cat hairs on all of our clothes and the furniture.

Sophie claws the front of the kitchen cabinets and we've tried everything to stop her but it's no use.

I sometimes think Dad is pleased about this, the cabinets are quite old and Mam would like new modern ones, but whenever Sophie is being chased away for clawing the front of the old ones Dad always says: "It would be a waste of money buying new cabinets with her around! Just think if they had been brand new!"

Mam never says a word just gives him one of her funny looks. Perhaps she thinks he somehow puts the cat up to it.

If Sophie had her way she would sleep all night on my pillow just above my head. Mam and Dad go crackers, they search the house for her just before bedtime but she knows this and hides in my room. Once they have gone to bed up she pops and jumps on to my bed, curls up and purrs very quietly, she purrs that quietly you can barely hear her.

Now Ben is a Marmalade Cat (Ginger Tabby) and has perfect markings. He purrs like a speed boat engine all the time, in fact you can hear him at the other side of the room if there is no music or T.V. on! He's far too fat and he loves company but not strangers. If anyone he doesn't know comes into the house or the doorbell rings he shoots straight upstairs and disappears.

You have to watch him though. He comes up to you very friendly and purring and you start to stroke him, then he half closes his eyes in contentment, the next second he's attacking you.

My sister has bought this cloth goldfish. It's on a piece of string at the end of a short rod and she teases and teases him driving him mad, then when he attacks her she runs crying to her Mam who comforts her saying: "That naughty cat, I'll get him" if she's not too busy she comes in and chases him until he hides under the table. Ben has no idea why he is being chased of course.

Adults and children yell at cats and dogs as though they could understand you. They say things like, "You're very naughty if you ever do that again you're for it," or something similar.

What the cat or dog hears of course is something like, "'#'#'@#@#'#'@ '#'@ @#' #' '#" > '>'@@ #'@#."

Mam says the cats must not be allowed upstairs in the bedrooms, but of course they always manage somehow or other to get upstairs usually to my sisters or my bedroom. Ben gets under the duvet and you can't tell that he's there and once or twice I have accidentally sat on him.

David's thoughts were interrupted when his sister reappeared.

"Mum says you've got to let me help you."

"No she doesn't! You're lying!"

"No I'm not lying! What are you looking for? I may know where it is."

"Just go away!! I'm not looking for anything."

"You must be looking for something you wouldn't pull the whole garage to bits for nothing."

"Just go away." Yelled David, who was starting to get annoyed.

"Ah well if you don't need my help." His sister smiled a curious knowing smile and turning walked back into the house.

Meanwhile a few miles away, Jenny's Mum was calling out to her.

"Jenny! Jenny! Where are you Darling? Your cousins want you to play with them."

Jenny sighed. She couldn't ignore her Mum much longer, oh how she wished she was back at Crinkles she couldn't take much more of this. She hadn't been able to study or practise any spells since the start of the Holidays.

Her cousins had come to stay for the first two weeks of the Holidays while their Dad was away on business and their Mum had gone with him.

For two weeks Jenny had gritted her teeth and done everything her Mother had told her to do. Her cousins were polite, friendly, and always smiled at her Mum. Always willing to help, butter wouldn't melt in their mouths.

Jenny thought she would burst with frustration if she heard her Mum say just once more: "I wish my Jenny was as polite and helpful as you dear children are."

Dear children! They were two faced, lying, sly, treacherous, scheming little brats!! Last night Jenny's heart sank as she heard her Mum on the phone saying: "Of course they can stay another week! That's no trouble at all and it's such nice company for Jenny. I can't wait until you get back to hear how lovely the place is! I'm so glad the business went so well. No.

No problems! Just you two enjoy yourselves! See you soon. Bye!"

Jenny had been hiding all over the house, she knew her Mum was planning to go shopping in town and thought that if she couldn't find her she might take the two monsters with her and leave Jenny all on her own in total peace and quiet! Oh, what bliss that would be!

Jenny decided perhaps hiding again might buy her a few more minutes of peace, so she settled down in the back bedroom in a little corner and pulling the door towards her had wedged it with her hankie.

Her daydreaming was interrupted after only a couple of minutes by Daphinia's voice shouting in her ear: "I've found her! I've found her! I've found Jenny Aunty Moffatt!"

"Oh, good girl Daphinia!" said Jenny's Mam appearing in the doorway. "Right then Jenny I've got some good news for you! Daphinia and Peter Michael are staying with us for another week! Their Dad has finished his Business and as the weather is so nice and the place so beautiful they're staying on for a little holiday."

"I'm running late and must dash Jenny. I'm leaving you, Daphinia and Peter Michael here while I do some shopping, it's 12 o'clock now, I will be back about 6.00 to make the tea. I have arranged for Mrs. Peters' daughter Nicola to look after you all when I'm out."

Jenny could not believe her ears, Nicola Peters was worse than Daphinia and Peter Michael put together, and she would 'unofficially' bring her boyfriend that slug Neil Green.

"But Mum I can look after Daphinia and Peter Michael myself." (Jenny never thought she would hear herself say that).

"No! You're all too young to be on your own."

"But Mum!" Pleaded Jenny.

"No Jenny! And that's final! In fact here is Nicola now, perfect timing!"

Jenny's Mum opened the door, Nicola gave her mam a big smile. Jenny felt she was going to be sick.

"Come on in Dear. Now I've made lots of sandwiches and there's plenty of crisps and pop for everyone. I'll ring a couple of times just to see that everything is okay, will that be all right Nicola?"

"Oh yes Mrs. Moffatt! That's fine! I'll sort out lunch after you've gone and since it's such a lovely day we'll play out in the garden."

"Excellent Nicola, Well I'm off now everyone! Now behave yourselves while I'm away and we'll have a nice tea when I get back."

Jenny's Mum was soon driving down the road with everyone smiling and waving her off. But as soon as she was out of sight Nicola's face changed to a scowl as she looked at Jenny and said: "You had better not give me any trouble this time or you're for it!"

Nicola had been 5 or 6 times to Jenny's house when her Mum and Dad were going out to the theatre, or for dinner, and each time had been worse than the last.

Hopefully her boyfriend wouldn't be coming round today. But hardly had the thought left Jenny's mind when he turned up with that fixed stupid smug grin on his face.

"Now you two" Nicola spoke in a soft and pleasant voice to Daphinia and Peter Michael.

"You can keep a secret, can't you?"

"Oh yes! Yes we can!" They replied.

"Well, this is my boyfriend Neil."

Daphinia and Peter Michael began to giggle.

"Now no-one's to know he's been here."

"We won't tell anyone! No-one!"

"Good, and the same goes for you!!" She spat out at Jenny.

Jenny just stayed quietly in the background and said nothing.

"Just wait till you see all the food Mrs. Moffatt has laid on, come and see Neil," and Nicola took his hand and led him into the kitchen.

"Boy!" said Neil "This looks good!"

"No Neil! Don't start eating it here we're going to eat out on the patio."

"I'm having some now!"

"No Neil!"

"Only one or two sandwiches there's plenty here," said Neil grabbing them.

"Remember there are five of us! Mrs. Moffatt only made the food for four," said Nicola.

"Yeah, But she made plenty for four! Anyway you two don't want much do you?" Neil asked Daphinia and Peter Michael.

They were quite frightened of him and shook their heads in response.

"As for you!" He turned to Jenny, "You don't want any do you?"

Jenny said nothing and looked at the floor.

"I'll tell her Mam she felt sick and didn't feel like eating anything." said Nicola.

All four of them thought that was really funny and roared with laughter.

Jenny's dog Jessie who is a three year old Golden Labrador had come bounding up to her. but when she saw Neil she started to growl.

"Go on clear off!!" He shouted.

"Get that dog away!" Said Nicola. "You know it doesn't like me, or Neil."

Jessie's got good taste thought Jenny.

"Yeah! Get it away from me before I kick it like I did the last time!" Neil went towards Jessie and lifted his leg as though he was about to kick her.

Jessie went low on her front legs and the growl turned to a snarl as she showed her teeth.

"It's going to bite you Neil!! Keep away from it! It's a vicious dog!" said Nicola taking his arm and pulling him away, though in fact he didn't need much encouragement to move.

"Come here Jessie!" said Jenny. Jessie slowly got up not taking her eyes of Neil until she was next to Jenny. Then her tail started to wag and her eyes twinkled as Jenny patted her on the head, she just managed not to say 'good girl' and instead said in a sweet loving voice: "Naughty dog. You've been a very naughty girl."

"Lock it in the garage!! Go on! Lock it in the garage." said Nicola.

Jenny took hold of Jessie's collar and led her to the garage. "It's far too nice a day for you to be locked up in here but it won't be for long."

Jenny put a bowl of fresh water down for her and gave Jessie a couple of pats and a big hug. Jessie put her head to one side and with large sad eyes looked at Jenny who had stood up to leave, Jessie leapt up to follow her,

"No girl! You've got to stop here!" Jenny said as she pushed Jessie back and closed the garage door.

"Where have you been? Come on hurry up and help to take the food outside!" yelled Nicola at Jenny. Jenny washed and dried her hands ignoring Nicola.

Help take the food outside of course meant Jenny doing all the work.

Soon everyone was tucking in except Jenny, who after a few minutes decided she'd try and get a sandwich and reached across the table.

"Greedy, greedy!" Yelled Neil, grabbing her hand. "Drop it! Go on, drop it!"

Jenny dropped the sandwich.

"Oh go on," said Nicola. "Let her have something to eat."

Neil smiled. Jenny knew that when Neil smiled it usually meant trouble, he picked up a picnic plate and put sandwiches sausage rolls and crisps on it.

"Here you are Jenny, for you."

33

Jenny reached across, not that she had any intention of eating any food he had touched.

But before she could take hold of the plate he deliberately dropped it onto the paving stones. Everyone including the obnoxious Daphinia and Peter Michael laughed loudly.

"Look what you've done! Get down and pick up the mess!!" Yelled Neil.

"Don't even think of moaning to your Mam! She won't believe you!" Added Nicola.

Jenny cleared up the mess and went into the house to put it in the pedal bin, then as she washed and dried her hands Jenny looked out of the window watching them all still eating and laughing. A smile started to spread across Jenny's face,

"Enough is enough!" she mumbled to herself.

No one noticed Jenny reappear. They didn't see the Wand in her right hand or hear her soft chant. Neil took a bite out of yet another sandwich and started to munch. Nicola's eyes grew larger and larger as she saw fat green caterpillars slowly emerging from the sandwich in Neil's hand! Before she could say anything he took another bite, then his eyes opened wide, his face changed to a strange expression and he started to spit and cough the remains of the sandwich out of his mouth.

"What have I eaten! What have I eaten!!" He cried.

"There's caterpillars in your sandwich!!" Yelled Nicola.

"I'm going to be sick!! I'm going to be sick!!" Neil shouted.

He leapt to his feet and started to run around the garden. The others looked at the sandwiches in their hands and Daphinia realised that she had some of her sandwich in her mouth. They all felt relieved when there was no sign of any caterpillars!

It was then that the first spiders started to crawl out of the sandwiches - and two spiders started to crawl out of Daphinia's mouth.

They all leapt to their feet at the same time, knocking the table, chairs, and the remaining food in all directions, and screamed and screamed and screamed!! So much so that Neil stopped running around and stood watching them with his jaw dropping.

No one had noticed Jenny laughing and laughing, but Jenny had stopped laughing now, in fact she was quite frightened as all four people were going totally berserk in the garden. The only thing she could think of doing was to put a 'freeze spell' on them.

One minute they were jumping about screaming and the next they were as rigid as a stone statue. Peace at last descended on the garden.

Jenny looked at her watch, it was 1.00 p.m. Her Mum wasn't due back until 6.00. She looked at the mess all over the garden and was very tempted to tidy everything up using Magic, but decided that she had used enough Magic for one day.

So she set about tidying the garden, washed the dishes then put all the used food and the unused food (you don't know who may have touched it) into a bin liner and popped it all into the wheelie bin.

Jenny went to the garage and let Jessie out, who in a wave of excitement at being free leapt up and tried to lick Jenny's face, then bounded ahead of her towards the back garden only stopping to make sure Jenny was following.

It was such a beautiful day that Jenny decided she would have a few hours relaxing, do a little sunbathing and perhaps read one of her spell books.

She got out a sun-lounger and settled back to watch Jessie running around the garden enjoying the freedom.

Jessie had started sniffing the strange objects that had appeared in the garden. She sniffed at Daphinia, Peter Michael and Nicola.

Then she came to Neil, she sniffed and circled him a couple of times then lifted her leg and wet all over him. Jenny couldn't stop laughing.

"Good girl! Come here!" Jessie came bounding across panting and wagging her tail.

"Sit." commanded Jenny. Lying with her eyes closed in the warm sunshine Jenny thought 'what a perfect day' as she patted Jessie who was curled up on the grass next to her.

'I've got hours and hours yet of peace and quiet before Mum comes home.'

I'll restore the new garden statues back to their original irritating form around about 5.00 to 5.30 Jenny decided. That seemed about the right time, pity though that it couldn't be longer. She made herself more comfortable and peacefully started to read one of her books on Magic while Jessie lay contented at her feet.

Whilst Jenny was relaxing in the sun David stood looking at an almost empty garage and a drive and front garden full of assorted junk. All that work and no sign of any Wands, now he had to put it all back again! It would take ages, then his dad came out to see what he was up to.

"Was all that in the garage?" he asked scratching his head. David looked at his Dad, does he think I've gone around all the neighbours collecting their junk as well.

"I hope you're going to put all that stuff back properly," said his Dad, picking up odds and ends and examining them. "I forgot I had that! Oh, look at that! I could have done with that last week! Where on earth did you find this David?" His Dad continued to go on and on as he discovered more 'lost' items that apparently he had desperately needed only recently.

Now his Mam appeared and told him that while everything was out of the garage he had to give it a good sweeping and hose it down but he mustn't put anything back until the floor was dry! Then he would have to have a bath when he came in.

"But Mam!! Protested David in dismay. "My favourite space film is on T.V. in an hour."

"But nothing David! Get started!" Said his Mam, turning and walking back into the house.

His little sister was enjoying every minute of this and stood smirking. After their Mam and Dad had gone back inside he asked his sister if she would give him a hand.

She pointed out that she had offered to help him earlier but he had told her to 'go away' and that was exactly what she had done, and was going to do it again, just go away and watch the space adventure on T.V.

"But you don't like space adventures!" Said a glum David.

"I do now!" She said, grinning.

David looked at the mammoth job ahead of him. Why oh why had he started it, what a complete waste of time it had been. Even if he had found his mam and dad's wands he knew they wouldn't use them or allow him to, so what had been the point other than curiosity.

"Bye David." Said his sister in a bright cheerful voice. "I'm off now, don't want to miss the start of 'The Film'."

CHAPTER FOUR

International Wizards Federation

Well, here I am again, Brian your storyteller. As I mentioned before I'm the caretaker-come-handy man, in some ways I'm the guy who keeps the whole place ticking over, well laugh if you must but it's true.

You see I know more about what is going on than anyone else at the School in my job I can go anywhere and everywhere, the lofts, the classrooms, dorms, cellars, master's rooms even the Heads and Assistant Heads.

No one thinks it's suspicious when I appear because in a very old place like this there's always something needing fixing, unblocking, easing, or there's something lost that needs finding and Magic aside I'm the guy they turn to.

Everyone came back from the summer break glum at first but soon cheered up when they met their friends. Lots of tall stories were told about what went on during the holidays into the early hours for a day or two and then everyone settled back to normality.

I should mention here that normality in this School is perhaps, well, let's say it's normally abnormal, or is it abnormally normal? Well, it's a bit different from your school, or is it? Perhaps it's not. I'm starting to get myself confused here; I think it's probably best to get on with the story.

It was a very quiet term, I noticed that Miss. Hutchinson and Mr. Scorn still had very little to do with each other and David and Jenny seemed to dislike one another.

A rather unpleasant gang had now formed from two existing gangs. One had been led by Lisa Grey, in it was Catherine Jones and Paul White then a third girl Christina had joined them, the other gang had one girl and five boys and was led by a boy called Eric. Unfortunately this meant more people for me to keep a close eye on.

Before we knew it Christmas was almost here and another year almost gone. It had been another quiet peaceful year to join all of the others, the only excitement being Cecilia and Ian joining the School, and of course the School Concert.

The same as everyone else around the World we all wondered what the year 2000 might bring but that was still 4 weeks away.

I love Christmas and do my best to make Crinkles have a great 'Cosy Christmas Feeling', the old building really lends itself to a really great Christmas atmosphere.

We always have a very large real Christmas Tree fully decorated and with ten sets of twinkling lights on it. It stands in the Main Hall and smaller ones are dotted around the School and although I say it myself the decorations looked the best ever that year.

The Gardener Harry and myself have the miserable job of taking all the decorations down while everyone is away on their Christmas Holidays. Mind you, we don't take them down until January 4th even though there is only the Head, Miss. Millthrop, Smithers, Harry, Cook, three other teachers and myself left in the school over Christmas.

It's nice to keep the place bright and cheerful for as long as possible as the School is incredibly quiet at Christmas when all the pupils are on Holiday. It always feels far quieter than in the Summer Holidays.

The Christmas Holiday's flew over and when everyone returned what with the School looking so dreary without the decorations and the grey, wet, cold weather, everyone was really glum. They had eaten too much and watched too much television, played too many computer games and didn't want to start lessons again and that, as they say, were the teachers - the pupils being even worse.

But after a week or so although the days were still short we did have some bright sunny weather. So no one seemed to notice the cold so much and everyone seemed to brighten up a bit, and of course Cook's wonderful warming meals also helped our morale.

However, the cheerful atmosphere was not to last for long, it dispersed with the arrival of the letter from the I.W.F. (The International Wizards Federation).

Now you would think wouldn't you, that Wizards and Wizard Schools would send messages that appeared in the mirror as you brushed your teeth or appeared on a notepad from nowhere. But no, they come through the post along with gas bills, offers on furniture with 50% off the price and a year's free credit (if you apply within seven days) and all the other assorted mail.

I pick up the post from the big letterbox in the Hall and distribute it throughout the School.

I take it upon myself to help the Headmaster out with all the mail that he hasn't a clue about enabling him to concentrate on the important stuff.

When I saw the I.W.F. logo, I thought 'Now then, I can't remember the last time the I.W.F. wrote to us so it must be important'. I left it in the centre of his desk and kept the other mail back so as not to confuse things.

When I took the Heads mail in the following day he was snoozing in his big winged back chair and I was surprised to see the letter I had left yesterday was still unopened on his desk.

I coughed a few times as I usually do when I find him snoozing, and he awoke.

"Ah! Brian, is that the post?"

"Yes Headmaster," I replied, "but you haven't opened the letter from the I.W.F. which came yesterday!"

"Well you see Brian I've mislaid my glasses. Didn't even notice there was anything there. Perhaps you had better read it for me."

"Are you sure Headmaster? It may be private."

"Stuff and nonsense Brian, you're part of the family here just go ahead and read it."

You know, I have never felt as proud as I did when he said I was part of the family.

I began to read the letter and suddenly a grey depressing feeling seemed to engulf me and I knew when the news started to circulate as it somehow always does that the whole School would feel the same. The letter read:

The International Wizards Federation.
Federation House.
Wizards World Avenue.

January 10th 2000.

Crinkles Academy.
Town End Farm,
England.

For the attention of,

Dr. Christian Emanuel Philpotts. I.W.M.M. F.Inst.M.W.

Dear Headmaster,
It is with regret that we note the following,
You have not replied to our previous
letters of:
10th January 1985.
10th January 1990.
10th January 1995.
The situation referred to in those letters has not improved in
fact it has to our dismay deteriorated even further.

The position to date being:

There has been no representation to The International Wizards Federation Annual National Convention for over 400 years. You have in fact failed to attend for the last 404 meetings.

There has been no attendance over the same period for any of the Business Seminars, Group Discussions and Social Functions, which took place over that period of time. Namely, there have been 2,828 occasions when either you and/or one of your colleagues should have attended.

We also note that for the last 127 years there has not even been a communication advising us that no one was to attend. You have not competed in any of the sporting events in the last 80 years, having been unrepresented on a total of 320 occasions.

Lastly, but most seriously, you have not had a Wizard Qualify at any standard for 30 years.

It is therefore the intention of the Executive Council, to consider at its next meeting <u>Withdrawing our Financial Assistance to the Academy</u> at the end of Summer Term 2000.

Your grant is currently as follows:

Namely, the £150,000 per annum pupil grant and the £30,000 per annum building and maintenance costs allowance.

At the moment there are a number of members of the Executive Council who are requesting that we demand repayment of the sums paid to you for all the years since 1969, when no student qualified, plus interest for those years. If this motion is carried I regret to tell you that it is calculated that a repayment of £6.5 million will be required.

This payment would be due within 90 days of any motion to this effect being passed by two thirds of the reigning Executive Council.

We await your reply and point out that any delay in replying, or not replying at all as has been your practise in the past, will be viewed very badly by your few remaining supporters in the assembly.

We remain your colleagues at The United Universal Council of Wizards.

On behalf of The International Wizards Federation,

A. Wizard Wandless.

Clerk to the Federation.

I looked at the Headmaster he looked so old and tired. Tears slowly ran down his face. I put the letter down and quietly left his office.

CHAPTER FIVE

Magic Lessons

Outside the Headmasters Office is a small anti-room. Now I have all sorts of little jobs that need doing there all put off for an emergency such as this.

You see, I can hear everything that's going on when I'm working there.

It's not that I'm nosy or mischievous, I love this School and all the old fossils that work here. In fact I live here in a flat on the top floor.

My intentions are the well being of the School. Most of the staff live in their own little worlds and are so out of touch with the 'Real World' they want to do some pretty stupid things from time to time. Because I usually learn of them in advance whilst working in the anti-room I'm able to stop minor disasters without embarrassment to anyone.

Having taken my tools up to the anti-room I had pottered around most of the morning waiting for something to happen.

Eventually Miss. Millthrop arrived and some whispered conversations took place then shortly afterwards she was followed by a stream of teachers.

It was mid-afternoon when Miss. Hudson the maths teacher appeared and for the first time some meaningful discussions took place.

Apparently the School many years ago had well over 300 pupils but was now down to just over 160, of which 58 were boarders.

The Wizards Federation was still under the impression the School had over 300 pupils and was funding it as though it had.

Nearly two thirds of the pupils did not pay to attend and the annual income from School Fees was only about £29,000 other than the income from the Federation.

So the situation was that for years and years we had been paid for pupils that didn't exist. Even with that extra funding we always struggled to make ends meet! Nothing new was bought it was always patch up and mend.

I was patching up the patch up patch ups. The heating was rarely on even in the middle of winter and apart from Christmas the place was barely lit. As for salaries, the Masters, my own and all the others couldn't be any lower.

Everyone's clothes were long past their best. I've become used to it and don't notice but a stranger would think 'what a shabby bunch of people'.

We all worked at the School not for the money, it was our home. We all felt part of Crinkles, the only thing that the Head didn't run on a shoestring was the food, he believed in good wholesome food for everyone. But all in all despite spending as little as possible, Crinkles would have closed years and years ago if we had only had the funding for 160 plus pupils. It was the ghost pupils that had kept us going.

It wasn't until the following day that I learnt to my amazement that the Old Library at Crinkles was said to have the finest complete collection of Wizards Spell Books in the entire World.

The Headmaster was convinced that it was this 'Valuable Library' that some members of The Executive Council were after.

They knew full well a ridiculous amount of £6.5 Million couldn't be raised, they may as well ask for £650 Million! But the Library was priceless, many of the books being the only ones in existence and most of the other books being the original manuscripts.

The morale of the Masters was nil. Rumours spread like wildfire around the School, a new one everyday, and each new one more depressing than the last. The School was not a happy place, the future looked very bleak and I personally could see no solution to a problem of this size.

Days passed by and there was still no plan of action, everyone was moody and solemn all the time. It felt as though the life was draining away from Old Crinkles Academy.

Another week had started already, two weeks had gone by and I was worried about the threat of the Headmaster losing his supporters if a prompt reply was not made to the I.W.F. letter.

Then on Wednesday I was surprised to be asked to attend a meeting at 3p.m. on Friday in the Headmaster's Study. Was I going to be made redundant? No, surely not! But I couldn't be sure. I thought 3 o'clock Friday would never come but of course it did.

I made my way to the Headmaster's study early and at exactly 3 o'clock I knocked on the door, it was opened by Smithers and I was surprised to find all the teaching staff already there. I had assumed it would be the Head other members of the support staff and myself.

"Come in and sit down Brian." said the Headmaster. "We've been here some time discussing the situation you're already aware of with regard to the I.W.F letter sent to the School."

The Head continued "Not all the staff believe you should be here, but I feel you should. You've always been a very loyal member of the non-teaching staff, although I've known all along how you eavesdrop on me! But I know you think it's for my own good and I accept that."

"The reason I feel you should be here is that I want some opinions from a Non-Wizard that we can trust. Now please tell my colleagues and myself what you think we should do? Ask any question you want an answer to."

I sat taken aback, with everyone staring at me, and I was surprised to hear my own voice reply. "Well everyone here knows there is no way that Crinkles could pay back £6.5

million we don't have that sort of money, and even if it was possible to pay back the arrears how could you keep the School open with so little future income?"

"You're correct; we could not possibly pay back that sum nor keep the School open without the assistance of the I.W.F.! So you can think of no solution then?" said the Headmaster with a sigh.

"Well, no apparent solution at first glance." I found myself saying. A lot of the Masters had been glumly looking at the floor but now everyone was looking at me.

"Go on." said the Headmaster.

"At least you know there is only one path you can take."

"What path is that?" asked Miss. Millthrop.

"You have to persuade the I.W.F to keep on funding you and drop the refund claim."

"How on Earth can we do that?" asked Mr. Scorn and quite a few other Masters mumbled an assortment of negative comments.

"First, we find out how much time we have before the proposed I.W.F. Meeting by the Headmaster contacting one of his friends who is a board member. Then we send a representative to the I.W.F. Conference, we enter the Inter- School Games, we enter a 'Team Quadro' team in the International Junior Team Quadro Championships, and we select people to represent us at any other gatherings that we are entitled to attend. Lastly we enter students in this years Wizards Exams."

The Headmaster looked around the room, "That would still leave major problems Brian," said the Head. "Even if funding was granted it would almost certainly be on a temporary basis, we would have endless inspections, endless forms to be filled in, endless assessments and every penny to be accounted for twice over. Strangers could even be based here listening to every word we spoke and watching every move we made, none of the staff could live with that nor could the pupils."

"Then Headmaster, not only must we do the things that I have suggested we must excel in them! We must be the best, so that there would be no need for endless strangers poking their noses into our everyday lives."

I felt exhausted, and very surprised at what I had said and the confident way I had said it! There was total silence for what seemed like hours, the silence was finally broken by the Head-masters voice that to my surprise sounded enthusiastic and very young.

"I have listened to everything that Brian has said with great interest, and I hope everyone else here has done the same. If we want to be sure of our jobs, or, more importantly in my mind if we want to save old Crinkles..." He paused and slowly looked at everyone. "...In my opinion old Crinkles' is more important than all our jobs put together, however saving Crinkles could also mean saving ourselves. If this is what we want to do then we must fight, and the course of action I put forward to every-one here today is that suggested by Brian whose contribution we should all be indebted to."

The Headmaster once again slowly looked at everyone.

"Tomorrow we make a start, we start by Teaching Magic." One or two of the teachers looked fidgety.

"But Headmaster." blurted out one of the teachers, "We haven't taught Magic of any kind for years!"

"Then we shall have to brush up on it won't we? There is no alternative." replied the Headmaster in the same strange enthusiastic voice.

I was sitting there amazed, are my eyes deceiving me or does the Headmaster look younger! He certainly didn't look so stooped.

"A vote then, a show of hands will do! Do we accept this course of action? All those in favour," the Headmaster said enthusiastically.

A few hands shot up immediately including mine and then slowly, one by one the others followed.

"I declare the vote unanimous."

I found myself surprised once more to hear my voice....

"Headmaster, you asked did I have any questions, I do have some. Why did you not tell the I.W.F. that we were down to so few pupils? Why did you accept money you strictly weren't entitled to? Why have we never attended any of the meetings? Entered any of the sports competitions? Or trained any Wizards?"

The look of amazement on everyone's faces frightened me! 'I have over stepped the mark here,' I thought. Then I realised the Headmaster had a genial smile on his face.

"I knew I was right in wanting you at our meeting Brian, none of the others here would have dared ask one of those questions never mind all of them. All of those questions will be asked by the I.W.F and I have valid answers to them all which I can't disclose here. I must keep some cards close to my chest."

"Well!" said the Headmaster, looking around everyone present. "From this moment in time we fight back from what looks like a poor position now, but what could be a lot stronger than many suppose! Let us hope so, ladies and gentlemen the meeting is closed."

The Headmaster rose and strode to the door, was this really the same broken man of two weeks ago? He seemed years younger, he had left us all sitting in his study looking at each other, everyone sat in silence for some time, then, one by one left the room, they had all suddenly realised that after years and years of the same quiet no stress routine all of their worlds were about to be turned upside down, as indeed was mine.

A different feeling started to filter through the School, optimism and hope started to blossom everywhere. There was a constant coming and going to the Library, the teachers were reading mysterious books every evening and at weekends.

Then two weeks after the meeting in the Headmasters study there pinned on the School Notice Board was a new timetable! A new timetable at this stage in the School Term was unheard of.

Within minutes you could not get near the notice board, there was a semi-circle six deep around it. Could this be correct?

Lessons and periods had been juggled about and now everyone, yes everyone, had a period of Magic every School day. The excitement in the School was unbelievable, no one could sleep at night, everyone was wishing the weekend over so that Monday would arrive and with it the first lessons in Magic!

I had never seen the teachers so active, dashing here, there, everywhere! Frantic searches for lost Wands, frantic reading and rereading of basic Magic so long forgotten. Then that weekend the experiments started, old skills to be rediscovered and polished.

Talk about things that go bump in the night! The whole place should have been cordoned off as a danger zone, had any of these people ever really been Wizards? I personally had very grave doubts and tried to keep well clear of them all, as I'm very happy just being me! I had no desire to be turned into a Toad or find myself walking backwards instead of forwards!

Anyway I had a problem of my own. I was given instructions to find as many old Wands, Cloaks, and Wizards Hats as possible. But where they'd been put no one could remember.

I searched the whole place from top to bottom twice but only found two damaged Wands and one old Cloak that had been used to stop a draft from a badly fitted window.

Come Monday morning my sad tally was just the same. On top of which, four Masters could not find their Wands and three others their Cloaks though we did appear to have some extra Hats.

It was then that I remembered that two of the pupils always had their Wands handy; albeit discreetly, and when I noticed young David outside class 4b I beckoned him over. I explained that I had not been able to trace any Wands, Cloaks or Hats despite searching all weekend and could he possibly help me with a little Magic.

"Why not try the Masters?" he suggested quite reasonably.

I replied by giving him a 'look', which he fully understood.

"I can't help but I think I know who can. Meet me here in one hour after old Harrison's lesson is finished."

I nodded and walked away with a feeling of relief. I had not been looking forward to telling the Headmaster of my failings. One hour later I was at Mr.Harrison's door waiting for the pupils to come out. David was the first out and looked a bit panicky.

"Quick!" He said. "We haven't much time before Jenny's next lesson."

It was a surprise to me that he knew where and when Jenny's next lesson was, as half the pupils didn't seem to know their own lesson times or locations especially since the timetable changes.

We hurried along one corridor, up two flights of steps and along another corridor just catching Jenny before she went into class 6c.

She looked very surprised to see David who quickly explained my request to her. She hesitated, frowned, and then whispered into David's ear, he repeated the spell aloud. She shook her head, looked annoyed and whispered it again but before he could check that he had got it right this time, the Master called Jenny's name and she disappeared into the class-room and the door closed behind her.

David looked a little unsure of himself, then asked me where I would like the Wands, Cloaks and Hats to appear.

"Oh! In my little workshop." I said.

He closed his eyes raised his Wand and chanting pointed in the general direction of my cubby-hole.

"That's the best I can do, I hope they turn up!" He turned and dashed off.

I couldn't wait to get back! I nearly knocked over Miss. Winthrop in the Hall.

"Brian! I'm surprised at you! She shouted, we are always telling the pupils they must not run through the Hall you know we must set an example."

"Yes, you're quite right Miss. Winthrop I'm very sorry!" I gasped, still running. I turned the corner and there was the door leading to my little workshop. I put my hand gingerly on the handle, gently turned it and slowly opened the door, peering cautiously into the room. My heart sank! There was nothing there! Nothing on my bench and nothing on my table apart from its normal clutter!

'Well I thought, David did say he wasn't sure it would work and it hasn't.'

There can't be many people who have had over two hundred Magic Wands of assorted lengths, diameters and colours rain down on their heads, followed by Cloaks and Hats.

What I had forgotten of course was how small my little workshop is and how full of junk it already was. Nor had I realised that you can't stop a spell once it's started, well anyway I can't, in seconds I was buried under Cloaks, Hats and wands, and they were still raining down. I could hardly breathe and had to fight my way out through the pile that was as tall as me.

As I gasped for breath the last Wizard's Hat floated very gently down onto my head and although I say this myself, I suited it!

I went to the Headmaster's office and told him I had everything.

"Excellent, excellent!" he said. "Where were they?"

I hesitated, it would have been nice to take the credit but I decided to explain, he listened to my whole story and smiled.

"That's very interesting, very interesting indeed."

Now dishing out Wands, Cloaks and Hats, isn't as easy as you would think. I had set up in the Main Hall as per the Headmaster's instructions, obviously Cloaks have to be matched according to size the same with the Hats. Surprisingly this took a whole day

Then it was time to dish out the Wands, simple you would think! You've a pile of Wands a queue of pupils and you hand out a Wand to each pupil as they pass. At first everything seemed to be going well in a very short time I had handed out 40 or 50 Wands. Curiously, although I was handing Wands out the pile of Wands seemed to be growing! Then pupils started to arrive back panting and talking a load of gibberish, some of them even appearing to be in a state of minor shock! The garbled message I was getting was that the Wands were returning of their own accord.

I was trying to make some sense of what the pupils were telling me, when suddenly the main double doors leading into the Hall burst open and young Sam Glover came hurtling in like an express train. He was flying around the room about six feet off the ground, holding his Wand in front of him. At first we all just stood and gasped, sometimes having to duck as he plunged lower.

Then he started to shout. "It's the Wand!! It's the Wand!! It's pulling me round and round."

"Drop the Wand!" We shouted! "Drop it!"

"I can't it won't let me!" Sam was looking greener and greener any minute now he was going to be sick.

"Boys", I cried! "Grab hold of his legs as he goes past!" and they did, first one boy grabbed Sam then another, then boys grabbed other boys. Sam Glover was still circling round and round the room, true he wasn't travelling so fast but he was still travelling. Eventually with more than 20 boys and girls hanging onto Sam and each other we managed to bring him to a halt.

But we couldn't get the Wand out of his hand, and then young James Carruthers who was holding his own Wand came near to Sam to see what had been going on. Hey presto! The Wand whipped out of his hand and at the same time the Wand in Sam's hand flew into James's hand.

Everyone, including myself was relieved to see that James was remaining stationary though he wasn't looking too happy.

The pile of pupils on the floor had started to untangle themselves and all appeared to be unhurt apart from Sam who had a few bumps and bruises and was moaning and groaning. Matron was called and after a careful examination declared that no serious damage had been done. She patted Sam gently on the head and said: "No bones broken Sam."

Then she turned to me. "No thanks to you Brian." She snorted.

"B...b..but Matron." I stuttered.

"But nothing Brian! You do realise that the well-being of these pupils is your responsibility when you have been put in charge, albeit for a short time."

"Well you see Matron…" I tried to explain, but Matron was having none of it, she was insisting on the stretcher being brought despite Sam's assurances that he could walk. He was lifted onto the stretcher by many willing hands too many willing hands actually!

The children were really enjoying this and so I suspected was Matron, her favourite word was stretcher, she was never happier than when she was organising a stretcher party.

Sam was embarrassed by the indignity of it all and pleaded to me with his eyes for help, but against Matron I'm powerless. James who was standing next to me and was apparently now feeling safe from any sudden take off said quietly "I bet now he wished he hadn't moaned and groaned so much."

Matron led the way through the crowd of pupils with the four stretcher-bearers behind her. She paused when she reached the door, turned to look at me and declared in a loud voice:

"The Headmaster will be hearing about this!" Turning back she led her little army victoriously away, and so young Sam was left in the care of and under the eagle eye of Matron for a few days.

It took two days to distribute all of the Wands with many minor hiccups along the way. Finally to my great relief each pupil had a Wand that would accept them.

For the next two weeks, Matron, the Gardeners, the Cook, all the other non-teaching staff and myself tried to keep well out of sight. A Wizards School practising Magic from one end to the other with most of the pupils practising Magic for the first time and the instructor's not much better, is not the safest place to be.

CHAPTER SIX

The Wizards Journal

Crinkles had just started to settle down and get back to something like normal when the monthly copy of the Wizard's Journal arrived. Now normally I pick it up with the rest of the post and leave it with the Headmaster who then passes it on usually unopened to the staff room. There one or two of the staff may occasionally glance at it before its inevitable early end in the waste paper basket, the waste paper basket that I empty every day.

So of course I take this opportunity to read them, I probably read more of the Wizard's Journal than any of the Wizard's.

I was on my way up to the Headmaster's study when part of the headline on the front page caught my eye, sliding the brown paper cover off I unfolded the Journal, there it was the main headline.

"CRINKLES ACADEMY to attend
the forthcoming INTERNATIONAL
WIZARDS CONVENTION!"

For the first time in over 400 years Crinkles Academy is to attend this years International Wizard's Convention in New York!

However at the moment no details are available as to who will be representing Crinkles Academy at the Convention.

Very few readers will remember, indeed very few will have heard of Crinkles Academy.

They will therefore be surprised to learn that Crinkles was many centuries ago one of the World's greatest Schools of Wizardry, and to this day it is believed to have one of the finest Libraries of Wizard's Magic in existence indeed some say it is the finest.

It would seem strange then that such a School faded into obscurity. In next months issue we will be looking into Crinkles Academy in more detail.

We invite any readers who feel they have something to contribute which would enlighten us as to Crinkles History to contact the Editor for inclusion in next month's Journal."

I was so excited that I burst into the Headmaster's study without knocking, and thrust the Journal under his nose.

"Look Headmaster!! It's us, it's Crinkles." I cried.

The Headmaster jumped, startled. Then taking the Journal he started to smile as he read it, whilst I quietly slipped away.

Within the hour the news had spread throughout the whole School, of course one of the main topics for discussion was who would accompany the Headmaster to New York. Just think of it - New York! (We were all assuming that he would not be going on his own).

It was with great excitement that the whole School awaited the next issue of the Wizard's Journal.

When the next issue did arrive the postman was none too pleased when he had to deliver well over 100 copies.

I should mention here that to anyone other than a Wizard this Journal appears to be a well-known monthly gardening manual or sometimes a car magazine. It is only when on the premises of a Wizard's School or held by a Wizard that it changes to what it really is and can instantly change back.

This issue caused even more excitement. The Journal was packed with reader's letters about Crinkles Academy, apparently it was the biggest postbag they had ever had about any topic.

The Editor apologised to all the contributors whose letters had not been printed due to the lack of space. He commented that this was the case even after they had allocated more than double the normal space for reader's letters.

They had selected 20 letters at random and the letters ranged from 'Memories of happy days at Crinkles', 'What my Grandmother told me about Crinkles', 'My Great Uncle taught at Crinkles', 'Was there a Carforth Crinkle and if so what happened to him?', through to stranger letters such as 'What was the 'Mystery' of Crinkles' and 'Was Crinkles founder a Wizard, a Super Wizard, or a Fraud?' etc.

Two of the letters in the Journal I really enjoyed, the first was about a Master who many years ago when making his way to bed had been shocked to see a Ghost at the top of the central staircase on the second floor. He kept this to himself but upon seeing the Ghost a second time about a month later and twice more the following week he could stay silent no longer. He mentioned it in the Master's Common Room one night and was at first made the object of jokes and scoffing, but as the night wore on more serious discussion took place.

If it was a Ghost who could it be? And why should it suddenly appear? As the evening grew late all of the ladies insisted that one of the Masters escort them to their rooms.

The later and darker it gets the more plausible a ghost story becomes. What is a good joke at lunchtime becomes a more serious matter at midnight.

Soon of course the whole School knew about it. The more adventurous and brave pupils and quite a few who weren't but had to put on a brave face rather than appear to be a wimp volunteered to stay up all night in an effort to see the ghost.

Most I suspect hoping that they wouldn't, and vastly relieved when they didn't. They sat up night after night, unofficially of course, mostly in groups of 2 or 3 with the very brave on their own. After a few weeks of no ghost appearing it all became a bit boring.

It was now time for some of the less brave to have a go, to try and impress some of their friends and that meant it was now time for the pranksters to begin!

Now to anyone wide awake and able to be logical it would have been obvious that someone was wearing a white sheet and moaning loudly. But, in a dimly lit corridor, when it's 2 or 3 in the morning and you are awakened from a sound sleep whilst sitting in what was called the 'Ghost's Chair' by a tapping on your shoulder and there in front of you stands a Ghost, you don't think! You run! And you run fast.

If you had the nerve to look back you would have seen a group of older pupils in hysterics and putting the 'Ghost Chair' back in the dining room with all the rest.

One enterprising trickster had rigged up a glove stuffed with paper, and dangling it at the end of a fishing line after a little practise could gently tap the side of the face of the poor sleeping pupil, who awoke to find a hand floating on its own, just level with his eyes. I leave it to your imagination what it did to those poor pupils. It was fortunate that no one suffered a heart attack.

First year pupils, some of the second year and all the girls were terrified to go up or down that staircase even during the day to change classrooms. They would run up or down in groups of two or three at a time for safety, others preferring a much longer detour to avoid those stairs. Eventually of course the pranksters were caught and a stop put to their nightly escapades.

The whole mystery was solved a few weeks later when the Master who had been seeing the Ghost saw it once more.

This time however it was earlier in the evening and he had not been enjoying the usual 'hospitality' of the 'Masters Common Room'.

What he had actually seen as he came to the top of the stairs was his own reflection in a long full-length mirror in the Master's Room directly ahead when the door was slightly ajar.

So late at night, one door left slightly ajar at the top of the stairs, one full-length mirror, dim lighting and one slightly intoxicated and tired Master and you have one Ghost.

It caused great disappointment for some at the School and great relief for others including all the lady teachers.

Sadly, a few months later the Master concerned left the School having grown tired of the constant ribbing.

New pupils of course were still told of the Ghost for many years to come and the odd one tricked into sitting in the 'Ghost's Chair'. But they soon found out the true story and gradually the whole thing faded away.

Although I have noticed that some pupils after reading the Journal show a great reluctance to use that staircase after dark.

The second letter that I really enjoyed was about a pupil whose friend's mother ran a little corner shop.

Apparently one day he was invited to tea and just before he was about to leave someone mentioned it was good manners to take a little gift to say 'Thank You'. He decided he should take something but what? He had left it too late to find anything suitable!

As he made his way out he noticed the table was being laid in the Dining Hall for the 'Master's Saturday Afternoon Tea'. He went back into the Dining Hall and seeing a large plate full of scones and no-one around he scooped up half a dozen wrapped them in napkins and gave them to his friend's Mum when he arrived at her house.

She was delighted and told him that she wished she could sell scones of that quality in her shop. "They are absolutely delicious," she said, and wanted to know where they came from. He told her that his Mother had made them and he could probably get her some on Wednesdays and Fridays if that was okay.

She told him it certainly was and she offered what seemed a very generous price for the scones, and said she would accept as many as his Mother was able to make, within reason.

Now the only problem he had was getting the scones. Wednesday and Friday were scone days at the School for Masters and pupils but how to get them?

The following Wednesday he deliberately passed the Kitchen knowing it was time for food to be taken up to the

Dining Hall. He asked the Cook if she wanted a hand. She said, "Yes, that would save my old aching knees." "It's no problem", he said. "I'll do it whenever I can". Strangely, Cook never seemed to notice that it was always on a Wednesday and Friday that he appeared.

He helped himself to some of the scones on the way to the Dining Hall, however his friend's Mother was always asking if he could provide more as three dozen each time didn't go far. But as he was already taking more than half how was he going to get more scones? He decided to tell Cook that her scones were 'favourites with everyone' and 'they' wished she would make more, she was delighted to have her scones so appreciated and said, "I'll see what I can do!"

Cook made an additional two dozen scones every Wednesday and Friday eighteen of which went to the shop and six to the Dining Hall.

Everything was going very well until one-day Cook popped into the corner shop and was surprised to see scones on sale that looked liked hers. She bought two and once outside the shop took a bite from one of them. Yes there was no doubt about it, these were her scones.

The pupil, let's call him 'Simon', was caught and he confessed everything, the Head decided that Simon should return all of the money he had made and that a present should be bought for Cook with it. She was presented with a beautiful mantelpiece clock and Simon was told that he must help Cook every evening after School for one month.

For the first few days they didn't speak other than the Cook telling Simon what she wanted him to do. After a while her good nature, his pleasant attitude and his willingness to do what ever she asked of him without any complaint soon found them both chatting again to each other.

A few years after he left Crinkles Simon and his wife opened a little Coffee Shop in Whitby specialising in home made cakes and pastries especially scones. Every year Cook who by then had been retired for some years spent a few weeks with them.

She was supposed to be on holiday, but of course couldn't resist helping to make the scones!

A lot of us have tried to work out who 'Simon' really was. Some of the teachers must know but they aren't giving anything away!

Perhaps Crinkles was never the boring place it seemed to be.

There was more excitement for Crinkles on page 4, where the headline read,

"MASTER WIZARD MERLIN is to attend THIS YEARS CONVENTION."

This article caused as much discussion as the letters pages had! It stated: "Last month we informed our readers that 'Crinkles Academy' was to be represented for the first time in centuries at this years Convention. Now we are able to inform all of our readers that the Master of Master Wizards, Merlin is to attend this year's Convention.

For several centuries Master Wizard Merlin has never made a public appearance and has made no contact with anyone to our knowledge.

However, as we are convinced no Wizard would dare to claim to be Merlin without dire consequences, we are sure that this is Merlin himself. This then begs the question: Why should Merlin wish to attend any Convention in modern times? Especially this one, although of course important issues will be discussed that effect Wizards it's a less important Conference than some in recent years.

So your Editor asks the question again. Why this Convention? There is only one unusual aspect about this convention and that is the attendance of Crinkles Academy. Surely this could not be the reason for the greatest (in my humble opinion) of all Master Wizards to attend.

I should mention that the Convention Organising Committee have told us that as yet they have not been informed who will represent Crinkles and they point out that all names must be submitted within two months or attendance will not be allowed."

As if this wasn't enough excitement for one issue of what is normally a pretty boring publication, in the 'Stop Press' column the following announcement brought excitement to fever pitch, it read:

'Stop Press': The Editor has just received information that there has been a request from a very high level that this year's International Convention should finish with an 'Oriliance'.

An 'Oriliance', as some of our older readers will no doubt remember is a battle of skills between Wizards. Any Wizard attending may be challenged. The challenged Wizard may elect another to accept the challenge on his or her behalf. Any Wizard refusing a challenge either directly or by election can be downgraded one level for up to five years. Any Wizard accepting a challenge and losing will hold onto their title but of course they could lose some of their standing in the fraternity.

'Oriliance' was banned many years ago as it had become the sole reason for many people to attend the Convention and had turned into a series of grudge battles, the Magic having turned from 'humorous and entertaining' to 'serious', and then to what one could only describe as 'sinister'.

Your Editor, and I'm sure all of our readers wait with baited breath for the decision of the Council.

Full details will appear in next month's issue and we would be very pleased to print your comments. Personally I have never looked forward to a Convention so much.

Then when one turned to the sports pages that surely must be an anti- climax, but no, here was even more exciting news we were mentioned yet again. Crinkles application to submit a team for next years International Junior 'Team Quadro' Championships had been accepted.

It told the readers that Crinkles had not taken part in any competitive 'Team Quadro' games for over 80 years, but they were sure that many readers would still recall the numerous Championships won by the School in the past.

The whole School was alive with excited chatter. Perhaps I should mention here that from what I have been told no one seems to know exactly what happens to Wizards when they grow very, very old.

Wizards seem to fade away - to disappear in fact. But some sources claim that they then reappear and not always looking as ancient as they were before. In fact sometimes looking quite young, so one of the things everyone was wondering about was how 'old' would Merlin look?

Would he look 'old and frail' or 'young and energetic'? Why has no one heard of him for so long? Where has he been? What has he been doing?

I wish that I was allowed to go to the convention but then so do all the teachers and of course they are Wizards. Where would all the money come from even if we could attend? We may all enjoy our jobs but 'well paid' we aren't.

CHAPTER SEVEN

Mischief and Magic

There was always a little bit of mischief going on at the School here and there. However, now some of the mischief started to be linked to Magic, a good example of this was the antics of Dianne and some of her classmates.

Dianne had smuggled her Alsatian puppy Mindy into the School and for the past 3 weeks she had managed to feed it, take it for walks, and completely spoil it with affection, without being caught out.

Her main teacher Edith Young appeared very strict but was in fact very easy going.

She was very absent minded always leaving things all over the place that she then found she desperately needed.

This absent mindedness suited Dianne and her classmate Christopher, as Edith normally would send them on little errands for her.

Usually, two or three times a day one or the other would be sent to find her reading glasses or some other item. This gave them the opportunity to check everything was okay with Mindy so the puppy was never left to long on her own.

Two of the boys in Edith's class were a bit of a handful: Daniel and Adam Gregg. Daniel always wanted to answer every question the teacher asked whether he knew the answer or not.

"Miss! Miss!" he shouted continuously during every lesson. His brother Adam, not wanting to be out done had started to join in.

Between the two of them they managed to cause uproar and disrupt the whole class.

Edith spent a lot of her time calling out: "Boys! Boys! Settle down!"

"But I know the answer Miss!" Daniel would shout back.

"So do I Miss!" Adam would join in.

"But I haven't asked anyone a question so how can you know the answer?" Edith would reply in desperation.

"I do Miss! I really do!" Insisted Daniel, and so it went on - day in - and day out.

No one is sure who originally had the idea, but when teaching 'Magic' was started again in the School, Dianne, Christopher, Daniel and Adam hatched a 'Magic' plot.

Adam started to quieten down; Dianne and Christopher were extra-attentive to all of Edith's needs. Meantime Daniel was deliberately being more boisterous and disruptive than usual.

Whenever Daniel was out of the class, Dianne and Christopher started to suggest jokingly, that Edith should use some of her 'Magic' to turn Daniel into a Toad, or a Frog, as a punishment for his misbehaviour and to shut him up.

Edith laughed at them and said "I wouldn't do that, even if I could" and she certainly couldn't manage Magic like that.

Then Dianne made a further suggestion. Why didn't Edith pretend she was going to turn Daniel into say, a puppy dog, utter some spell-like words then tell him if he didn't behave himself he might at any time suddenly become a puppy.

Edith told everyone not to be so silly and stop all this nonsense.

Over the next couple of days Daniel went his 'ends' he was ten times worse than usual.

Edith started to think more and more about what Dianne had said. The naughtier Daniel became the more appealing the idea became.

Finally she thought to herself, 'Why not? After all no harm would be done and it might just work, for a while anyway.'

The following day Daniel was that troublesome that Edith decided enough was enough.

"Daniel!" She said, "I'm going to put a Magic spell on you, and if you don't quieten down and behave yourself you could change into a puppy and you might stay like that for days."

A hush fell over the whole class. Daniel looked shocked, and when Edith started to rattle of some hocus pocus words and waving her arms around like some demented windmill then pointing directly at Daniel, he looked terrified.

For the rest of the morning the classroom was almost in total silence. 'This is Heaven, sheer Heaven, thought Edith.'

Dianne, Adam, Daniel and Christopher, could hardly contain themselves in class, Daniel had 'ants in his pants' not being able to talk.

None of them could wait for lunchtime to get together and talk things over. At last the lunch bell rang then there was the usual race for the door.

"Don't run! Walk." Shouted Edith, not that anyone took any notice.

A couple of minutes later the gang of conspirators were deep in conversation.

Lunchtime was over and the children returned to the classroom settling down at their desks. Daniel's was in the centre row near the back.

Edith hadn't noticed the bag Dianne carried into the classroom.

The lesson had hardly started when Daniel began his usual noisy antics. Edith looked up from her desk. "Daniel, remember the spell I put on you."

"Yes Miss, but I only wanted …."

"Daniel, keep quiet, you have been warned." Edith got up and turning to the blackboard started to write down the maths questions. Daniel got up quietly and hid behind the desks next to the wall.

While he was hiding Dianne got Mindy her puppy out of the bag and put her on Daniels desk. Christopher who sat behind Daniel held the puppy there and stroked her so she wouldn't jump about.

Then Adam shouted out, "Miss! Miss! Look at Daniel!"

Edith recognized Adam's voice.

"Keep quiet Adam!" she replied, but didn't turn around she just went on writing on the blackboard.

"Hurry up," whispered Christopher. "Mindy is starting to wriggle all over the place. Oh no! She's had a wee now! It's all over my hand."

"But Miss!" Adam cried out louder. "Look at Daniel! Look at Daniel!"

Edith sighed to herself, 'One peaceful morning … that's all I had!' and turned around.

"Well Adam, what about Dan........." she stood stunned into silence, looking at the puppy standing on Daniel's desk.

She screamed "Daniel! Daniel! Oh!!!....... What have I done?" She screamed again then fainted.

The whole class burst out into laughter, but after a few seconds became a little worried.

Dianne picked the puppy up and put her inside her bag,

"Here Christopher. Take Mindy back I'm going to fetch Miss Millthrop," and off she dashed.

Daniel was with the other children who had gathered around Edith when Dianne arrived back with Miss Millthrop.

Edith was just starting to come around and the first face she saw was Daniel's.

"Daniel!" She cried, "It's you! Are you all right?"

"I feel great," he said. "In fact if I had a tail I would wag it!" Edith gave a loud groan and passed out again.

Christopher was sent to get Matron and soon Edith was tucked up in bed.

Miss Millthrop had talked to Edith and knew that she was totally incapable of such a spell. She put two and two together and had a good idea of what had been going on, she told Edith she was probably suffering from overwork, and that she must take it easy for a few days and she would take care of her class.

Miss Millthrop concentrated on Edith's class, especially those who she suspected had been the cause of all the mischief and made them work harder than they'd ever had to work before.

"I knew something like this would happen, I wish we had old Edith back!" moaned Adam.

"Shut up! It's only for a couple of days!" said Christopher. It lasted 3 days but everyone felt they had done a terms work. When Edith returned she found her class polite and very well behaved.

They had become a pleasure to teach and 'Surprise! Surprise!' the children found they enjoyed their work more and more.

Dianne decided she had better take Mindy back home that weekend as she didn't want to push her luck.

The odd time Edith felt the class starting to become a little unruly she would casually mention Miss Millthrop. It always did the trick.

Meanwhile, Miss. Maria Harrison the P.E. Teacher was also about to have some problems.

She had the idea that if the School could produce a 'Team Quadro' team then the School could also produce a decent 'Netball Team'.

Maria's heart was in the right place, but how she thought she would be able to organise even a passable netball team when she constantly struggled to organise the P.E. lessons is a mystery to me. Passing bean bags to each other was about the most successful thing achieved so far.

Lisa Grey was the first who volunteered for the team and soon made sure she was indispensable to Maria. She would rush to do this and dash to do that, nothing was too much bother.

Abbey wanted to be Lisa's friend and also hoped she would let her join her gang. She followed Lisa everywhere, and ran any errand Lisa requested.

Bethany and Sophie were also on the netball team and although they were good friends of Abbey they weren't very keen on Lisa.

During netball practise Lisa said to the other girls, "Wouldn't it be fun if I put a spell on the ball so that every time we made a shot at the net and missed (which would be every time) the ball would shoot across towards Maria."

Abbey thought this idea sounded great fun. "Yes! Yes! Let's do that! Let's do it now!"

She suddenly looked puzzled. "But how do we do it? I don't know a spell that would do that."

Lisa smiled "But I do!"

"I think it's a stupid idea," said Bethany.

"I think it's stupid as well and I like Maria! I don't want the ball to hit her!" added Sophie.

"It's Miss. Harrison to you two. I knew you wouldn't like the idea you're both mamby-pambies."

"We're not mamby-pambies, and why is it that you can call the teacher 'Maria' and we can't?" asked Bethany in an annoyed voice.

"Because she said I could, that's why," said Lisa smurking.

Lisa turned and walked away, followed by Abbey.

"Are you still going to put a spell on the ball?" Abbey asked Lisa.

"Of course I am, and I'm going to do it right now."

"Ready girls!" called out Maria, "Let's line up and start the last practise session for this afternoon."

Maria blew her whistle and the practice commenced.

A couple of minutes later Lisa threw the ball towards the wall just above the net. The ball hit the wall, bounced back and then flew straight at the teacher. It hit Maria with a hefty whack on the head, she staggered backwards and felt a little unsteady, then recovering called out: "Play on!"

Four minutes later it happened again this time hitting Maria on her brow. She staggered and swayed more this time but still managed to call out a very shaky, "I'm okay! Play on!"

Abbey and some of the others thought this was great fun and had started to giggle. Lisa had a smirk on her face and was trying for a third time to get the ball to hit Maria.

Bethany and Sophie were both disgusted at their friend Abbey, they couldn't believe that she would join in and support Lisa and wished they could do Magic powerful enough to turn the tables on her.

Once more Lisa hit the wall behind the net and once more the ball hurtled if anything faster than before towards Maria who this time was standing just in front of the door leading to the corridor.

At this point the door opened and in stepped Dr. Philpotts. As he did, Maria who had her back to the Headmaster having seen the ball coming this time ducked, the ball flew over her head and hit the Headmaster full in the face.

He stumbled back into Miss. Millthrop who was following him through the door, they were on an informal tour of the School.

I was behind Millthrop with my little notebook jotting down various odd jobs the Headmaster wanted attended to. Down went Millthrop on top of me the Headmaster on top of her.

We lay in a pile on the floor with the children screaming and Maria running amok shouting, "Is everyone alright? Will I call Matron?"

Although a little shaken we all scrambled swiftly to our feet at the mention of the word Matron. With a note of panic in his voice the Headmaster said, "No! No need to call Matron! Everyone is alright Maria."

I breathed a sigh of relief and so did Miss. Millthrop, as Matron was the last person we wanted here.

The Headmaster paused and looked around. Everyone had gone very quiet and most of the children were looking at the floor although I noticed Lisa was looking slyly at Miss. Millthrop.

"I can't apologise enough Headmaster I'm so awfully sorry." Maria stuttered.

"Now don't upset yourself Maria these things happen."

Miss. Millthrop was looking at the ball that was in the corner of the room and very slowly spinning around. She walked towards it and it started to move away.

"I thought so." She said to herself, and discretely took her wand out and spoke quietly.

The ball gave off a few wheezing noises and it crumbled as all the air inside was released.

She turned around and walked over to Lisa. "In my office in half an hour." She whispered in her ear.

Lisa's face changed colour, she had hoped to get away with it. Miss. Millthrop then walked up to Abbey, "In my office in half an hour." She whispered. Not only did Abbey's face change colour but she also started to shake.

No troublemaker could escape Miss. Millthrop. A sixth sense guided her, and she could read a face like a book, she was a walking lie detector!

Just as things had quietened down Matron burst in, the jungle telegraph had reached her and faster than Superman, Super Matron was on the scene. The Headmasters jaw dropped!

"Oh, Dr.Phillpotts!! Just look at that huge swelling on your brow! We can't have you standing up! You must rest! Temperature's to be taken, pulse to be checked! I'll organise a stretcher to get you to sick bay!"

This was Matron's moment of glory. A stretcher for the Headmaster would need four teachers!

"What's this I see? Look at your face Maria! ...an even bigger bump on your brow! And what's this great lump on top of your head? You could suffer from aftershock, best to get you by stretcher up to the sick bay!"

"I'm alright Michelle! I really am! Just leave me alone... please Michelle."

'Michelle', so that was Matron's name. I had never heard anyone mention her name before, she was always known simply as 'Matron'.

Well, Michelle, or Matron as I will still call her was determined that this would be her finest hour. A 'stretcher convoy' to the sick bay!!

The Headmaster protested and asked for Millthrop's support.

"Tell her I'm okay," he pleaded. But to his surprise Millthrop said: "Matron probably knows best I would follow her instructions, I must go now as I have some other matters to attend to back at my office."

No amount of protesting was going to stop Matron getting her way, "After all Headmaster," she said, "What example are you giving to the teachers and the pupils if you don't obey your own rules."

That having been said, the Headmaster and Maria gave in and the 'Great Convoy' was organised and formed up.

Six senior pupils led it to clear a pathway along the various corridors, (now thronged by pupils and staff trying to see what was going on and to find out what had happened). Then came the Headmaster on a stretcher carried by four Masters, with Matron alongside as proud as a General leading a Victory Parade. They were followed by six more senior pupils then Maria on a stretcher carried by four Masters and a rear guard of six more senior pupils to stop anyone crowding in.

It just so happens that the sick bay is about as far away as you could possibly get from the gym.

The convoy wound its way along corridors, up stairs, down stairs, between groups of pupils and staff who in turn fell in behind when it passed them so that the convoy grew longer and longer.

The Headmaster and Maria were relieved when they finally found themselves in the sick bay lying comfortably on beds with pristine white cotton sheets and pillows on them, and everyone else being ushered out.

Magic, or none magic authority of any kind, no matter how powerful could alter the fact that this was Matrons domain where she ruled supreme. I called around to see if everyone was okay, but was told in no uncertain terms to: "Clear off Brian."

Lisa was banned from the netball team but Abbey was allowed to stay in the team on condition that she did not misbehave. Strange to tell, Maria (after the two bumps on her head) seemed to have found new confidence and ability. With the enthusiastic help and skills of Abbey, Bethany and Sophie she eventually went on to create a very successful 'Netball Team'. But that's a story for another day.

CHAPTER EIGHT

The Containment Book

It was a couple of days after the excitement of the Wizards Journal that I was asked to pop up to the Headmasters Study to have a look at his chair which had developed an annoying squeak.

So armed with my toolbox just in case needed and an oilcan off I went. I knocked on the door and was summoned in and told to close the door behind me.

"Ah, just the man I want to see."

"Yes your chairs squeaking." I said.

"No, that's not why I want to see you." He answered very softly.

Then he took out his Wand and muttered a few words.

I looked on in amazement; I had never seen the Headmaster use his Wand before, what was he doing?

"That should do it, just a little spell to guarantee we won't be heard, I can't be too careful at the moment probably not needed but best to be safe."

I stood waiting, but the Headmaster now sitting at his desk seemed miles away and I was afraid to interrupt his thoughts.

"Ah!" He said looking up. "What do you want Brian."

"It's you who wants me Headmaster."

"I do?" He looked thoughtful, and paused. "So it is, so it is," he said. "You must forgive me Brian I have a lot on my mind at the moment."

"Well now Brian you've been with us for some years now."

"Yes 20 years." I replied.

"Time flies, 20 years, you've always been reliable but do you love the School Brian?"

"I certainly do Sir, none more than me." I replied.

"I believe you Brian, that's why I want you to say yes to something you would rather say no to."

The Headmaster paused and looked at me intently, there was what seemed to be a long, long silence, eventually broken by me.

"I'll do my best for the School sir you can rely on it, just tell me what you want me to do?"

"You're very popular in the School Brian with everyone, Masters, Children, Parents, everyone."

"I'm going to ask you to do something that will make you disliked, perhaps even hated by the children and you could find a very negative response from some of the Masters." he paused

"I want you to appear to be vindictive to Jenny and David."

"Jenny and David!!" I cried out. "But they're great children."

"I know, but I need a reason to have you all here in my study from time to time, this could be essential if the School is to survive." He paused and looked out of the window.

"The only way I can think of doing this without attracting suspicion is for you to have supposedly complained about them. This will give me the excuse to have everyone in my study, so you must pretend to dislike them and them to dislike you."

I stood there stunned, he didn't face me, but continued to look out of the study window.

"Are you sure this is necessary." I queried.

"Yes, I'm sure. Unfortunately there is no other way, there must be at least one spy in the School probably more, who they are is anyone's guess! It could be a Master, or Masters, who have been here for years and years or it could be one of the new Masters or even some of the children. What I'm sure of is that you're on the School's side, you and the two children are the only people I can guarantee are 100% loyal at this moment in time."

"I don't really understand what you're talking about Headmaster, but if it's for the good of the School I will do it."

"I was banking on your support Brian. I want us all to meet after the evening meal, I will send for Jenny and David and later for you. Till this evening then when you will fully understand the problem."

I nodded and left the Heads office, spending the rest of the day in a sort of daze trying to work out what it could all be about.

Strangely all day to my embarrassment I seemed to be bumping into Jenny and David.

It was with relief I picked up the phone in my little office come workshop at 7.30 that night and heard the Headmaster's voice summoning me up to his study, when I arrived Jenny and David were already there looking a little puzzled.

"Well Brian." Said the Headmaster, "I've been explaining to Jenny and David some of the problems the School has at the moment which you are already aware of." The Headmaster paused. "I have also explained my plan to enable us to gather here from time to time as we have tonight and avoid suspicion and rumours.

Jenny and David are as upset as you Brian that you can no longer be openly friendly. Hopefully it will not be for too long, now it's time to explain why all three of you are here"

I noticed the Wand in the Headmaster's hand and realised he had been doing an anti-eaves dropping spell once again.

The Headmaster continued, "I need all three of you to be my spies, every piece of gossip or anything that doesn't feel right or seems a little strange I want you to tell me about it on a regular basis. I mean anything, even if on second thoughts you may think it too trivial to mention. That's why we need regular meetings here in my office, I want all of us to hear the information at the same time because it's possible one of us might be able to put something useful together that the others had missed."

"Now I'm going to take this opportunity to tell you a little more about Crinkles."

"As you all know no Magic has been taught at Crinkles Academy for a long, long time, this was not by chance but by choice. You see all Magic has a touch of evil in it as you know Jenny."

"I know Headmaster?" Said Jenny embarrassed and looking at the floor.

"Yes Jenny, your Summer Holidays, you did break the rules although I agree you were provoked, that's why I overlooked it."

"You knew!!" Gasped Jenny, she had thought he was talking about the School Concert.

"Yes I knew, there's not a lot that escapes me and no one from my Academy can do any Magic without me knowing about it. I won't mention the School Concert."

Both Jenny and David started to blush and looked at the floor, the School Concert? I must remember to ask them about that I thought.

"We must press on, I don't want you here that long that it starts to look suspicious." The Headmaster stood up and started to walk around his study pausing now and again to tap the large globe standing in the corner, a figurine or a book.

"No doubt you have all read the current issue of the Wizard's Journal and read the name Carforth Crinkle and Crinkles Academy, however it has been in existence for many more centuries under a different name."

"Carforth Crinkle did indeed establish Crinkles Academy as we know it. He was a truly talented Wizard, the best there ever was in Spell Neutralising and undisputed Master of Spell Translations." The Headmaster started to tap the top of his desk.

"Long, long ago, in the midst of time, when motor cars, trains, aeroplanes, T.V's, telephones, computers and all the other developments we know today didn't exist." He paused and started to spin the globe we watched the Countries of the World pass by. "Magic and Wizards had become very powerful second only to Kings and Emperors."

"Some very Influential Wizards felt that they should be the 'Most Powerful People in the World' and dabbled more and more in dubious and evil spells to achieve their goals."

"Forcing Good Wizards to band together, and soon a Wizards War was in progress, it raged for years until eventually the Good Wizards won but not before a terrible price had been paid. This Victory ended the huge power the Evil Wizards had held."

"Our Library holds not just books on spells, but historical books telling the stories of great battles won and lost by Wizards in every corner of the World."

The three of us all looked at the Headmaster in wonderment. He had always seemed so uninteresting and the Library so dusty and dreary, yet here was the Head telling us that the Library was full of books on great battles and wars of which he probably knew every word.

"Although defeated, the Evil Wizards still had great power to do mischief, an agreement was finally made that they would give up all their evil spells on condition that they were to face no further punishment."

This is where Carforth Crinkle played his crucial part; he created the 'Containment Book'. This contains all of the Evil Spells and the Good Spells that defeated them. So although the Evil Wizards still knew their Evil Spells and could pass them on through the centuries right up to the present time, they were useless as long as they were held by the Good Spells in the 'Containment Book'."

"If Evil Wizards could get their hands on the 'Containment Book' then they would be able to study the Good Spells and possibly devise spells to overcome the Good and release the Evil."

"So it was essential that the book be kept in the safest place possible and that is why the book is here at Crinkles Academy."

All three of us sat in silence, totally amazed.

"You mean here at Crinkles is the most 'Important Book in the World'!!!" Gasped David.

"Yes precisely!!" Replied the Headmaster. "As far as Good and Evil Wizardry is concerned."

The Head thought for a while then said,

"In my opinion it is the 'Most Important Book in the World' as far as everyone is concerned, if the Evil Wizards regain their old powers they could destroy the world as we know it today. Centuries of democracy and freedom would disappear, everyone would become slaves to their way of thinking."

David was no longer listening to the Head, he was thinking about the Containment Book and where it was hidden.

"Headmaster!!" He shouted in excitement "Here at little Old Crinkles, we have the 'Containment Book', where is it hidden? Is it in a secret vault with walls incredibly thick?"

"I bet it's guarded by Dragons and buried deep, deep underground, with secret passages and huge winged bats and......." Jenny added excitedly but tailed off when she realised the Headmaster was laughing.

"No. I'm afraid not children. Dramatic and romantic as that may seem none of those things presents a problem to powerful Evil Wizards, 10, 20, 30 foot thick walls, an army of Dragons no problem at all."

"Then where would be safe?" I found myself asking. "Or are we not allowed to know?"

"I don't see why you shouldn't know, after all our enemies know and you are my army, the army for good."

"But some tea and cakes I think, I don't know about you but I'm ready for some refreshment."

Tea and cakes at a time like this, I thought, and looking at David and Jenny I knew they were thinking the same.

The Headmaster waved his Wand and before us appeared a selection of cakes and beautifully decorated cups full of hot tea.

I looked at the cakes but my personal favourite Fruit Cake was not there, so I decided to have a slice of Battenberg. I reached out and picked up a piece of Battenberg and to my amazement it turned into a slice of Fruit Cake. I looked at the Headmaster who gave me a large grin.

Although it seemed strange to be having tea after hearing such startling news I must admit I enjoyed it very much.

"Back to work I think." said the Headmaster, and just as suddenly as it had appeared, cups, saucers, the remaining cakes and plates all disappeared.

"Now you want to know where the 'Containment Book' is." The Headmaster looked at us, we could hardly wait to find out, every second we waited felt like an hour. He was smiling and taking great delight in making us wait for the information, finally he told us,

"It's in the School Library."

"LIBRARY!!!" We all shouted.

"Yes, the Library."

"But anyone could just walk in and take it!" Jenny said.

"Anyone could just walk in, but take it, 'NO', at least at the moment no-one can.

"You see the 'Containment Book' itself is stable and untouchable, and will remain so as long as it is surrounded by 'ordinary everyday basic Magic Books' in a Wizards environment where the Wizards are Good Wizards." The Head paused to let it sink in.

"That's why Crinkles Academy was chosen to be keeper of the book." He continued.

"It had then and still has the biggest single collection of basic everyday Magic Books, rare and unusual Magic Books and almost all of them the original manuscripts which have far more power than mere written or printed copies."

"There has never been a pupil from Crinkles who turned into an Evil Wizard. That's why to safeguard us and hence the 'Containment Book', we were guaranteed financial support forever in the original agreement."

"It is also why we gradually reduced teaching Magic until we taught none at all, and why we did not keep contact with other Wizards or Wizards Schools. By doing that we reduced to almost nil the possibility of any Evil Magic no matter how small developing in the School and therefore never likely to produce an Evil Wizard."

"Now it's become obvious the Evil Wizards want to ignore the original agreement hence the ridiculous demand for £6.5million repayment. This can only mean the Evil Wizards have gained control or almost gained control of the Executive Council."

The Headmaster looking very angry continued:

"I can't understand how they have been allowed to do this. Is it because of laziness, complacency, or incompetence on the part of the other members of the Executive Council? Whatever the cause they have managed to endanger centuries of peace, allowing the enemy to come virtually to our door. All they have to do now is overcome a handful of us here at Crinkles to win.

We are forced to make a last stand at 'The International Wizards Convention' that's why I asked Merlin to attend and thankfully he agreed."

We all looked at each other, the Editor of 'The Wizards Journal' had been right, Merlin was attending because of Crinkles, well because the Headmaster of Crinkles had asked him.

To think that our apparently dozy old Headmaster had Merlin as a friend, we were brought back down to Earth when the Head said we must not tell anyone about Merlin or anything else we had been told in his study that night.

"I was afraid when you and David joined the School Jenny."

"Afraid of us!!" Jenny and David looked amazed.

"Yes, very much so, you were the first pupils for years and years who had any real interest in Magic, I was afraid of what it might lead to, now it turns out that we are going to have to rely on your Magic."

"Our Magic!!" They exclaimed.

"Yes, you're coming with me to the 'Wizards Convention' in New York."

The children sat totally silent. I was the one who spoke up.

"Headmaster!! They're only children they won't understand anything."

"Very true Brian, they will probably be bored out of their minds during the Conference but they aren't going for the Convention, they're going for the 'Oriliance'."

"'Oriliance'!! But that's heavy stuff from what I read in the Wizards Journal, surely not suitable for children." I spluttered out.

"Yes, very heavy stuff indeed, even for Master Wizards, but all we have are the children."

"Surely children won't be allowed to attend anyway?" I said.

"There's no rules saying children can't attend, no-one ever thought any child would want to or that any adult would take children," replied the Headmaster. "It's dangerous yes, but there is no alternative."

"But their skills will be too limited they wouldn't have a chance to succeed. You can't rely on the children Headmaster."

"Their strength lies in never having called on any real evil in any spells they have done so far only a little mischief, and the fact that they are born Wizards. They will have help from myself and other Wizards there, of that I am sure, or I would not commit them."

"There is also the strength of the 'Containment Book', which if we are able to protect it, is a truly great force on our side."

"What do you mean? If we can protect it Headmaster, is it in danger?" I asked.

"I'm convinced there is more to the Containment than I have been able to explain here tonight."

"For some years I have been afraid that Evil Wizards may have been studying ways of breaking through the Containment. Now I must conclude that I was right in my assumptions which were based on various small pieces of information I have been receiving from friends and contacts around the World during the past year, then the letter from the International Wizards Federation followed by the announcement that there was be an 'Oriliance' at the International Wizards Convention confirmed my worst fears."

"The Evil Wizards feel powerful enough to make their move against Crinkles!"

"It would appear that centuries of inactivity by the Evil Wizards have concealed a huge build up of frustration and anger. Once more they want their power over people and events. It was a terrifying power all those centuries ago, in the 'Modern World' we know today the damage it could do does not bear thinking about.

"I myself have devoted a lot of my time in trying to fathom out how the Containment really works. You see Brian I have not merely been sitting here in my big comfortable chair daydreaming or snoozing, that is what I wanted you and everyone else to think. But I have failed! I had hoped others had failed also, now I see that they are almost at a point where they may succeed."

"You see, Carforth Crinkle could not leave instructions with anyone on how his Containment really worked. The only way he could try to guarantee its complete safety was that only he knew the secrets of how it works."

"If only we could contact him, but he vanished hundreds of years ago probably to protect his system. Personally I think he Dewizarded."

"Dewizarded? What does that mean?" I asked the Head.

"He gave up being a Wizard. In which case he will have been dead for centuries." replied the Head.

"But now, if we don't fully understand it, we can't fully defend it."

"Shouldn't we be guarding the Library Headmaster?" I asked.

"We probably should, but with whom? Who do we trust? And how will we guard it all-day and everyday? Where would we get all the guards from?"

"I think the books will warn us somehow if they are in danger, but I don't know how. Perhaps something built into them by Carforth Crinkle similar to a burglar alarm system but of course not visible."

"Unfortunately the only way that we could test this theory would be to have some Evil Wizards try and steal the books whilst unknown to them we observe them, unfortunately this we can't arrange."

"I have no doubt," the Headmaster continued, "That we have Evil Wizards or should I say followers of Evil Wizards in the School. But we can't put in a request on the School Notice Board for them to come forward and assist us in an experiment."

"How can we be sure there aren't any really Evil Wizards at the School Headmaster?"

"I would sense powerful Evil of the magnitude that truly Evil Wizards have. Probably even you would Brian."

"No, they would not be able to slip someone that powerful into the School for fear of detection. The people they have in our School are simply afraid of not obeying them, or feel that they have been overlooked in life. Promising them greater status in return for their assistance when required would probably be enough to persuade some of the Masters. Being overlooked in life could possibly cover every Master at this School."

"If some of the pupils are involved it could be a parent or a relation who has been promised greater things if their children co-operate in some way or another. Or perhaps the child sees itself as a leader and enjoys the feeling of having secret powers, who knows?"

"As for the teachers Headmaster, I suspect it's more likely to be a relative newcomer."

"Not so Brian! It could be someone who's been here for years even longer than me."

"Teachers who have been here longer than you Headmaster!" I asked in amazement.

"Yes, there are two. You're thinking in your timescale Brian, you must think in Wizards time. 200 hundred years to us is like five years to you. Someone could have been planted at the School years and years ago just waiting for the right opportunity."

"From what you have told us I am more than ever convinced Headmaster that what you propose is too dangerous for David and Jenny."

David and Jenny had just sat quietly listening to the Head and myself.

The Head nodded in agreement then said, "I can't believe it myself Brian how much pressure I'm putting on David and Jenny at their age. Unfortunately there are no other options open to me and what makes this harder on all three of you is that you must not mention or discuss any of this with anyone else. I mean anyone, Mams, Dads, best friends, no one, only amongst ourselves!"

"But there must be other options open to us Headmaster." I said

"I'm sorry Brian, I have thought through even the remotest options time and time again, this is the only realistic one open to us. There can be no more discussions on this matter. We have been here too long already. David, Jenny, Brian, remember not a word to anyone! And I mean anyone! That's all for now, Goodnight."

I felt annoyed and a little hurt at the Heads sudden abruptness. He stood up and opened his study door, the three of us left without staying a word to each other and went our separate ways.

I felt very uneasy and a feeling of dark foreboding came over me, so how must David and Jenny feel?

To this day I still don't know if the Headmaster put a spell of silence on us or not. All I know is much to my surprise I found I didn't want to talk to anyone about it.

All I could think about for days was – 'who could be a spy?' Spy sounded as good a word as any, although when I looked at the Masters, which I was doing all day long, none of them seemed to have it in them to be a spy.

They all looked so harmless, though I suppose that's what makes a really good spy. So forget the shifty very sly-looking ones and forgot the tall handsome dashing full of confidence people. Concentrate on the quiet and respectable looking ones, and those that wouldn't say boo to a goose, so as the Head said, this narrowed it down to every Master in the place.

Then again, though highly unlikely some member or members of the general staff may be involved.

As for the children, it could be some or all of the mischief makers, but that seems to easy. Once again the same as for the adults it could be some of the quiet or timid ones.

In truth it could be anybody.

CHAPTER NINE

Miss Millthrop's Garden Fete

There was a bright cheerful atmosphere about the School, however this was not shared by me because a rumour had spread (as it was supposed to) that I had a grudge for some reason or another against David and Jenny and that any excuse would do to report them to the Headmaster.

We had all attended two more meetings in the Headmaster's study, mainly he wanted to know in minute detail every rumour circulating in the School and any conversation we may have heard no matter how trivial, but he would also give us what I would call a pep talk.

A favourite saying of his had become: "Keep your ear to the ground."

He would repeat it five or six times every visit. On each visit he gave David and Jenny books on spells, two each the first time and three each the second time, saying: "Try your best, read through them then read them again, when you have finished swap your books with each other. Remember you must return them on your next visit to me."

Strangely he never asked how much they had managed to learn from them, he simply took a book in both hands and sat silently holding it for a few seconds, if he smiled you knew they must have done well. Of the four books returned so far it was three smiles and one nod for Jenny, but unfortunately only one smile one nod and two scowls for David.

The books were not reissued but taken back and new ones handed out.

The Assistant Head, Miss. Melissa Millthrop had become so enthusiastic about her Magic abilities that she had organised extra evening Magic Classes on Mondays and Thursdays. She charged 50p each entrance fee, 20p for pop or crisps, 25p for tea or coffee and 2p each for a biscuit, 5p for a chocolate one, all money received to go into the School Fund.

At first a lot of the boys went, but after a while they realised there was more talk than Magic and most of it girl talk, so soon it became 'girls only' evenings.

Then one day she had a brain wave, why not have a 'Garden Fete'? A marquee could be hired and possibly a folk band, there could be craft demonstrations, outside amusements, a tug of war etc and her speciality would be the cake stall. She was in fact a very good cook and I for one was looking forward to the cake stall.

She certainly put plenty of effort and enthusiasm into it, insisting on everyone helping, everyone apart from me that is.

I was told, "We can manage very well without you." That hurt because we had always got on so well, then the following day when I overheard two teachers discussing me and the following comment: "I don't know why the Head doesn't get rid of him he always was pretty useless."

Pretty useless! I felt like thumping them. When I think of the favours I had done for both of them in the past! I crept off to my cubbyhole where I sat feeling sorry for myself. I made a cup of tea to cheer myself up, but there were no scones these days because cook had heard about my supposed bad treatment of David and Jenny.

I had to check everything in my cubbyhole now. Already my mug had been glued to the workbench; brown poster paint had been mixed in with my coffee; work boots filled with treacle; wellies with water and my newspaper often swapped with yesterday's or pages removed.

Most annoying of all my tools had been emptied into a huge pile in the middle of the floor along with my assorted screws, nuts and bolts and bits and bobs. That took me two full days to sort out. I had now fitted two large padlocks on my door, a door that I never used to lock.

Meanwhile Jenny and David were the 'School Heroes' something that under normal circumstances they probably would have enjoyed. Whereas under the actual circumstances that were known only to the three of us they were going about with faces as long as fiddles. Everyone else of course thought they were looking so miserable because of me.

So I was not happy when I was summoned yet again by the Headmaster. This would make the situation even worse, and to be frank I had taken about as much as I could stand. It was people either not talking or barely talking to me that bothered me the most.

It wouldn't have seemed as bad if some startling information had come to light, as far as I could tell there had been nothing of any importance emerge from all this eves dropping we had been doing.

As it turned out the Headmaster was right, some apparent useless gossip proved invaluable two years later when we were in South America of all places.

Once more we had to tell the Head everything that had been happening, he then collected the books from Jenny and David and I could see how worried David looked. The score this time was Jenny 4 smiles and 2 nods but David's was one smile 2 nods and 3 deep frowns it was obvious to everyone that David was struggling.

The Headmaster picked up two very thick books from his desk. "Only one book each this time, this will be the last book I want you to study."

David's face said it all, one book, but look at the thickness of it. "However," said the Headmaster, "You can't possibly study this and do your normal school work, so as a punishment for your latest misbehaviour I 'm telling your teachers that you are to report each day to me where you are to clean and polish every book in my personal library. You will of course be studying this last book."

"But Headmaster!! When this gets out I will be blamed again and my position will be impossible at the School." I was surprised at how angry my voice sounded.

"You must hang on one more week Brian, you must. I will only have your eyes and ears out there now during the day." He said this in a quiet and calm voice. I knew there was no point in arguing and nodded my reluctant agreement. He smiled and added. "Time for tea I think."

But this time even the Headmaster's Magic afternoon tea did nothing to cheer me up. I knew the following few days would seem endless and the only thing that did cheer me up was the thought that I didn't have to study those musty old books.

The children had left the Headmasters study, and as usual I was staying behind for a few minutes before leaving myself.

The Headmaster was studying a book and did not seem to be aware that I was still there,

I grunted a little to attract his attention.

He looked up, "Ah Brian you haven't left yet."

"I'm just about to leave Headmaster. I know it's not my place to query any of your decisions but I can't help wondering do the children need to learn what I expect is Advanced Magic? Especially seeing the strain it's putting David under.

I thought the Headmaster would be annoyed at me, but instead he looked a little sad and nodded.

"I hope and trust they won't need any of it Brian, it's a sort of insurance policy, hopefully it may assist them if anything goes wrong." He finished with a smile and a nod and returned to the book he had been studying and I realised that he was not going to explain any further. It was time for me to slip out of his office.

As I made my way back to my room his words swirled around and around in my head, especially the end of his sentence, "Hopefully it may assist them if anything goes wrong". If anything goes wrong!! Suddenly everything was becoming deadly serious, I knew I wouldn't sleep very much that night.

Saturday arrived the day of the Garden Fete. Fortunately the weather was looking good, though emergency plans had been made to hold it in the Main Hall and the 'Large Marquee' which had been erected a couple of days earlier in case the crowds were large and the weather turned bad.

I had been puzzled for some time at how helpful our gang of troublemakers had been to Miss. Millthrop, here they were again today bringing out and setting up the trestle tables in the marquee, putting table cloths on and laying out knickknacks and some of the food, and what mouth watering food it was Miss. Millthrop certainly knows how to cook.

Once everything had passed her inspection everyone was ushered out and the flaps on the door tied not to be opened until about 12 noon.

With just about 10 minutes to go until 10 a.m. everyone was on standby, everyone except me that is, apparently there were still no jobs at all for me to do. I would have just sat in my little office come workshop until it was all over but the Head was insistent that I circulate and keep an eye on what was going on.

At 10 a.m. the school gates would be opened and the entrance fees collected, apparently there was a very large crowd already forming, so much so that the local Bobby was patrolling outside just to keep an eye on things. The local Traffic Warden looked like a youngster on Christmas day about to open presents, he was almost rubbing his hands with glee no doubt expecting a good haul today as people struggled to find a place to park their car.

The Headmaster was out and about with the Mayor and Mayoress. They had been invited to open the Garden Fete officially at 10.30 a.m. and at the moment were having a look see at what outdoor activities were taking place. After the official opening they would then be going to the marquee with the Masters, various Councillors, the Chief Constable and Fire Officer along with the Local Press.

Inside the marquee they would have first choice of the food and a selection of drinks was to be laid on. After they had finished enjoying the refreshments it would be zero hour and the lesser mortals would be allowed in, the lesser mortals only happened (as is normally the case) to be the people who would be paying for everything including what all the free loaders had been enjoying.

I had a big surprise when I first saw Miss. Millthrop. I am so used to seeing her in a tweed costume that I barely recognised her in a flowery summer dress with her hair in a different style and a wide brimmed hat, she actually looked quite pretty.

She spotted me staring and she gave me one of her looks that meant 'you're dog's dirt on my foot' so I beat a hasty retreat.

It was fabulous weather, blue skies and comfortably warm, everyone seemed in very good humour and it rubbed off on me. With such a large crowd milling about no one noticed me and for the first time in days I felt I could relax.

I had a couple of goes at the penalty kick, half a dozen goes with the bean bags and won a plastic key ring for knocking down 6 cans. I had a good few tries at roll the 10p piece and before I could turn round I'd spent £5! Then I noticed the tug of war was about to start.

There was to be a fancy dress tug of war for the younger children followed by a junior and then a senior tug of war. But first the Mayor and the Civic Dignitaries on one side would be matched against some of Crinkles Masters on the other.

Miss. Millthrop led the Crinkles Masters team, and faced the Mayor and his team, the local Sea Cadets had kindly lent a white ceremonial length of rope for this event with a red scarf tied in the middle. The local newspaper's photographer had already taken a dozen or so shots and was now in position for the starting pose.

"Take up your positions, take the strain." called out the referee. The rope was now taught. "Back a bit on my right, a bit more, stop, hold it there."

The red scarf was now exactly above the centre line of the three white lines painted on the grass. Flashes went off as more photographs were taken.

Then the referee called out "Take the strain, when you hear my whistle blow start to pull. Are you ready? Steady."

The whistle blew and both sides started to pull, the photographer swung into action. More flashes, more pictures then SNAP!

The rope parted much to the amusement of the assembled crowd who began to cheer!

On one side lay 3 Council Officials with the Mayor in a heap in all his official robes (on top of the Chief Constable and the Fire officer). On the other side 5 of the Masters lay in a heap (with Miss. Millthrop on top).

The photographer was making the most of it, he may be able to make a bob or two here he thought if some of the pictures are bought by the Sunday Papers. Headlines flashed through his head such as: 'Mayor Lands on His Dignity' or 'Power of The Law in Action'.

As for myself without thinking I rushed across to help Miss. Millthrop to get back onto her feet, and save her from any further embarrassment. Bearing in mind that unfortunately her dress had split and she was showing her underwear to a large crowd of laughing faces! She had also managed to find probably the only patch of mud on the whole field.

When I reached her she was dazed and flustered, I helped her up and was about to offer her my jacket when she realised it was me and immediately attacked me with her already crumpled hat, yelling:

"Unhand me! I might have known you would appear."

So I beat another hasty retreat but not before I got a lot of funny looks from the crowd and an unpleasant knowing smile from the photographer. Fortunately I didn't have to run off like an idiot, as I was soon lost in the ever-increasing crowd as other people arrived to see what the fuss was all about.

It turned out not to have been an accident! The Sea Cadets were very annoyed when it was disclosed someone had deliberately cut through the rope leaving only a couple of strands and had hidden the cut with the red scarf.

I never did find out who was declared the winner. The Mayor and others took it in good spirit and departed for the refreshment marquee where Miss. Millthrop reappeared a little later in her usual tweeds.

The rest of the morning passed off without any other mishap, and then it was time to open the refreshment marquee to the general public. I had made my way over a little earlier as I was feeling rather hungry and looking forward to some of Miss. Millthrop's home made sausage rolls and pie followed I thought by a nice slice of home made cake.

I was about third in the queue and as I entered the tent I noticed Lisa Gray appear from under one end of the trestle table Miss Millthrop was now approaching with the final cake, a huge home made gateaux that she was about to place in the centre of the table.

Out of the corner of my eye I saw Eric White now appearing from under the other end of the trestle table. It suddenly clicked, so that was it! I rushed forward shouting. "Miss. Millthrop!! Don't! Don't put that cake down! Don't!"

She turned her head towards me but too late! Down went the last cake and with it the trestle table collapsed along with all the other cakes, pies and sandwiches and Miss. Millthrop in the middle.

There was total silence, then Miss. Millthrop screamed louder and louder and shouted:

"Look at the state of me!! Look at all the lovely food, look at it!! It's ruined!!"

She stopped screaming and her eyes searched the crowd, some people looked down at the ground and a bunch of young girls had started to giggle, slowly she turned her head until she faced me.

"YOU!" She cried out. "YOU!! Are the cause of this, LET ME AT HIM!!!"

I was off like a rocket, you don't stand and argue with a raging bull, so you definitely don't stand and argue with Miss. Millthrop. But boy could she run, despite her size and age she was gaining on me. I was running flat out towards the School Gates then I heard Miss. Millthrop who was literally breathing down my neck shout:

"Oh, no! Oh, no! The parents! What will they think?"

She had suddenly realised that she was covered from head to toe in gooey cake with the odd mini sausage roll sticking out here and there.

I realised she had stopped chasing me and was now running back towards the disaster area.

I stopped running myself and found that I could hardly stand up, my heart was thumping like a pile driver and I could hardly breathe, and yet there she was running back flat out. What a woman! I was holding onto the gates huffing and panting and near to collapse.

"What's going on?" Someone asked.

"Yes what is happening?" People were shouting from the crowd.

"What's up Brian?" Asked Finnigan a teacher who was helping take entrance money at the gates.

I told him a little about what had happened between gasps for breath.

Apparently the grapevine had been in action! Word had got back to the Town that the Garden Fete must not be missed and the crowds were pouring in. I had now recovered sufficiently to make my way back to the marquee to see if I could help, but I was intent on staying out of Miss. Millthrop's way. I'm not that brave.

When I got back I was very surprised to see all the tables back in position and everything as clean as a new pin! Not a sign of any of the mess!

There stood Miss. Millthrop without a single mark on her clothes. I was thinking what on earth is going on, then I saw Miss. Millthrop raise her Wand and all the food reappeared as if by magic! Well of course that's exactly what it was. Magic!

My heart sank. She had spotted me.

"This is no thanks to you." She hissed, "Think yourself lucky I don't turn you into the Monkey you are, I'm seeing the Head about you once the Garden Fete is over. I would sort you out myself now but enough of the day has been ruined already."

The cakes and pastries did look good, as good as before. Knowing how delicious the Headmasters teas were I wanted to try some. However Miss. Millthrop was rooted to the spot standing guard directly in front of the stall.

The first customers were appearing at the cakes and pastries stall as Miss. Millthrop and a couple of assistants skilfully cut up the cakes and pies and placed them on party plates. Miss. Millthrop was starting to smile thank goodness for that!

Money was changing hands, teas being poured, little plastic forks placed along side mouth-watering cakes. In went the forks and 'PUFF' went the cakes, no one seemed to know what was happening at first but I knew! Then for the second time that day I was off like a rocket this time heading towards the School's Main Entrance.

The Magic had either failed or worn off, or she hadn't got the spell right, but whatever the cause I would get the blame. I was almost inside the School when I heard her bellowing,

"Where is he...? I'll kill him!!"

I didn't stop, I didn't look back, I headed for the only place where I knew I would be safe - the Head's study.

I rushed up the stairs two at a time along the corridor up the next flight (two at a time) and on to the end of the corridor where I stopped outside the Heads study. My head was spinning and I was gasping for air, I had done far too much running for one day. I raised my fist to hammer on the door but it swung open before me.

There stood the Headmaster.

"Come in Brian". He didn't seem to be the least surprised. "We are just about to have afternoon tea, please join us I think you must be ready for some."

I sat down but was still unable to speak because I couldn't get my breath. Eventually I had recovered enough to try and explain what had happened, but the Head just raised his hand and said, "I know what happened, just enjoy your tea."

I decided not to argue with that, and I nodded to Jenny and David who were sitting opposite but I couldn't face any food. As I sat there I found myself feeling very sorry for Miss. Millthrop she had tried so hard.

The Head told us she had been up at 4.30a.m baking the cakes. She had done so much hard work and put such an effort in to see that everything was perfect, and had looked so pretty in her new dress and hat. It was a great shame there had been so many mishaps, he intended to have some pupils in front of him tomorrow for a severe dressing down at the very least.

Annoyingly I could not explain to Miss. Millthrop what had actually happened. Fortunately it turned out that the Garden Fete had been a huge success, when everything was finally counted up a few days later apparently more than £6,500 had been raised. Everyone agreed it had been a great day out, and the 'Local Newspaper' was full of praise and said it was looking forward to next years 'Garden Fete'.

The Head decided it would be a nice gesture to donate £500 to the Lord Mayor's charity fund and £250 each to the Police and Fire Service benevolent funds. A further £200 was to be given to the Sea Cadets.

He thought it only fitting that the person who had the idea and organised the 'Garden Fete' as well as doing most of the hard work should be the one to present the cheques.

The following day the Headmaster told Miss. Millthrop about the cheques and that as she was facing a very busy week of public duties it was only right that she should look her best. She had looked so pretty in her floral summer dress that could he suggest she buy another one, of course the cost must come out of the School Funds, as without her efforts there would not have been over £4,500 going into those funds (after various expenses had been covered).

When the Head made the announcement at Monday morning's School Assembly the children and masters all applauded! But when the Head mentioned Miss. Millthrop, the children also cheered and many of them stamped their feet. It took the Head nearly five minutes to settle everyone down again, and I noticed he had a large boyish grin on his face whilst Miss. Millthrop went crimson and started to cry.

As for the photographs, fortunately no Sunday Newspaper was interested in them as apparently a political scandal had just become public and they didn't need any fill in pieces.

What no one knows is I bought the negatives from the photographer for £50 but not before he gave me the prints he had developed. I destroyed most of them but kept a couple. I won't say which.

This was a very miserable time for me, it was the companionship of the cats that kept me going. We have three cats at Crinkles. There's Molly (a grey tabby), Casper (who is jet black) and the third cat is Humbug (a ginger tom). It was Humbug that helped save the day at Crinkles - but that comes a little later. They don't like each other very much and all three are as bad as each other for causing trouble.

Often one will lie in wait for one of the other cats to appear and then jump out, there's a chase that always ends in a lot of snarling and spitting until they get bored and back off from each other. Then they will wait until there is a safe distance to turn and walk away, each one with a look that says, I'm the 'Boss' around hear.

Fortunately they don't actually viciously attack each other it's more like play acting. The only time you will see them all together peacefully is in the Autumn and Spring when the sun comes out, then they sunbathe on the flat roof just below my workshop window which is sheltered and is a proper suntrap.

I know how they feel, I could often do with a lie there to ease the winter aches and pains in my old joints. You're all supposed to say, "But you aren't that old Brian." None of you did of course, Ah well, never mind.

I love the cats, you see Crinkles is so very old and has so many nooks and crannies which to be honest are very creepy, very creepy indeed. Every now and then I have to visit one of these spooky places to do repairs, or search for some long lost item the School now decides it needs urgently. When I go to work in these odd places usually one of the cats will turn up, they love to plonk themselves down on top of the tools I'm using, curl up and watch me.

I can't understand the cats, they love their comfort yet they can lie on top of my tools which you would think must be really uncomfortable, half close their eyes and purr in contentment as though they were lying on the softest cushions.

It's when I'm working in a creepy place that the cats help me. For example not long ago I had to go up into the 'Old Bell Tower' to check for damage to the roof tiles. I had put the job off for weeks. I hated going up there, and the only way to really check the tiles is to go up with your torch and ladder switch your torch off and look up to see where chinks of light are shining through.

I'd struggled up there and set the ladder up, put my torch down and switched it off, then I peered up at the roof and yes there were a few tiny chinks of light, so small you wouldn't have thought they would let much rain through.

I reached for my torch but couldn't find it, I searched around in the dark but no torch and then I began to panic! A weird feeling had come over me I had to get out of there.

Beads of cold sweat had broken out on my face, then I saw the two yellow piercing eyes, moving slowly towards me, they disappeared and I felt something rubbing against my leg and heard a low purring noise it was Casper.

I bent down and felt his head and stroked him, he lifted his head and there were the two bright yellow luminous eyes.

Suddenly I felt totally calm, if Casper was happy up here then I was also.

Within a couple of minutes I had found my torch and made a note of the roof damage. Then my little helper and I made our way back to my workshop where Casper had a well deserved bowl of milk, after which he settled on my desk on top of the papers I was going to work on. Ah well, there's always something else I can do, sort this work room of mine out for starters.

I looked around, where do you make a start? It would take a week at least and all those decisions to make. Will I keep this or that? It may come in handy one day. International sods law number 107942/02/1102 amendment number 077 EU Statuary Code 447/07 of course would apply. Which states keep an item and you will never need it again. Dispose of it and you will immediately need it. Amendment 078 additionally states that it will prove to have been of great monetary value.

Well I certainly couldn't face sorting this lot out at the moment. So I pulled a chair up to my desk and gently stroking Casper I felt totally relaxed and stress free as I listened to his gentle soft purring.

CHAPTER TEN

Sabotage

It was very early Sunday morning and so very peaceful after yesterday's Garden Fete.

I had spent the night in the Head's study sleeping on the settee. Jenny and David were still sound asleep in two of the Head's guest rooms. We had spent the whole evening discussing the day's events and now I was creeping back to my own rooms listening for any sound that may warn me of impending doom in the shape of Miss. Millthrop, who I was hoping was sound asleep.

But who could tell? She may be prowling about looking for me waiting to pounce. She had been up to see the Headmaster yesterday and it had taken all his powers of persuasion to calm Miss. Millthrop down, even hidden away in the Head's study I had felt vulnerable. Now I felt totally unprotected.

She had left the Heads study mumbling that I was some-where in the School and that she would eventually find me.

Taking no chances I had taken my shoes off so that I didn't make a sound and I was returning to my room the long way round as an extra precaution. This took me past the end of the corridor leading to the Library, as I was about to pass this point I heard the faintest of noises.

I stopped and listened intently, yes there it was again only just audible. Slowly, very slowly I peered around the corner, at first I could see nothing it was so dark. Gradually as my eyes adjusted to the darkness I could vaguely make out what appeared to be someone passing something to someone else who was standing just inside the Library doorway.

What were they passing into the Library at this time in the morning? I have no idea how long I stood there or at what point I realised it was books that were being passed. Obviously there was something very wrong here but what should I do? I could rush up to them and take them by surprise, but then what? How many people were there inside the Library?

I decided informing the Headmaster as quickly as possible was the action to take and rapidly made my way back to his study, gently tapping on the door I waited and waited. There was no reply or even a sound from inside. I started tapping louder and more insistent than before this time I heard movement from inside the study but still no one opened the door.

Desperately searching through my pockets I found an old petrol receipt and a pencil and wrote on it – 'It's me – Brian'. Tapping again on the door I slipped it underneath and waited for what seemed like an age.

"Is that you Brian?" It was Jenny's voice very faint.

"Yes it's me." I whispered back, and heard a bolt being withdrawn. The door swung open and I saw the relief on Jenny and David's face when they saw that it really was me.

Jenny flung her arms around me.

"Oh Brian! We're so pleased that it really is you, we were terrified, we both have this strange feeling something's wrong."

"But where is the Headmaster?" I asked.

"We don't know." Replied David, "Just after you left he received a phone call and dashed out saying wait here until I return."

"Did he say when he would be back?"

"No, just told us to stay here." Said Jenny.

"Why are you back?" Asked David.

So I told them the full story.

"What do we do now?" Jenny murmured in a frightened voice.

"If only I knew."

It was then that David jumped up and said, "I'm going to see what's up!"

"Oh no, you're not!" I shouted, but he was out of the door before I could stop him.

Jenny and I had both leapt up at the same time to catch him and collided with each other, by the time we had sorted ourselves out there was no sign of him. We also decided to go to the Library in case David needed help. It was a surprise to find him on his way back before we even reached the Library corridor.

"Come on!" He said, "Let's get back to the Heads study." We made it back to the study without anyone seeing us although the School was now starting to come to life.

"What happened?" We asked David.

"Well you were right Brian! I ran in my stocking feet along to the place where you had been and it was just as you had told us, so I turned and crept back along the corridor for a few yards. Put my shoes on then making a lot of noise and singing I went back and turned the corner and merrily walked along the passage towards the Library."

"I heard the door close and the click of the lock. I then ran to the stairs opposite but there was no sign of anyone, however I did find this!" He said grinning, and held up a small book of spells.

We all looked at the book, but of course it didn't tell us anything.

"Where do we go from here?" Asked Jenny.

"Let's put our heads together, let's tackle this as though we were Sherlock Holmes." Suggested David and so we did. But in the end the only thing we could come up with was that I visited the Library in my capacity of School Caretaker.

It was nearly 9.00a.m now and I knew old Smithers, Smitkrausermann to be exact, would be there. He seemed to live in the place no matter what day of the week it was.

I made my way to my workshop totally forgetting about Miss. Millthrop.

I put my overalls on and picking up my toolbox went back to the Library. Sure enough Smithers was there when I arrived.

"Morning Mr. Smithers!" I said cheerfully.

He turned and eyed me up and down. "Oh, it's you." He said.

"What did you want fixing?" I asked.

"Nothing, I don't need anything fixing. Who said I did?"

"I was sure the Headmaster mentioned the Library to me the other day along with other odd jobs that needed doing."

"There are no odd jobs or any other jobs for you here! So be on your way boy!" (He called everyone boy).

"Mr.Smithers."

"Why are you still here?" He mumbled. "Didn't you hear me tell you to clear off?"

Ignoring that I continued, "Would you know if a book was missing from the Library?"

"Would I know if a book was missing!!" He looked at me as though I had just run into the back of his old banger of a car.

"Nothing goes missing in this Library!! I can tell what books are out just by looking down the rows of shelves." He went on to demonstrate and by Jove he could.

"What if you had extra books, would you know if you had extra?" He stared angrily at me I thought he was going to explode.

"Extra books! What extra books? Where from? You're an idiot boy, a rambling idiot, get out of my sight."

"Well what about this book?" I said holding it up.

"Where did you get that book? Your not suppose to have books on Magic even if it's that rubbish."

"Is it an extra book?" I asked. "Would you check it for me?"

I was banking on arousing Smithers curiosity and fortunately it did, he grabbed it from me and walked away mumbling to himself that he was surrounded by idiots before disappearing down one of the Library aisles, a couple of minutes later he reappeared.

"Yes, we've got it." He said.

"Are you sure it's exactly the same?" I asked.

"Exactly the same! Of course it's not! Ours is the original - this is just a copy!"

Suddenly I knew exactly what was going on.

"So that's it!" I said out loud.

"So what's it?" asked Smithers.

"Oh! Nothing really." I replied.

"Are you deliberately setting out to waste my time boy? Do I go around wasting yours?"

Before he had a chance to ask where the book had come from, I quickly picked up my toolbox and said, "Sorry to have disturbed you Mr. Smithers, now it was my turn to grab the book back. You have been a great help, thank you!" I was disappearing around the door as I spoke, knowing that he now thought me the stupidest person in the whole School.

I couldn't get back fast enough to tell David and Jenny what I had discovered, when I got back I was disappointed to find that the Headmaster had not returned.

We knew now what 'they', whoever 'they' are, were up too.

They were trying to reduce the 'Containment Level' on the Evil Wizards Spells locked in the 'Containment Book' by switching books, replacing originals with copies. But how many had been switched? Was last night their first time or had it been going on for days? The questions were endless.

How did they smuggle the books out of the School? Or are the books still in the School hidden somewhere and if so where? All these questions! And no answers!

We decided there had to be at least three people involved, one passing books from the top of the stairs to one person in the doorway then to someone inside the Library.

"But why not just carry a load of books into the Library in one go instead of all this passing one at a time?" I asked.

"I think I know why." said Jenny. "Do you remember what the Head said about Carforth Crinkle and a sort of burglar alarm? I think the Library may have some kind of invisible shield that would set off a protective alarm or barrier if a large number of extra identical books to those used for the 'Containment' were brought in, or a large number of originals taken out at anyone time."

"However, by bringing only one replica in and taking one original out at the same time the alarm protection system is not triggered."

"If that is correct." said David, "then you would have to get the original copy out of the Library as a replacement came in."

"Also you probably can't allow them to pass each other whilst doing this." I suggested.

"Could well be." Said David.

"How did they get the books out Brian?" asked Jenny. "Both you and David didn't see any coming out only going in, and there's only one door into the Library."

"But there are windows!" said David. "Good grief that's how they did it, the books must have been passed out through the window. That means more people must have been involved it may be as many as five or six." David looked shocked at what he had said." Five or six traitors…" he said quietly almost to himself.

I was standing by the window in the Heads study watching a team of men dismantling the marquee that had been hired for the Garden Fete. They were starting to load a large white van parked nearby and were nearly finished.

I turned to face David and Jenny. "If only the Headmaster were here! He'd know what to do."

I looked back at the men working below, then it dawned on me, it was so obvious, so obvious.

"The marquee!!" I shouted out "Of course - that's it! The marquee!"

"David! Jenny! Come here. Look at the marquee, what windows are directly above it?"

"I'm not sure." Said David.

"Nor am I." Replied Jenny.

"Well I'm sure! That's the Library windows and that's the windows they used, a book was dropped out of the window onto the roof of the marquee at the same time as a replacement was passed through the door. The book would slide down the sloping roof to a waiting accomplice or accomplices. And as for how are they going to get them out, they're inside that van, I'll bet a year's pay that's where they are, probably hidden under rolls of canvas."

"Another ten minutes and they'll be away! What are we going to do?" asked David.

Jenny's face lit up, "I could do some Magic to stop the van from moving."

"No you couldn't." I replied.

Jenny looked very hurt and annoyed. "I could, I certainly could!" She shouted.

"It wouldn't work Jenny, because there is someone here at Crinkles who I think can do a lot more powerful Magic than you. In fact I'm sure of it. That's why the Headmaster was called away, he would have been the only one with Magic more powerful than the Evil Wizards at the School, remember although we can't see them because we don't know who they are they will be watching that van and watching us."

"Well that's it then!" Said Jenny still peeved.

"No it's not! I can stop that van leaving without the need of any Magic so no one will suspect that there is anything wrong, but I need a diversion!"

"A diversion?" queried David.

"Yes, you see all those aluminium tent poles waiting to be placed in the van?"

"Yes we see them." Chorused the children.

"Well I want you and as many of your friends that you can muster to pinch them and run off in all directions towards the back of the School. Hopefully the men loading the van will chase you. I only need about five minutes then you can drop them and run off."

"But what will we tell our friends?"

"Anything you like! Off you go. Time is not on our side!"

We opened the study door and the children dashed off down the passage whilst I locked the door and made my way downstairs.

I was out on the front lawn walking as casually as I could manage with my tool box in one hand and a spanner in the other.

The last of the canvas sides of the marquee had been rolled up and three men were passing it up to two men inside the van.

"Nearly finished?" I shouted cheerfully.

"Yeah." One of the men grunted.

"You should beat the rain then" I nodded towards the darkening sky.

The men outside the wagon followed my gaze but said nothing. I was desperately trying to hold their attention.

"Is that something moving inside the van at the back? We have loads of rabbits and hedgehogs here."

The two men inside the van started to look around and the men outside were also peering in.

"I can't see anything." said one of them.

There was a clink as some aluminium poles knocked against each other. One of the men turned towards the noise.

"Sorry!" I said, shrugging my shoulders. "I caught your van with my toolbox." But then there was another clink followed by another.

"What's going on?" Said the one man left outside the van, the other two having jumped into the van to help heave the heavy canvas into the position they wanted it. The man outside walked around the open van door.

"Strewth!" He cried, "Hey lads! Those sodden school kids are pinching our poles." and he was off after them and the other four were scrambling down from the back of the van to join him in the chase.

"All these b'#'#' school kids are the same, the boss will go crackers if we lose some more gear! Come on! Get them! Get them!" He appeared to be the one in charge.

I looked over the field to see what looked like half the school's pupils running in all directions with poles pointing straight up straight ahead and some being thrown like javelins.

Hopefully any Evil Wizards watching would be concentrating on the children. I was straight into the cab and up with the bonnet lock, back out, quickly round the front, up with the bonnet and out with the distributor head then down with the bonnet.

I opened the cab door again. YES! I had seen them, they were in the ignition, the ignition keys! 'That will do very nicely' I thought as I removed them. Then I closed the cab door and just for good measure I did a little trick that I had better not mention here, just a case of double belt and braces.

As I walked quickly back across the front lawn to the School intent on enlisting the help of some of the Masters to search the van I was amused to see the five men trying to collect the poles, they were scattered far and wide it would take them at least ten minutes to sort it out!

However my amusement was short lived as I looked up at the leaded windows of the School at least two dozen faces were peering out.

There was no way that some of those faces hadn't seen me disable the van! But were they friend or foe? Not that I had any friends at the moment.

Before I reached the Main Entrance steps, a number of teachers were already making their way towards me.

"What's going on Brian?" called out Thompson, a Geography teacher. "What on earth are the pupils up to?"

"There's no time for lengthy explanations!" I replied. "But there's valuable School property in that van and we've only just been in time to stop it from being stolen!"

"The man's crazy!" I heard someone shout. "They're only workmen going about their business."

"You've got to look inside that van!" I cried.

"We don't, and won't, do anything of the kind." replied Ian, "That van is not our property."

"No but what's inside is!"

"And what might that be, pray?" Someone shouted.

"BOOKS!" I cried out in panic "Our valuable books from the Library!" This was all going badly wrong, it looked as though no one was going to help us search the van.

"Perhaps we should check?" It was Graeme, the Woodwork teacher.

"Yes perhaps we should?" shouted out a couple of the other teachers.

"It will only take a few minutes." I said. Then disaster struck!

"If that little rat's involved don't believe a word he tells you!" It was Miss. Millthrop.

The men were back at the van now and had already loaded most of the aluminium tent poles leaving only a few odds and ends left to put in the van, the driver climbed into the cab ready to start the engine.

"Where are the damn keys?" The driver had realised the keys were missing! He got out checking his pockets and the floor beneath the steering wheel.

"I'll tell you where they are! He's got them!" It was Miss. Millthrop - pointing at me!

One of the other men jumped down from the van and grabbed me by the throat,

"What's your little game then?" He said, with his face an inch from mine.

"Let's get out of here Ted!" cried one of the other men, "Or we'll never get to the club... and I'm dying for a pint!"

"I, me too." said Ted, kindly leaving go of my neck.

"I'll use one of the spare keys," the driver announced triumphantly, climbing back into the cab he pulled down the sun visor and removed the key which had been taped to the back. He quickly put the key into the ignition to start the van.

"I don't believe it! The '#'#'#'# engine won't start! It'll be those damn kids again!!"

"PLEASE!!" I cried, "Please check the van for the 'Stolen Books'!"

"What stolen books?" Everyone turned. It was Smithers. "Come on, what Stolen Books?"

"Brian claims there are stolen books belonging to the Library in the back of this van." explained Ian.

"Stuff and nonsense, No books have been stolen from the Library. If anyone knew books were missing it would be me, and I say none have been stolen."

"There, what did I tell you? This is a troublemaker! He was the cause of unbelievable problems yesterday." It was Miss. Millthrop.

"I think you will need this." Ian was handing the distributor back to the driver. "I saw him take it out of your engine and throw it away."

"You're dead right we need it mate, thanks!" In no time at all the distributor was re-installed, the engine started and the van began to move off.

I looked over to where all the pupils were gathered a short distance away. Jenny was crying and David had his arm around her shoulder. He was looking straight at me with a look that said 'We've lost'. The van was now almost at the School Gates.

"You know we should have checked that van." It was Edith the English teacher.

"YES!! YOU SHOULD HAVE!!"

Everyone was startled and turning round there was the Headmaster. He was looking so angry it was frightening, because he always looked so gentle.

At that moment we heard the van spluttering. Turning around once more we watched it judder to a halt.

A group of pupils ran across the field yelling loudly at the top of their voices, nothing in this world was going to stop that van being searched.

The van was completely surrounded by pupils and now the Masters had also reached the van, the five workmen had climbed out and stood swearing and threatening one and all.

The Headmaster had pushed through the crowd and told the workmen they were going to search the van.

"No one's searching our van!" growled the driver. "and anyone trying will be sorted out by me!"

"Get those back doors opened!!" commanded the Headmaster and a couple of Masters and about a dozen pupils rushed to obey.

"Touch those doors and you're all for it." It was the biggest of the workmen who was holding a three-foot piece of aluminium tube threateningly.

"Get the Police on your mobile Bob." shouted another workman.

"Yes, you had better back off or we'll call the Police."

"Go ahead call the Police. I've no doubt they'd be very interested in finding property stolen from the School in your van, very interested indeed." replied the Head.

"Hey!" One of the workmen was nudging the driver. "We don't want cops sticking their noses in."

"No, we don't need that hassle." said another with a very worried look on his face.

I was close enough to hear him whisper to the driver, "We've no road tax remember? It's failed its M.O.T, and we haven't sorted the two baldy tyres out yet."

The driver was becoming very angry, but he knew he was beaten. Still defiant he shouted: "Okay you can search the van, but you'll have to pay for any delay at double time and we aren't unloading it."

"If we don't find our property on your van, I will be happy to pay treble time!" said the Head.

The driver still looked very angry, but the others now looked very pleased at the thought of treble time.

The van doors were opened, and the tent's aluminium side poles were soon out with the many willing hands eager to help.

The rolls of canvas however were a different proposition. Much to the great amusement of the workmen who were now standing around with great smiles on their faces, no matter how hard we tried we couldn't budge the rolled canvas.

We had chased the pupils out of the van and mustered all the younger Masters, the gardeners and myself. However that still meant we could muster only six people and we simply could not budge any of the rolls.

Truthfully, we just didn't have either the strength or the knack needed.

"You will have to help us." The Head told the driver, who was obviously the man in charge he was also the only one still scowling,

"I told you we weren't going to help."

"Ah come on! Let's give them a hand. There's no way they'll ever do it on their own!" One of the men said to the driver.

"I'm helping nobody take the stuff out or help put it back." said the driver, folding his arms across his chest.

"Well we are! Come on lads!" and surprisingly the others followed him, they all had big grins on their faces. Two of the men climbed into the van and told us to shove off in no uncertain terms we climbed down and before we could sort ourselves out the first roll of canvas sheeting was emerging from the van.

The Headmaster peered into the van as sheet after sheet was removed, but nothing was revealed, eventually the van was completely empty except for the very large and heavy main tent poles and we had found nothing.

Jenny and David were standing next to me, their faces had gone from jubilation to despair.

"There's nothing there." They both said looking at me. I nodded.

"But there has to be something there." Whispered David.

"Perhaps only a few books had been taken and they could easily be smuggled out. We somehow got the idea that it was a case full." I replied.

"I was expecting at least a tea chest full of books hidden under all that canvas." added Jenny.

"Another waste of everyone's time, I warned you! I told everyone not to take any notice of him!" It was Miss. Millthrop, screaming and pointing towards me.

A low mumble of agreement started amongst some of the Masters.

"Satisfied?" said the driver smugly to the Head. "Remember treble time you said! This will cost you mate." He added with a satisfied grin on his face.

"Right lads" He looked around at the assembled crowd enjoying the embarrassment on our faces. "Let's get this lot back on the van and away from this loony bin."

They all grinned at each other, and one whispered to his mates, "Not too fast lads, remember, its treble time."

The grins on their faces broadened, and they started to stroll slowly towards the first canvas bundle. They lifted it and moved towards the van.

"No, no! Put that one down. I think this one should go in first."

"Oh I don't think so." replied one of the men. Another suggested "Perhaps that one over there."

"That one over there, don't be crackers more like that far one." and so it went on, arguing over which should go in first. The longer it took the more money they made, and anyway they were enjoying every minute of it.

The driver meanwhile was sitting in the cab smoking. He had turned the wireless on playing it at full blast.

"Are you going to make a start!! Do you intend doing it today? Or are you all planning to camp overnight?"

We all turned, we knew that voice. It was Miss. Millthrop, standing with her hands on her hips, her voice booming out.

Even above the din from the radio in the cab every word was crystal clear. The ground almost shook.

"Who does the old bat think she is?" one of the workmen said to his mates.

"I'll show you who I am if you don't make a start!!" Millthrop's voice boomed out again and this time no one made any comment, deciding it was best not to argue with such a formidable foe, they knew when they had met their match, just as I did.

They were about to make a hasty retreat from Millthrop by loading the van as quickly as they could just as I had when I had to run for my life. Okay for them I thought, they'll soon be out of her range of influence whereas I had to exist alongside this 'Dragon Lady' every day.

Some of the Masters, pupils and other staff had started to walk back to the School.

I noticed the Headmaster handing the driver some money. "This ain't treble time for five people." He complained.

"It's all you're getting, I didn't see five people working." Replied the Head.

The driver snorted and stuffed the money in his back pocket.

"What else did you do to that van, Brian?

I hadn't noticed Ian come up behind me and I must admit I had forgot about my double belt and braces bit.

"Me?" I tried to look and sound as though I had no idea what he was talking about.

"Yes! You Brian. I think you'd better undo it and quick."

All the others had forgot that the van packed in just as it was about to go through the School Gates, my last hope of delaying the van's departure any further had now gone. If only Ian had also forgot. I nodded in agreement and replied, "I'll sort it out now Mr Scorn."

One folded roll of canvas was already in the van and the others soon would be. Only minutes remained before the van would be ready to leave.

David was coming towards me looking excited. "Do you think the books could be folded up in the canvas Brian?" he asked.

"No I'm afraid not David. I'm sure of that, they couldn't risk damaging them with all the tugging and heaving required to handle the sheeting."

Only Jenny had noticed Humbug, Crinkles ginger cat jump up into the van, he had been sniffing around the outside of the van for some time.

She went to the back of the van and watched him sniffing here, there, and everywhere. He went further into the van and stopped at the back wall, his nose went down and he sniffed all along the bottom of the back wall, then he did it again! Then he pawed it and started to hiss.

The men were approaching with another roll of canvas and Humbug startled jumped down from the van and ran off. But Jenny stayed and stared into the back of the van. Why had Humbug acted so strangely? There must have been a reason.

Then she saw the reason! But was it her imagination or a trick of the light? She turned to look for me, seeing me she rushed over shouting:

"Brian! Brian! Whilst tugging on my arm.

"What Jenny?"

"Look inside the van Brian!"

"At what Jenny?"

"At the back wall!!" Jenny dragged me back to the van.

"Look at the back wall!!" She shouted.

"Well! What about the back wall? What am I supposed to be looking at?"

"Can't you see it!! Can't you see it? It's disappearing then coming back again!! " Yelled Jenny in desperation.

I looked again, it all looked alright to me.

"Don't be so stupid Jen....." Then I gasped. I couldn't believe what I was seeing! She was right! The solid-looking back wall was turning hazy then it would look solid again then it would turn hazy again.

"Get out of the way!" The driver pushed me to one side but not before a box at the back of the van had appeared. The box had not been there before, or should I say we hadn't been able to see it before.

I turned to look for the Headmaster but he was almost at the Main School Entrance.

I grabbed an arm, but was surprised when I realised it wasn't David's but Jonathan Dent's. I realised he wouldn't have a clue what I was talking about.

"Listen Jonathan!! You must bring the Headmaster back and as quickly as you can! Tell him we've found the books!"

"You've found the ….." Jonathan looked at me as though I was stupid.

"No time to explain, bring him back NOW!! Tell him we've found the books!" Jonathan gave me one last puzzled glance then he was off, and boy could he run!

"That boy! Stop running." It was Ian. But Jonathan didn't stop, however the Headmaster did he turned to see what all the commotion was about.

"Headmaster! Headmaster!" gasped Jonathan. "You've got to come! Brian says he's found the books!"

The Head didn't ask Jonathan any questions but immediately made his way back, shouting as he did:

"Stop loading that van! Stop loading!"

"What the heck is going on now?" Growled the driver, "You had better '#'#'#'# stop loading."

Jenny and I had been trying to stop them but had been over-ruled by Miss. Millthrop who claimed that I could cause more trouble in a weekend than a normal person can in a lifetime.

When the Headmaster arrived everyone was standing around looking annoyed and Millthrop absolutely furious.

The Masters and pupils who had left were now reappearing from the School to see what was going on, and in no time a large crowd had reappeared.

"Look!!" Said Jenny pointing into the van as the Head approached.

"At what?" He asked

"At the back wall of the van." Said jenny

"But it's just the back of the van dear girl." said the Head, with disappointment and frustration in his voice.

"It disappears, Headmaster!! Watch it." The Head turned to look again at a blank solid wall, and then once more it was starting to fade. "There!! There's a box!" said Jenny pointing.

The Head turned, Graeme the Woodwork Master was standing next to him.

"Check that out for me Graeme." He said excitedly.

Graeme climbed into the van and walked towards the back, he stood with his hand against the back wall and turning shouted.

"There's nothing here Headmaster. It's good and solid."

Suddenly he fell sideways. The wall had started to disappear again and Graeme had fallen through.

It reappeared and looked solid again, and there was no sign of him then we all heard his voice.

"There are two boxes here full of books!!"

Graeme had reappeared, the powerful Magic that had been used to hide the boxes having completely worn off.

"What books?" Enquired the driver.

"Never mind what books! Enough to say they're our books." Replied the Head.

"I know nothing of any books mate, nothing at all! Anyway the van was empty wasn't it? We all saw that didn't we lads?" He turned to his men who were all nodding in agreement.

"Was the van left here last night?" Enquired the Head.

"Yes it was parked up next to the marquee."

"Why was it left?" asked the Head.

"We were running a bit late and we wanted to get back smartish because there was a good comedian on at the club. So we left in Bob's car rather than take the van back to the depot."

As everyone talked I discreetly fixed the van to speed their eventual departure.

"There's no need for cops or anything like that is there? I swear none of us knew anything about these books." said the driver nervously.

"No Police need be involved." Replied the Head, "But I want the van unloaded again and there is a little matter of the return of some money."

"Oh, Gordon Bennet! Has there ever been a job like this! Load the van. Unload the van. Load the van. Unload the van. He paused. Double time squire?" The driver asked. But he didn't try and argue when he saw the look the Head gave him.

"Unload the van again lads!" He shouted.

"You're joking!!" Shouted back the fed up crew.

"No I'm not!! Get started and let's get out of here!"

The van was once again unloaded and now the boxes could clearly be seen for the first time, Myself and some of the Masters scrambled onto the back of the van and many eager hands dragged and pushed the boxes to the end of the van.

"How on earth didn't we see that?" Asked the driver.

"Beats me." chorused the others.

"Can we lift them down?" Asked the Head.

"Not full we can't! Unless you want us to do our backs in! Empty some of that stuff out lads." ordered the driver.

"No, no!" cried out the Head. "Some of that 'stuff' as you call it is old and could easily be damaged beyond repair! We will take the books out!"

While he had been talking the Head had been looking at the crowd and was relieved to see the School Cook watching the proceedings.

"Mrs. Houghton, our Cook, will make you all something to eat you must be very hungry."

"But we want to get to the pub!" complained the driver.

The Head ignored this. "You can arrange something Mrs. Houghton can't you?" the Head shouted across to her and without waiting for a reply said "Good, good, excellent."

She turned and walked back to the School looking non-to-pleased.

"Some of you senior boys kindly escort these gentlemen to the junior dining room and stay with them." The Head instructed.

Connor, who although only 16, was as big as the van driver, volunteered his services. The workmen trudged off reluctantly, Connor lead the way with a big grin on his face they were followed by more than a dozen boys and girls.

"Right now staff, to work! We must lighten these boxes and I want everything covered and put in the....." The Head paused and quickly scanned the grounds. "...and put them in the potting shed for now."

"The potting shed?" Quite a few Masters voices queried the proposed destination.

"Surely you mean the School Headmaster."

"No I mean the potting shed." Repeated the Head.

I looked around for Smithers, I was surprised that he'd made no comment. He was standing next to the books with a look of complete amazement and puzzlement on his face, I knew exactly what he was thinking, 'How did I not know that all of these books were missing?'

I felt sorry for Smithers but I wasn't going to quietly walk away leaving him to his thoughts. Over the years I've had to accept his sarcastic remarks and his endless put downs, in his eyes being the School Caretaker meant I was of no importance, someone to be scoffed and sneered at whenever an opportunity arose.

Everyone made excuses for his behaviour, but in truth he was plain and simply a grown up bully. It was now time for some revenge, I walked over and stood beside him and looked down at all the books. He glanced sideways at me and said nothing, still looking down at the books I thought to myself boy am I going to enjoy this.

"Mmmm, stuff and nonsense eh? So no books had been stolen from the School Library? Well you should know you've been Librarian for how many years?" I paused to let it sink in, he didn't reply and just stared at the books.

"Strange though," I continued, "That looks like a mountain of books to me, it would be too much to expect an apology or a thank you Brian from you, but you know that without me,

David and Jenny you would have lost those books forever. You would have been the Librarian of copies, a laughing stock amongst your fellow Librarians. Thank you Brian and will you thank David and Jenny for me you saved the day, and I will be eternally grateful. There I've said it for you, you miserable old sod."

I turned and walked away, I had said my piece and I knew every word had struck home, he was still standing motionless staring at all the books, the way I felt at that moment he could have stood there forever for all I cared.

When the men returned to the van there was no sign of the boxes or their contents.

They'd enjoyed their meal and quickly reloaded the van, it started without any problems and they finally drove out through the School Gates and onto the main road and Freedom!!

It would be hard to say who was the most relieved, the men in the van at last free of the School, or the School at last free of them.

We now had time to tell the Head the full story and he agreed with us about how the books had been removed. He decided there was no point in taking any chances to try and save a few hours putting the books back. So we would put them back the same way they had been taken out.

CHAPTER ELEVEN

The Empty Box

Everyone thought we were finished for the day but it was not so.

"Right" Said the Head, "Now we have to get the books back into the Library, and there's no time like the present, the weather is dry and there is still plenty of daylight left."

"Couldn't it wait until tomorrow Headmaster? I think we've all had enough excitement for one day." Said Carruthers, the Geography teacher.

"No it can't!" Replied the Head. Everyone looked surprised at his sharp reply but no one spoke. The Head was already striding out towards the potting shed.

Half an hour later found a ladder up against the open Library window. At the bottom of the ladder was the first box once more full of books with Carruthers standing next to them. Cecilia was on the bottom rung Ian was half way up and I was at the top.

The Headmaster was on the inside of the Library window, Smithers the librarian stood inside the Library, Miss. Millthrop was standing just inside the Library door and Brownly was standing outside in the passageway.

"Are we all ready?" Asked the Head. A chorus of Yes's came back. "Right then let's get started." Commanded the Head.

Carruthers lifted a book out of the box passed it to Cecilia who passed it to Ian who passed it up to me. I held the book outside the Library window with the title towards the Head.

The titles were in Latin, Greek, Arabic, Hebrew and other languages I hadn't even heard of.

As the Head read each title out Smithers the librarian took out the book that had replaced it and gave it to Miss. Millthrop, then the Head shouted,

"Change books."

I handed him my book through the Library window while at exactly the same time Miss. Millthrop passed her book out of the Library door to Brownly who was stacking them at his feet. The Head then waited until Smithers told him the book was back in its rightful place.

So it went on book after book until we had reached book number 20. Then Smithers called back, "No matching book!"

"Pass that book back down Brian" said the Head "and tell Carruthers to put it to one side."

Number 34 was also a 'no match', as were numbers 51 and 68 from the first box. I noticed that the Head wasn't happy about this. There were four more 'no match' books in the second box, numbers 101,118,134 and 150.

Eventually we came to the book that I had been looking for, the last book! And was I pleased! In all a total of 160 books of assorted sizes had been matched and swapped over.

It felt more like 1,600 books had been swapped over, I thought it was never going to end. There were a total of 8 books unmatched.

With the last book safely in place it was time to put the ladder away. I heard the Library window being locked as I started to put the extension ladder down, soon I had the ladder back in the potting shed and came back to collect the empty boxes. Carruthers had taken the 8 books left over to the Head's study.

The Masters working outside had now all gone indoors for dinner as had the pupils and masters who had been watching us and wondering what on earth was going on, why didn't we just take the books back to the Library through the School?

Inside the School Smithers and Brownly were transferring the stack of books lying outside the Library door into the

Library cupboard which was on the opposite side of the passage. Smithers wanted to eventually check every book before deciding what to do with these duplicates.

Meanwhile, I was about to take the empty wooden boxes back to the potting shed as the wood might come in handy I thought. This was the first time I'd lifted one empty, I was surprised at how heavy it was for an empty box, it suddenly dawned on me 'It's too heavy to be an empty box.' I lifted the other box and it was the same, too heavy.

I looked about and thank goodness there was Harry the Senior Gardener pottering around. I called him over and asked him to guard the box I had to leave behind as I couldn't handle two at the same time. I told him it was vitally important not to let anyone near it until I came back, he nodded but didn't say anything or give any indication of curiosity. I started to walk away carrying the other box.

Then I thought, he's pretty old and there may be something valuable in the box, what if someone attacked him. I turned and asked Harry if he would be alright, he smiled and said,

"I'll be alright, anybody giving me any trouble and I'll smack'em one with me spade."

That will do me I thought, and shouted as I hurried on, "I'll be back as soon as I can." I had done an 'about turn' and was now heading back to the School and the Heads study. When I got there I tapped on the door and I found him studying the 8 unmatched books.

"Hello Brian, I thought you'd be off for your dinner I think everyone else is. Ah, you've brought up one of the boxes! But there are only the 8 books here that we couldn't match so we won't need a box."

"I didn't bring the box up for the books Headmaster, I brought it up because it's not empty."

The Head looked surprised. "It's not empty?"

"It looks empty but it's too heavy to be empty." As I spoke I took out my tape measure and measured the inside. "It's 21 and a half inches deep inside before the lid goes on. But it's nearly 27 inches deep on the outside, even allowing for the thickness of the wood which is 1 and a half inches, that leaves a difference of over 4 inches. "This is a dummy base" I said.

"There has to be something hidden underneath."

"I've been puzzled about these 8 books left over and now this mystery! But at least we can solve this mystery." said the Head.

"I'll nip down and get my tools and fetch the other box."

"No need for any tools Brian! But on your way back I want you to tell Miss. Millthrop and Mr. Smithers I would appreciate if they can spare the time to come and see me as soon as possible this evening."

They were just about to start their deserts when I arrived to give them the Head's message.

It made them annoyed having to leave a delicious chocolate mousse and even more annoyed at having received the message from me. Their temper didn't improve when I didn't go direct to the Heads Study but back to collect the second box and to thank Harry for guarding it.

"Have you had any problems Harry?" I asked.

"No problems, no one came anywhere near the box." and he nodded and grunted a greeting to Smithers and Millthrop. Smithers scowled and Millthrop smiled in return.

"What's going on? What's this all about?" growled Smithers, "I thought we were going to see the Headmaster urgently not wasting time mucking about with old wood boxes."

"We're off to see the Head now." I said, striding out as fast as I could.

I knew of course Millthrop would have no trouble keeping up with me but old Smithers was puffing and panting and moaning and groaning, I looked back and shouted,

"Come on Mr.Smithers get a move on we don't want to waste time do we?"

By the time we reached the Heads study Smithers was miles behind. His study door was still fully open so we just tapped on the door and walked in. Once inside Miss. Millthrop immediately let rip.

"Headmaster!" she shouted. "I don't know what he's been saying about me but I've seen through him and it's about time you did."

"It's alright Miss. Millthrop! It's not about you, and I can assure you Brian has done this School proud. One day soon you will learn the full facts and probably regret many of the things you have said about him."

The wind had been taken out of her sails. "Mmm! That's as may be!" She replied quietly.

The Head just ignored that. He asked her to look at the eight books on the bureau beside his desk and tell him if she recognized any of the titles.

Miss. Millthrop walked across and picked the books up, we all sat silently as one by one she carefully studied them, after about 10 minutes the Head said.

"You're very quiet Miss. Millthrop which is not like you." There was still silence then she replied, "If you just give me a few more minutes Headmaster."

Smithers was looking very annoyed and was about to complain about sitting around doing nothing whilst Millthrop looked at stupid useless books.

However, before he could say a word the Headmaster who had sensed he was about to interrupt put his hand up to keep him quiet.

So we sat for what seemed like hours but was probably only about another five minutes. Smithers was becoming more and more irritated and looked about ready to explode at any moment.

Then Miss. Millthrop looked up and said, "I thought I recognized them! I know why these books were in the chest, they were put there as 'sleepers'."

"Sleepers" I queried.

"Yes sleepers, they were put there to absorb any 'adverse energy' the other books may have generated, energy that would have endangered the spell cast to create the dummy wall at the back of the van."

Miss. Millthrop looked at us and was pleased to see our admiring glances even Smithers was nodding in agreement.

She went on to explain that she had in fact read all 8 books. They were written as light romantic entertainment for Lady Wizards and in themselves had no Magic power. However being neutral they would readily absorb (just like a dry sponge will absorb water) any Negative Magic radiating in a confined space around them.

Perhaps she suggested if more sleepers had been used the 'Concealment Magic' may have held for longer.

"I think you're correct" said the Head, "It's thanks to Brian, David and Jenny that more books were not removed and more sleepers added."

She told us that she could detect no sign of any Magic of any kind within the books, and if it were acceptable she would keep them, as she didn't like to see any books being destroyed and was certain that Mr.Smithers wouldn't want them in the Library.

"You're certainly correct there, I don't want silly rubbish like that in 'my' Library." retorted Smithers.

"The School Library." said the Headmaster smiling at Smithers.

Smithers grunted in reply.

"Take them by all means Miss. Millthrop, I'm indebted to you for solving one mystery from a list of mysteries which I feel is going to grow and grow." said the Headmaster as he gently patted her hand.

She looked the happiest I had seen her for many a long day.

"There is one more thing I would like you to do for me while you're here, can you read out the titles of those books on my desk?"

Miss. Millthrop picked up the books one by one and was starting to look puzzled.

"I'm afraid I'm a little embarrassed Headmaster. I don't even recognise the languages the books are in apart from the one in English. As she spoke Miss. Millthrop was taking a closer look at the one in English.

"So I won't be of any help to you if you want translations." She paused,

"Well I never! I didn't recall the title at first, I must have been only ten or twelve when I read this book, it was written by an Aunt of mine." She lifted it up and showed it to the Head.

"Your Aunt!" said the Head holding out his hand to take the book. He slowly flicked over the pages. "Incredible." He muttered. "The Children's Book of Happy Magic by Rose Cadwell. I hadn't realised it was there, how strange it should turn up in that pile of books."

The Headmaster looked very sad and said, "I knew the author of this book, I knew your Aunt very well, so well that I had intended to ask her to marry me. Perhaps I'm being vain but I felt she would have said 'yes'."

We all looked shocked, that had come out of the blue. The room had fallen silent then Miss. Millthrop said:

"Marry my Aunt!" Gasping for breath she continued in a whisper, "What happened? Why didn't you ask her?" She asked eagerly.

"Another time perhaps?" replied the Head. "That's enough book titles I think."

The Head now turned to Smithers. "Would any of those titles have presented a problem to you Mr.Smithers?"

"You know full well they wouldn't Headmaster."

"So you would have no problems translating them?"

"I wouldn't go as far as to say no problems, but I could do it."

"Excellent." said the Headmaster. "Then please do so, I want to see if there is anything in those books that could shed some light on this business and I already have others to study myself."

"I feel there is something else you want to say to us Headmaster, am I correct?" Asked Smithers.

"Yes you're correct. I've been waiting for a suitable moment to discuss some important matters with you and Miss. Millthrop and I suppose this is as good a time as any." The Head looking a little uneasy continued "I have known for some time that there are people at this School who want to see the end of Crinkles and what we stand for, how many and who they are I don't know, so I was forced to suspect everyone."

"People plotting to bring about the end of Crinkles and you suspected ME!! to be part of the conspiracy!!" said Smithers. "I don't believe the insult I have just received."

"Calm down Mr.Smithers. I had not singled anyone out, I had to suspect everyone."

"You suspected me as well Headmaster?" asked Miss. Millthrop in the softest of voices. I think she was about to burst into tears.

"I had no option Miss. Millthrop, although it would have hurt me deeply if you had proved to be against Crinkles. But I'm very happy to tell you that I now don't have any doubts about your loyalty."

"But you do have about mine." Smithers stated in the voice of a defeated man. He still hadn't been able to come to terms with the stolen books humiliation and now this.

"You are the only other adult person here at the School Mr. Smithers apart from Brian who would have caused me great pain if I found you untrue to Crinkles.

I know there is no love lost between us but your devotion to Crinkles I have never doubted. However if you had aligned yourself to a dark force to get at me I now know that after seeing what that force was up to today, removing a large part of Crinkles Library, your Library as you like to call it Mr.Smithers, that you would have ended all connections with that outside force and be as loyal to me and Crinkles as any member of staff could be."

Both Miss. Millthrop and Smithers looked relieved, the Head then went on to say that he would be relying on them to protect Crinkles when he was away at the Convention and that may put them both in some danger.

Miss. Millthrop wanted to know how they would be in danger. The Headmaster told them he did not know what form it would take, but if anyone wished to step down (and he also included me here), then now was the time to do so.

He said he would think none-the-less of anyone who decided to step down. The Head looked at all three of us, there was a long silence. I was waiting for the others to reply but when no one did I decided to speak up.

"You can rely on me Headmaster."

"And Me." Said Miss. Millthrop.

The Head was looking at Smithers. "Yes me too!" Mumbled Smithers.

"Excellent!" Said the Head, "Then let us move to tonight's business. Brian put one of the boxes on the floor in front of my desk please."

"Well now." He said. "Let us see what else is inside this apparently empty box." The others looked surprised.

I moved the box to the front of his desk and we all peered inside the 'supposedly' empty box. No one saw what Magic the Head did but the box collapsed into a heap.

We all jumped back with surprise, but soon recovered and started to lift away parts of the box to reveal its contents. The base had two compartments and each contained a block of mahogany.

I eased one out, it was nearly 2 inches thick by 18 inches in height by 15 inches long with polished sides and front. There were five grooves in the front of the block and four off set holes top and bottom which had obviously had screws in them at one time, but there were no grooves or notches at the back nor was the back of the blocks polished. I handed it to the Head, he examined it then past it to Smithers.

"I know what these are! They're book dividers." said Smithers. "The fronts are grooved to match the pattern grooves on our library bookshelves." He handed it to Miss. Millthrop.

"If they are just book dividers why protect them so well in that box? Look at the base of the box, separate compartments have been made to take each of them and look how neatly they fit." said Miss. Millthrop, placing it back in the base of the box.

Meanwhile the Head had passed the other divider to me. I was looking closely at what I thought was a fine crack in the back of the book divider I was holding, but the 'crack' looked too straight for my liking and as I turned the book divider I could just make out a fine line - running completely around the top, down the front (on the inside of one of the grooves) and along the bottom.

I decided to see if it would separate into two halves along the fine line. I opened my penknife and using the smallest blade which is very thin I gently eased it into the fine line at the back of the divider. Everyone was watching in complete silence, it gave way slightly so I followed the line around slowly and gently easing it open until the divider was in two halves.

"It looks like a piece of clay." I said. We all looked at the two halves of the book divider in my hands, one empty and one filled with the 'clay' insert.

"Let's have a look at the other divider to see if it's the same?" said the Headmaster. Once again there was the fine line running completely around the book divider.

So I eased open the second book divider and inside was a similar 'clay' insert.

"Time to check out the other box I think." said the Head. So the second box was brought and the Head's Magic used to collapse it, it also contained two book dividers.

I eased them open as before and once again we found the clay inserts inside.

"Why don't we try and get one of the clay inserts out?" I asked, and the Head agreed.

He cleared some space on his desk to give a reasonable area to work in.

We turned one of the shelf dividers over so that the clay segment faced the desk and as the Head held it just clear of the desktop, I gently tapped the back but nothing happened.

"Perhaps a little harder Brian." the Head said.

This time he rested the outer edges of the book divider on pieces of wood from one of the boxes this enabled us to keep the clay segment well clear of the desktop. The Head pressed down to stop it from moving and with a piece of the box on the back of the book divider to stop it being damaged, I was ready with another piece of wood to give it a good hard thump. We all held our breath.

"Ready Headmaster?"

"Yes ready Brian."

So I gave it a good hefty whack, but after 6 attempts nothing had happened.

"I'm going to see if I can ease it a bit with my pen knife."

There was no comment from anyone so I went ahead, slowly moving the blade of my pen knife in and out as I followed the inner shape to break the clay bonding that held it to the sides of the book divider. Once more we set it up as before and on the second hard thump it fell away from the book divider on to the desktop.

The Head put the book divider to one side and he picked up the clay insert, it was in the shape of a quadrant he turned it over and over in his hands.

"This looks and feels like clay." He said, "But the same as the supposedly empty boxes it's far too heavy there's something inside. Give me your pen knife Brian."

I handed it to him and he gently started to scrape away some of the clay. The Head was scraping away slowly but steadily at one of the straight edges of the quadrant, he had scraped off about an eighth of an inch when a chunk of clay fell away and exposed a section of the quadrant that glinted faintly as the light from the Heads desk lamp caught it momentarily.

I gasped!! "I think that's GOLD!!"

"We should remove the remainder of the clay or whatever it is from this quadrant." said the Head.

"Why don't we wash it off in water?" Said Smithers, "That would mean we wouldn't damage any inscription or carving there may be on it."

"That's a good idea." Said the Head, "That's why I didn't scrape away any clay from around the outer radius because that's the most likely place to find an inscription. Washing the clay off would solve the problem."

"NO!! I don't think we should."

Everyone turned to look at Miss. Millthrop.

"But why on Earth not?" Asked Smithers.

"Because I think we should try and save as much of the clay or whatever it is as we can."

"Save the clay! What rubbish," snorted Smithers.

I suddenly felt Miss. Millthrop was right, so I spoke up.

"It's probably that the clay was the polystyrene or bubble wrap equivalent protection of the day, and that's all it was a protection against damage." I looked around the group, "But what if we were wrong? What if it served another purpose? Also what if it's not clay as we know it? Why take the risk? Let's keep it, soften it if we must to help remove it but don't wash it away."

There were a couple of minutes of silence then the Head said.

"Yes I agree with Miss. Millthrop and Brian, we will save as much as we can including what I have already scraped off."

It took a lot longer softening the clay with a damp cloth and working it loose with our fingers. Occasionally a largish dry piece would break away, we managed to save about 95% of the clay that had surrounded the quadrant and stored it in old clean jam jars the Head found.

I say found, there were that many of them in a cupboard in his office I think he was starting a collection or intending to start jam making.

Eventually the complete 'Gold Quadrant' was revealed and what a surprise it gave us. On a closer inspection it had become obvious that it was actually a layered construction. We gave it a final gentle cleaning with a soft damp cloth and dried it with another soft cloth.

We each in turn held it. I wondered how many people in the whole World had seen it before us, never mind held it, very few I bet. It was late and we were all growing tired, but we were afraid to just leave the cleaned quadrant and the others over night locked in the Heads office.

Now that we had fully cleaned the first quadrant we felt ill at ease wanting them all cleaned and any information recorded then safely back in the Library were they belonged. We agreed to work on, three of us cleaning a quadrant each whilst Smithers took down any information he could find on each one.

The Head said first we must have some refreshment courtesy of himself and some delicious sandwiches and piping hot tea appeared.

Then it was down to work, finally we had all four quadrants completely cleaned and we placed them together on the Heads desk. It was breathtaking. We all sat quietly staring at them, to think that they had always been in our Library hidden away from sight for possibly hundred of years. Smithers must have passed them thousands of times, he would have walked past them numerous times every single day.

The top of each quadrant was engraved either with North, South, East or West and each one had an inscription around the outer edge. We felt sure that this was Gold about one inch thick, then a layer the Head thought was Platinum about a quarter of an inch thick and finally a layer of what we now know is 'Blue Emororite' again about a quarter of an inch thick.

This final layer was not the exact size of the quadrant although it wasn't far out, in fact spot on in some places. This reinforced my later theory that the 'Blue Emororite' was not being machined but pieces selected that were as near as possible to the shape required.

We all realised there was still something missing, namely 5, what I would call locking pieces. The corner of each quadrant was notched and a locking piece not unlike a piece of a jigsaw puzzle would fit in and hold each corner together.

This left a notched centre hole into which would fit the 5th locking piece which would be circular and hold all 4 pieces of the quadrant together in the centre, but at that moment in time we had no idea where the locking pieces might be.

"I tell you what Headmaster." I said, "If word gets out about this being in the School you'll need more than the Magic of the 'Containment Book' to protect them. We'll have every rogue in the country coming here to try their luck."

"Very true, Very true Brian, I never thought of that. This must not go any further than the four of us." We all nodded."

I was thinking four pieces of Gold with a Platinum backing, all four of us could be very, very rich.

Money didn't seem to mean much to the Head he was as happy as he could ever be as Head of Crinkles and he knew it. With Smithers and his Library it was the same. As for Miss. Millthrop - I wasn't quite so sure.

But for myself, well I've never had any real money, always penny pinching by necessity and never ever likely to have any real money unless I win it. Now this could change my whole life, even I realised that it wasn't simply the value of the gold itself but also the rarity and antiquity that would make each quadrant very valuable, if not priceless. Now put all 4 quadrants together and you must be talking a Kings ransom.

We need never ever worry again about money, all of us could go anywhere in the World that took our fancy, and as many times as we wanted. Travelling in luxury, have fabulous homes in exotic locations, expensive cars (I've never had a new car, always old bangers, other people's hand me downs). We could have whatever money could buy.

Had the Headmaster read my mind? I don't know. But he said:

"It's harder for Brian than the rest of us. We all understand the meaning of real contentment and happiness, we don't need or even desire the things that Brian might long for."

"All I can say Brian is that your job here at Crinkles is yours for as long as you want it, and when the day comes that you want to retire there will always be a place for you to live here at Crinkles, amongst friends that really care for you."

He looked at me with a kindly look and continued,

"Remember Brian, you would always have companionship and never feel lonely."

"Thank you Headmaster." I replied.

Miss. Millthrop actually gave me a kindly look.

We all stood looking and touching the gold quadrants. It was Miss. Millthrop who spoke first.

"I know what this is."

"You do!" all three of us shouted in amazement.

"I do, but never thought I would ever see any of them, they belong to a little known legend lost in the passing of time, or so I thought."

When, oh when, is she going to tell us what they are?

"If my Aunt's stories are correct, these are the 'Compass Points of the World' or at least that's what she called them."

"As you can see there are four gold quadrants each representing a point on the compass North, South, East and West."

"Perhaps it might be advisable to make sure we know which shelf divider held each quadrant." We all nodded in agreement, it probably didn't matter but why take the chance.

Smithers had been studying the inscription on the North quadrant for some time then he declared.

"I think I know roughly what the inscription on the side of the North quadrant says: It's a very ancient language from which ancient Hebrew and Arabic partly originated." Said Smither's excitedly, I had never seen Smither's excited about anything before, angry, irritable, bad tempered yes, but excited never.

"We have one book in our Library written in this language which I have studied on and off for many years with only a limited amount of success but I think this roughly translated means:

'Without Others I cannot stand'."

We all stood quietly as he studied the next quadrant,

"The Eastern quadrant appears to be: 'I Will One Day Meet My Brothers', or perhaps it could be, 'See My Brothers'." He paused deep in thought, "Then again it may be, 'One Day Pass My Brothers'."

There was another long pause as he studied the third quadrant.

"The Southern quadrant is something like: 'I Hold Always My Position', or perhaps, 'I Held Always My Position' or something similar."

"That only leaves the West." I said.

"The West appears to be, 'I Am What I Am'. Or it could be 'I Am Where I Am'.

I'm not really completely sure about any of these translations. I would have to spend a lot more time studying them."

"I think Headmaster," said Smithers, "The 'Compass Points of the World' as Miss. Millthrop calls them have been in our Library to give support to the 'Containment Book' ever since Carforth Crinkle first set up the 'Containment' itself."

"I agree with you." Said the Head, "and as they were obviously removed along with the books. I suggest we check to see what has replaced them."

"If we have these 'Compass Points of the World', where are the locking pieces? Do we also have them?" I queried.

"It always seems to be more questions than answers Brian." Said the Head.

"There is one certainty." I said, "The Northern book divider will go into the bookshelves on the North wall probably somewhere in the middle of the centre row and the same would go for the others on their respective walls."

"That makes sense to me." said Smithers, "You're not as stupid as I thought boy." He said smiling.

"Then" Said the Head, "I suggest we put the quadrants back in the two halves of their respective book dividers and each take one and we depart for the Library."

Everyone agreed to this, but Smithers requested a few minutes to take a copy of the inscriptions on each quadrant so he could study them later.

While he was doing that I popped into the anti-room where I had a box of tools and collected some screwdrivers.

Smithers seemed to be so slow, I understood that he didn't want to make a mistake but the rest of us were itching to get moving, finally he said that he had all the information he could obtain.

We each put the two halves together of our book divider with the respective quadrant inside, and left the Heads study waiting while he locked the door, then made our way to the Library.

To put it mildly I felt a little uneasy, it was very late now and very quiet, it had also turned quite cold.

The School felt a lot spookier than usual, the passage ways a lot darker and I felt someone was watching us all of the time.

Somebody probably was, I certainly would be watching the Head if I was on the other side.

We finally arrived at the Library. Smithers unlocked the door and put the lights on.

Blimey I thought, it's even creepier in here.

Have you ever been in a poorly lit library after dark? I don't recommend it.

Row after row of musty old books gave the place a strange smell, and at this late hour a very strange feeling, I nearly jumped out of my skin when a tiny spider hanging down on its thread touched my face.

I grabbed Miss. Millthrop who went rigid,

"Sorry." I whispered, "I tripped."

"You gave me a terrible shock." She whispered back.

I don't know why we were whispering it just seemed right somehow.

"This is the West wall." said Smithers, "The sun always sets through this window."

I put my back to the West wall.

"That would make the wall on my right the South wall and the wall on my left the North and the one straight ahead the East." I added.

"Right!" Said the Head, "We each know which wall is ours let's go to it."

"Just one thing Headmaster, I think it would be best if we all went together to each wall just in case anything goes wrong. I don't know what could but why take any chances."

Let's face it, I wasn't too keen to be on my own out of sight of the rest, surrounded by nine feet high book cases in a really creepy place.

"Fair comment." said the Head, "Let's all stick together then."

I could see the relief on Miss. Millthrop's face and I have no doubt it showed on mine. For the first time I felt we were comrades in arms.

We started with the West wall, selecting roughly the centre of the forty-foot long wall and took the centre position of the bookcase and there it was on the 18-inch height shelf.

"This should be the one Brian." said the Head, "According to your reckoning."

"Let's have a look at it before we disturb it." and I examined it closely. It didn't quite match the mahogany of the bookcase but it was close, very close.

I very carefully removed some of the books from each side of the divider, and Yes! that's what I had been hoping to see, the dust slightly disturbed not just at the front which could be caused by a book being removed for normal use but also right at the very back.

Just to be doubly sure I checked another two dividers on that wall and no dust had been disturbed at the very back.

"Yes that's definitely where it came from." I told the others.

I selected the correct size screwdriver and found the screws came out easily as they had candle wax on the threads.

Now to put the original one back we reversed the procedure, the screws going in as easily as they had come out. We replaced the books on either side of it and went on to check and replace all the others. I had checked the book dividers we had removed and satisfied myself that they were what they seemed, solid wood.

"That's a job well done." Said the Head, "I have no idea of the exact role they play in the Library but I'm very pleased that they are back where they belong."

"Now is probably as good a time as any to tell you it's here in the School Library that you Miss. Millthrop and you Mr.Smithers will defend Crinkles on the home front. You must both be here not later than midday on the second day of the Wizards Conference and remain here until at least midnight."

"Lock the Library door and keep it locked, you must both remain in the Library neither of you must leave it, not even for a minute under any circumstances what so ever.

It may be that someone or a group of people want to come into the Library, no matter what argument is put to you to open the Library door, you must not open it. So it's just as well we have toilet facilities here." "Well we have." Said Smithers, "but they don't work."

"Brian." Said the Head, "A little job for you I think." I nodded in reply.

"Remember to bring plenty food and drinks with you." continued the Head.

"Brian will be on the outside but he may be otherwise engaged so you will have to be self contained."

"Can you not give us any idea what you expect may happen and what action we should take Headmaster?" asked Miss. Millthrop.

"I would if I could, but I have no idea what might take place, hopefully nothing, but I rely on your judgement and abilities to handle whatever situation may arise and that applies to you also Brian."

"Well its long past all of our bedtimes." said the Head as he put the Library lights out. Mr.Smithers locked the door and we all started to make our way back to our rooms.

"Do we check tomorrow to see if the locking pieces are also in the Library?" I asked.

"It's very late." said the Head, "Why don't we discuss it tomorrow."

We were now back outside the Heads study, he smiled at us and said:

"Goodnight everyone, and I thank you for your invaluable help." We all said goodnight and started to go our separate ways.

"Miss. Millthrop, I go your way may I accompany you?"

"Yes, it would be very nice to have some company, thank you Brian."

So I saw Millthrop safely back to her room and the brave lad that I am after I left her I shot along the corridor, up the stairs, and along my corridor to my room before any Hob Goblins or Spiders could get me. Was I ready for bed? Was I not. I was totally worn out what a day it had been. On top of everything else I had actually seen Smithers excited and he gave me a smile, wonders never cease.

CHAPTER TWELVE

The Compass Points of the World

The following evening after dinner we gathered again in the Heads study.

This time it was to discuss what we had decided to call Locking Pieces. I suggested that we got the Gold Pieces out again.

This did not go down well especially with Smithers who didn't want the Library disturbed yet again. He pointed out that if we went on like this taking a book divider out every five minutes we wouldn't have to bother soon because they would just fall out. So I asked the Head that if I could find the Locking Pieces could we then get the Gold Pieces out again.

"But where could they be Brian?" asked the Head.

"I've been giving this some thought and I'm almost sure Headmaster that there's a book divider directly in line with those with the Gold Pieces inside but two shelves higher and I think this would be the logical place to start."

It was agreed that we should once more depart for the Library.

We went straight to the divider with the Gold Piece inside on the North wall and sure enough the shelf above did not have a divider in line but the one above that did.

After removing the books from either side I quickly unscrewed the divider. Sure enough there was the faint tell tale line showing that this divider was also actually in two halves. I carefully parted them and there it was, a beautiful blue coloured piece of metal similar in shape to a jigsaw puzzle piece.

While we were there we decided to remove the divider containing the Gold Piece. To stop Smither's worrying about them becoming slack the Head said he'd remove one using Magic, the spell was cast but nothing happened. The Head tried again yet still nothing, Smithers, Winthrop and the Head all tried at the same time yet again nothing happened.

"It's not going to work is it?" said the Head. "It must be the quadrant inside blocking it."

So once again I removed it and then continued to collect all of the other dividers from East, South and West along with the dividers for the locking pieces.

"That leaves one piece to find Headmaster." I said. "The one that goes in the centre and I think we will find it in the centre of the Library."

It took a while to get the exact centre of the Library, but once we had, we simply counted up from the floor to the correct shelf level and there it was.

A book divider exactly where I had hoped it would be. I removed it and once again there was the very fine line telling us it was in fact in two halves.

We departed to the Heads study and opened up the other four book dividers being careful to note which divider had contained each piece.

The Head once more placed all four quadrants together on his desk but this time also putting the four outer locking pieces in position. They appeared identical but in fact only the correct one would fit. "Well now." He said. "All that is left to do now is put the centre piece in."

The Head had picked it up and was considering the correct position for it.

Suddenly fear and apprehension gripped me and I shouted out:

"HEADMASTER!! Please don't put the centre piece in."

"Why not Brian?" Asked the Head.

"I'm not a Wizard I can't do any Magic, but a sixth inner sense is telling me we shouldn't put the centre piece in."

"Stupid boy what possible harm can it do." Sneered Smithers.

"I don't know." I replied.

Millthrop to my surprise supported me.

"You shouldn't call him stupid boy Mr. Smithers. In the past few days he's been right more times than we have."

Smithers nodded and gave one of his famous grunts, that decoded meant okay I was wrong. The Head put the centre piece down and said:

"Well it hasn't been in position for possibly hundreds of years so a few more won't matter." He then took out one of the outer circle Locking Pieces and said:

"I wonder what these Locking Pieces as Brian calls them are made of." He was turning it over in his hand as he spoke.

"I don't know." Said Smithers, "But I know who could tell us, Mr. Abbott."

"The Physics teacher" Millthrop queried.

"Yes there's not much he doesn't know about Geology, Geochemistry and Mineralogy it's his hobby, in fact it's his life. He's studied it for years and years and spends every spare second with his books and collection." replied Smithers.

"I'm amazed." Said the Head, "I had no idea." He turned to Miss. Millthrop, "It's gone seven he would have finished his evening meal, do you think you could pop out and find him."

Millthrop nodded and dashed out returning in just a few minutes.

"He's in his classroom working on his own apparently." She told us on her return.

"Excellent, excellent, could not be better let us all join him. But first we must put the book dividers with the Gold Quadrants and Locking Pieces back, I only feel at ease when they are safely where they belong. We will take this locking piece with us."

The Head had wrapped the centre locking piece in a handkerchief and slipped it into his pocket. He led the way out of his office and locked the door, so once again our merry little band departed for the Library and we soon had the eight book dividers back in place and then we all followed him to Mr. Abbott's classroom.

The Headmaster knocked loudly on the classroom door and Simon called out: "Come in."

He turned when the door opened and was more than a little surprised to see the Head and the rest of us.

"Good Evening Headmaster."

"Good Evening Mr. Abbott."

"This is a surprise, no one ever visits me in the evenings and here I am with four visitors."

"It's not a social call I'm afraid we are hoping you will be able to help us Mr. Abbott."

"My pleasure, if I can help I will, but I can't think what I can help with."

The Head took the handkerchief out of his pocket and handed it to Simon as he said:

"We wonder if you can identify this."

Simon moved over to the bench where he had been working and unfolding the handkerchief looked at the locking piece. He picked it up and I sensed his instant excitement though he didn't show it.

"If you can give me a few minutes Headmaster." said Simon in a strange trembling voice.

The Head nodded in agreement, and I wondered was I the only one to sense Simons excitement, and the slight trembling of his hands.

Simon turned it a few times then switched on a lamp on the workbench and with a magnifying glass he took out of his pocket he began a close inspection.

Then he weighed it, took out a ruler and a micrometer and took various measurements then he started numerous calculations. We all stood watching his every move, he had now gone over to his desk and was rummaging around inside, boxes and trays were being taken out the contents examined as he searched for something obviously in vain.

"Can we help?" I volunteered.

"No! No! No! Just give me a minute or two."

He had put his desk top down and was sitting in his chair with his head resting on his left hand. We all stood as quiet as possible not wanting to interrupt his train of thought.

"Ah!' He said. Stood up and strode across to a wooden chest of small drawers, one after another he opened them and took out small cardboard boxes, peered inside, grunted, then put them back.

Until at last he opened one looked inside then took something out and immediately turned and walked over to the workbench, he started rubbing the locking piece with whatever he had in his hand. He did this for sometime and repeated it until finally he seemed satisfied.

"Just one more thing to check Headmaster, don't be alarmed."

As he spoke he was putting a wood block just below the jaws of a large vice and now placing the locking piece on top and tightening the vice whilst pressing down on the locking piece to prevent it from rising from the wooden block.

Walking away he rummaged through some assorted tools and returned with a hard tipped hexagon bodied punch and a large adjustable spanner. He tightened the spanner on the hexagon body of the punch and turning to me asked would I position the punch in the centre of the locking piece and hold it in that position with the spanner.

"Keep well away from the punch Brian." He walked away rummaging through more tools and returned with a large sledge hammer, "Keep back Brian."

Everyone looked alarmed, what was he doing? But before the Head could say 'STOP', down came the sledgehammer, the force through the large spanner heavily jarred my wrists.

"Ready Brian, I'm going to do it once more, hold the punch nice and steady."

The sledgehammer came down again with even more force than before.

"That will do Brian."

I looked at him with relief. I wasn't sure if he had broken my wrists as both hands were completely numb. Simon was peering down at the locking piece in the vice.

"Excellent." He said, "Just going to double check though."

He removed it from the vice and gazed at it for some time under the lamp with his magnifying glass.

"Not a mark on it, incredible. Well Headmaster." He said turning to face us. "You have made me 'one of the happiest men in the World', definitely the happiest person who is fascinated by Geology and Mineralogy, who would have thought it? Working here at Old Crinkles as I have done every night for years, then you just walk in and you completely change my world."

We all looked at him puzzled what on earth was he talking about.

Simon Abbott was now beaming and smiling and almost jumping about. I couldn't remember the last time I had seen someone as excited and happy.

"This Headmaster is 'Blue Emororite'!!! I never thought I would see a piece never mind hold it in my hand. As far as I know no-one has ever seen a piece before, in fact many say it's a myth." He paused, "But they are wrong Headmaster, here it is in the palm of my hand. I can hardly wait to tell my fellow Geologists and Mineralogists.

"That I'm afraid must not happen." said the Head. "The only ones ever to know about this are the five of us standing in this room, it's absolutely crucial that no one else knows of its existence." The Head was holding his hand out for its return. Simon looked devastated, from being on top of the World, his World had collapsed around him in a mere twelve seconds.

"Then may I hold it for a while." He asked in a sad almost feeble voice, the Head nodded and Simon slowly turned it in his hand then said:

"There is one thing puzzling me, you see 'Blue Emororite' is harder than any other material, harder than diamonds yet this has been machined and very intricately at that, how could this be? It's not possible!"

"May I have a look Headmaster?" I asked.

The Head nodded and indicated that Simon should pass it to me, this time it was I who studied it under the light with the magnifying glass.

"Yes it looks as though it has been machined, but I don't think it has. I feel it's been selected because of its shape that some how or other has been formed naturally.

A bit like the Giants Causeway in Ireland, blocks of stone in near perfect hexagonal sections appearing to be manmade but which in fact are an unusual natural phenomenon."

"But what about the rest." said Smithers, "There identical, and to have such complex forms identical is asking too much natural phenomenon or not."

"There's more!!! How did you get them?" Simon was reeling from this disclosure.

"There are a few more, I'm afraid I can't tell you where they came from." said the Head.

I turned to Smithers, "But that's just it Mr.Smithers they are not identical, they are very similar but not identical, remember only the correct one fits. If they had been machined in some way then they would be identical there would be no reason why they shouldn't be."

"There could be a reason that we aren't aware of." He replied.

"There could be but I doubt it." Oh dear, that made Smithers go in a huff.

"How many more pieces are there!!" Queried Simon "And what do you mean only the correct one fits?"

"Not many." Said the Head being deliberately evasive.

"Mr. Abbott." I said, distracting him from his second question, "There's something that I can't understand."

"Well go on Brian." said Millthrop.

"How can you be sure that is Blue whatever you call it if no-one has seen it before? Where did all this information come from?"

"Good point." Said Smithers and Millthrop nodded in agreement.

"Well that's all down to one incredibly clever and incredibly beautiful young lady. When we were students she worked ten times harder than any of us, read every book she could lay her hands on and researched and researched." Simon paused, "We were all madly in love with Rose Cadwell."

As soon as he mentioned the name I turned to see what the Heads reaction would be as had Millthrop. He had gone very pale and his jaw had dropped.

"But we didn't have a chance" continued Simon, "she was in love. She never stopped talking about her boyfriend, none of us ever actually met him we didn't even know his real name, but we all felt we knew him. Rose had given him a nickname, it was 'Potty this and Potty that' she was driving us pot...ty!" Simon paused, he looked shocked and very uneasy, suddenly, we all knew who Potty was. We looked at Dr. Phillpotts his face was bright red.

I was the only one to hear Simon softly say to himself, "I can't believe it, all these years and it never dawned on me, it seems so obvious now."

"I was Rose's boyfriend." Said Dr. Phillpotts, "We were deeply in love with each other, then one night we had a lovers tiff over something so trivial that I can't remember what it was. Unfortunately we were young and arrogant, Rose didn't apologise and neither did I. I was determined not to back down and waited for Rose to contact me, which she never did. No doubt Rose was determined also not to back down and was waiting for me to contact her, which I never did. Oh what stupid, stupid things, pride and so called principles can be."

The Head continued. "Shortly after that I joined Crinkles and found that I never had any spare time, the years rolled on and I assumed she had found someone else, I knew she was always very popular whereas I was not a one for mixing, preferring my own company if I'm truthful. I could never understand what attracted her to me in the first place. It's all probably been for the best, although I often think of her and wonder what she's doing now."

We all stood in silence. Millthrop was crying and I had a lump in my throat and even old crusty Smithers looked sad. Perhaps he had a similar story to tell and that this had opened up long forgotten memories, maybe that's why he's always so miserable and bad tempered, it may all stem from some sad episode in his life that happened years ago. I looked at poor Simon he looked so ill at ease and embarrassed.

"Have you kept in touch with Rose?" The Head asked Simon.

I thought Simon was going to collapse, his jaw dropped and he fidgeted from one foot to the other.

"You, you, you, don't know then!!" He stuttered and sounded surprised..

"Know what!" Asked the Head.

"Rose dis, dis, dissappeared."

There was silence as we all took in the word disappeared. The Head broke the silence.

"'DISSAPEARED!!' what do you mean DISSAPEARED?"

Simon swallowed hard and tried to pull himself together.

"Well strangely it was all to do with 'Blue Emororite'."

"How can that be!!" Queried the Head.

"Apparently she had been told that some had been found abroad."

"By who and where?" asked the Head.

"No one knows, Rose wouldn't tell anyone. All we knew was that she made arrangements to go abroad on her own to check it out, there were plenty of volunteers willing to go with her including me, but she would have none of it. Rose told us she was leaving on the Tuesday and had only a few final arrangements to make. She had packed all of her personal bags and scientific cases and they were in her room at the College. On the Saturday she went into town to get a few odds and ends and was never seen again."

We all stood in silence, totally stunned.

"How did I not hear anything about it in the newspapers or something?" Asked the Head

We all knew the answer to that of course, he never read any newspapers or watched any television or listened to the radio.

"There wasn't much coverage in the papers about It." said Simon. "As some major news items from abroad were emerging and I think only the local papers mentioned it and even then it was buried away in the middle."

"Was there not an investigation?" asked the Head in a hesitant voice.

"Well yes, but what could they investigate, she left no letter or note, all her personal papers were checked but apparently no clue was found there." Simon paused, he felt as though the Head was blaming him personally for Rose's disappearance the way he was looking at him and his tone of voice.

"Is that it!! Is there no more?" Asked the Head impatiently.

"Well I know she didn't disappear in England."

"What!! How on earth can you know that? And if you did know was the Police informed?" Queried the Head.

"Yes I informed the Police but they didn't share my opinion. In fairness to them if I was correct and Rose had disappeared abroad, where abroad? There was no indication whatsoever as to her intended destination."

"What made you decide Rose hadn't disappeared in England?"

"The Police called in Rose's parents to go through her personal cases which provided no clues. They then wanted someone to check through her scientific luggage and as her Mam and Dad had no idea what they were looking at I volunteered. I found that all the equipment you would expect to be there was there, except."

"Yes! Yes! Go on." Said the Head impatiently, "Except what?"

"Except five of the items were obviously brand new." Simon replied in a sad tired voice.

"Brand new! So why did that matter?" Asked the Head.

"The items they had replaced had belonged to her Grandfather and she always took them with her, they were a sort of good luck charm, she would never have left them behind.

I think she had no intention of leaving on Tuesday, we were meant to think that while Rose in fact quietly slipped away on the Saturday.

"Why would she do that?" asked the Headmaster irritably.

"That way, there was no chance anyone would be following and discover her destination, no doubt Rose had a second set of luggage and scientific equipment at some other location. Also there was no passport or any other travel documentation ever found, I'm sure she had them all with her on the Saturday."

"But why the need for such precautions? Why would anyone want to follow Rose?" asked the Head.

"Because Rose might lead them to 'Blue Emororite'." Simon explained. "It's unique, it has properties no other material has. It's priceless."

"As Brian said, how do you know all this?" Queried the Head.

"I can only go on what Rose told me but I believed her, I still do. The danger was that if Rose had been able to find this information then so could someone else."

"Has there been any further developments?" asked the Head hopefully.

"The only other thing I know is that Rose hasn't made any contact with her parents since she disappeared. I go to see them from time to time but not very often as my visits upset them." Simon paused to gather his composure before continuing, "When they see me they think I have brought news of Rose, their disappointment when I tell them there is no news is terrible to see. Then we talk covering the same ground we've covered so many times before and always it's the same dead end, I come away depressed and leave them depressed." Simon looked at the Head "I'm sorry I can't tell you anymore you know all that I know."

I couldn't help feeling sorry for Simon. The evening had started with such jubilation for him, his whole life would have changed, and then in such a short span of time those hopes were dashed and the evening ending in great sadness as old memories had been vividly revived.

It was the same for the Head he looked bewildered. He had not remotely expected any of these revelations and as for Millthrop she appeared as shocked as everyone, I can only assume she also didn't know her Aunt Rose had disappeared. The Head turned to Simon,

"Thank you very much Mr.Abbott. I'm deeply indebted to you, we will leave you in peace now, thank you, Goodnight."

"Goodnight Headmaster." Simon replied in a quiet voice as he watched us leave the classroom.

I've no doubt he was relieved to have it all to himself again, there was certainly plenty for him to think about.

Millthrop looked at the Head and knew he needed some time alone, as indeed so did she.

"It's getting late now Headmaster I think we should call it a day."

"Yes, you're right Miss. Millthrop, Goodnight everyone."

"Goodnight Headmaster." We all replied and with a slight nod to each other went our separate ways. Although very tired I could not go to sleep as today's events went back and forth through my head.

The centre locking piece was left in the Heads office overnight, but early the next day when everyone was having breakfast I put it back in its correct place in the Library.

The following day no one mentioned the previous evening's events and for a while we tried to avoid looking at each other.

As the days went by it was never talked about, everyone must have decided it was best to leave the revelations in the past and get on with normal day- to- day life.

This suited me very well, and soon other events pushed it further and further to the back of our minds.

The Headmaster and Mr.Smithers returned to studying musty old volumes whenever an opportunity arose to try and find out some information on what we had decided to call the 'Compass Points of the World'. Now of course also looking for any reference to 'Blue Emororite'.

Unknown to anyone else, Miss. Millthrop had made contact with her Aunty Rose's parents and arranged to go down and see them.

Whilst there she had persuaded them to let her have all of Rose's scribblings, notebooks, book roughs and finished books that she could find and brought them back to Crinkles, having promised to return them as soon as she had read them. So she too was now studying masses of documents and books in the same search.

Was I not half glad not to be involved in all that reading and studying business.

I think I've explained before but no matter I should re-mention it.

At Crinkles when we talk about time, there are two times. Our time, 24 hours per day where one can live to be over 100 years old. Then there is Wizards time, again 24 hours per day but for all I know Dr.Phillpotts could be 300, 400 years old, or more.

His romance with Rose could have been 40, 50 years ago or longer our time. One never ever talks about that side of it, enough to say Dr.Philpotts is here at Crinkles and to all intents and purposes appears to be in his late sixties and living in our time.

It can become complicated, so not only do I not talk about it, I try not to even think about it.

CHAPTER THIRTEEN

The Bonfire

The Head asked me to collect the wooden cases from his study and ask Mr.Graham the Woodwork teacher if he could put any of the wood to good use.

I had sorted out some old hessian sacks to put the pieces in, halfway through filling the second sack an idea dawned on me.

The Head wasn't in his study so I pottered about waiting for his return, by the time he came back I wasn't so sure it was a good idea anymore but I decided to give it a try.

I greeted him as he came in through the door, "Good morning Headmaster."

"Good morning Brian."

"Headmaster I've been thinking, we all more or less agreed that it required at least 6 people to smuggle the books into and out of the Library that means there are at least 6 people who are working here that are enemies of Crinkles."

"I'm afraid you are right Brian and we have no idea who they are. We know a few people who are definitely on our side, but as for the rest your guess is as good as mine, we shall just have to be very watchful until someone shows their true colours."

"I have an idea Headmaster that might at least expose one, hopefully more."

"Then let me hear it Brian."

"It all depends on whether you can use your Magic to put the boxes back together as they were before."

"No problem there Brian tip out all the bits of the box you have in the sacks and I'll do it now, but how does this help us detect the enemy?"

"We've found the Gold Quadrants." I said, "But if they see the boxes thrown out they can't be sure the quadrants aren't still in there, they must make an attempt to find out."

"Yes I see, well let's get the boxes back together then."

"Hang on Headmaster I need to find the bases first, because I think it may be a good idea to put something of similar weight to the Gold Quadrants into the compartments then I'll nail the base into position. They probably have a good idea how the boxes should feel weight wise and if they feel too light will just put them back down, they must take them away and ideally we want to catch them opening the bases up."

I watched in amazement as the parts all sorted themselves out lined themselves up and locked into place, leaving only the dummy base for me to nail down.

The Head could make a fortune putting together assemble your self furniture for people.

"What are we going to use for the dummy gold quadrants?" asked the Head.

"I think I know just the thing, Miss. Millthrop has about 8 glass paper weights left over from the Garden Fete she was given 12 free of charge from the local gift shop to sell on one of the bric a brac stalls, two in each compartment should be about right."

"Could you ask Headmaster if you could have them? As I'm only on probation, and she'd ask me all kinds of questions."

"Good point Brian, it's almost time for the mid morning break I'll call along and see her."

A few minutes later the Head returned with 8 glass paperweights. I popped them into the compartments in the base with some cardboard as packing to stop them rattling about then fitted in the base and nailed it down.

We examined it and decided that it didn't look as though it had been disturbed.

"Now Brian, Where do we put it? Somewhere like the potting shed where anyone can get easy access to it?"

"I'm afraid not Headmaster, we don't know how many people might get involved, so we would need 2 people ourselves in case of physical trouble."

"Physical trouble, I hadn't thought of that." replied the Head looking worried.

"The other problem with the potting shed is that you would have to watch it night and day this would be impossible as we don't have enough people."

"But would we have to watch it night and day Brian?"

"Yes Headmaster, you could bet your last 50p that even if it were left unguarded for only five minutes that would be the five minutes that they would turn up. I have given it quite a bit of thought and I think the only solution is a Bonfire."

"A Bonfire! With just two wooden boxes that would look a bit odd Brian." said the Head

"There would be more than the boxes Headmaster. Eric the junior gardener has been trimming the trees and collecting dead wood and was planning to have a Bonfire this week."

"So if I have a word with him."

"Exactly Headmaster, it's Tuesday today, if you ask him to tidy the place up a bit he'll tell you about his proposed Bonfire, ask him to do it on Thursday night after the evening meal is over. That means he will build the Bonfire during the afternoon."

"Yes I know the pupils love their Bonfires." said the Head.

"I think the best idea is for me to make my way to the Bonfire with the boxes and put them on top as the children are making their way to the School Hall, most of the pupils will see me doing this especially as I will have to make two journeys. While everyone is eating and the yard is deserted our enemies should arrive to remove the boxes before the fire is lit."

"We will be hiding discreetly and catch them at It." added the Head.

"That's it exactly Headmaster."

That evening the Head called us all together. Smithers, Millthrop and myself. It was becoming a regular knitting circle, this time David and Jenny were also there, he explained our plan and everyone agreed it was worth a try.

It was Smithers who pointed out that we should sketch a ground plan to make sure all areas were covered we did this and realised we were one short.

Some time was spent trying to decide not only who we could trust but who would also support our plan, it was beginning to look as though no one would fit the bill.

Then Millthrop suggested Harry the senior Gardener. This amazed us, he was very old and had poor eyesight so we rejected her proposal out of hand.

But she insisted we heard her out.

"It's because of his poor eyesight he could be invaluable to us." She said, "He's compensated for that over the years and can recognise someone by the way they walk. I've got good eye sight but he can tell me who's coming long before they are close enough for me to recognise."

"There's other things in his favour." Added Smithers, "He will do anything for you Headmaster and the School, and won't even ask why."

"You're right." said the Head, "I will ask him tomorrow."

So there it was, the Magnificent Seven and not a gun or a horse between us. The Head reminded us for about the fourth time that nobody was to try and stop or detain anyone only observe.

The following day was endless I couldn't wait for the evening to come, it felt like November the 5th when I was a boy. Waiting and waiting for it to get dark enough for the Bonfire to be lit and the Fireworks set off, ten minutes felt more like ten hours.

At last it was time for me to carry the first box from the Heads Study to the Bonfire. I made sure as many people as possible saw me, there was certainly a good crowd passing when I placed it on top of the Bonfire.

There were not many people about when I returned with the second box, but I knew everyone in the School would have seen at least one box.

Soon the courtyard fell quiet as everyone was in the hall for the evening meal, although all the pupils and some of the Masters liked Bonfires fortunately they all enjoyed their food even more.

In approximately 45 minutes the Bonfire would be lit. I looked around and knew the others would be watching but I couldn't see anyone else, we were all well hidden.

If anything the time seemed to be going slower than before, the first 5 minutes seemed endless. 15 minutes went by – nothing. 30 minutes went by – nothing. 40 minutes went by – nothing. Pupils were now starting to arrive back, 45 minutes had gone by and a crowd had gathered around the Bonfire. Eric arrived and soon the Bonfire was well alight, within a few minutes you could hardly see the boxes because of the huge flames around them.

We had been wrong, no one had come to rescue the boxes so they must have known we had removed the hidden contents, but how could they? I couldn't believe they'd not tried to check if they were indeed empty.

The crowds were thinning now and 10 minutes later there was only two or three here and there looking at a pile of grey white ash and glowing embers. We started to make our way back to the Heads Office.

By the time we arrived what a sorry looking bunch we were, none of us had seen anything unusual, how could we have been so wrong. Harry the gardener was the only one not there.

"He's probably off to bed." said Smithers, "He's getting on and gets up very early so he goes to bed early and bed is where I should be. There's nothing left here to talk about, next time boy keep these ideas as you call them to your self." He was staring at me with his usual miserable grumpy look as he spoke.

"Yes we may as well call it a night." said the Headmaster.

Just as we all got up to go there was an urgent knocking on the door, the Headmaster opened it and there stood Harry the gardener puffing and panting, gasping for air.

"Is this School going crackers!! Did you tell those pupils to rake those hot ashes Headmaster? If you did it was a bit daft, someone will end up with nasty burns the way there going on. The other day it was Chamber Maids carrying armfuls of books across the playing field at five in the morning, the whole Schools going bonkers, it's not the School it was, tain't the School I remember."

But no one was listening to him, we were all racing back to the remains of the Bonfire, how stupid, stupid, we had been, they didn't need to try and retrieve the boxes just wait until it was a pile of ashes and when everyone had gone rake through them to recover what they hoped was there.

If the Gold Pieces had been in the boxes surely they would have melted with the heat I thought, obviously they knew something we didn't.

Could it be that the clay type material they had been covered in would have stopped them from melting? Or would it have been the Platinum layer working in conjunction with the Blue Emerorite layer?

Unfortunately for them Harry the Gardener had hung around in the shadows after everyone else had left. He had still been there when pupils had appeared with rakes. When he'd stepped out and challenged them he had been told that the Headmaster had asked them to rake out the ashes.

The question now was had Harry reached us in time for us to get back to catch them?

The answer was unfortunately NO.

By the time we arrived back at the site of the Bonfire it was totally deserted.

"Now we'll never know who it was." said the Headmaster.

"I do." said Harry who had only just arrived panting and gasping for breath. "Well I know, gasp, gasp, two of them, puff, pant, there were four pupils altogether."

"Then tell us." said the Head.

"Give me a few minutes." He gasped and wheezed, "To catch my breath."

We had forgotten that poor old Harry had ran flat out both ways. He finally got enough breath back to tell us that there had been one girl and three boys.

The girl had been Lisa Grey who he recognized because she was always hanging about with a boy called Eric. It was Eric who had told him they were acting on the Headmasters orders and it was Eric he was forever chasing for playing football on his beautiful lawns.

Harry could tell us no more, he had not recognized the other two boys and he was looking really tired. The Head was worried about him and asked Millthrop to see he got to his room safely.

"I'll talk to Lisa and Eric tomorrow." The Head told us. "Perhaps I can get the names of the other two from them though I doubt it. Well, yet another meeting tomorrow in my office after the evening meal, once again it's time to say Goodnight everyone."

We all chorused back "Goodnight Headmaster".

The following evening we discussed the previous night's events. The Head told us Lisa and Eric insisted they had not noticed any other pupils raking the ashes, they also insisted no one had asked or told them to rake the ashes, they just happened to be passing and noticed the rakes lying on the ground and couldn't resist using them. Eric claimed he had told Harry the Gardener the Headmaster had given them instructions to do it because he thought they were going to be chased by him. We all knew it was lies of course and that someone who hated Crinkles had control over them.

All we could do was to watch these two very closely and keep an eye out for any clue that may tell us who the other two may be. I then brought up Harry mentioning the two Chamber Maids carrying books early in the morning.

The Head thought this highly unlikely as the Chamber Maids had worked and lived here at Crinkles for years and years. However Millthrop pointed out that the two present Chamber Maids had only been here a little over two weeks apparently Gladys who has been with us over 30 years was on leave visiting her sister who is poorly. Maud who has been with us over 25 years was away on Holiday visiting her Brother in Sydney, Australia, who she hasn't seen for over 15 years.

Two replacements had been hired from an agency to give temporary cover and they were living here at Crinkles until the end of the month when Gladys and Maud should be back. The two temporary Chamber Maids were obviously part of the enemies team, but the Head felt they would be such minor members that they would not have any information that would be of value to us, he also felt that as they were both about to leave and old reliable trusty hands return no further action should be taken.

So as the Headmaster said, "Who'd have thought that Harry the gardener the last choice for our team would be the top goal scorer?" The Head felt we had uncovered four of the enemy.

He asked me to bring Harry to his study, a few minutes later Harry was standing very embarrassed and looking at the floor as the Head praised him.

We all started to clap which embarrassed him even further, he mumbled a thank you to everyone and asked did we mind if he left and went back to his work. The Head said by all means, but it would be appreciated if he kept a sharp eye out and his ears to the ground and report directly to him if anything strange or unusual happened. Harry reassured the Headmaster that he certainly would.

CHAPTER FOURTEEN

The Broom Cupboard

Two or three days after the mention in the 'Wizards Journal' of Crinkles joining the 'International Mixed 'Team Quadro' Junior League' next season, a team pre-selection list appeared on the Schools general notice board.

It simply requested any person who was interested to put their name and form number on the list.

There was no rush by anyone to put their names down; you see 'Team Quadro' isn't the main game played these days at Wizard Schools.

In popularity it's a bit like cricket compared to football. One week later the list consisted of only three names (which were later crossed out) and the usual applicants: Donald Duck, Roland Rat and I. Pump. Alot etc. added.

The list was taken down and the following day the Head spoke at the morning assembly requesting support from the School.

He explained a little about the history of the game and introduced Ian Scorn as the coach for the new team.

Apparently Ian had been an exceptionally good player just a few years ago. He had been in the European Semi Final twice the Quarter Finals three times and had also been Team Captain on two occasions.

A new list was to be put up that morning and the Head said he knew that there would be more support this time, by the end of the day twelve boys and six girls names had appeared on the new list.

The following morning the Head told us he was still very disappointed at the response, pointing out once again that there had to be an 'A' Team and a 'B' Team, plus 'reserves' for both teams and a reasonable number of pupils required if two good teams are to be fielded.

He also pointed out that there was to be a deadline of 6.00p.m that day, after which no further applicants will be considered. It would be no good wishing you had put your name down later tonight or tomorrow morning as it would be too late.

That seemed to do the trick (excuse the pun). About a dozen new names appeared before lunch having been added by pupils dashing from one classroom to another.

At lunch time there was a queue waiting to sign and by 6.00p.m that night the list had 42 boys and 17 girls' names along with Donald Duck, Roland Rat and friends who had appeared once again.

Crinkles had certainly changed. Gone are those tranquil peaceful days of times past, it's all go (and in all directions) now.

Perhaps I should explain the basic rules of the game of 'Team Quadro' here, but I feel the back of the book is a better location. There you can find:

The full set of rules for playing Team Quadro

A drawing of a Team Quadro Pitch

A drawing of a Team Quadro Post; and

A typical Pole Watcher's Score Sheet

Over the next two weeks one by one many of the applicants were eliminated, some had only put their names down because their friends had, others realised they weren't really cut out for 'Team Quadro'. Some just couldn't remember the rules!

Eventually the 59 names were reduced to 24 and serious training was about to begin.

However there was one major problem. Unfortunately Crinkles doesn't have a 'Team Quadro' pitch, the land having been sold many years ago to raise money for essential repairs to the roof.

Ian had started practise sessions at the back of the School out of the view of any passersby.

The practise sessions consisted of flying back and forth with everyone taking turns on ten old brooms which we had lovingly cleaned and restored. These had been in the general stores for years where they had lain alongside paint tins, stepladders, old desks and other piles of assorted junk 'that various people including myself thought might come in handy someday'.

It soon became apparent that a further two pupils were never going to be Flyers and one of them was Jenny, this was a relief for the Headmaster as he was afraid that Jenny or David may be injured. A further three soon followed because they said it was so boring, and it was!

It was boring out of necessity as none of the pupils had ever flown brooms before. They needed to learn the absolute basics: coordination, balance, patience, distance judgement etc.

An old telegraph pole was adapted, it was painted and pegs inserted in the appropriate places. A hole was dug in the lawn at the back of the School about 5 feet deep and the pole inserted then concrete was poured in and a couple of 2inch by 2inch wood batons nailed in position to keep it square until the concrete had set. Once set we removed the 2x2's then we replaced the topsoil around the bottom of the pole and stamped it firmly down.

Some original quoits were even tracked down, we found a huge box-full in one of the big cupboards under the main staircase along with some old photographs of past teams.

The Head thought it would be a good idea to display the photographs although they were very faded, they had never been that good a quality even when first developed.

I made a display board and fastened it up next to the School notice board, many of the Masters spent quite a bit of time carefully studying them but could not recognise anyone.

So the practising continued: flying up, turning, flying down, turning, swinging right, swinging left, lift up, lift down, steady straight ahead, zig-zag ahead, stop dead, accelerate forward, side flying, etc., etc.

On and on this went, then came practising quoit-snatching from the pole with various manoeuvres, then on to replacing the quoit onto the pole with various manoeuvres.

Eventually from total shambles things started to improve. Then, quite rapidly there was a real improvement similar to when you're learning to drive a car, at first there seems that much to do at once, then it clicks and you find you've mastered the clutch and the gears, you are judging the traffic better and you are on your way.

One or two of the Masters would come out from time to time to see how things were going and once or twice even offered some advice much to Ian's annoyance.

Groups of pupils would sometimes gather for a while but soon got fed up and wondered off.

I'm sure what kept the group of Flyers together at this stage was more the fantastic teas that Ian and Cecilia provided after practise.

At the end of one of the practise sessions Ian told everyone to gather round and said he was sure that they were ready for the next stage.

Now the next stage was really something. Because the front of Crinkles could be seen from the road and having no 'Team Quadro' pitch the Flyers would have to fly around the School at night completely in the dark to avoid being seen by passersby.

I doubt any other Flyers have practised night flying around their School.

Three nights every week everyone had to stay inside the premises whilst the Flyers practised flying faster and faster then closer and closer to the building, swooping up, swooping down, grabbing quoits from the old telegraph pole and putting them back.

We had the best night Flyers in the World, unfortunately 'Team Quadro' is played during the day. It was decided very sensibly that it was too dangerous to practise flying towards each other at night.

This meant we had no experience of flying towards each other because practise during the day would have aroused too much curiosity from people sitting on the top deck of the buses that pass the School.

Eventually Ian felt he could improve the Flyers no further at this stage and it was time for a team selection: 8 'A' Team members and 8 'B' Team members, out of 19 Flyers (14 boys and 5 girls).

That evening the Head came down to see them flying, most of the School from time to time had been watching at night, peering through the windows to catch a glimpse of the Flyers swooping past - just a foot or two from the building. I must admit I enjoyed watching them practise.

When they had finished that night's practise session the Head asked everyone to follow him and he led the way up to his study.

Reaching the study door he told everyone to wait in the corridor and to put their brooms on the floor. The Head went into his study and everyone started asking each other:

"What's up?"

Ian told them to stop chattering and to stand still, as now annoyingly everyone also seemed to have the desire to shuffle about.

The Head had reappeared with a large old ornate brass key and walked past us to a cupboard built into the panelled wall, I was amazed I never knew it was there.

Mind you the cupboard blended perfectly into the panelling and if it hadn't been for the keyhole into which the Head was now inserting the old key you wouldn't think there was a cupboard there.

He turned the key and there was a loud click, by now there was a crowd behind the Head all trying to be the first to see what was inside.

The Head started to open the cupboard but then stopped, and turning towards us gave a big smile and said:

"This is what I call a 'Broom Cupboard'." Then turned back and opened the doors to reveal 8 Brooms.

Each Broom was neatly resting at a slight angle in over behind a polished mahogany ledge at the bottom and resting in two mahogany notched racks, one 2 feet up from the ledge and one 4 feet up, the whole cupboard including the back of the doors was covered in dark green baize.

There were highly polished brass-retaining clips across the Brooms, one on the top rack and one on the bottom rack where they rested in the notches.

The Brooms looked as though they had just been made, they looked too good to use.

It was Ian, who talked first,

"Headmaster, I've never seen Brooms like these before, they're 'MAGNIFICENT'!!"

The pupils just stood staring, for once totally speechless and motionless.

"These are the finest Brooms in the World." Said the Head smiling.

"You mean they're the fastest? Faster than all the super new Brooms?" A pupil excitedly shouted.

"Ah!" said the Head "No they're not as fast as all the new super powered Brooms.

What I should have said is that they are the best 'Team Quadro' Brooms in the World."

Disappointment appeared on all the children's faces, the Head noticed their disappointment but ignored it and went on to explain.

"These Brooms were made by Hercules Swift who was the Master Craftsman of all Broom Makers, and these are the finest

Brooms he ever made. He only made eight of these Brooms four for our 'A' team and four for the 'A' team reserves."

"Have they ever been used? They look brand new." Queried a boy.

"Oh Yes, they have been used." Said the Head, who paused for a while then continued,

"In the past they have won every major 'Team Quadro' Tournament throughout the World."

"Then why did that bloke…?"

"Hercules Swift" The Head interrupted the boy.

"Yes, Hercules Swift, why didn't he make any more?"

"He never made another broom after these because a boy died."

"A boy died." Gasped one of the girls.

"Yes, a boy died flying one of these Brooms." Said the Head patting her on the shoulder.

There was total silence, until a quiet voice from the back asked what everyone else wanted to.

"Which one, which Broom killed the boy?" The Headmaster looked at the children.

"No one knows which of these Brooms the boy was on, whichever one it was it had no intention of harming the boy in any way. In fact, the exact opposite, it was trying to save him from being injured." The Head said very quietly but very distinctly.

We all looked at the Brooms. They stood quietly and majestically lined up in front of us. Everyone was thinking the same thing, which one of them killed the boy? Which one? They all look the same which one could it be? We had of course chosen to ignore the Head's remarks.

The Head, looking at our faces knew what we were thinking and continued. "Before a dozen stories start to circulate throughout the School, I will tell you the true story."

Everyone looked intently at the Head. You could have heard a pin drop.

"The boy was a pupil at Crinkles his name was Albert Huntington. Some of you may have noticed a plaque to his memory in the Main Hall on the left as you go in. Crinkles in those days was a force to be reckoned with in 'Team Quadro', every Stadium we played in was always full to its capacity and beyond.

We had four teams in those days. The A and B teams who obviously had our best Flyers in them and the C and D teams which were our up and coming Flyers.

Albert Huntington was in the C team, he was a capable Flyer but unfortunately he was of the opinion that he was a superb Flyer and should be in the A team.

The C team was playing in the Finals of the Second League. He decided just before the match that all he needed to show everyone that he should be in the A team was to win this game almost single handed and to achieve this all he needed was a better Broom."

"So he simply helped himself to an A team Broom. In those days they were not locked away, however as Brian our Caretaker found out you can't just hand out wands to anyone. It's the same with these Brooms - you can't just pick one up and ride it, the Broom has to accept you."

"The game was into the final Quarter of the fourth Period and it was a draw at that stage, both sides having played very well.

Albert Huntington was our Flyer for the fourth game, he started nice and steady the Broom doing all he asked of it. Then he decided to show everyone that he was the 'Star Flyer'.

He tried to get the Broom to fly as it did for the A team but the Broom wouldn't respond knowing that he didn't have the flying skills.

His frustration built up and he started to hit the Broom. The Broom stopped dead and Albert Huntington flew off, very unfortunately he hit his head full force on one of the pegs in his pole then fell some 12 feet to the ground."

"The game of course was abandoned and Albert Huntington was rushed to hospital but it was already too late.

The following season the heart went out of the teams, C and D teams were disbanded the A and B teams carried on for two more seasons but got nowhere.

With each poor result the morale dropped lower and lower and when the two Masters who coached the teams left us the A and B teams also disbanded and we have not had a 'Team Quadro' team since then."

The Headmaster paused, and then continued enthusiastically, "But that's all in the past,

We Are Back!! and Mr. Scorn tells me you're excellent Flyers. We have the best Brooms and we're going to make an exciting new future for Crinkles and 'Team Quadro' World wide."

The Headmaster had decided to act before any indecision set in and anyone dwelt to long on Albert Huntington. He knew everything must be positive.

"So we're going to select the 'A' team and their reserves tonight, here and now!!" Ian couldn't believe his ears he was totally shocked.

"But Headmaster!! I wanted to run through my notes on the Flyers with you before I made my final decision, I thought by tomorrow afternoon I would be in a position to give you the names." Ian's voice had a touch of panic in it.

"You've done an excellent job selecting the final group of flyers, teaching them the basic and intermediate skills, all excellent. However we have now reached the stage where there is no need to consult your notes Ian." The Head paused, "The Brooms will pick the team!!"

"THE BROOMS!!" Ian shouted in amazement. "LET THEM PICK THE TEAM!!"

The Headmaster didn't reply but flipped over the two latches on the first Broom and lovingly lifted it out.

"Children please form a straight line standing with your backs to the wall."

The Flyers shuffled into line excitedly, wondering what was going to happen next.

"I want each of you to hold this Broom in turn until I tell you to pass it on." The Head handed the first Broom to young Smithfield who held it gingerly. He was obviously relieved to be told to pass it on. It went to the next Flyer.

"Pass it on." Said the Head. Then it went to the next Flyer. "Pass it on." Said the Head and so the Broom was passed on down the line until it came to number 11 - Lorraine Leigh. "Pass it on." Said the Head.

"I can't Sir!!" Said Lorraine "I can't let go of the Broom and it's becoming warmer and warmer in my hands."

"Right Lorraine come and put the Broom back in the cupboard." Lorraine followed the Head past the other Flyers to the Broom Cupboard and gently placed the Broom into the one empty space in the mahogany rack. "That's it, now put the latches over, good! good! Right Lorraine that's your Broom now and it belongs to no-one else." Said the Head.

"But I couldn't let go of it before Sir so how was I able to put it back in the cupboard?"

"Don't worry about that, the Broom has chosen you and it will never let you fall. You are now a 'Swift Flyer', the Best, the Very Best!!"

Ian stood silently watching in amazement as one by one the Brooms were taken down from the cupboard and one by one the Brooms selected their Flyers until there was only one Broom left. It was passed on down the line of those left waiting to see if they would be picked as the last Flyer.

The Broom had reached the end of the line and no one had been selected the Head collected it and started at the first pupil again. For the second time the Broom went down the line and still no one was selected.

"Is there someone missing?" queried the Head. Ian looked down the line of the remaining children and at everyone who had been selected.

"No. Everyone is here Headmaster." Said Ian.

Everyone went deadly quiet, and some of the children were beginning to think as was one or two of the Masters, could this be 'the' Broom?

Daniel's voice chirped out, "David's not here Sir." Ian turned to the Head, "You asked for him to be taken out of the team contenders Headmaster."

"Yes you're correct I did, but we had better get him back I'm afraid."

Ian turned to Daniel, "Go and find David and be quick."

He didn't have to go far because David and almost the whole of the School were hiding around corners and in doorways just further along the passage all trying to hear and see what was going on.

"I'm here!!" Said David, popping up from a group of boys and walking towards the last boy in the line who was still holding the Broom. He took it from him and walked towards the Head,

"Give it to me David." said the Head, stretching out his hands.

"I can't Sir! Sorry."

"Put it in with the rest David." David walked to the cupboard and gently put it in the one remaining empty place then swung over the brass retaining latches into the locked position. He still had one hand gently on the Broom. 'My Broom' he thought and softly said: "My Swift Flyer."

David stepped away and the Head who had been patiently waiting moved forward, closing the cupboard doors he inserted the key turned it until the lock clicked, removing the key he placed it in his pocket.

He turned to Ian and said, "Well there you are Ian - 8 Flyers. I leave it up to you as to who goes in the 'A' team as match Flyers and who are reserves. I've no doubt I'll hear from you tomorrow, shall we say tomorrow afternoon, goodnight everyone!" He smiled, and then turning strode down the hall and into his study closing the door behind him.

"Right come on! It's long past everyone's bed time and I think we've had enough excitement for one night!" said Ian, who had started to usher the pupils along the corridor.

The five boys and three girls who had been picked by the Brooms to be Swift Flyers were still hanging around near the Broom Cupboard reluctant to leave.

Ian looked at them. "That means you lot too! The first practise on your new Brooms will be at 7.00p.m tomorrow! Come on, away you go!"

A couple of minutes later the corridor was silent and empty. The Head opened his study door and looked down the hall at the Broom Cupboard, paused for a while, thinking of years gone by then switched off the hall lights and closed his study door behind him.

As I walked back to my room I wondered if anyone else had noticed that the last Broom given out number 5, wasn't the last Broom in the cupboard. The Head went from 1 to 4, then missed out 5 and went to 6, 7 and 8. Strange I thought, very strange.

CHAPTER FIFTEEN

Match Practice

The following morning the School was a buzz with tales of what had happened the previous night at the Broom Cupboard.

Everyone added his or her own little bit extra, here, there, and everywhere, until the truth was barely recognisable.

It's interesting to note that the number of pupils who are full time borders had nearly doubled in the last few months. This was because no one wanted to go home – just in case they missed anything!

The Speed Flyers had slept very little and felt more than a little uneasy all day about the pending training session that night. The whole School could hardly wait for 7.00p.m.

When practise time did come it was a bit of an anticlimax initially. The teams went up to the Head's study with Ian where the Head was waiting for them, he already had the Broom Cupboard key in his hand.

He smiled, nodded and unlocked the cupboard. The players took out their respective Brooms then the Head relocked the cupboard and returned to his study.

The teams followed Ian down to the Main Hall and out onto the grounds, this was to be the standard procedure in future.

Every window around the entire School seemed to have a face peering out though most disappeared after half an hour as absolutely nothing appeared to be happening.

Ian was talking and talking to the assembled Flyers with the odd pointing here and there, it was 8.00p.m before he finally told everyone to mount their Brooms.

At first the Flyers had been terrified to even carry the Brooms never mind attempt to fly them.

Now perhaps that endless boring talking had been Ian's secret plan or maybe it was accidental. But by the time he said "Mount up!" everyone's fear had been forgotten by boredom and they didn't give it a second thought.

They stood at the left side of their Brooms holding the Brooms with their left hand at 45 degrees, swung their right leg over the Broom shank and holding on with their left hand they rested their right hand on top of their right knee then quietly said. "Hover".

All the Brooms levelled to a horizontal position with the Flyers feet still on the ground, and then they rose slowly and gracefully to a height of about 5 feet.

"Right." said Ian. "Now relax totally and put both your hands on your knees." He paused while they sat there for a few seconds.

"Now take your left leg and swing it over your Broom. Shuffle your bottom if you wish until you're comfortable. Don't worry! You won't fall off!" He waited until everyone had followed his instructions.

"Now tell your Brooms to 'free fly' and you can tell them to stop whenever you want to."

A few more faces had appeared at the windows as word got around that something was about to happen.

A chorus of Flyers voices said,

"Free Fly."

The Brooms climbed higher and smoothly flew off in whatever direction the Broom felt like going in.

A couple of the Flyers felt a little uneasy as they rose higher, and higher, deciding to take their hands off their knees and grip the Broom tightly on either side, they all preferred facing forward, not sideways.

"Don't grip the Brooms!" shouted up Ian. "Put your hands back on your knees!"

David, who had been one of the Flyers gripping his Broom tightly, reluctantly let go.

"Now!" shouted Ian "Think your Brooms to 'Swoop'. Don't talk to your Broom. Think your Broom to 'Swoop' and think your Broom to 'Lift' when you want it to."

There was a reluctance to carry out this command, when you feel you are about to fall off at any second when flying in a straight line you aren't too keen to 'Swoop' and 'Lift'.

Ian shouted up again. "Keep your hands where they are! Don't grip those Brooms! Think your Brooms to 'Swoop'"! Go on! Do it! Do it now!"

One by one they had a try and were relieved that they did not slide about, tip forward or backwards or fall off. In fact this was fun, 'Great Fun'.

"Excellent" said Ian, "Now think your brooms to 'Lift', that's good, very good."

After about ten minutes Ian decided there had been enough 'Swooping' and 'Lifting' so he called up to them. "Level off now! But keep your hands on your knees!"

He waited until everyone was levelled off.

"Now, say to your Brooms: NWOD EDISPU EM YLF."

The children followed his instructions and the Brooms all rolled through 180 degrees. It had happened before the children had time to think about it and here they were flying upside down and holding on to nothing. All the spectators peering out of the School windows wondered how they didn't fall off the Brooms they couldn't believe it possible, it was as though they were glued on.

"Now tell your Brooms to 'Speed Fly', 'Level 5'. Do it now!" Ian shouted

"Speed Fly, Level 5." said David. The Broom leapt forward. David could see nothing, everything was a blur and he was starting to feel sick! 'Oh no!' thought David, I'm going to be sick and now Ian is shouting more instructions.

"Speed Level 7, Command level 7!" shouted Ian to the Flyers through cupped hands

"Speed level 7." David commanded his Broom in a half-hearted voice.

He felt the Broom accelerating. 'If only I hadn't eaten so much dinner', thought David.

"Command - Circle Building! Command - Minimum Ground Level!" Ian's voice boomed out, "Go on, DO IT! And DO IT NOW!!"

Everyone in the School was now looking out of the windows and agreeing it was a fantastic show. They had never seen the like of it before and although no one knew it at the time they would never see the like of it again.

"Command - Maximum Speed Level 10!" shouted Ian.

"Speed level 10." David whispered to his Broom. The Broom 'SURGED' forward, David felt as though he couldn't breath.

Flying upside down in the dark at Maximum Speed Level 10, whilst circling a solid building at minimum ground clearance with your hands resting on the top of your knees, looks absolutely incredible.

The watching pupils could hardly believe their eyes, and were constantly gasping and pointing out various flyers as they flashed past.

However it actually means very little to the Flyer, who can only see a constant blur through barely open watery eyes and feel the Broom swing sharply every few seconds as they turn a corner of the building and the sudden sharp rises and equally quick falls as the Broom adjusts to clear obstacles and maintain minimum height.

Obstacles such as a plant pot only 6 inches high, David swears he felt the long grass parting his hair.

It was with great relief that the Flyers heard Ian call out. "Reduce speed gradually to Speed 2, gain height and level off at 15 foot ground clearance." Then finally to hear those lovely, lovely words, "Fly upright."

The Flyers gave the commands to the Brooms and they all slowed and rose to a 15 foot flying height. Then, as it was completely safe to do so rolled back through 180 degrees.

David felt relief, but could not stop himself commanding his Broom to roll him through 360 degrees. Round and round David went. The others started to laugh!

"Give me 90 degree turns with stops." David commanded his Broom. His Broom stopped rotating then rolled 90 degrees to the right stopping dead, then a further 90 degrees stopping dead, then a further 90 degrees and stopping dead and so on as he flew around the building. Then at the 90-degree point, David commanded "Keep it there, and fly me around the building at Constant Speed 4."

The Broom followed his commands and David flew round and round the building sideways, which looked even funnier than upside down.

"David! Cut out that goofing about!" shouted up Ian, as David flew past.

Ian had been going to stop David as soon as he saw what he was up to, but had decided to let him carry on for a while and end the practice session on a light note.

"Time for everyone to land!" called out Ian, and one by one the Brooms and Flyers came in.

The Brooms hovered a couple of feet off the ground until the Flyers stepped off then each moved into a vertical position and waited for their Flyer to collect them.

Now I know this sounds silly, but I tell you I'm sure those Brooms were laughing at the Flyers, who now back on firm ground found their legs didn't seem to want to support them or go in the direction they wanted them to.

They staggered around as though drunk, they felt dizzy and light headed, first one then another decided to sit on the grass or fell over onto the grass.

All the Flyers were now either sitting or lying on the grass moaning that they felt ill, felt sick, and felt weird. But Ian just stood there smiling.

The whole School had poured out, and surrounding the Flyers they were enthusiastically shouting and cheering.

"What a show!" "It was great!" "When are you doing it again?" A chorus of voices praised their heroes who still lying on the grass didn't feel like heroes.

The Brooms had stayed vertical but had moved discretely away from the surge of people and now stood in a group under an old Oak tree waiting to be collected by their respective Flyers.

One by one the Flyers had started to recover getting back up onto their feet, each one to the cheers of their fellow pupils. The Masters had started to try and usher everyone back into the School.

"Come on Flyers, Time to collect your Brooms and put them away." Called out Ian, striding towards the Oak tree where he had spotted the Brooms grouped together.

Although the Brooms would look identical to you or me, somehow the Flyers seemed to recognise which was theirs. The Brooms certainly recognised their Flyers.

Ian gathered everyone around him,

"Now Flyers, I want you to listen to me very, very carefully! You are never, Never again to repeat tonight's flying. You now know how unique your Brooms are, they are totally reliable, tonight's flying was to give you complete confidence in your Brooms. In future anyone showing off or playing the fool will be thrown off the team."

"Your Brooms will look after you and will never let you fall. But that does not mean you can abuse your Brooms abilities, it does mean that you look after your Brooms and I mean look after them! Does everyone understand?" He looked around noting the Flyers heads nodding that they did understand.

The Flyers carefully wiped down their Brooms with a damp cloth and dried them having first carefully inspected the brooms for any damage. Ian had stood watching and was satisfied that everyone had given their Brooms the correct attention.

"Right then, let's go!" said Ian.

The Flyers put their Brooms over their shoulders and marched behind Ian to the Broom Cupboard carefully putting them back and swinging the latches into position.

The Head had appeared outside his study and once again locked them all safely away.

"Mr. Scorn, a moment of your time please." called out the Head.

"That will be all Flyers, you can go now." said Ian. Then he turned and followed the Headmaster into his study.

"Sit down Ian." The Head pointed to an easy chair.

"Ian!" The Head looked at him sternly. "This morning when I explained to you what the Brooms were capable of I never imagined you would provide a full scale demonstration. You took some very serious risks tonight, and before you try and give me excuses I'm as much to blame as you."

The Head paused and tapping the top of his desk, continued:

"But never again Ian! I understand why you did it, to give the Flyers total confidence in the Brooms, that's why I didn't stop you, but on reflection that flying was too dangerous in anyone's books and once was once too many. We were very fortunate to get away with it without even a scratch to any of the Flyers. Hopefully when it gets back to some of the relatives and parents they will assume youthful exaggeration and over-active imaginations are at play. Let us hope so. "

Ian felt he should say something, but couldn't think of anything appropriate and his mouth was so dry that he doubted that he would have been able to speak. So he just sat silent.

After a while the Head added: "I won't keep you any longer no doubt you have things to do." The Head moved across the room and opened his study door. Ian got up, said goodnight to the Head and left breathing a sigh of relief.

The 1999 'Team Quadro' International Junior League had experienced the worst year ever in its recorded history for injuries, so much so that the final game of the season had still not been played by the end of February 2000.

The four finalists were teams from Germany, France, The USA and Greece.

Greece could not field a team for the final due to injuries. The USA wanted the final to be decided 'on the most points to date' - meaning they would win by ten points! The others of course, refused to accept this.

France wanted it decided by 'the team that had won the most individual quarters', which meant France would win. Naturally, Germany and The USA would not agree to this.

In Germany's case it had been considered the favourite to win, as it had been improving dramatically with every game.

The T.Q.I.J.L. organisers then decided that the solution was to form a replacement team for Greece, from other teams Worldwide. However, whatever team was put forward it never suited all three opposing teams.

With a new season about to start in May 2000 the T.Q.I.J.L. had given an ultimatum to the three teams.

The game was to be played by the end of March 2000 or be abandoned, with no winner being declared for the 1999 season and hence no cup or medals awarded. This had never happened before in the History of 'Team Quadro'.

It was then that the T.Q.I.J.L. came up with the idea that if Crinkles agreed they could provide the fourth team, subject to their inspectors being satisfied that the Crinkles players were skilled enough to avoid unacceptable risks to themselves and other players by taking part in the final. That could be a workable solution for all concerned.

The T.Q.I.J.L. had approached the other three teams to see if they had any objections to this proposal. As none of the three teams could see any serious competition coming from Crinkles they saw no reason not to accept. Crinkles would simply be there to make the numbers up.

Crinkles was contacted by the T.Q.I.J.L. asking them if they would be willing to put forward a team to replace Greece in the Finals.

Ian was all for it, but the Head felt that perhaps Ian's judgement was clouded by the fame taking part would give him as coach, whereas Ian had talked a great deal about the good publicity it would bring the School.

The Head was worried about the children's safety he didn't want anyone injured. After all they had never played an actual game of 'Team Quadro'! In fact the team had never actually been on a 'Team Quadro' field. It was even possible that none of the team had ever seen anyone else play 'Team Quadro'.

Another thing that bothered the Head was that the game was to be played in a neutral ground - in Milan, Italy. It was true the Q.I.J.L. had promised to cover all costs, but still – Milan! In Italy!

The Head and Ian had just finished their fifth meeting discussing the pros and cons. Ian was adamant that should they go David had to be on the team as Ian knew he was their best male Flyer, whereas the Head certainly didn't want David on the team he wanted him in reserves.

He was afraid David might be injured and he was relying on him and Jenny for the 'Oriliance', but of course he couldn't tell Ian this.

The Head pointed out to Ian that if they did go it was not to try and win but simply taking part as an act of goodwill. They were there only to enable the final to be played and as such did not require star players.

It was 11.00p.m. Ian had just left the Head sitting in his large winged backed chair, he was resting his head on his left hand whilst leaning on his desk and tapping it with his right hand.

The Head sat there for some time trying to decide what he should do. A reply had to be made by tomorrow at noon, otherwise the decision was made for them and the Championship would be cancelled.

They had received numerous phone calls from the American, German and French teams. All asked the same question.

Had they made their mind up yet? Each mentioned how they would have a great time, no worries, and just great fun.

In fact the American's had rang five times that day the last time late in the afternoon.

"Gee man, you're leaving it late deciding! If some guy had offered me this sort of action I'd be grabbing his hand and off like a shot." On and on this man prattled. He had asked what the problem was then didn't listen to a single word the Head had said in reply! The Head felt totally exhausted when he finally rang off.

'If they can exhaust you like that on the phone what can they do to you on the 'Team Quadro' pitch?' thought the Head.

This was normally the Heads favourite time of the day. Quiet, peaceful and serene, a half hour or so of freedom from pressure or so it should be. As he sat at his desk he absentmindedly opened the drawer containing the Broom Cupboard key.

He sat tapping his desk with his right hand and thoughtfully looking at the key in the drawer.

Picking up the key he stood up and made his way to the study door, as he opened it a shaft of light escaped from his study and dimly lit the long corridor.

The Head walked to the Broom Cupboard and unlocked it, he opened the doors and stood looking at the Brooms. The half light, half shade, seemed to intensify their shape and size.

"Hercules Swift's Brooms." he said quietly as he gently touched each of them. "How I wish one of you would let me fly, I envy those boys and girls the greatest freedom of all!" He paused, "I have never flown not even when I was at School, College and University, now I fear I'm probably too old."

The Head and Ian both knew, that if it wasn't for these Brooms, Swift's Brooms, they would not be having any discussions at all as to whether Crinkles should or should not go to the finals. The answer would be a definitive 'NO'.

Out loud the Head talked again to the Brooms.

"Do you remember the glory days? The sun, the rain, the wind, the enormous crowds, the cheers and the clapping the days when we were the best, unbeatable." said the Head

"Do you remember O'Connor? What a flyer! I wonder which of you was O'Connor's Broom?" The Head caught just the slightest movement from one of the Brooms.

"Ah, Number five! So it was you! You're the fastest, you're David's Broom!" The Head rubbed his chin.

"Do you know we have the chance of some fame again? We've been asked to play against America, Germany and France in Italy at the Milan Stadium in the 'Team Quadro International Junior Championships'. Do you remember Milan? What a stadium!"

"What should I do? Should I say yes? If only you could tell me! It's your skill and match experience that will be needed. The children haven't even practised on an actual 'Team Quadro' pitch never mind play a game on one against other teams! These teams are not just 'other teams'. They're the 'Best in the World'."

"Our old pitch and its beautiful grounds are long gone now; houses and shops have been built on them, that is why you had to fly the children round and round the School building."

"I have to make my decision tonight, what should I say? Should I say 'Yes', we will take part? " The Head paused and stood looking at the Brooms.

The polished brass retaining latches on the first Broom started to sparkle then the second and then the third until all the latches sparkled like diamonds.

The Headmaster turned his head away from the Brooms to see what additional light was causing the latches to sparkle, there was none, when he looked back the sparkle was gone. Had it been a trick of the light coming from his open study door or had the Brooms been trying to tell him something?

The Head nodded to the Brooms as he closed the doors and locked them. Returning to his study he closed the door behind him and placed the Broom Cupboard key in its drawer in his desk closed it then retired for the night.

The following morning the Head was waiting to have a word with Ian. He told him he had decided to go ahead and except the T.Q.I.J.L. invitation and it would probably be best if Ian made the announcement to the School that morning at assembly.

Ian made the announcement and the pupils cheered and clapped for more than three minutes. The Head informed the T.Q.I.J.L. by telephone that morning and said he would confirm it in writing that he did later that day.

Once again Crinkles was to field a 'Team Quadro Team'. History had gone full circle.

Following the positive response from the School an inspector arrived from the T.Q.I.J.L. within a couple of days to assess the Flyers' skills.

Fortunately the weather that day was atrocious with strong winds and very heavy rain so it would have been impossible to play 'Team Quadro' outside, and as the Inspector didn't ask to see the pitch he never found out that we didn't even have one!

Ian suggested that the Flyers demonstrate their skills in the Gym.

As chance would have it Ian had known the Inspector for many years, and had often played against him in the past.

The Inspector had arrived at just after 10.00a.m. By the time Ian had introduced him to the Head and finally got started in the Gym it was 10.30a.m. The demonstration of individual and team flying skills went very well. As did the answers to his questions on the rules, and at about 11.45a.m Ian suggested 'perhaps a pint' and 'a bite to eat' at the local pub and 'why not slip away now to beat the lunchtime rush'.

The Inspector thought this was a good idea. 'As everything seems okay here why not get away early!' So off they went. Once inside the pub Ian kept him talking about the old days, about this game that game and how he had always admired his skills and enthusiasm.

Soon it was a case of: "My goodness is that the time! I'm afraid I must dash Ian, I'm sorry there's no time for me to call back and say my 'goodbyes' to the Head, please pass on my regards. I'll be reporting back that the flyers are very competent and there are no problems here, it's been great seeing you Ian we must get together again soon."

"We certainly will," grinned Ian. They shook hands enthusiastically and he escorted the Inspector to his car. "Have a good journey back." Said Ian, waving as the Inspector drove off.

Ian stood outside the pub until the car disappeared from sight. He breathed a sigh of relief and went back into the pub and ordered another pint. 'I need this' He said to himself thankful that it had gone so well. Another five or ten minutes thought Ian and I wouldn't have been able to think of another single thing to say. I can't believe he didn't ask any questions not even asking how many games we have played and where!'

Well that's one hurdle over thought Ian as he finished drinking his pint. He was considering having another, but decided he better get back to Crinkles and tell the Headmaster the good news.

CHAPTER SIXTEEN

Outside Help Needed

The 'Team Quadro International Junior League' acknowledged the Head's acceptance to take part in the 1999 final between America, France and Germany in Milan. They informed him that travel, hotel and other arrangements would be made on behalf of Crinkles.

There would be some incidental expenses which would have to be born by Crinkles but all the main costs would be covered and paid for by the T.Q.I.J.L.

The Head called in Ian and gave him the letter to read. They then discussed the new problem the letter had raised, namely the paragraph that said:

"As is normal practise these costs would be paid 60 days after receipt of Crinkles' invoices. Therefore an action fund is advisable and previous experiences suggest that a minimum of £8,000 should be allowed for.

"It just seems to be one problem after another Headmaster, have we any money available?"

"We have £4,700 in the kitty at the moment all thanks to Miss. Millthrop's Garden Fete and her evening Magic lessons. She has really put the rest of us to shame, but I'm afraid I can't think of any way to raise the extra money."

"I can't think of any way either Headmaster, we can't have another Garden Fete so soon after the last one, how long have we got to raise the money".

"We really need to have the funds in place within a month."

I found this out shall we say by chance, and for some reason that I'm still not sure about I decided to tell David and Jenny.

Perhaps I felt they would be able to find a solution if anyone could.

Later Jenny and David sat thinking about what I had told them.

"How does Brian find all these things out?" David asked Jenny.

"I don't know, but I do know its best not to ask."

They both fell silent racking their brains but a solution eluded them. It wasn't until the following day that David told Jenny he knew what they should do.

"There is only one person that I can think of who will have that sort of money and who may help us."

"Who's that David?"

"Big Heck!" Said David triumphantly.

"Heck who?" Asked Jenny puzzled.

"You know, Big Heck's Quality Used Car Sales."

Jenny looked at David in amazement, "Why on earth should he help us?"

"He went to Crinkles Academy. He's one of the old boys."

"Yes but that was years and years ago, I doubt he has ever bothered coming back since."

"But we're always in his mind's eye. Every time he looks across the road from his showroom he sees the School."

"That's true David, but does he look across at the School with affection? From what I've heard when he was a pupil here he was always in trouble, always late and had the worst record of attendance in the whole School. Then a few years ago he had a big barney with one of the Masters who wanted his money back after buying an old banger from him, so I don't think he'll be very sympathetic to our cause."

"Well have you any other suggestions?" asked David, starting to get annoyed that Jenny was turning his brilliant idea down, his only idea really.

"No I haven't any ideas, not even one as daft as that."

"It's not daft, anyway, daft or not it's the only we've got." David paused, " Let's give it a try, we have nothing to lose he can only say no!"

Jenny didn't look convinced.

"Come on Jenny! It's not as though there's lots of time the money has to be found from somewhere - really quick!"

"Okay! We'll give it a try. But when?" asked Jenny.

"After school today."

"Today! Why not tomorrow?" Suggested Jenny hopefully.

"Because the sooner we do it the better, it will be just as scary tomorrow."

The lunch break was over now and they made their way back to their lessons.

Neither concentrated much that afternoon on school work, running this and that possible eventuality through their heads.

When they met up after school the questions they asked each other were...

What are we going to say? How much should we ask for?

They finally decided to simply ask outright for a loan. If a minimum of £8,000 was required and £4,700 was available then the shortfall was £3,300.

It was almost a certainty that more money would be needed and they wouldn't be able to go back a second time, so in for a penny in for a pound, £5,000 seemed a good round figure to ask for.

As they walked away from the School they felt more and more uneasy. Once they had crossed the road and approached Heck's showroom they felt they were in his territory.

Their legs had turned to jelly and they had a funny sinking feeling in their stomachs.

"I don't think this is a good idea David, let's turn back." Pleaded Jenny.

"No we're nearly there just keep going."

Posters were everywhere in black or white letters on gaudy florescent backgrounds.

'More for LESS!'

'Big Heck Guarantees Satisfaction!'

Dave prodded Jenny,

"What?"

"Look at that one." said David. Someone had added 'Di' in front of 'satisfaction' in pencil.

On the cars standing outside the showroom signs proclaimed, 'More CAR For Your Money.' 'VALUE, VALUE, None Better.' 'BIG HECK Wants to Help YOU Find Your DREAM CAR.'

They were standing now in front of the large glass doors leading into the Car Showroom.

"Don't you think we should come back another day? He looks busy." said Jenny.

"Looks busy!, there's no-one in there except him and he's lounging against a car eating a bar of chocolate."

By now they were in the actual Showroom where there was a large semicircle of cars all beautifully polished. Potted plants were dotted here and there and a few low seats placed around coffee tables which had the usual assortment of car magazines on top.

A pleasant aroma of fresh coffee came from a little machine in the corner with cups, saucers, and spoons in front and little tubs of milk and packets of brown sugar at one side. Above the machine a notice said 'Welcome to Big Heck's, Customers Please Help Yourself.'

"I wouldn't mind a coffee." said David.

"You just dare!" Before David could make any move towards the coffee machine Jenny started pushing him towards Big Heck who had his back to them. "He's not big at all is he?" whispered Jenny.

Indeed he wasn't, and numerous good lunches and endless chocolate bars during the day had succeeded in making him really tubby.

He was wearing a dark grey suit with a pale pink striped shirt and a maroon bow tie, he was clean shaven apart from a pencil thin moustache, his dark hair combed straight back and shining from hair cream, dark grey shoes highly polished matched his suit perfectly.

Heck was leaning against a beautiful looking Red Sports Car with its hood down to show off its black leather interior, chrome trim, mahogany-veneered dashboard and leather-covered steering wheel and gear lever.

The same as all the other cars in the showroom it had the price boldly displayed on the windscreen £3,500. Alongside the price was a card stating, 'Car of The Week.'

Most of the other cars in the showroom had similar announcements such as, 'Best Value.' 'Unbeatable Value.' and 'Best Buy.'

David was looking at the gleaming Red Sports Car with its polished chrome bumpers, side flashes, wing mirrors and hub caps.

"What a smasher." David had spoken louder than he had intended and Heck turned round, David and Jenny froze to the spot as two dark beady eyes looked them over.

A sarcastic grin spread over his face as he looked at David.

"Have you been saving in your piggy bank eh? Wanting to impress your girlfriend?"

Both David and Jenny could feel themselves going bright red. Heck loved this,

"That's clever!" He said. "You've both turned the same colour as the sports car. Why not take a look at the green car over there you might change colour to match that - green with envy."

And he started to roar with laughter at his own joke.

"Let's go." said Jenny trembling. "Please David let's go."

"No, we're here now, let's see it through." replied David.

Heck had stopped laughing but still had the sarcastic grin on his face.

"So what do you two brats want?"

"We've come to ask you for help." Said David, quite force-fully much to his surprise.

"Help for what? No, don't tell me, you want Money!"

"Yes! How did you know?" Gasped Jenny.

"How did I know, because it's always for money!" Said Heck scowling

"You mean you've been asked before?" Queried David.

"Asked before! Of course I have! You don't think you're the first do you? Kids are in here all the time. It's always Money! Money! Money!"

"Money for the Scouts, Money for the Guides! Always after money for something or other and the answers always the same! NO! And guess what, it's 'NO!!' To you lot, so clear out now!" said Heck with a large sarcastic grin on his face.

He turned to greet a young couple that had just come into the showroom.

"Come on David." said Jenny in a despairing voice, "Let's go, at least we tried."

"Hang on a minute Jenny! That couple are interested in the Sports Car."

"So what?" Said Jenny.

"Let's just stay a couple of minutes I'm just curious to see if they buy it."

Reluctantly Jenny followed David. They hid behind a dark blue family saloon car out of sight but in earshot of Heck.

Heck walked across to the young couple giving them a big friendly smile,

"Good afternoon Madam. Good afternoon Sir. Can I be of any assistance?"

"We are just looking at the Sports Car." The young man replied.

"Isn't she a beauty!! One of the best cars I've ever had in my showroom. In fact she's my personal favourite."

Big Heck had produced from his pocket a large yellow duster and proceeded to gently flick off some non-existent dust from the highly polished bonnet of the car.

The young lady smiled and gripped the young man's hand tighter.

Heck hadn't missed this. He missed nothing when it came to selling cars.

"You know." He said softly, looking around as if afraid of being overheard. "This is a lover's car." The young lady blushed, "It's a car for a young couple to take onto the open road, the wind in their hair, the sun on their faces and their whole life stretching ahead to the far horizon."

"Sit inside, see how comfortable it is." He urged in a friendly pleasant voice opening the passenger door for the young lady. She followed his instructions and slipped into the car.

"There you are, now that's perfect isn't it?" The young lady was now beaming with happiness.

Heck nearly ran around the car to the driver's side. He opened the door and smiling ushered the young man in,

"Your car awaits you Sir." The young man returning Heck's smile sat behind the steering wheel, he was admiring the polished dashboard and scrutinizing the instruments.

"How many previous owners?" he asked.

"Only a few very careful owners who treated her as a lady should be treated."

The young Lady started to blush again.

"He's jolly good isn't he?" David whispered to Jenny.

But Jenny was looking at a mechanic who had appeared from a door that obviously led to the workshop, he was trying all ways to attract Heck's attention.

"It has a very high mileage?" The young man said in a slightly worried voice.

"For other cars, yes, But for this car, this model, the engine has barely been run in, good for a lot more miles around the Mediterranean yet, Paris, Marseille, Nice, Venice, Pisa and Rome." Heck was looking out of the showroom window visualising driving across Europe or so he hoped it would appear to the young couple.

It worked. At first they had looked at him taking in every word but thinking what's he on about! Now they looked straight ahead, they were driving along the Cote d'Azur with a turquoise blue sea before them and tiny beautiful white villas with red pan tiled roofs all clinging to the hill sides, wild flowers in a blaze of colours cascading above and below the villas and farmhouses, the road twisted and turned past field after field of lush green Olive bushes.

The mechanic seeing the couple daydreaming in the car seized this opportunity to nip across and grab Heck's arm. He pulled him to one side uncomfortably close to where Jenny and David were hiding.

"Boss you can't sell that car! The engine's a bag of hammers, the big ends gone. It's totally shot! You need to fit a reconditioned engine! The hoses are split, the fan belts snapped and the water pump's useless!"

"No more! Don't tell me anymore! You're supposed to be the mechanic not me, what do I pay you for? You'd better buck your ideas up or you're for the push."

"Don't make me laugh!" replied the mechanic. "Who would you get to do this work for you? Doing these old wrecks up for what you pay me! Anyway I've been trying to tell you about this car for days."

Heck was half keeping an eye on his two young customers, he noticed they were starting to get restless.

"I'll sort you out later." He said to the mechanic. Then he strode out back across the showroom beaming and smiling at the young couple."

"Sort me out!...He couldn't sort out his old Granny." Mumbled the mechanic to himself as he made his way back to the workshop.

"Now." Said Heck. "Why not have a think about the car and pop back in a couple of days?"

"We don't need to come back, we've made up our mind we want this car now...TODAY!" replied the young man.

"TODAY!!" repeated Heck with a touch of panic in his voice.

"Yes today!" replied the young man.

"If you can just start her up I'll check the engines okay."

"Ah, we seem to have mislaid the ignition key." Flustered Heck.

"It's here in the ignition." Said the young man.

"But that's not the actual key!" Bluffed Heck. "We were just trying it hoping it might fit. You do realise its £3,500? And there's no discount on this model."

Panic was gripping Big Heck, his brain was in turmoil, somehow or other he had to persuade this young couple to buy a different car.

"That very smart Silver Grey Coupe over there is only £3,200 and I can give you £500 off for cash. It would be cash wouldn't it? "

"Oh yes, it would be cash! But this is the car we want!"

"Why not just let me show you that Blue Saloon over there, it's a real beauty." Said Heck in desperation.

"We don't want to see any other cars. This is the car we want!!" Said the young man."

"NO!! Don't touch that key!" Shouted Heck panicking.

Too late! The young man turned the ignition key and a strange noise came from the engine.

Heck looked desperate. He could see £3,500 cash going down the drain.

He watched helplessly as the young man tried again. 'VROOM'...vroom, vroom, vroom. The engine burst into life and just purred.

"Listen to that engine!! Isn't it beautiful?" The young man said in sheer delight.

"Yes!! Beautiful, Beautiful! It's the best engine I've ever heard." Gasped Heck with relief showing all over his face.

"I had better just take a look under the bonnet, now where is the bonnet lock?" The young man was feeling about under the dashboard.

"Ah, that's it I think!" Click. "Yes that's it!"

'Oh no!!' Thought Heck. Under the bonnet will be disaster; there goes the £3,500 again!

"Come and look at this Darling!!" Called out the young man.

Heck's face dropped. 'Here we go', he thought.

"Oh." said the young Lady. "Isn't it lovely, so clean and shiny!"

Heck looked over the lady's shoulder at the engine and gasped in amazement. It was immaculate!! Factory new condition!!!

'When I get my hands on that brainless mechanic I'll kill him for what he's put me through', thought Heck.

Shortly after, the couple left arm in arm smiling happily on their way to arrange the car insurance and to their bank for the cash.

Meanwhile Heck was equally happy knowing he would soon be clutching a wad of £20 notes. He was never happier then when he had a wad of notes in his hand.

"Mr. Heck!" David and Jenny had come out of hiding and were standing behind him.

He swung round surprised to see them still in the show-room.

"Why are you two still here? I told you to clear off!! Are you deaf? Now hop it, go on hop it!"

David and Jenny just stood and looked at him.

He suddenly thought, 'Well I've had a good afternoon … I'll give them something.' He rummaged around in his pocket.

"Here!" He said, and gave Jenny a £1 coin.

"That's only one pound." said Jenny.

"Well how much do you want for the Guides or 'whatever'?"

"£5,000." said Jenny.

"£5,000!!" GASPED Heck.

"Yes £5, 000, it's not for the Guides or Brownies it's for Crinkles!"

"For Crinkles!! Why should I want to give anyone £5,000? Least of all Crinkles!!"

"We need a loan just for a few months about three we think." Answered Jenny.

"Then go to a Bank, or did you not know that they're the people who lend money. What's that old fool of a Head thinking about - sending you children out asking for money?"

"The Head doesn't know we're here." said David.

"He doesn't eh, well he soon will!"

"No! No! Don't tell him!" pleaded Jenny.

"I can't wait to tell him!" laughed Heck.

"Look!" Said David, "We aren't asking for the money for nothing."

"Oh! You would be paying me interest would you?"

"No, not quite." Mumbled David.

"No! I didn't think so."

"We sold that car for you!" added Jenny.

"WHAT CAR?"

"The Red Sports Car." said David

"Don't be stupid!" Heck couldn't believe his ears.

"Well how do you think the engine started and ran so smoothly? And how was the engine compartment so perfect?"

"Just pass that over me again!" laughed Heck. "I thought you said 'YOU' made that engine run!"

"We did!" David and Jenny chorused.

"You did!! By Magic I suppose?"

Jenny looked annoyed, "Yes! By Magic!"

"That's it you two! I'll give you five seconds to clear out or there will be real trouble and give me that £1 back! Come on! Out! Out of my showroom!" growled Heck.

Vroom! Vroom!, VROOM!, VROOM!! A dozen car engines burst into life! Heck's jaw dropped. He turned and stared at the semi-circle of cars all with their engines running! It was true! They 'HAD' started the Red Sports car's engine!

"Okay! Okay! Stop those engines! I believe you! Come with me into the office." David and Jenny followed Heck into his office and he closed the door behind them.

The mechanic had rushed into the showroom, he stood looking at the cars rubbing his chin with his right hand and scratching his head with his left.

'Am I going nuts?' he thought. 'I'm sure I heard engines running?' He turned and walked across to the Red Sports Car that still had its bonnet open and looked inside.

'I'm losing my marbles! I must be going crackers! This can't be the engine I looked at this morning? It's, it's brand new!'

He put the bonnet down and walked back to the workshop muttering to himself.

"Right you two! Firstly I want to know why you need £5,000."

"Not us," said David, "the School needs the money."

"Well the School then."

So David and Jenny told him the whole story, as far as 'Team Quadro' was concerned.

"It was never like that when I was at Crinkles! I hated it! I was always in trouble for something or other.

My ambition if I win millions on the lottery is to buy Crinkles, demolish it and build a really huge 'Second Hand Car Salesroom'. The 'Biggest in the County' if not the Country and chop down all those trees and turn the front lawn into a giant car park!"

"You're only joking aren't you?" asked Jenny looking shocked.

"Only joking, Well perhaps I am." replied Heck. "Anyway where am I going to get £5,000 - just like that?"

"You've already got £3,500." replied David.

"Well yes. But I've got expenses and things, what will you do for me if I did manage to raise the £5,000?"

"We will help you sell ten of your cars." Jenny told him.

"Twenty cars." Replied Heck. "And we have a deal."

"No. Ten." Jenny insisted.

"Then no money."

David tried to sound assertive, "Twelve cars."

"Fifteen." Heck snarled at them, "No less than fifteen."

David looked at Jenny. She nodded.

"Fifteen cars then." said David.

"It's a deal!" cried Heck. "But remember I also want my £5,000 back. It's only a loan! Let's shake on it."

They shook hands, Jenny and David felt like real business people.

It was then that they realised there was still a problem. How could they give the School the £5,000? At first they thought Heck could give the money to the School as a gift. But then they would have to pay him back, how could they, they had no money. If it was given to the School as a loan the School would have to pay him back and the School had no money. It hadn't been a good deal they weren't real business people after all. They left Big Heck's Autos deflated.

In the end very reluctantly David and Jenny had to agree to help Heck sell a further fifteen cars in return for the School keeping the money.

All the following day David and Jenny expected the Head to call them to his office and ask what they had been up to, having detected the Magic they had used, but nothing happened. That night they sat talking in the games room,

"I can't understand." said David. "How did the Head know you practised Magic on your holidays and that we had helped the singers at the School Concert yet he hasn't picked up on yesterday!"

"I think," said Jenny. "It was because we were the only ones doing Magic then. Now everyone is doing Magic at the School, there's usually some Magic going on most of the time - and ours must just get muddled in along with the rest."

"Hmmm." said David. "You could be right."

"Are you two going to play table tennis or not?" It was their friend James.

"Yes." David and Jenny replied. "We're coming now."

Two days later the Headmaster was very surprised to say the least when he opened one of the envelopes in his mail and found a typed letter inside from Jonathan Heckinwicker, stating that he had great pleasure in enclosing a cheque for £5,000 in appreciation for the help and education he had received at Crinkles Academy some years ago, which he felt sure had given him the ability and confidence to go into business and become as successful as he is today.

He hoped they would accept the enclosed cheque and he was certain they could find some good use for the money. He would like to take this opportunity of offering a 10% discount off the marked price of any car in his extensive, fully inclusive range, to any member of the School staff who may be considering buying a car.

The Head informed Ian that the 'shortage of money problem' was unexpectedly solved and that they could press on with all the arrangements immediately.

The Headmaster's Secretary sent a grateful thank you / acknowledgement letter to Big Heck, signed by him, Miss. Millthrop the Assistant Head and Ian as the 'Team Qaudro' Coach.

The letter told him it would be the new 'Team Qaudro' team that would benefit from his amazing generosity. It concluded by giving him an open invitation to join them at Crinkles for afternoon tea whenever he choose.

Big Heck had a grin on his face like a 'Cheshire Cat' when he read the letter from Crinkles. He immediately had it framed and hung on the office wall above the water cooler. He was very pleased with the open invitation to join everyone for tea whenever he wished, although it was unlikely he would be taking up that offer as the very name Miss. Millthrop gave him nightmares.

David and Jenny honoured their agreement and a steady stream of very satisfied customers left 'Big Heck's Super Autos' with beautifully running cars. But of course Heck soon returned to his old ways, he didn't want to lose 'the goose that laid the golden eggs'.

David was surprised to be told that there was a telephone call for him and even more surprised to find it was Heck, telling him, not asking him, to call with 'that girl' to see him immediately after school that afternoon.

As soon as his last lesson was finished he raced to catch Jenny and told her of the phone call and Heck demanding to see them.

"What can it be about?" asked Jenny.

"I think I know, but let's wait and see what he has to say."

There was a group of people in the Showroom when they arrived so they hung about until everyone had left. When they went in Heck was waiting for them.

"I saw you two lounging about out there! Come with me I have something to discuss."

Once again they followed him into his office.

"I'll get straight to the point." He said. "No sense in hanging about, I want you to sort out more cars for me."

"That's what I thought you were going to say." replied David.

Heck was smiling. He was going to be a very, very, rich man. Why hadn't he thought of it before? If they can put engines right they can also put car bodies right. He would be able to buy really grotty cars for next to nothing and have them transformed into little beauties.

He would also be able to save more money by sacking that idiot mechanic who wouldn't be needed. He could see the money rolling in, all of the other dealers would be furious they wouldn't be able to match his prices or quality.

"No." said Jenny. "We're not going to 'sort' as you put it any more cars for you."

"You had better or I will contact the Head and tell him what you did to get the money."

"BLACKMAIL!!" David yelled.

"You can call it blackmail, I call it good business."

"No! We won't do it!" said Jenny defiantly.

"I think you will, I'll give you a couple of days to think it over. Now off you go! Go on, hop it! The business conference is over."

David and Jenny left his office and made their way back to the School. David looked and felt gloomy yet Jenny was smiling.

"What are we going to do Jenny? We're right in it now."

"No problem." said Jenny. "I'll handle it."

"But how?" Questioned David.

"Don't worry about it, I'll handle it." She refused to say anymore.

The next morning Heck drove into work feeling on top of the World. The World was a great place, well for him anyway.

'Who would have thought a few weeks ago that I'd be making so much money! You never know what's around the corner.'

He settled into the big leather chair behind his desk and glanced at a newspaper. Then suddenly his office door flew open.

"Hey!" Heck looked up it was his mechanic:

"There's the biggest load of junk I've ever seen in my life just been delivered out there, two car transporters full! You've had me fixing rubbish for years,... but that lot! What am I supposed to do with them? Other than put them through the crusher at the scrapyard."

"Nothing." replied Heck.

"Nothing!" said the now confused mechanic.

"Yes nothing, because you won't be here."

"What are you talking about?"

"You're finished, that's what! There's your money and card's."

"That's it, sacked just like that! After all these years! You're a proper little @#@#!!!"

The mechanic opened up the packet, "What's this? There's only one week's pay here! Where's my redundancy money?"

"What redundancy?"

"I've been here for years and years."

"Yes but not continuously, you'll find you have everything there that you're entitled to."

The mechanic stormed out of the office slamming the door behind him.

Tut, tut, said Heck to himself smiling smugly.

The phone rang and he eagerly picked it up.

"Hello! Big Heck's Motors." He said cheerfully. "How can we be of service?"

"Service!" said a very angry voice on the other end of the telephone. "I'll give you service when I bring back the heap of scrap you sold my son three weeks ago!! You better have the £4,000 he paid you ready for me to collect when I come around this afternoon!" The phone was slammed down.

Heck gulped. He hadn't quite taken it all in when the phone rang again.

"Hello, Big Heck's Autos." He said, in a less enthusiastic voice.

The woman on the other end of the telephone broke into tears!

"My husband's coming to see you about the state of the car we bought from your garage. It's dropping to bits!"

Heck was trying to understand what was happening when his office door was flung open and in came a walking mountain, six foot six and as broad as he was tall.

"Right! You pile of cow dung! You'd better sort out this car I bought from you last week or I'll ring your neck!!" His huge fists came thumping down onto Heck's desk. "Next time it will be your head! Come out and take a look at it!"

"I'll be out in a minute Sir I'm sure we can sort out any problems, just a minute or two until I'm finished on the phone." The man grunted and left the office.

Heck was still holding the telephone from the last call.

"Sorry Madam I have to go!" He put the phone down and could feel himself breaking out into a cold sweat, what on earth am I going to do? What's going wrong? He wondered.

Jenny was having Maths when the School Secretary put her head around the door. "Sorry to interrupt the class Miss. Nichols there's an urgent phone call for Jenny."

"Away you go Jenny, but straight back." said Miss. Nichols.

"Yes Miss!" Jenny leaving her seat walked out of the class smiling to herself, she knew who it would be and deliberately took her time walking to the Reception and picking up the phone.

"Hello, Jenny here!"

"Jenny! Jenny! Its Big Heck! I think there's been a terrible misunderstanding, it was all a joke the other day. Just a joke! If you sort things out for me we'll say no more?"

Jenny remained silent. Big Heck nearly jumped out of his skin! The big guy was thumping the outer window of his office and indicating 'Come out now!' Heck put his hand up and tried to smile at the man. 'Just a minute', he mouthed. The man scowled in response.

"Jenny!! Jenny!! Are you there? Can you hear me?"

"Yes." she replied. "I can hear you."

"Can you sort it out?" gasped Heck in desperation.

"Can I sort it out? What?"

"Can you sort it out 'PLEASE'?"

"What was that? I didn't catch it."

"PLEASE!! PLEASE!! Sort it out."

"I'll think about it." Replied Jenny.

The big guy had reappeared and was making his way around to the office door hitting the metal panels of the office wall with his fist as he went leaving large dents in each one.

"PLEASE Jenny!!! Do it now, there's no time to think! It's almost life or death!!"

"I take it that we won't be hearing from you again." said Jenny.

"Never again I promise!! But do something 'NOW'!! PLEASE!! PLEASE!!"

He could say no more as he was lifted bodily out of his chair.

"You've kept me waiting too long!" growled the man.

"Now let's go and see this so-called car."

"Yes! Yes! Certainly! We'll go and see it now." said Heck, who was experiencing the worst day in his whole life.

"You bet we will!" Said the huge man, as he frog marched Heck out of his office across the showroom and out onto the garage forecourt. The big guy now had his hand on Heck's shoulder to make sure there was no 'quick escape'.

"NOW!!" He said. "Feast your eyes on this load of rubbish just around the corner here." They turned the corner and the big guy's mouth dropped open, there stood a car in absolutely immaculate condition. He stood there speechless! His hand dropped away from Heck's shoulder and Heck quietly slipped away back to his office.

Back in his office he spent the rest of the morning and most of the afternoon sitting at his desk afraid every time the phone rang it would be more trouble.

He was relieved that all the calls for the rest of the day had come from customers interested in buying a car, or suppliers wanting to be paid accounts which as usual! Were long over-due

Late that afternoon he decided it was time to bite the bullet, time to phone his ex-mechanic. He picked up the phone and dialled his number.

"Hello Bill, its Heck here! When you come in tomorrow forget the cars that came in today I'll sort them out, just work on the two in the workshop."

"What are you on about? I'm fired. Or have you forgot?"

"Oh take no notice of all that silly business! It was just one of those things, I'll see you when I get in tomorrow."

"Not on the wages you've been paying me you won't."

"Okay! I'll give you a rise an extra £1 an hour!"

Heck couldn't face all the hassle of trying to find another good mechanic. He remembered all the mechanics who had walked out after only a couple of days just because he shouted at them the odd time! Actually he shouted at them all the time.

"Make it three and you're on."

"£3 an hour EXTRA! I'm not made of money!"

"Make it £2.50 then."

"Okay, okay, an extra £2.50 an hour."

Heck put the phone down. Normally he would have made every effort to reduce his mechanics wage increase to as little as possible but not today as he was totally drained. 'What a day!' he thought. You never know what's around the corner.

Later that day Jenny caught up with David.

"It's all sorted David you can relax, we won't be hearing from Big Heck anymore."

"What happened then Jenny? I've been dying to see you and find out."

"I'll tell you first chance I get I've got to dash now!"

"But Jenny...."

"Later David, tell you later!" And she dashed off.

David stood there stunned. That's a typical girl he thought! Here I am desperate to know what she's been up to and she can't spare a minute to tell me. It would be different if it was the other way round.

"Hi David" It was one of his friends. "Going to have a kick about with us?"

"Yeah I may as well." He said, as his friend threw the football to him.

David missed catching it and then saw his friends making a quick getaway, he had an uneasy feeling and turned slowly, there stood Miss. Millthrop holding the football.

"Ball games in the Hall!!" She thundered. "50 lines, - I must not play any ball games on School premises only outside at the rear of the School." She stared at him. "I want it on my desk tomorrow by 9.00 a.m. sharp!"

"But Miss..." David's voice tailed off when he saw the look on Millthrop's face. 'I'd better shut up' he thought 'or it will be 150 lines'.

"Right Miss, Sorry Miss, on your desk 9a.m sharp." he turned and as he walked away he thought this is all Jenny's fault!

CHAPTER SEVENTEEN

The 'Team Quadro Final' (Part One)

Brian begins the story:

The excitement was mounting throughout the School as the day of the match grew closer. Unfortunately it was too far to travel for most of the pupils and Masters.

One hundred tickets had been sent to the School but only 10 people were going. Tickets were like gold dust, the Final in the past was always a complete sell out but in recent years the Stadium was usually only half full.

This time all the three main contenders had big followings and non - stop publicity over the last two months had helped to make it a sell out.

The black market for tickets was working overtime, a ticket could fetch up to 30 times the face value if the seat was in a good location and at least 10 times the face value for a poorer location.

The Head had noticed that all the tickets he had been sent were poor locations, this didn't stop dozens of phone calls every day from all over the World wanting to know did we have any spare tickets? Any location would do just name your price.

The Headmaster had double checked that no one else was in a position to attend the match, this resulted in two more tickets being taken up.

The Head told us at the morning assembly that he had donated the remaining 88 tickets to the Wizards In Need Charity and added:

"Sad as it is, that so many of us are unable to go to the 'Team Quadro' Final it's a comfort to know that a reasonably large sum of money will be raised on our unused tickets to help a very worthwhile Charity."

What was really going to hurt was that the game was to be broadcast live on T.V. on the Wizards channel W.C.W.W.

But we don't have a T.V. at Crinkles, so we were elated at our team going to Milan on the one hand and despondent about not being able to go and support them or even see it on T.V. on the other.

The Head informed T.Q.I.J.L. how he had disposed of 88 of our tickets to the W.I.N.C. and the reasons why as per the rules.

When they commented that at least we would be able to see it on T.V. the Head had to tell them not so as we didn't have a television set.

You can imagine our excitement and joy when we were informed by the T.Q.I.J.L. that a T.V. set tuned to channel W.C.W.W. was to be delivered on loan in time for the match.

Soon we had worked out where the T.V. was to go in the Main Hall, organised the seating and the catering. We planned piles of food and drinks this was to be a really great day.

It was the evening before the team left for Milan the School lay quiet and peaceful.

Finally the last pupil had stopped their excited chatter and fallen asleep.

The Head had been working in his study and was finishing a hot drink before he went to bed.

He paused, put down the drink and taking out the Broom Cupboard key left his office and opened up the Cupboard, the light escaping from his study once more made the Brooms look larger than normal.

"Tomorrow Brooms you will be on your way to Milan, I ask only one thing of you, bring your Flyers back safe and sound," he spoke quietly as he patted each Broom in turn then took one last look at the Brooms before locking the Cupboard.

Four days before the match the names of our team's players and the order in which they would fly was posted up on the School Notice Board it read:

Lorraine, Liam, Adam and David the 'A Team Flyers' and the reserves were Debbie, Lauren, Christopher and Daniel.

They were to be accompanied by Ian Scorn the Coach and Cecilia Hudson as the Assistant Coach to take care of the girls.

The Swift Brooms were placed in their carrying cases which apparently had also been made by 'Hercules Swift' and stored at the School directly below the 'Broom Cupboard' which again because of the wood panelled walls was virtually hidden. I certainly never knew it was there.

Each Broom had its own beautifully polished mahogany case and could not be fitted into any other.

At 8.00a.m on the dot the mini bus arrived and suit cases, holdalls and Broom Cases all safely loaded on board. The Flyers and Masters said final farewells and boarded the mini bus and set off for the Local Airport.

The whole School, pupils and staff gathered outside to see them off and cheered and waved like mad.

We watched the mini bus go down the drive and through the School Gates, it waited for a gap in the traffic then turning right it was soon out of sight.

Suddenly the atmosphere changed, it all seemed so different, no longer electrified, in fact we felt and looked a bit glum.

It didn't help mind you that the T.V. as yet had not arrived and it was now Wednesday and the match was on Saturday. By Friday panic was setting in as we still had no T.V.

The team had been in touch with us on their arrival at Heathrow, from the Hotel where they were staying overnight and again on their safe arrival in Milan on Thursday afternoon.

Everything had gone smoothly and everyone was feeling well but of course nervous.

On Friday morning the team was going to visit the Stadium and meet the other teams.

Whilst back here the Head had decided he had better check up on the televisions none arrival, it actually arrived as he was on the telephone and I dashed up to tell him.

Shortly afterwards the Head came down to the hall and we positioned it as previously planned.

I got my longest extension cable and there we were, the new Television Set in position, the extension plugged in, the power on and 'No Aerial'!

No one had thought about an aerial, we scanned the Local Phone Directory for T.V. aerial erectors, yes a few could come today (We didn't want to chance it as late as Saturday) but the cheapest was going to be £58.

There was only £15 in the School Petty Cash Box along with eleven I.O.U.s totalling £140.

We had no option but to ask for a whip round, we finally raised £65 that gave us a bit extra just in case. Most of it seemed to be 10s, 5s, 2s and 1s, it looked like a small fortune piled up on the old Reception Desk.

It only illustrated what a hard up bunch the Masters were, they could hardly muster £15 of the total, mind you I only had 70p and the Head had nothing at all.

It was only after all this running about that young Mc.Intosh told us his dad did aerials and had a little place on the trading estate just down the road.

It took a lot of will power for us to keep our hands off him. We contacted his dad who called after tea and fitted an aerial, it cost us £47 leaving us £18. In our panic to raise the money we hadn't recorded who had given us what, so we had no idea how much should be returned to each contributor (apart from the Head and myself that is) in the end we decided to spend it on extra crisps, biscuits, chocolate bars and so on for 'Saturday's Match Feast'.

David now takes up the story:

After the long journey and all the excitement of being in Italy for the first time the team was exhausted when we arrived at our Hotel in Milan, having had a light meal earlier we decided to unpack our cases, check our Brooms and then went straight to bed.

Friday morning we all got up early for breakfast then it was across the city to have a look at the Stadium. We all found it very daunting the Stadium was so huge, a guide took us on a full tour then we had lunch in the restaurant with a panoramic view overlooking the playing pitch.

After lunch it was time to start meeting the other teams. Our team found them all reasonably friendly, but they all seemed far larger than us especially the Americans who looked about 17 or 18 years old.

The players from the other teams talked constantly about this great win or that great win, fortunately they all preferred to talk about their own achievements and hence no-one asked any embarrassing questions about our team, although we were always on edge in case anyone did.

The Americans insisted on always calling our team Wrinkles and the girls usually added 'how cute'. After about a dozen attempts to explain that it was Crinkles our team gave up trying.

That afternoon each team was allowed 45 minutes practise and familiarization on the actual pitch, fortunately we were going on last this meant the other teams probably wouldn't bother hanging back to see how we played.

The Germans were playing first then the French followed by the Americans. After the Americans finished there were still some German and French players hanging about but once the Americans started to leave the field they also started to drift away.

The usual 15 minutes between one team leaving and another starting was usually long enough for most people to get bored and leave unless of course they had some specific player who they wanted to keep an eye on possibly to check their current form.

In our case no one had ever heard of any of our players never mind their current form.

Just to play safe we gave it another five minutes before we came out onto the pitch because we didn't want the embarrassment of people seeing how amateurish we may be.

The Stadium apart from a few grounds men appeared totally deserted so we went out onto the pitch to start our practice session. We had 40 minutes left to practise picking up quoits and placing quoits whilst Flyers were coming towards you. It was very, very scary, we had never had Flyers coming towards us before because that would have been too dangerous in the dark.

What a strange feeling it was to be flying in what seemed like a huge bowl, the 40 minutes soon passed and we would have liked more time.

As it happens there was no-one around and we probably could have just gone on flying but Ian thought there may have been an official that we couldn't see hanging around somewhere timing us, and it wouldn't do to cause any controversy over having more practise time than the rest. So we stopped, had a shower and got changed, then checked and carefully packed our Brooms and returned to the Hotel for our evening meal.

Shortly after we had finished our meal we all went on a very interesting though rather short sightseeing bus tour, there wasn't even time for us to get off the bus and walk around even one of the city squares or visit any place of interest.

Ian stayed behind, he said he wanted to keep an eye on our Brooms and would not have enjoyed the tour knowing that they had been left unattended.

Everyone was in bed by 10.30 p.m. not that any of us slept, we shared rooms, the three girls were in one room, three boys in another and two of us had a large room to ourselves Ian and Cecilia both had their own rooms.

We spent most of the night whispering to each other, we finally fell asleep only to be woken up what seemed like 10 minutes later, all of us felt like just turning over and going back into a lovely deep, deep sleep.

But it was time to get up, shower, have breakfast, gather in a small conference room and have a pep talk from Ian.

After Ian's pep talk which also included some discussions on tactics we went down to the Hotel Gym and did some light exercises then it was back up to our rooms, pack our playing gear, check our Brooms, freshen up again and down to the Hotel Lobby to wait for our lift to the Stadium. The mini bus picked us up at 11.30a.m prompt, the match was to start at 2p.m but all the teams had to be at the Stadium for 12 noon.

Brian and others continue the story:

Meanwhile back here at Crinkles we had all been watching the build up for the Match, the Hall had a brilliant atmosphere the trestle tables groaned under the weight of all the food and drinks.

Everyone was here, even the old fogey Masters seemed as excited as us.

At the moment on T.V. two sports broadcasters discussed the merits of the opposing teams.

Hugh Branigan was talking to Tom O'Hanlon:

"Well Tom, this is the match I was beginning to think we'd never see."

"Too right Hugh, but here we are and in a couple of hours we shall see just who the Champions are, will it be the Germans the favourites? Or the French who I feel might surprise everyone, they have a very powerful team I think we haven't seen the best of them yet."

"So your money is on the French?" said Hugh.

"Well" Tom grinned, "I have it on good authority that if you're a betting man which of course I'm not that the Americans are the ones to back, then of course we have the also ran Crinkles, you've got to hand it to them it's a great sporting gesture."

"Yes." Agreed Hugh "But let's hope they don't end up with egg on their faces, a trouncing could take a long time to live down, people may soon forget their sporting gesture but remember their embarrassing total defeat."

"Hang on Hugh, who says total defeat."

"Let's be practical here Tom, look what they're up against, I can't remember the last time we had three teams out of four so closely matched."

"Okay Hugh, point taken I'll give you that, but my researchers tell me Crinkles have a glorious past, true it is way, way in the past, but perhaps we will be surprised."

"Yes surprised if they don't bomb out Tom, well its 30 minutes until the start of play and time to have a word or two with Julia to get the Ladies view point."

"Thank you Hugh, hello Tom, well viewers this is a really exciting day, no one has mentioned something that is of great interest to us ladies, namely that Crinkles are fielding three lady players out of 8, this is statistically the most female players any 'Team Quadro' Team has ever fielded and not all of them are in reserve. In fact the player for the first quarter from Crinkles is a girl called Lorraine Leigh, the Germans have one lady player the French and Americans both two but they are all in the reserves. I hope that these ladies taking part will act as encouragement for more of you girls to come forward to play 'Team Quadro'."

"Tom and Hugh have mentioned the brilliant electrified atmosphere here in the magnificent Milan Stadium, which is second to none, but no matter how impressive the stadium if it is only half full the event feels like a damp squib," Julia continued, "Damp squib this is not, It's 'Fireworks Day'!! the Stadium is full to its 60,000 capacity with an estimated 5,000 people outside just desperate to get a taste of the atmosphere. Now then Tom, Hugh, why do you think there's so much interest in the match? Bearing in mind that in the past few years a 40,000 plus crowd was thought to be very good."

"Well." replied Tom "The Germans and Americans always have a good following and the French supporters are of course fanatical."

Julia smiled, "Yes true, but it was estimated 45,000 to 50,000 max. So where have all the extra fans come from?

I know there has been an exceptional amount of publicity because of the delays controversy, which no doubt transformed into more interest and more supporters."

"Whatever the reason." interrupted Hugh "This can do nothing but good for 'Team Quadro' which has been left in the shade in recent years."

"My thoughts." said Julia "Are that the extra interest and support is due mainly to Crinkles taking part."

Tom gave one of his trademark knowing winks. "Well that's an interesting thought, but it's almost time for the game to start so unfortunately we can't go further into why Julia thinks that, but I know she will join Hugh and I in wishing the best of luck to all the teams taking part in this '1999 Team Quadro Junior Final'."

"With a special best of luck to Crinkles." added Julia smiling.

"Yes just so." said Tom with Hugh nodding in agreement "Now it's time to hand you over to Steve Dunnett for our in match commentary, Julia, Hugh and myself will of course be making our match comments during the five minute intervals, but now it's time to say, sit back, enjoy the match, and over to Steve."

"Good afternoon Ladies and Gentlemen, Boys and Girls, we have only five minutes to the start of the 1999 Final of the 'International Junior Team Quadro Championships' and what a season it has been. Some surprises early on but nothing compared to the surprises waiting for us at the end of the season, NOW! What surprises are in store for us today? We will soon know, there's just enough time to show you the team lists for all four teams and their coaches."

Up on the screen came the names of the Schools, the names of the their players and coaches with the games played in the tournament so far and their total score to date along with their best score in any game so far, and individual players best game score.

Back here at Crinkles we had cheered every time Crinkles name was mentioned and the game had not started yet so already we were hoarse.

Every time the boys and girls cheered the Head would stand up, face us, and say:

"Now, now, we don't want them to hear us in Milan."

Whilst flapping each hand up and down, in an attempt to quieten us, of course every one of the pupils (and myself) cheered all the louder.

The Head would just smile and sit back down he knew when he was defeated.

Our name was coming up now on the T.V. screen

CRINKLES ACADEMY - ENGLAND

Then up came the team players names, with Ian as coach and Cecilia put down as his assistant.

Games played: NIL
Points to date: NIL
Highest game score: NIL
Individual players' best score: N/A.

A hush fell over the Hall you could have heard a pin drop, we all suddenly realised how absurd it all was. Should we have submitted our fellow pupils to the forth coming indignity, what chance did they have to make even a reasonable score?

Back to David:

We arrived at the Stadium just before 12 noon, first we all went to the Ground Floor Reception and each one of us received a badge and a special pass. Then we went to a Welcoming Reception on the second floor, we milled around in a large conference room being introduced to various players, coaches and an endless army of officials.

Photographers and journalists arrived and photographs were taken of various individuals and groups.

I lost count in the end how many times my photograph was taken.

The large beautiful Silver Trophy which would be held for one year by the Winning Team was on a stand, surrounding it was the Gold Winner's Medals, Silver runners up medals and Bronze medals for the team coming third. All of which would be presented at the game's closing ceremony.

Then more photographs and journalists all asking the same questions to which I usually just nodded or shook my head and tried to smile all the time. Someone pointed out that time was getting on and the teams were led away to the changing rooms.

It was now 1.30p.m and we all decided that we desperately needed to go to the toilet at the same time, no sooner did we get back then we had to go again.

We had opened our Broom Cases and checked our Brooms, then very carefully, gently dusted them not that they needed it, it just felt right to be doing it.

Cecilia brought in a large carry all and took out our Flying Cloaks, I was a bit disappointed in fact I think we all were.

The Cloaks were black with a yellowy gold coloured sash that fastened at the front and went over our shoulders getting wider until it was about 8 inches wide at the back of the Cloaks. Embroidered on the front was our School name CRINKLES in gold they looked so old fashioned compared with the others.

During our practise the day before when we had just worn our own Flying Cloaks, the Americans had blue cloaks with white stars on them and a red sash, the Germans burgundy with a gold sash, the French white with a red sash edged in blue.

I don't know about the others in our team but I hadn't even thought about our Flying Cloaks until I saw the competitor's cloaks yesterday, apparently they all have two or three competition cloaks each.

Ian gathered us around and told us:

"Go out and play fair, play by the rules."

Then he said to us what every Mam and Dad tells their children in a situation like this and really there is no better advice that can be given:

"Do your best, no-one can ask for more,"

Ian looked around the room, it must have shown on our faces how nervous we all were. He smiled and said:

"I don't know about you but I've got butterflies in my stomach and my legs have turned to jelly." We all gave a half hearted laugh. To be honest at that moment I would have given anything to be back at good Old Crinkles as a spectator.

Ian looked at his watch. "Almost time to go." Looking around at everyone he said "Just think of the tea we will have when we get back home."

A few of us smiled, I thought to myself that's all everyone seems to think about at Crinkles having tea.

"Oh! One last thing, some of you may have been disappointed when you saw your Flying Cloaks. Well I would just like to say that these are the Cloaks that our Star Flyers wore when playing in the games that gave us our 'Glorious Victories' in the past. They have been worn and hence flown in every 'Major Quadro Stadium' in the World, they have seen more Victories than any other Cloaks. They are as unique as our Brooms. Miss. Millthrop has lovingly looked after them, that's why although very old they are still in as new condition."

That came as a big surprise, it was a great confidence builder to think our cloaks had been worn by some of the greatest ever 'Team Quadro' Flyers at Famous Stadiums all over the World.

The other teams had brand new Flying Cloaks, but only our team had historic ones and fancy our Cloaks being looked after lovingly by that old goat, it only goes to show how surprising people can be.

I was visualising crusty old Millthrop ironing and carefully folding our Flying Cloaks when there was a loud rap on the changing room door.

"All competitors out on the field please."

We all trooped out with our Brooms, Ian was in the front with Cecilia at the back it was then that I noticed how smart they both appeared in their matching blazers. We came out of the dressing room into the tunnel, the French team was ahead of us and the Germans behind.

The tunnel was well lit and had a white ceiling and walls with a light grey floor.

But when you came out into the brilliant sunlight and saw the 'Huge Stadium' in front and all around you, it seemed as if the tunnel had been pitch black.

The American team was already on the pitch all smartly lined up along with their officials.

It was then that I realised they had more officials than team members, but then so had the Germans and the French, where had they all come from and what did they all find to do?

We lined up beside the Americans with the French on our left and the Germans on their left. For diplomacy reasons no doubt we were in alphabetical order, A. E. F and G.

The crowd had applauded each team as they came out and the noise was unbelievable.

I may be wrong but I think unlikely as it sounds we got the most applause.

Over the loud speaker system the crowd was welcomed to the finals and each team introduced in turn and once again there were huge roars from the crowd and applause.

There it was again, when the announcer said,

"From England, the team from Crinkles Academy." the roar from the crowd was incredible.

CHAPTER EIGHTEEN

The 'Team Quadro Final' (Part Two)

David, Brian and others continue the story:

The announcer's voice boomed out over the public address system.

"The 1999 International Junior 'Team Qaudro' Championships Final is about to start, would the first team members please take up their positions on the pitch and the others make their way to the team seats."

There was no more preparation to do, no more practicing, this was it, reality time was here. Our first Flyer Lorraine Leigh would be under way in just a couple of minutes.

It would be 1 hour and 33 minutes plus any injury time before I went on and I didn't feel I could last out that long, the pressure of waiting would be so intense. I wish I was on first or even second, but last.

We sat in our allocated seats, Ian was at one end then seven Flyers, an empty seat which was Lorraine Leigh's and Cecilia at the other end, but Cecilia had now moved up and was sitting in Lorraine's seat.

All the eight Pole Watchers had taken up their positions and the Overlooker was talking to the four Flyers in the centre of the pitch, now they had stopped talking and made their way to their respective start positions.

The Overlooker was now in the air about twice as high as the Pole watchers and in the dead centre of the pitch.

All four Flyers had reached their respective poles. Ours was Red, the German's Blue, Americans Green and the French Yellow.

The Flyers were all on their Brooms hovering about five or six feet from the ground, first one Outer Pole Watchers arm went up then another, then the other two. This indicated the Flyers were in the correct starting position. The Overlookers whistle blew. That's it! They're OFF!! 'The 1999 Junior Team Quadro Final' had finally started.

The crowd had been almost totally silent it was really rather eerie, but now it broke out into a huge roar the moment they heard the whistle blow, a roar louder than anything I had ever heard in my life.

Back at Crinkles with all the excitement we could barely contain ourselves, we couldn't imagine how our team must be feeling, no-one was eating or drinking we just sat mesmerised looking at the T.V. screen.

I realised that unintentionally we were mimicking the crowd in Milan, we didn't realise that Crinkles had the greatest cheer from the crowd because we were so busy cheering ourselves we never heard it.

It wasn't until I heard Hugh Brannigan the T.V. Commentator say,

"Well now that's a surprise already, I think Julia I'm going to have to say you could be right about Crinkles support, they definitely had the loudest roar of any of the teams both on coming out onto the pitch and for the team introductions."

Steve Dunnett was starting the game commentary:

"They're Off!!" Steve Dunnett had a crystal clear voice and could talk faster than anyone I knew.

"This is fast," said Steve, "this is very fast, and first circuits completed, first quoits on, no drops, America, France and Germany neck and neck. Crinkles girl flyer a bit behind. Across into the centre, reverse flying, wow, that was close, Germany and France nearly collided, no love lost there, both have quoits on heading back to outer posts, America now quoits on, Oh!, Crinkles failed."

"This game is so fast it could cause rule book problems if they can keep this pace up, ah, pity Crinkles failed again, Crinkles young Flyer Lorraine must be a bundle of nerves but is it surprising considering the standard of the opposition."

"Germany and France have second quoits on, now America on second, Crinkles dropped couldn't manage a quoit on."

So it went on, cheers from the crowd when their respective teams got a quoit on and oh's and ah's when Crinkle's failed.

"Well we are now five minutes into the game and I have never in all the years I've been commentating on 'Team Quadro' witnessed flying this fast, surely this pace can't be kept up for a full period."

At the bottom of the T.V. screen the score read.

America 20, Crinkles -20, France 30, and Germany 30.

And so it went on until at the half way mark it read:

America 50, Crinkles 10, France 60 and Germany 60.

Steve said he thought he detected a slight slowing in the game but only slight, he did add you have to hand it to the young lady Flyer, Lorraine from Crinkles she has guts, but I'm afraid is totally out classed, indeed a couple of times she appeared to be putting other Flyers as well as herself in danger because of her much slower speed.

"The American." said Steve, "got off to a poor start but has nearly caught up with the others, ah! A quoit on for Crinkles the crowd appear to have appreciated that."

"Here we are almost at the end of 15 minutes playing time and I'm almost relieved to say that the speed of the game has definitely slowed, it was dangerously high, more so when you have an inexperienced Flyer taking part."

"Fifteen minutes gone, five minutes to go, the score:

America 70, Crinkles 30, France 70 and Germany 80."

"America still unable to close that gap." continued Steve "Apart from Crinkles who have dropped two we have not had a single drop by the main teams, here we go!! The last quarter has started."

Sitting here on the bench we felt for Lorraine, her flying was great but the competition was just too good, only another five minutes to hang on in there and it's a job well done.

Steve was telling viewers there was less than four minutes to go, "No surely that can't be correct! Check that please, my colleague has just handed me a note telling me that Lorraine the Crinkles Flyer has just flown the fastest round in this section, it is in fact equal to the starter speeds, well I'm blowed !"

As the minutes ticked by the other Flyers were slowing down and Crinkles Flyer was speeding up, at the end of the fourth quarter, of the first period, viewers saw Steve sit back in his chair shaking his head and saying, "Incredible! Absolutely incredible! My researchers inform me that the Crinkles Lady Flyer Lorraine has flown the fastest ever recorded circuit here at Milan Stadium and in the last three minutes managed to bring her score to 70."

"The final score for the first period being:
America 90, Crinkles 70, France 100 and Germany 100."

The first period Flyers had now left the field to rapturous applause from the crowd.

The cameras had been showing pictures of the crowd and had now gone back to the media box where Hugh was commenting on the match,

"What a game!! And with no added time for injuries, France and Germany neck and neck what a score for a first period."

"Very true." added Tom, "And America no matter how hard they tried could not make up those last 10 points, your comments Julia,"

"Yes a great game so far and the crowds appreciating the skills we are seeing out there, but what about that young lady flyer from Crinkles, look at her speed in the last five minutes and look at her score at 70 points, remember she had to make up 20 lost points according to me that puts her up with the top players."

Back at Crinkles it was pandemonium everyone clapping and cheering, we hadn't done bad, not bad at all, in fact we had been 'Great'.

On the bench we all stood up and applauded Lorraine Leigh when she came off the pitch and so did the crowd, they loved her.

As she passed us we could see tears streaming down her face, Cecilia went with Lorraine down the tunnel to the changing rooms.

Our second Flyer was Liam, he was tall and very studious, a little gangly and didn't look the part of a Flyer, until he was on his Broom that is.

The second period was as furious as the first, at the five minute mark the Germans and French still battling it out neck to neck, the Americans only ten points behind and we plodded steadily on.

In this period it was the fifteen minute section that was the fastest, the Americans had finally after a super human effort managed to catch up and at the end of the twenty minutes and the end of the second period the score was:

America 180, Crinkles 100, France 180 and Germany 180.

Liam had flown very well, and had a good round of applause when he left the field.

Lorraine was now back on the players bench in her track-suit, and was the first to congratulate Liam who was smiling happily until Cecilia gave him a kiss.

Liam was already flushed but now went bright red and I mean bright red, being kissed is bad enough, but in front of a huge crowd is more than any young man can take and he ran off down the tunnel followed by Ian to the changing rooms.

Just twenty-five more minutes and I would be out there, I hope I don't let everyone down, the match had been that excit-ing that the time had flown over which meant the waiting hadn't been too bad.

At Crinkles we had cheered Liam as much as Lorraine and now all of us had sore throats, we weren't going to last the match out at this rate and if our throats got too bad we might not be able to eat all that gorgeous food.

Adam was our next Flyer. He's a lot shorter than Liam and just a little tubby with a round cheerful face.

"Give it to them Adam." I shouted as he passed, he turned and smiled and put his thumb up.

Adam is a very good Flyer but the pressure on him to do well because the two other Flyers achieved so much was tremendous and proved to be too great.

At Crinkles we had all sat hushed waiting for the third period to begin, but poor Adam was struggling almost from the start. We knew he was trying his best but it just wasn't working out for him. Our hearts went out to him but we cleverly disguised this with cries like, "Stupid idiot." "I could do better than that."

"Anyone could do better than that! My Granny could do better than that." And so on.

Adam had missed the pins and dropped two quoits in the first five minutes, strangely though the other three teams had all dropped one quoit.

There had only been six quoits dropped in the first forty minutes playing time and now five quoits had been dropped in only five minutes and so it went on.

As the commentary team said:

"We thought we might be in for some surprises today and we haven't been disappointed, now what do we make of this surprise, for the third period the game completely slowed down. Yet all four players dropping quoits right, left and centre and that of course is reflected in a remarkable score board at the end of that quarter:

America 210, Crinkles 110, France 210 and Germany 210."

"So now three quarter way through the game, that's three Periods giving a total of 60 minutes playing time behind us we go into the final Period of four 5 minute quarters with America, France and Germany all on the same score.

"What a battle between these three giants, at the end of the second Period they were neck and neck and the same again here at the end of the third Period."

"Crinkles have played exceptionally well far better than most of us thought they would, but at 100 points behind have no chance of catching up."

"With the 'Best Three Teams' in the World going into the fourth and final Period of the game with equal scores and only 20 minutes left to play this has to be a breath taking final."

We all applauded Adam as he came off the pitch (he had actually done very well under the circumstances) but he looked totally defeated. He didn't know that the others hadn't done too well either, Ian put his arm around him as they went to the changing room.

Now it was my turn, now that my turn was finally here I'd rather it wasn't. I looked at the reserves they must have been as keyed up as the rest of us and not one had played because surprisingly there had been no injuries, thank goodness.

The rest of the team all smiled and gave me thumbs up as I started to walk across the pitch to my pole.

I stood there and looked at all the quoits in position, I didn't hear a single noise the crowd was making.

All I could think about was what if I failed the team, failed Crinkles.

What would I do if I failed, run away, that's it run away. I was brought back to reality with a start by the voice of my Pole Watcher calling,

"Get in position Flyer."

I patted my Broom. "We're Swift Flyers." I said quietly.

I rose about 6 feet off the ground and held my position, the German Flyer I faced looked so far away, I couldn't stop my legs trembling or my arms from shaking. I wondered how he felt.

Then I heard the whistle blow. We Were 'OFF'!! This was it, no turning back.

In twenty six minutes time it would be all over for good or bad, I would settle for just okay, yes okay would do me.

The German Flyer flashed past in a blur, he's not half travelling I thought but when I over took the American I realised it was me who was flying so fast. The outer circuits completed and with a quoit in my right hand I was now flying to the centre circuit, reverse direction, one full circuit complete and then two full circuits completed quoit pole coming up, steady, steady, got it.

If the first circuits were fast now that David had his first quoit safely on it's peg his confidence grew and his speed was now phenomenal, first outer circuit, second outer circuit in to the centre, reverse direction, first full circuit, second full circuit, a quoit on.

David was already on his way back to the outer circuit when the French boy was the first of the other Flyers to reach the inner circuit.

In the commentary box Steve visibly gasped as he was handed David's first quoit on time. He said to his 'World Wide Audience', "This 'IS' Speed Flying, perhaps that round was a nervous fluke we shall soon see."

"Crinkles Flyer quoit on, quoit on, quoit on." David's Pole Watcher was calling out time and time again and indicating with an arm signal.

"The other players are flying incredibly fast, at any other game their performance could be said to be breathe taking." said Steve. "But the Crinkles Flyer David is so fast he makes the others look very, very slow."

"Germany quoit on." cried his Pole Watcher.

"America quoit on." cried the American Pole Watcher

At the end of the first five minutes the individual Flyer's scores read:

America 40, Crinkles 60, France 40 and Germany 40.

The Americans having had a quoit dropped earlier in the game.

The overall score now standing at:

America 250, Crinkles 170, France 250 and Germany 250.

Back at Crinkles we were jumping for joy this was great stuff, the pupils had started to chant, David! David! David!

The Head and the other Masters telling everyone to Ssshhh!, But it was no use.

Even Matron who was always known for her lack of humour of any kind and stiff unemotional manner was chanting "Come on David, come on." with great enthusiasm.

The other competitors had sensed the danger and instinctively their game had become more aggressive.

The second quarter found the three other players blocking David at every opportunity and the mood of the crowd was changing more oh's and ah's and feet stamping.

Steve commented on how poor that quarter had been and how it was worlds apart from the first quarter. The brilliant flying of Crinkles first quarter now reduced to a shambles by the other teams blocking tactics. He went on to say that nothing had actually been against the rules but it produced a poor round as far as spectator value was concerned, and a disastrous round as far as Crinkles was concerned.

The second quarters score being:

America 30, Crinkles 20, France 30 and Germany 20.

Giving an overall score of:

America 280, Crinkles 190, France 280 and Germany 270.

The third quarter made the second look good as far as Crinkles was concerned, there was nearly three mid air collisions, two between David and the German Flyer and one between David and the French Flyer.

The individual score for that quarter was:

America 40, Crinkles 10, France 30 and Germany 20.

Bringing the overall total score up to:

America 320, Crinkles 200, France 310 and Germany 290.

Steve was reviewing the possible final outcome of the game to his T.V. audience, he pointed out there was only five more minutes of flying time left with no injury time to play, which was a remarkable feat considering the very dangerous quality of the play in the last two quarters.

The Americans who many saw as favourites at the start of the game just in the lead by 10 points ahead of France, starting to fall back now Germany 30 points behind America.

Can Germany pull out all the stops or are we to see the final a battle between two very skilful teams, America and France? Not that we have witnessed very much skill in the last 2 quarters. What had been a wonderful exciting final reduced to brute force with three teams joining forces in what was intended and has proved to be a successful attempt to keep Crinkles out of the game.

Crinkles sadly are now well out of it, having starting the first period with great promise and the first quarter of this final period with exceptional skill they now trail 120 points behind the leader.

Back at Crinkles we all looked very solemn, from total exhilaration to total despair in just twelve minutes.

On the players bench the Crinkles team felt helpless, the reserves full of admiration for David's first quarter had now all decided how well they would have done in the second and third quarters if only they had been given the chance.

The American team bench was jubilant just five minutes until celebration time, five more minutes and the cup was theirs.

"For sure man! For sure!" As one player kept shouting through his cupped hands, then punching the air.

David stood looking up at the top of his outer pole with all twelve quoits in position and only five minutes left to play. The other players had more nerve than he did, they simply flew straight at him and didn't back off so he was the one who had to take avoiding action.

This meant losing the flying line and valuable seconds as well as over shooting his turning point or quoit peg, losing yet more valuable time.

But what should he do? If he didn't back off and they didn't it would be a head on collision with the obvious serious consequences. Already there had been three near misses.

David looked down at his Broom,

"Well my Swift Broom, what have we got to lose? Let's go for it."

The bell rang for the fourth and final quarter,

"Thgieh muminim deeps xam ta thgirpu ot seerged ytenin ylf." said David patting his Broom.

The German Flyer was already half way towards him and David hadn't moved an inch, then, 'WHOOOOSH', David was off like a rocket, both Flyers hurtling towards each other head on.

At the point where David would normally break away, this time, in a fraction of a second he rotated through 90 degrees and dipped to almost touching the ground.

He flashed underneath the German Flyer, three seconds later he passed the American and then the French Flyer as though they were standing still.

Accelerating even faster on the second outer circuit he completed it then shot up to grasp his quoit and back down, across to his pole in the centre circuit swiftly touching it he shot off clockwise completing the first circuit then the second then rising up:

"Quoit on." David's inside Pole Watcher shouted raising his arm.

There was utter silence both from the T.V. commentator and in the Stadium and back at Crinkles we all sat stunned.

Then Steve started to speak, "Did I see that? Or imagine it? In all the hundreds and hundreds of 'Team Quadro' matches I have watched, never have I seen such flying."

"Flying sitting upright at that speed would be incredible but to fly lying sideways at that speed defies belief, and so low, so low to the ground, what can I say!!"

"I don't believe it, in the time it has taken me to tell you about that run, its 'quoit on' again."

The crowd roared into life, a few started to chant, "Crinkles! Crinkles!"

Soon to be taken up by more and more spectators it spread like a tidal wave, it ran down the terraces up the terraces and rolled around the Stadium.

"Crinkles! Crinkles!" then another huge roar when, David's Pole Watcher put his arm up yet again indicating a quoit on for David.

Here at Crinkles we jumped up and down with excitement, "Go for it David! Go for it!" We all cried out.

"A quoit on." shouted Steve from the T.V. presenters box, "I make that four 'quoits on' in one minute fifteen seconds I think that has to be a world record."

"Just over three minutes left to play David is almost a blur, if it wasn't for his black cloak streaming out behind him and the gold sash which seems huge and is gleaming in the sun we wouldn't be able to see him at all" Steve gasped, "That's seven 'quoits on' in two minutes fifteen seconds."

"The tension is unbearable, another 'quoit on' that's eight in two minutes thirty five seconds, what a game!" Said Steve, "There's two minutes twenty five seconds to get four 'quoits on'."

To the left of Steve's shoulder was the large countdown clock showing the remaining time for the last quarter it was two minutes two seconds.

"Quoit on" Shouted Steve, "One minute thirty seven seconds left to play, WOW!!! Another 'quoit on', that's a total of ten. COME ON DAVID!! COME ON!!" Steve shouted, "YOU CAN DO IT!! One minute two seconds 'quoit on', one more 'quoit on' and it's incredible, it's unbelievable but CRINKLES COULD WIN!! They actually could WIN!!!"

"It would be a 'Full Pole' in 'Less Than Five Minutes' and that would make it a DOUBLE SCORE!!!"

The crowd knew it to, roaring David on,

"Go Crinkles! Go Crinkles!! GO CRINKLES!!!"

Every member of the crowd was out there on the circuit flying with David, as were the people all over the World watching it on television, just like us back here at Crinkles Academy.

For a few wonderful seconds we were flying, it was us, not David, but every one of us.

David was completing his last full main circuit, one more quoit, just one more he was thinking, I mustn't miss it, I mustn't miss.

Up, up he soared, grabbed the quoit, plunged back to ground level and streaked around the course on his last full circuit.

His competitors were powerless to stop him, no one dared to fly as low.

The American and German Flyers had been doing exceptionally well but no one not even their own supporters were watching them, all eyes followed that blurred Black and Gold streak which was David on his 'Swift Broom'.

David was now in the centre circuit, one complete circuit, the second complete circuit, then rising swiftly.

A hush fell on the Stadium and in sitting rooms around the World and here at Crinkles Academy everyone held their breath.

David swiftly reached out with the last Quoit but misjudged it and missed the peg, the Quoit

was tumbling towards the ground.

"Oooh" the crowd cried out as though it was one huge voice.

The Broom took over, reacting instantly it dropped at lightning speed moved sideways and caught the Quoit before it reached the ground, rose swiftly back up levelled off just below the top peg and David grabbed the Quoit and threw it, it landed perfectly on the peg

"Quoit on." cried David's Pole Watcher and raised his arm. The whole Stadium was quiet, that quiet it could have been completely deserted not full with 60,000 plus people all looking at the Pole Watcher.

The Pole Watcher now raised both arms and crossed them and shouted,

"POLE FULL." a thunderous roar broke out in the Stadium.

"Double Score!! Double Score!!" The crowd started to chant.

Back at Crinkles, we jumped up, shouting and cheering with excitement and danced with each other, we had done it, we had been there, we had flown that last quarter, it had been us not just David, it had been all of us, we had all won, the Headmaster, Matron, Miss. Millthrop, everyone.

Steve beaming and smiling was announcing on T.V., "We have all been privileged to see History made today, History that I never thought I would see, and History that will become a Legend."

"I have never before seen flying like that, and doubt I will again, Crinkles Academy is the worthy winner of the 1999 'International Junior 'Team Quadro' Championships' and the Flyer mainly responsible is that young man David."

"On behalf of everyone here in the commentary box, the fans in the Stadium and viewers around the World, 'Congratulations'!! David to you, your Team and Coaches. Thank you all for such an incredible event."

"The score for that final quarter is: America 20, Crinkles 240, France 10 and Germany 40."

"Giving a total score for all four quarters in that Period in that round including David's double score for completing a full pole in less than five minutes is:

America 130, Crinkles 330, France 110, and Germany 120.

"This gives a Total Final Score for all Four Periods of:

America 340, Crinkles 440, France 320, and Germany 330.

"David achieved a full pole of 12 quoits in four minutes 21 seconds a 'World Record' and the fastest quoit on in 17.01 seconds which is also 'Another World Record' beating the previous record of 21.98 seconds which has been held by the French Flyer Per'e Lammon for the last twenty years."

"Well Viewers," said Steve, "I'm told, that the Official Announcement is about to be broadcast."

David had flown off the pitch after completing the full pole leaving the others to play on until the game's end.

He landed at his team mate's feet and held his broom tight in his right hand. Ian, Cecilia and his team mates crowded around him as Cecilia attempted to throw a jersey over his shoulders.

They hoisted him shoulder high to the cheers of the crowd sitting behind them. When David left the pitch there remained only thirty-six seconds to the end of the game which meant it was impossible for the others to catch up.

The German Flyer had a 'quoit on' five seconds before the end of the game but apart from the official score keepers no one noticed.

The Stadium was Jubilant, what an Exciting, Fantastic, and Incredible Game it had been.

The loud speakers crackled into life and the Official Stadium Announcement was made.

"Ladies and Gentleman, boys and girls, we have witnessed an incredible day's sport, we have seen History made here to-day which will be remembered and talked about for the rest of our lives, all of us who have been here at the Milan sta-dium and witnessed these events should consider ourselves privileged, and now the Official Final Score in alphabetical order:

America, 340 points.

England, or as everyone here knows them Crinkles, 440 points.

This was greeted by a huge roar and applause from the crowd.

Back at Crinkles Academy it was greeted with, "Yes! Yes!! YES!!!"

The announcer continued,

France 320 points.

Germany 330 points.

When the applause finally subsided the announcer continued.

"Because Crinkles was a Guest Team introduced only to enable the finals to be played, and they had not competed in the normal manner to win a place to play here today, we announce the official '1999 International Junior 'Team Quadro' League

Champions' as America, with Germany second, France third, and Crinkles an honorary fourth place."

There was total silence throughout the Stadium, then a lone voice heard only by a few people around him, cried out,

"Shame! Shame!"

The people close to him heard this and joined in, "Shame, Shame! SHAME!!"

Within less than a minute the whole 60,000 strong crowd were chanting,

"SHAME! SHAME! SHAME! SHAME!"

Then the foot stamping started, hardly audible at first then a little louder and then it sounded like an express train in the distance, it built up and UP until you could feel the noise, and feel the vibrations running through the Stadium Flooring.

Thump, Thump, Thump, …. SHAME, SHAME, SHAME,

Thump, Thump, THUMP, …. SHAME, SHAME, SHAME,

Thump, THUMP, THUMP, …. SHAME, SHAME, SHAME,

THUMP, THUMP,THUMP, …. SHAME! SHAME!! SHAME!!!

At Crinkles we just sat stunned looking at the T.V., we wanted to be able to stamp our feet we wanted to shout shame, but we weren't there so we sat silently.

Steve in the T.V. Broadcasting Room in the Stadium with Hugh, Tom and Julia spoke up,

"The way all of your broadcasting team here today feel, and I suspect the way all of our viewers around the World feel is best put by the crowd." they all sat quietly as the cameras panned back to the crowd.

A request was made asking the crowd for silence so that the 'Official Award Winning Ceremony' could commence and the Cup and Medals given out to the Winning Teams. This caused the volume of protest to increase considerably.

Forcing the Officials to announce that there would be no award winning ceremony on the pitch, it would take place at a later date away from the Stadium.

There now followed an official request that people left the Stadium in an orderly manner but apart from a handful the majority would not move and still sat chanting and stamping their feet.

Despite repeated appeals by the organisers and repeated explanations as to why Crinkles could not be the winners it was nearly an hour before the majority of the people started to leave, and well over two hours before the Stadium fell silent, but for the rustle of plastic cups being blown about in the light breeze that had sprung up.

As the Headmaster said, the organisers were correct of course, but it didn't seem right on the day and it will be argued about forever.

The Head said we did win, everyone knows that, it is an indisputable fact and everyone can be proud to be part of Crinkles Academy.

He then suggested that we partake of some of this delicious food that awaits us, and so we did, we tucked in with a vengeance and talked about the game,

"Did you see that?" "What about the speed of that flying," "Did anyone notice...?"

Everyone had an opinion, and everyone wanted to talk at the same time. We talked and talked all evening and into the early hours of the morning, and we still had the excitement of the team arriving home in a couple of days to look forward to.

Obviously the team initially felt devastated, but Ian and Cecilia talked to them in much the same way as the Head had talked to us.

The team carefully checked their Brooms and put them safely away in their boxes.

"You're the best, the very best, I owe it all to you and so does Crinkles." David said to his Broom as he gently laid it in its Travelling Box and closed the lid.

The team showered and dressed, and their disappointment lessened a little. Picking up their Broom Boxes they left the dressing room and started to make their way to the Foyer but stopped.

The passage way leading to the Stadium was deserted, so they decided to take one last look at the now empty Stadium, walking back along the tunnel they came out into the huge open space and looked at tier after tier, row after row of now empty seats rising to the sky, with one last look at the empty 'Team Quadro' pitch. They could all here the ghost crowd in their minds cheering and cheering, urging them on. They turned and made their way back.

Back through the tunnel and along the passage, then they turned the corner and there stood six large security men who all started to grin when they saw them.

They opened the doors and went ahead of the team trying to make a passageway through the huge crowd.

Officially they may not be The Winners, but unofficially they were. It was mayhem, from the quiet of the deserted Stadium half the World now seemed to be packed in front of them.

There were Photographers, Journalists, T.V. crews, well wishers, Presidents of this Company, Executives of that Company, TV, Radio and Cinema Stars, Sports Personalities, Teenagers, Children and Politicians.

Everyone wanted to congratulate them and shake their hands whilst asking a million questions. When they finally got back to the Hotel it was the same again, people, people, people,

Questions, questions, questions "What did they think of this? What did they think of that? What toothpaste did they use? Did the boys have girlfriends? Did the girls have boyfriends? Did the girls in the team argue all the time with the boys?"

The questions went on and on, finally with the help of the Hotel Staff everyone managed to get to their rooms and collapsed exhausted.

A little while later when hunger overcame exhaustion it was decided it would be safer to have meals sent up to their rooms rather than trying to push through the crowds both to and from the Dining Room.

After everyone had finished eating they chatted for a while, but felt too tired to talk for long and were soon in bed and sound asleep.

The following morning despite Ian allowing everyone a long lie in the team was still very reluctant to get up.

They were supposed to be returning home that day but events dictated otherwise, and the team found themselves on Local and National Wizards T.V. and mobbed wherever they went.

Crinkles was officially the losers but in the eyes and minds of the Wizards World they were undeniably the real winners.

People crowded round them wanting autographs, but they were all ushered away by the body guards that now constantly surrounded them. Lorraine, David and all the other Flyers felt bad about that, and often shouted "Sorry" to the disappointed fans clutching their autograph books and pens, but no matter how loud they shouted they could barely be heard above the noise of the crowd.

The Security Men acting as Body Guards explained it was too dangerous to stop, they had to keep moving otherwise they would be crushed by the crowd all trying to get near them.

Its amazing thought Lorraine, yesterday no one knew who we were, all these people would have walked past us in the street without giving us a second glance. Today it seems everyone wants to talk to us, be near to us, to touch us, it's a strange old World she thought.

Apparently very little interest had been shown by anyone in any of the other three teams who had become that embarrassed at being ignored they all decided to fly home early.

Finally our team flew from Linate International Airport Milan, bound for Heathrow London where it was decided we should stay overnight at one of the airport hotels.

Everyone was in bed by 8.00p.m and didn't stir until 11.00a.m. A light lunch then it was the afternoon flight back home.

No one spoke much on the flight back home, we were still trying to take it all in. The fact that we had travelled to Milan, played in the 'Final' of the 'International Junior Team Quadro Championship' game and won, WE HAD WON!!

Then all the unrealistic business of the crowds and the fame, so much had taken place in such a short space of time that it was hard to believe it was true, that all of this had actually happened to us. As we sat in the aeroplane we all felt left up in the air. (Excuse the pun). Exciting things had taken place so fast that many of our memories had already become a blur.

Back at Crinkles you can imagine the disappointed when we heard of a days delay in the teams return.

We had a huge reception planned; a large banner had been made and was now fastened to the front of the School it said in huge red and blue letters on a white background:

'Welcome Back, Welcome Home the Champions'

The gardeners had found yards and yards of old bunting and dozens and dozens of flags from the coronation, from which coronation no one was sure.

What a feast was organised, now this could have caused problems as it took us all our time to raise the money for the television aerial.

However for the past couple of days there had been a string of vans and cars dropping things off and leaving donations all from well wishers, the Headmaster had dozens of little notes saying things like, 'Just a little something for the party you will be having.' and so on.

The night before the team were due back everything was sorted and we were about to call it a day, when for no apparent reason I suddenly felt very sad.

I felt that it would never be as good as this again and glancing around I just knew I wasn't the only one thinking that.

It was 7.00p.m when everyone arrived back. It was a lovely sunny evening and we lined both sides of the drive up to the School's Main Entrance and waved our flags and cheered from the moment the minibus turned off the main road.

We rushed to surround the bus as the team got off and hoisted every member of the team aloft along with Ian and Cecilia carrying them Victoriously into the Main Hall.

The Hall was fully decorated with the coronation bunting and we sat them down as guests of honour in front of the feast of feasts, while other pupils unloaded the minibus and put all the cases and Broom Boxes in the Hall.

The Head welcomed everyone home and told them he could not express how proud he and everyone at Crinkles Academy were of their Magnificent Achievements.

He was even prepared to overlook a certain person ignoring his orders on dangerous flying confident that it would not happen again.

"Now enjoy your party, and tomorrow we will have a day off, no lessons."

Everyone cheered and cried out "Good old Head!!" The Head smiled and quietly slipped away to the Entrance Hall where I joined him and we carried the Brooms in their Travelling Boxes upstairs where we carefully put them and their boxes back one by one.

"That's grand Brian." Said the Head, "I'll lock up now, you get yourself away to the party."

"Are you not going back downstairs to party Headmaster?"

He smiled, "No Brian, no one's completely at ease at a School Party when I'm floating around, best for me to call it a day I think."

"I'm sure your wrong Headmaster everyone would want you there."

"It's nice of you to say that Brian and I know everyone would try and relax and make me welcome, however under the surface they would be a little uneasy and afraid to really relax and let their hair down. Best for me to have an early night I think, I am feeling rather tired."

"Goodnight then Headmaster."

"Goodnight Brian, and thank you for all your help."

"My pleasure Headmaster," I nodded and slipped away.

But I knew it would be a while before he closed the Broom Cupboard door and locked it.

I knew he would talk to the Brooms thanking them for looking after their Flyers and he would talk about the game in Milan. It's a pity they can't talk back, Imagine hearing an eye witness account of the game from the Brooms themselves now that would be incredible. I made my way back to my little cosy room, the noise of the party downstairs could be faintly heard.

I could go back down to the party and join in the fun and tuck into all of that lovely grub, as no one would feel they had to be on their best behaviour for me, but somehow I didn't feel like it, I felt I needed to be alone.

CHAPTER NINETEEN

The American Trip - The Toy Shop

David takes up the story:

Just two days before our trip to America Jenny and I had finished all our last minute preparations. I was really excited when we flew to Milan for the 'Team Quadro' game, that was the first time I had ever flown, although I hadn't mentioned this to anyone as I appeared to be the only one at the School who hadn't flown here, there, and everywhere. This would be even more exciting the first long haul flight I had ever made.

The Head had completely worn out the School Secretary, Mrs. Brown. For years she had been used to a fairly leisurely pace but over the past few weeks had been trying to track down as many old pupils as she could.

She seemed to be working night and day, letters had been sent out to all the parents of the present pupils at the School and all the old pupils that Mrs. Brown had been able to find and to old friends of Crinkles.

The letters were identical and rather strange, they read:

Dear (the persons name),   Date.

14 days from the date on this letter, from 12 noon to possibly as late as midnight, representatives of Crinkles Academy attending the International Wizards Convention at the conference centre in New York, may desperately need your assistance.

You will become aware of this need if it is required. If it is required please help us to the best of your ability.

243

Please do not contact the School in any way for more information as there is no more information available.

May we ask you not to discuss this letter with anyone else and to send the attached acknowledgement back to us in the stamp addressed envelope enclosed, <u>immediately</u>.

The acknowledgement simply read:

I have received your request for my/our assistance and will help if required.

No. of people   No. of people

    YES ☐   NO ☐

The Head had a chart in his office that Mrs. Brown marked up each day with the replies received.

I think a few more replies have trickled in today, but by yesterday lunch time just over 92% had replied, of which 22,540 people had ticked yes, can you believe it? Where did the Head find all of these people?

1,180 had ticked no and 287 hadn't ticked any box. (I wondered how Heckinwicker, Big Heck voted)

Quite a few apparently had put in little notes and a lot of others had requested more information despite being told not to.

The Head was very pleased with the response. I was even more pleased and very excited when the Head told us he had arranged for a window seat on the aeroplane. I was to have the window seat on the way out and Jenny on the way back to stop any arguing between us.

It was the last day at School before we left for America and the Head at morning assembly said that he hoped everyone would be wishing us every success on our trip.

Even those people who in the past may have been unsupportive of the School and some who had actively worked against it.

This caused quite a few murmurs and a lot of puzzled looks, what did the Head mean actively working against the School?

I glanced at one or two who I suspected for signs of unease but if they were feeling uneasy they didn't show it.

He then said that Miss. Millthrop would be in complete charge until he returned and he expected everyone, and he meant everyone, to give any assistance and support Miss. Millthrop may require without hesitation.

Mr. Smithers the Head continued would as usual have the very responsible position of being in charge of the Library, during the next few days that responsibility may well increase considerably and any assistance he may require should also be offered immediately without question.

He added that he looked forward to seeing everyone on his return as no doubt did David and Jenny.

With that he left, leaving most people there totally baffled, what had he been talking about?

It was almost time to go, we had finished a last minute check to make doubly sure we hadn't forgot anything. The Headmaster had the Passports, Flight Tickets, Hotel bookings and all that kind of stuff in a special pocketed black folder. Unknown to the Head Jenny and I had decided to always make sure that he had it with him as he was notoriously forgetful. The taxi had arrived and we bundled our gear into the boot settled ourselves in the back and wound the windows down so we could wave goodbye.

Most of the School had turned up to see us off, and much to the embarrassment of the Head, Miss. Millthrop planted a big kiss on his cheek.

I was having a laugh to myself when she went and did the same to me and Jenny. All my friends started to jeer and scoff I was glad when the taxi pulled away.

Everyone was waving and we waved back till they disappeared from our view.

Soon we arrived at the Airport to fly down to Heathrow, now the battle began as to which of us was to have the window seat on the flight down, as it happens neither of us had one.

I enjoyed the excitement of the take off but a few minutes later I felt sick and was glad when we landed.

Heathrow is huge there are so many people, and more planes than I had ever seen before.

But it makes you feel so small and sort of vulnerable, we were hopeless, we didn't know where we should be going or what we should be doing.

The Head was not used to this sort of place and got very flustered and confused. He would ask anyone who had a uniform on any sort of uniform would do for information, and many of them didn't even work there or were shop staff.

Eventually we would find somebody who could give him instructions and off we would go only to find we were lost again within a couple of minutes.

If we checked once we checked a hundred times the flight information shown on those TV. Screens dotted about everywhere.

The Head was always asking what our flight number was, it would appear on the screen but before we could read the information it would move up and we had lost it again.

We finally sorted ourselves out and to everyone's relief we found we were actually seated in the right seats, and on the right plane, an achievement which an hour earlier seemed impossible.

I thought being on a big Transatlantic Jet Plane with a window seat was absolutely brilliant, I enjoyed taxiing to the end of the runway and hearing the engines powering up, then shooting forward like a rocket to take off. I pretended I was the pilot and everyone was in awe of my incredible skills.

The view looking down on people, cars, buses, houses, roads and fields is great but then the plane climbs higher and higher till you can no longer make any smaller things out. Flying high over the Atlantic looking down on to White Clouds as far as the eye can see is very impressive. They looked like huge pieces of fluffy white candyfloss. I really enjoyed that at first but as time went by it got a bit boring and I was glad of the meals for a break.

I had taken some anti-sickness tablets before we set off and was feeling okay, otherwise I may have missed out on the food which was very good, I tucked in and also ate some of Jenny's that she didn't want.

Occasionally the clouds would break for a while and you could look down on the sea, now and again you could see a ship but it wasn't very often and it looked just like a tiny dot on the huge endless expanse of sea. Then the clouds would disappear altogether and it was blue skies and sea stretching for miles and miles.

It was sunset when we approached New York, it was breathtaking looking down at the City. We flew on then started to circle John. F. Kennedy Airport for a while waiting out turn to land. Then we started to descend, the excitement of landing was great, the bump as the wheels touchdown then the breaks applied so that we stop before the runway runs out. Once again everyone admired my coolness and skill as the Pilot.

We had arrived, and surprisingly we managed to sort ourselves out quite quickly perhaps we have already become seasoned travellers. We got off the plane and made our way with our fellow passengers with no problems through Passport Control then on to collected our luggage off the carousel. It then become embarrassing as three times the Headmaster panicking had removed someone else's luggage; the two security guards were starting to look at us suspiciously.

In the end it was simple, but only because there was only our luggage left on it. Mind you another couple of minutes and the luggage handlers would have removed our cases and started to fill the carousel with cases from the next flight in. The thought of then finding out how to collect our luggage and explaining why we hadn't collected it earlier with the Head panicking, becoming confused and talking mumbo jumbo (which he is very good at), Jenny would have been crying, I would of course have been the only one left to sort it out.

I was thinking all this to myself as we loaded up the luggage trolley; fortunately this hadn't happened and thankfully things began to fall into place quite quickly.

We soon found ourselves outside the Airport and in the queue for the Express Bus Service into town, after about fifteen minutes we were on our way into New York.

It took nearly an hour to reach 'Grand Central Rail Terminal' where the bus dropped us off. We weren't going anywhere by train but had a quick look inside, it's huge and decorated like some sort of Cathedral it was great fun, already the different atmosphere from back home was gripping us.

We then joined a long queue for a taxi, it wasn't that bad as they were coming and going so fast that it didn't take long for the queue to go down.

I don't think it was a long journey to our Hotel it only felt that way because most of the time we hardly seemed to be moving, or were just sitting stuck in the traffic. I really enjoyed this as it enabled us to soak in the atmosphere and really take in what was going on outside.

I couldn't believe it when for the first time I saw a New York Traffic Police Woman. She was standing in the middle of a very busy multi-lane road junction blowing like mad a whistle in her mouth and with her white gloved hands going berserk, signalling first that lane of traffic to move, then another, then another to move, stopping that one and that one then letting it move on again. In what appeared to be no apparent order.

I just couldn't understand how the drivers knew what to do, with all this confused (to me) hand waving, whistle blowing, and pointing to the ground, I'm sure some of them hadn't a clue what was going on. It was great fun to watch from the comfort of the bus as a passenger, but I wouldn't like to have been the driver.

I was starting to get very hungry and was glad when we arrived at our Hotel, it was huge and very impressive with a Massive Foyer, it had three lounges each with a different theme and totally different atmospheres.

Further on there was a large games arcade and an even larger shopping centre. A bell boy escorted us up to our rooms and after unpacking we were off downstairs for something to eat. Then Jenny and I played in the arcade for a while before we went to bed at about 10.00p.m.

We got up the next morning at about 11.00a.m, had our breakfast come lunch at the Hotel then the Head told us some important business needed his attention that afternoon, however he had been told of a fabulous Toy Shop that you could spend days in and never be bored.

If he took us there could we be trusted to behave ourselves and would we not be frightened on our own

We told him that sounded like great fun, and he need not worry we would be on our best behaviour and no, we wouldn't be frightened on our own, (anyone would think we were kids).

"Excellent" said the Head.

So off we went, the Doorman outside our Hotel hailed us a cab, and soon we arrived at this huge Toy Shop. We arranged to meet the Head outside the main entrance of the shop later that afternoon.

When the Cab pulled up we leapt straight out and rushed into the shop forgetting to even give the Head a goodbye wave.

Once inside the shop we just wondered around saying,

"Where do you start?" "Let's go into this department," "No I've changed my mind let's try this one first." "Look at this." Or "Come and see this." We wondered around in a daze.

The Head hadn't given us much money, he has no idea about the price of things anyway, and what prices he thinks he knows are from donkey's years ago.

So every time he bought something during the trip he always said:

"Oh dear, I didn't think it would be as much as that."

He had given each of us $20 and we had wondered into the electronic games area. All week the 'Toy Store' was promoting a range of games made by 'Super Master Electronic Games'. Apparently the 'World Champion Player' for these games had been demonstrating his skills everyday for nearly a week. Anyone could enter a competition free of charge to pit their skills against him.

The prize to anyone who could achieve 50% of his best score was an expensive package of a twin games console/monitor and a huge assortment of games and all sorts of other odds and ends what most of them were for I had no idea.

If you could reach1,500,000 points the prize was $15,000 and if you could beat 2,000,000 points the prize was $50,000, Jenny and I had been watching the 'World Champion' for some time,

"Boy, he's good Jenny, I want to put my name down and have a go."

Jenny was annoyed, "We haven't got time, come on let's go. We've got loads to see."

"We have time." I said, "What you do is take one of those tickets from over there put your name on the back and pop it in that drum."

"Every half hour they pick out 6 names, if you're not already here they announce your name over the customer information system and you have five minutes to turn up or they select a new name."

"So we can be looking around the store and if my name is called I'll just call back."

While I had been talking I filled in a ticket and popped it into the drum.

"Right," I said, "Let's look around the rest of the store."

The store was absolutely huge, they seemed to have every toy that had ever been made.

Many of the toys I had never seen before, and those that I had the selection available was incredible.

"Do you like this store Jenny?" I asked.

"I don't know?" Replied Jenny" "I think it's got too many toys, you think you want something then you see something else better and then something better again. In the end I don't know what I would choose even if I had loads of money."

"Jenny! Look at these train set layouts can you believe them? Their fantastic, I see what you mean though which one of those would you choose?"

"Strewth! Have you seen some of the prices?"

It was at this point that an announcement came over the customer information system.

"Would the following customers please make their way to the games department's 'Super Master Games' display area if they wish to compete against the 'Games Master', John Caines."

"Michelle Short, Sally Grey, Bruce Adamson," I felt glum I'm not going to be picked then he said, "David Taylor."

"It's me Jenny! It's me! Are you coming?" I asked.

"No, I'm going to look at these play houses and the miniature log cabins, meet me back here when you're finished and oh!, David no using Magic, that's cheating."

"Would I cheat?"

"Mmm." said Jenny.

"I'm off now, or they'll pick someone else." And I dashed away.

When I arrived back at the electronics game centre it was packed and I only just got through the crowd in time to register.

I handed over my half of the ticket I had filled in and a man checked it, handed it back and told me to stand over there pointing to where five other children had already gathered.

The 'World Champion' or so the games company claimed was at the centre of the stage. He had his back to everyone playing furiously on his games console as he was attempting to beat his own World Record.

Above him a huge screen showed his game in progress, and to the right of the screen his score so far and his time. Below that was shown the score and the time he had to beat which was supposedly the Official World Record for the Super Master Electronic Games, Premier League Console

He had set this record apparently two months ago and with 30 seconds of the five minute playing time left he was almost there, with 20 seconds left he was level with his old score.

An announcer declared, "YES!! This is going to be a new 'World Record'."

20 more seconds of furious manipulation and he had beaten his previous 'World Record' by 95,000 points, giving him 1, 695, 000 points in five minutes.

Everyone including me loudly applauded and cheered.

He stood up turned to face everyone and bowed, then waving and smiling he walked off behind some curtains at the side of the small stage.

"Would the next six competitors please step forward." said the announcer.

I moved forward, a lady who looked completely bored checked my ticket stub, she obviously wasn't a games fan.

In a sharp stern voice she said "You're with the next lot stand over there." She pointed to where the 'World Champion' had just disappeared.

The last six players had vacated their seats on the play consoles that had been arranged in a semicircle in front of the stage.

The same as the Champion you sat with your back to everyone and there was a screen above your head that the audience could see, at the side of the screen there was a score and time indicator.

Everything was identical to the one on stage that the Champion had been playing except that these had a much smaller screen, the best score for the group that had just left was a girl who had achieved 630,000 points this was the best score so far today. The best score for the week (this was the last day) was 645,000 points scored by a boy two days earlier.

Because of the 'New World Record Score' that had just been declared you now had to reach 847,500 points to win the prize of a games console.

The new group was in position and waiting to start.

From behind the screen near to where I was standing I could hear voices, I had not been trying to listen until hearing 'Dumb lot', mentioned.

I pricked up my ears, apparently the demonstration by the 'World Champion' was genuine enough but the sponsors just in case a brilliant player came along had the computers play consoles rigged to guarantee no-one could reach 2,000,000 points and only 2 of the 6 consoles able to reach the maximum possible of 1,700,000 points.

This reduced their risk in paying out even the $15,000 prize too almost nil.

Sales for the game had been incredible, as people bought it and practised like mad at home hoping to become that good that they could compete at the store.

Today an announcement was to be made that they would be returning in a month's time with even bigger and better prizes and so they were looking forward to even bigger and better sales.

I didn't hear any more as the last bunch of contestants were leaving the play consoles the highest score from that group being 610,000 points.

We were ushered forward to replace the previous contestants and I prepared to settle in.

"Everyone ready?" Asked the assistant, the clock and scoreboards read zero, "You're off." He cried.

Ten seconds had gone and I hadn't even started, I had been weighing everything up, now I was under way, sorry Jenny I said to myself.

Jenny was looking at a fantastic playhouse it was almost a real house in miniature it was very impressive indeed.

Yet she could remember having great fun making a playhouse out of a huge cardboard box, cutting out the windows and the door then painting it with some old emulsion paint her dad had given her.

Gluing plastic numbers on the door then taping along one edge with some wide reinforced tape her dad had for roof repairs.

Then pressing the other edge of the tape on to the front of the house so that it acted like a door hinge, she had spent many happy hours making it and with her friends had spent many more happy hours playing in it.

Then Jenny felt the faint vibrations, she was furious, she should have known he wouldn't be able to resist using Magic. I had better go and see what's going on she thought.

What was going on was I had spent one minute familiarising myself with the game's action movements and then started to speed my reactions up by using Magic.

I thought to myself, you've rigged it so that no one can win, 'well just you watch this'.

When I started playing the games area was full and although they had asked for quiet there was always a babble of chatter in the background.

At the end of the first minute my score was only 10,000 points the lowest of any of the six players, in fact the lowest all week for anyone at the one minute mark.

The best score at this stage in the game was 126,000 points but now my skills linked with the Speed Magic would double my score every 30 seconds.

By the end of the second minute my score was 40,000 points and the best in the group was a girl on 260,000 points, the nearest to me was a boy on 110,000 points.

By the end of the third minute I was on 160,000 points with the girl still leading on 420,000 points. 420,000 points was a very good score at this stage of the game.

The excitement was mounting and the crowd was growing a lot quieter.

The Organisers and the 'World Champion' had appeared from the side of the stage to see why the crowd had grown quieter and stood watching the young player.

By the end of the fourth minute the young girl was on 640,000 points a terrific score, everyone eyes were glued on her screen no-one had noticed my score was also 640,000 points until someone shouted.

"Look at number 2 player's score."

With one minute to go it was neck and neck, the young girl was a brilliant player but of course she could not compete with Speed Magic.

With 30 seconds to go I was now on 1, 280 000 points and the girl on 730,680.

There was total silence now in the games area and word had started to spread throughout the store, this meant more and more spectators arriving.

The Organisers and the 'World Champion' could not believe their eyes, the machine must have developed a fault as there was no other way that anyone could have such a high score.

At the end of the tournament there was huge applause and cheering.

My final score was 2,560,000 points and the young girl on game console number 6 finished on 840,000 points.

By the time the Magic signals had become strong enough for Jenny to pick up the game was already into its fourth minute, by the time she got anywhere near the game area it was over.

There was no way she could push her way through the crowds so she decided it was best to make her way back to the play houses area where she had told David to meet her.

It was almost deserted when Jenny got back and she could have had a really good look at everything, but she was that furious with David she had lost all interest in the displays.

Dear knows how long I might have to wait here until he arrives, she thought.

The 'World Champion' was devastated, an unknown kid had come along and scored 2,560,000 points, when his best ever score was now a mere 1,695,000, how could this be?

The sponsors were very annoyed at having to pay the prize money out, and were already implying that the Ex World Champion's Services may no longer be required.

An announcement went out over the intercom system informing everyone in the shop that the $50,000 prize money along with all the other prizes had been won by a young man named David Taylor.

Jenny was absolutely furious how could he, how could he do that, the cheat, I never want to see him again.

She was also annoyed that she had to stay until he came and that she had to work with him because the Head was relying on them.

Back in the games area the Store Manager had arrived along with a Publicity Photographer.

I was now on the small stage with the young girl who came second standing next to me and a small group of people from the store and the games firm.

The Shop Manager was now talking through a mike linked to the stores intercom system.

"Everyone here I'm sure wants to congratulate David from England, who tells me he is in New york on holiday with friends for a few days."

"Now I know we all want to hear what David intends to do with his $50,000 cash prize so congratulation's David." He shook my hand and pointing the mike at my face said, "Over to you David."

I hadn't really taken it all in, $50,000, just think what that would buy, I could buy one of those fantastic train layouts with 6 or 7 locomotives and still have plenty of money left, loads and loads of money left.

Then I remembered Jenny, I could be in big trouble.

"I think he's a little shy folks." Said the Store Manager, "Come on David let's hear what you're going to spend your money on, a lot of it in this shop I hope." He said with a big grin on his face and everyone laughed.

"Emmm." I said, then there was a long pause, "Eh, eh." Then at last I was able to get my brain back into gear, "First, I'd like to thank everyone." although I wasn't sure why I said that, but it seemed like the right thing to say as they always say that on all those TV presentations and award shows.

I looked around desperate for inspiration and saw how disappointed Sally was.

"I would like to give my full game's package to Sally here for being such a great contender and sport."

"Sally really deserved to win I just had a very lucky break." A lot of people started to applaud.

"That was very generous David." Said the Store Manager, But you haven't told us your plans yet for this $50,000 cheque we are about to make out to you?"

I was panicking, I realised I couldn't accept it but what should I do with it? It was then that I spotted the badge on Sally's top, that's it I thought.

Jenny could hear all this through the shop's intercom system and was growing more annoyed by the second, $50,000 for cheating, I still can't believe he would do that, we have betrayed Crinkles.

She was starting to feel that she should take some of the blame as she had guessed he couldn't resist using Magic, she should have tried to stop him entering the competition he may have listened to her then if she had been more forceful but now it's too late.

"I don't want the cheque for $50,000 to be made out to me. I want it to be made out to the New York Children's Fund and presented to them by The Store on my behalf."

Jenny breathed a sigh of relief when she heard him say that.

There was a gasp from the crowd then a huge cheer went up and everyone started to clap. Flashlights went off, the Store Manager and the Photographer shook my hand as did the Games Promoters and the 'World Champion' (up until 20 minutes ago).

They all realised this publicity was priceless, Sally threw her arms around me and much to my disgust started to kiss me, this brought more cheers from the crowd.

"This has been the most exciting day in my life." said Sally blushing slightly. "I have played alongside the new 'World Games Champion' and been given a fantastic prize by him."

Sally's face was now bright red "I can't believe this is happening to me I wish you were staying in America." She then threw her arms round David and kissed him yet again. The photographers loved all of this and took shot after shot. Another shouted "I think you've won another prize, an American girlfriend." And everyone started cheering.

The microphone was now being pushed in my face again, "So how does it feel to be the new 'World Games Champion'?" A reporter was asking.

Where are all these people coming from? I thought, this is all getting out of hand, I could now see T.V. news people arriving.

So I grabbed the microphone,

"I would like to make it plain to everyone that I'm not the new 'World Games Champion', nor do I want to be. My win was sheer luck and I know I would never be able to repeat it and I must go now as I'm meeting a friend and I'm already very late."

I handed the microphone back.

Reporters and Photographers were crowding around me.

"Just a few words please David." "Yes just a few questions." "You're on holiday aren't you?" "We all want to know what you think of New York." "Where are you staying?" "How long are you here for?" "Is this your first visit to New York?"

There were questions coming at me from all sides I didn't know what to say. In the end I said,

"I'm sorry I must go." and I started to push my way through the crowd although where I was going to I had no idea, then I felt someone grab my arm.

"David this way." It was the 'World Champion Game's Player', he pulled me behind the screen, "Follow me and I'll get you clear." We went through a 'staff only' door and along numerous corridors until we came to a fire exit.

"Through that door, turn left for 50 yards and you're in the Main Street turn left again and you're outside the Store's Main Entrance."

"But the friend I'm with - Jenny, she's expecting me in the miniature play house area."

"What's she wearing?" I told him and described her, "I'll fetch her, wait here don't wander away."

Off he went, and I wondered how long he would be. I was afraid that someone might come along and want to know what I was doing there but within ten minutes he was back with Jenny who gave me a very stern look.

"David," said the 'World Champion Games Player' "I don't know how you achieved that incredible score, it seems impossible to me. I would like to thank you for the announcement you made. Hopefully it's saved my job." And he shook my hand wishing me the best of luck "Away you both go but fast before the alarm goes off."

Jenny smiled and I nodded, we pushed down the bar on the emergency door and shot through, we were barely clear when it was slammed shut again and there had been only one little bleep from the alarm. We turned left and 50 yards along the alley there we were in the Main Street with crowds of people to melt into and not be recognised.

I looked at my watch, "Phew, that's lucky Jenny, 10 minutes to go before we meet the Head outside the shop." Jenny looked at me, I knew that look probably won't speak to me for days I thought.

We had turned left at the corner and had reached the Main Entrance to the Toy Shop. We stood to one side waiting for the Head to arrive.

I decided to tell Jenny the full story, she never said a word, never interrupted me as she so often did just listened in silence.

"Well that's it. You know the full story now." Still silence, "Well some good did come out of it." I added.

"Well all's well that ends well," still silence. I thought I would try one more time "It's all over now anyway."

Jenny looked at me, "Are you really stupid? Or do you just act that way? What about when the Evening Papers come out and the T.V. news comes on, with your face everywhere."

"I hadn't thought about that, are you going to tell the Head Jenny?"

"No, It's up to you to decide whether you tell him or not, here he comes now bang on time."

David had a sinking feeling in his stomach.

The Head approached us smiling. "I haven't kept you long have I?"

"No we've just arrived ourselves." Smiled Jenny.

"Did you enjoy yourselves in the Toy Shop?" Asked the Head.

"Yes it was really great." I said enthusiastically, then I noticed the look Jenny was giving me.

"There are some fantastic toys there." Said Jenny, "It was really interesting."

"Good." Said the Head, "I'm glad you've enjoyed yourselves it's nice to relax for a while."

Jenny looked at David, good to relax for a while! Some chance with that idiot about she thought.

"Actually Headmaster, we haven't spent anything." said Jenny as she gave the $40 back to the Head.

"I'm amazed, why didn't you buy anything?"

"There wasn't enough time." I said quietly, hoping Jenny wouldn't explain further.

The Head nodded "Ah well, perhaps another time."

"We had better head back to our Hotel, freshen up a bit then we're off to a 'Highly Recommended Restaurant' for our evening meal. After that it's an early night I think as we face a very busy day tomorrow. I'll just call a taxi."

"Can I do it Headmaster?" I asked, "I've always wanted to call a Yellow Cab I've seen so many people do it at the Cinema and on T.V."

"I don't see why not." answered the Head.

Despite what seemed like an endless streams of taxi - cabs it took nearly five minutes to hail an empty one. Eventually one pulled over out of the main stream and stopped at the curb.

"YES!!" I said, "That was great."

Is he for real? Thought Jenny, he's as excited about stopping a taxi as he was about winning the Toy Shop game. Jenny got into the taxi first then David tumbled in and finally the Head.

"Where to bud?" asked the taxi driver as he pulled away from the curb to rejoin the traffic flow.

Beep, Beep, Beep, the car he cut in front of wasn't too pleased, "Ah, get yourself a bike." Our taxi driver shouted.

CHAPTER TWENTY

American Trip - in the Restaurant

As told by David and Jenny:

After arriving back at the Hotel we freshened up and a couple of hours later we left for the Restaurant.

Apparently it wasn't far and as it was such a pleasant evening we decided to walk. There was a great atmosphere of hustle and bustle and the towering buildings are so impressive, they always had looked impressive in Magazines on Television and in Films, but in real life they were breath taking.

If you looked up for too long you began to feel really dizzy, I had to lean on a lamppost to look up.

"Are we going to see the Empire State Building before we leave?" asked David.

"We certainly are, and have a meal at Windows of the World followed by a trip on the ferry over to Manhattan and then to see the Statue of Liberty and much, much more." said the Head.

"Great." said David and Jenny gave a big smile.

Two large New York Policemen on patrol were approaching us.

"Excuse me." Said the Head, "But I wonder if you can direct me to this Restaurant."

Showing them a piece of paper with the restaurant's name on it as though they were French or Italian Policemen and may not have under stood him. They looked at the Head then at the name on the piece of paper.

"Sure." said one of them, "You're here." And pointed to a large dark green and gold canopy just about thirty yards ahead which stretched from the restaurant entrance to the curb and had the restaurant's name on the side in huge gold letters.

We all smiled a little embarrassed and thanked them, they smiled back and one touched his cap.

"Well here we are children." said the Head, walking towards the large brown smoked glass doors with their heavy gold frames and elaborate door handles.

Just as the Head was about to open the door it was opened for him by a Commissionaire in a splendid uniform.

We all walked in and immediately felt a little uneasy, the restaurant was very, very posh and everyone was expensively dressed, we were dressed casual but reasonably passable, then we suddenly realised the Head looked a little shabby in his old suit.

"Yes." A waiter, or Head Waiter, or whatever he was had appeared at our side. It's amazing how explicit that one word can be according to how you pronounce it.

What this one word 'yes' actually said in this case, was, who on earth are you lot and what on earth are you shabby people doing here in this restaurant?"

"We have a table booked for 7.00p.m. The name is Phillpotts." replied the Head.

"Phillpotts, Phillpotts." repeated the waiter.

"A problem?" another man had arrived wearing a white tuxedo with an air of superiority about him.

"These people say they have a table booked for 7.00p.m." said the waiter. The white tuxedo man looked us up and down with disdain.

Just then a couple arrived, the lady covered in jewellery and her companion in a black tuxedo.

White tuxedo turned and in a very friendly cheerful voice greeted them.

"Good Evening Sir, Good Evening Madam, how nice to see you." Still smiling he snapped his fingers and a waiter appeared from nowhere, "Ah, Renardo, please escort," he paused, smiling at the couple, "Mr. and Mrs...."

The couple smiled back, "Its Mr. and Mrs. Carmichael. We have a 7.30p.m. Reservation" The man said.

White tuxedo ran his finger down the evening reservation list, "Ah, here we are table number 10." He now turned back to Renardo, "Mr. and Mrs. Carmichael to their table please." and off everyone went beaming and smiling at each other. A 7.15p.m and 8p.m reservation had now also been shown to their table while we were left standing like empty milk bottles on a step.

"I don't think they must have been expecting us." said the Head.

I looked at my watch it was 7.05p.m, I was just about to say that I would rather go to a burger bar and have a triple whopper and a milkshake, when one of the two waiters who had been some distance away looking in our direction and talking to each other came over and said in an arrogant voice,

"Follow me."

They sat us down at a table tucked away in the corner, opposite us was a group of eight people talking and laughing that loud that almost everyone in the restaurant could hear them, they hadn't realised that we were now sitting opposite.

"Did you see that funny old man that has been standing over by the door?" One of the women said.

"You mean John." said another laughing.

"Hey, watch it, or you'll pay the bill." Said the man who was obviously John, this was greeted by laughter from everyone at the table.

"No the one with the two children, you wouldn't see John with any children he hates them"

"Where?" asked another one of the party.

"Over there, Oh! He's gone, no he hasn't he's sitting over there." and pointed at us, apparently this was also terribly funny as everyone started to laugh, Jenny and I just sat quietly wishing we were back at our Hotel.

The Head just smiled, perhaps he hadn't heard, we both hoped he hadn't.

We sat and sat, other people had arrived long after us and were tucking into their meals.

The Head had tried to attract a waiter's attention for some time as they glided past our table, the odd one would say, "In a minute." We noticed there was no 'sir', or any apology for the delay. We finally managed to place our order.

The Wine Waiter was serving the table opposite with yet more wine, this time when he finished he glanced in our direction and said, "You won't want wine." But before he could leave the Head said,

"Yes, I would like some wine." The Wine Waiter came over and gestured with his hand towards the wine list on our table, "Oh, I think the Red House Wine will do." said the Head, "I can never pronounce any of the fancy names anyway."

The Wine Waiter sneered as he turned and went on his way.

The table opposite had sat in silence listening to every word, they now started to mimic the Head, in such loud voices that almost everyone in the restaurant could here.

"House wine I think." roars of laughter.

"It is the 'cheapest', isn't it?" more laughter.

"If it's not Cola I can't pronounce the name." More roars of laughter, but now also from other tables nearby.

Jenny and I felt so sorry for the Head, we didn't know what to say so we just sat quietly.

The Wine Waiter returned, and knowing he had an audience from the table opposite and from some of the other tables nearby he made a great show of opening the bottle of wine and pouring out a little passed it to the Head.

"Does it meet your expectations? Sir." said the waiter with a mocking politeness.

The Head took a sip, "Yes perfectly acceptable." He said.

"Perfectly acceptable House Wine." one of the women opposite said in an exaggerated whisper so that half the restaurant could still hear. The others around the table started to laugh and had their wine glasses in their hands and were pretending to be sampling the wine.

"Will I pour, or leave the bottle? Sir" Asked the waiter with the emphasis on leave the bottle and a scoffing Sir, more laughter from the table opposite.

The Wine Waiter was playing to the audience for all he was worth, he was really enjoying himself.

"If you would pour please." said the Head.

"I might spill it." Said one of the men on the table opposite trying to mimic the Heads voice and the women all started to giggle.

The Wine Waiter with a nasty smirk on his face and using as much mock pomp and circumstance as he could muster started to pour the red wine into the Heads glass.

Jenny was knocking my foot, I looked in the direction she was looking in and there was the white tuxedo standing next to a waiter both smirking and looking in our direction, apparently we were providing entertainment for the whole restaurant.

The Head's glass was now about half full and wine still being poured into it, then the wine stopped pouring the bottle was empty, but the Head's glass was still only half full.

Jenny and I looked at each other.

The expression on the waiters face was unexplainable.

"I would like a full glass of wine please." said the Head with a firm crystal clear voice.

The Wine Waiter dashed off to get a fresh bottle of wine and the people on the table opposite had gone quiet, they weren't quite sure what had happened.

Within a minute the Wine Waiter was back this time without any exaggerated pomp he opened another bottle and immediately started to pour it into the Heads glass.

He was pouring that fast that the wine was jumping about in the glass and some had come over the side and stained the tablecloth.

The glass looked as though it was filling up but once the waiter stopped pouring and the wine had settled down the glass was still only half full.

He tried again, the bottle was empty now except for a few drops and the glass was still only half full.

"What is wrong with you? You call yourself a Wine Waiter yet you can't fill a glass with wine and look at the state of the tablecloth." The Head had said this in his sternest, crystal clear, Headmaster's – no nonsense voice.

The whole restaurant had heard the Headmaster's remarks, the Wine Waiter turned bright red and fled.

White tuxedo had now appeared along with one of the waiters,

"What seems to be the problem here?"

"The problem," said the Head, "Is that I was led to believe that this was one of the top restaurants in New York, yet we ordered our meals over an hour ago and we are still waiting for them to arrive, however you have managed to serve at least a dozen people who came in after us. I'm still waiting for my wine as your Wine Waiter seems incapable of filling my glass, what he has managed to do is cover the table cloth in wine stains. It's just as well we didn't go to one of the poorer restaurants."

The table opposite and the whole restaurant were listening to every word and watching every move, no one was actually eating or drinking. The White Tuxedo remained silent, he quickly turned and left our table but was soon back with yet another bottle of wine.

"I am the Maitre 'd', I will personally pour your wine and your meals are arriving now." Everyone in the restaurant was trying to get a better view some diners even standing up, those that couldn't see or hear properly were desperate to know what was going on.

White Tuxedo started to pour the wine, his faced changed from arrogance, to puzzlement, to disbelief. The bottle was empty and the wine glass still only half full.

A waiter had arrived with our meals on a large silver tray held on the palm of his right-hand level with his right shoulder, he started to lower it and with his left-hand lifted off one of the plates of food, the plate suddenly left his grasp and the other plates on the silver tray joined it, all flying in the direction of the table opposite.

In a fraction of a second the meals deposited themselves over the eight people sitting opposite, over their heads, shoulders, down their arms, there was food everywhere. The woman started to scream and the men to swear, they jumped up from their table, and one of the women slipped on some food on the floor, trying to save herself she grabbed at the corner of the table.

The tablecloth along with the remains of their meals and their glasses of wine landed on top of four people sitting at the next table down.

Another lady and a man who had been making their way to their table started to slide in the food which was now all over the floor, they grabbed hold of each other to try and regain their balance and slid into the White Tuxedo who in turn grabbed hold of the waiter and all four ended up sailing along the restaurant floor on their backsides, knocking tables and chairs over right, left and centre.

Other members of staff had rushed out to help, and the cooks and chefs had rushed out to see what was causing all the commotion.

One by one everyone lost their balance and so the chaos grew and grew. All the ladies shouting and screaming, "Look at my dress it's ruined, ruined, I've never been so embarrassed in all my life."

"My jewellery, my beautiful jewellery just look at the state of it."

"These shoes cost $800 look at them, look at the state of them, I'll never be able to wear them again." The women opposite shouting "Your shoes! Take a look at my $4,000 handbag it's not worth $4 now." Men angrily shouting "What's going on? Look at my suit, how am I going to get home in this?"

The more yelling and shouting the more slipping and falling, the more slipping and falling the more yelling and shouting.

"I think," said the Head, "It's time for us to leave, surely they won't expect us to pay for the meals we never received or drinks I never had, follow me children, but be careful, walk slowly."

So we did, we picked our way very carefully through the mayhem. We opened the smoke glass doors the commissionaire having left his post to discover what was going on inside. We were just leaving the restaurant when we heard someone shouting,

"Fire!! FIRE!! The Kitchens on Fire."

The staff having all come out of the kitchen to see what was causing the mayhem had obviously not turned everything off.

We found ourselves outside immaculately clean, there was not a speck of food on any of us, but we were all very hungry.

"Well," said the Head, "What about some Super Burgers? I seem to remember passing a Super Burger Bar just down the road."

"YES!!" Jenny and I both yelled.

A few minutes later as we walked down the street three huge Fire Engines raced past us with sirens blaring and red lights flashing.

We were all really hungry and the burgers tasted great, the Head certainly enjoyed his, he ordered a second one and so did I. Jenny only had one because she said they were huge, they were and you got a mountain of chips with them.

As we sat eating a Police Car raced past blue lights flashing and it's siren howling soon to be followed by three Ambulances, then another two Fire Engines then more Police Cars and more Ambulances.

After we finished our meal we had milkshakes and the Head a cup of tea.

When we left the Burger Bar we looked down the street, there was no sign of any flames but enough Flashing Lights to put Blackpool Illuminations to shame? The restaurant staff and patrons all yelling and shouting covered in food from head to toe were being ushered into the ambulances, everything seemed complete chaos.

We walked back to the Hotel and sat in one of the beautiful lounges to let our meals settle before having a reasonably early night.

The next day in the Newspapers and on Television News, there were reports of a 'serious fire in the kitchen' at one of New York's most 'Famous Restaurant's' due to a pan of fat over heating following a disturbance in the restaurant.

The reports went on to say that the restaurant had been full at the time and as Firemen fought the blaze the Police sealed off the road and redirected traffic. Everyone was evacuated and taken by a fleet of Ambulances to Hospital, where fortunately it was found that once all the food had been cleaned off them no one was serious injured, only a few minor cuts, bruises and some sprained ankles, all of the patients being sent home later that night.

There were great photographs of some customers, white tuxedo (the Maitre 'd') and some of his waiters covered from head to foot in food, wine and sauces. I doubt that they would ever live it down in the 'New York restaurant owner's community'.

Apparently it took three hours to bring the blaze under control and part of the restaurant and building was badly damaged. It was estimated that it would be closed for at least six months.

We had been sitting with other guests in the Main Hotel Lounge watching the news on Television while we waited for the delegate's buses to arrive to take us to the Conference. Once the news was over we found ourselves on our own. The Headmaster then turned to us and said, "Remember. I told you all Magic has Evil in it."

We knew what he meant, the wine glass that wouldn't fill seemed so harmless at first. Who would have thought it would lead to such dramatic events, though Jenny and I felt many of them had got there just deserts, (though none of them had a dessert, other than those who had it on their clothes.)

The Headmaster said he was popping into the shop to get some mints and asked did we want anything. We asked him to get some cheesy crisps, this was simply to give us more time to look at the morning Newspaper he had been reading, once he was gone we looked through the morning paper, the Head had only read the headline article about the fire.

There it was in the middle of the Newspaper, two full pages telling the story of David's $50,000 win on the games machine and there were 8 photographs 6 of them with David in them. The article finished by saying that Sally Hardacre the girl who David had given the games package to, the girl shown kissing David in the picture would like him to get in touch with her, the Newspaper said if David contacted them they would put him in touch with Sally.

"I hope you're not even thinking about doing that David." Said Jenny giving him one of her stern looks.

"No way, I don't want to be involved with any girls, I have trouble enough with you." David was surprised he made the last comment.

Jenny looked very annoyed and was just about to tell David what she thought of him when she spotted the Head returning. She told David the Head was coming back, David sitting with the Newspaper in his hands decided the only place he could hide it was beneath one of the large cushions.

"Here's your crisps, children" said the Head as he handed them two packets each "Have you seen my Newspaper I'm sure I left it here?"

"We thought you had it with you when you went into the shop" replied David

"No matter," said the Head "I have plenty that I should be reading here in my briefcase."

David and Jenny looked at each other feeling very uneasy and wishing the bus would come.

Our bus arrived 15 minutes late delayed through heavy traffic and it was no better on the way to the Conference by the time we arrived we were 30 minutes late.

It was fun sitting in the bus in a traffic jam watching all the comings and goings the arguments and the crowds of pedestrians.

If it was every day you would soon get really sick of it, but for a couple of days and in another country away from home it was fun.

The Conference's first day though wasn't fun, it was boring, boring. It was held in a large Conference Centre with car parks so big it was frightening. There was a Huge Reception Area with people standing in groups talking and people wondering around everywhere. The delegates all seemed to know where they were going but probably they were just like us and lost half the time.

We all had identification tags with our picture and name on them along with a reference number. The delegates came from all over the World and were every shape and size imaginable, they all looked very old, the youngest seemed to be at least 35 some about 535.

A few of the delegates gave us funny looks and others annoyed looks, they didn't think we should be there of course, and we wished we weren't. The Head had told us we must stick with him all the time and we did.

He seemed to know everyone, no sooner did he finish talking to two or three people then another two or three would appear, sometimes it would be a group of five or six.

The odd one would scowl at us, or smile, or pat us on the head, but once they started to talk they no longer even noticed us.

The Conference morning session finished for lunch at 1.00p.m. The food was very good, but unfortunately it was soon 2.30 and time to return to the Conference Hall.

The afternoon session finished at 6.00p.m and we were taken back to our Hotel by bus.

The traffic was just as bad on the journey back and it was well after 7.00p.m when we reached our Hotel.

We had a light meal, even David didn't feel that hungry because he felt so tired, it had been such a long, long, boring day, endless discussions that we didn't understand and didn't really want to.

"Is this the sort of thing that happens to you when you grow up Jenny?" asked a weary David

Jenny knew exactly what he meant, they went to bed really early and fell asleep before their heads hit the pillow.

CHAPTER TWENTY-ONE

The Oriliance' (Part One)

Told by Brian with information from the Head, David, Jenny and others:

The day after the Head and the children had left for America, Smither's during morning assembly informed pupils and staff that all books on Magic on loan from the Library had to be returned by 6.00p.m that day, and heaven help any pupils' who had not returned their books by that time.

He didn't actually threaten any of the Masters if they failed to return their books but as all the Masters were terrified of Smithers there was little likely hood of them not obeying.

He also announced no further books would be issued until after the Headmaster returned.

When the hour of 6.00 p.m. arrived six books were still missing and half the School searching for them, the pupil's whose books were missing were preoccupied imagining the dreadful punishments they faced if the books were not found by the new deadline of 9.00p.m.

But thankfully by that time only one book remained lost, but you would have thought it was the Crown Jewels. Smithers was ranting and raving insisting it was found and had everyone double checking everywhere.

It was Miss. Millthrop, who moving papers on Smithers desk to make some working space uncovered the missing book,

"Mr. Smithers," he turned, "Would this be the book you're looking for?" She knew of course that it was, and enjoyed every minute of his embarrassment as he stuttered and mumbled some sort of reply.

"I had better tell everyone the book has been found, shall I?" She was deliberately turning the screw. He mumbled away to himself. "Is that a yes?" asked Millthrop.

"YES." He replied and went off to hide in the Library while Millthrop went off grinning to tell everyone they could relax the book had been found on Smither's desk.

At the School Morning Assembly on the last day of the Conference in New York, Miss. Millthrop told everyone that from noon that day everyone should be thinking of the Headmaster, David and Jenny and give them all their morale support throughout the whole day in whatever way they could.

This left everyone puzzled, what was the old bat talking about? Had she flipped her lid? First it was the Head talking mumbo jumbo before he left and now her.

Think about David and Jenny and give them moral support, they are enjoying themselves in New York while we are stuck here at Old Crinkles, she should get real.

Smithers was none too pleased to be sharing his beloved Library with Miss. Millthrop, locked in together for twelve hours how could anyone stand that? Least of all him.

He had already explained that there was no need for her to be there, as in the highly unlikely event of anything happening he was more than capable of handling it. She let him finish and then told him that she noticed he had not said any of that to the Headmaster when he had the chance because he knew what the Headmaster would say.

She had been told to stay, and stay she would. Smithers retreated muttering to himself.

"You can cut that muttering out Smithers, I'm not putting up with that for 12 hours." She shouted after him as he left.

She had made a mountain of sandwiches, you name it, and she had made it, flask after flask of tea, coffee, chocolate, soup, along with bottled water and diluteable orange, in fact the lot, a feast fit for Kings.

I had to carry it all up to the Library and was almost wishing that I was being locked in with all that lovely grub to enjoy, just as well I had fixed the toilet. Even Old Smithers looked pleased when he saw the results of all the effort Miss. Millthrop had gone to.

It was 11.30a.m, I went off to fetch two comfortable chairs and a folding table and when I got back it was nearly 11.55a.m.

"We were just about to lock the door." said Smithers, "Where have you been all this time boy?" I handed Millthrop the table and a chair.

"Thank you Brian." she said.

"And what about my chair boy?" called out Smithers.

"I don't see any boy Mr. Smithers, it looks as though you aren't going to have a comfortable chair, you'll just have to make do with a rickety old Library one as 'oh dear' its 2 minutes to noon.

"All right! All right! Give me that chair Brian." I noticed there was no thank you as I handed it across to him, and immediately the chair was inside the Library the heavy wooden door was slammed shut and I could hear it being locked and bolted it was one minute to noon.

Suddenly none of this seemed funny anymore, and what was happening over there at the Conference in New York?

Jenny and David had been up since 8.00a.m and had just finished breakfast, in the case of David a huge breakfast.

"Where do you put all that food?" Asked Jenny.

"Actually I could do with some more." Replied David.

"He has hollow legs Jenny as my Mother used to say." Said the Head.

David and Jenny looked at each other, they had never thought of the Head as having a Mother, although now that they thought about it obviously he must have had one.

The Head had done his best to stop the children worrying or thinking about the 'Oriliance'.

What with their adventures and the dynamic atmosphere of

New York it had not been difficult, in fact the children had never mentioned it.

"Well children." Said the Head, "We will be leaving soon for the Conference, now this afternoon will be a little different, you must not be afraid no matter what may happen there are lots and lots of people on our side."

"I wish I could tell you more but it wouldn't help in any way. What you must do is think only of happy times at Crinkles, think about your Mam and Dad, your favourite Aunt's and Uncle's, your favourite days out, all the things you have and do that make you happy."

"Think of sunny days at the beach, playing with your friends, your favourite books, funny cartoons and films, blank everything else out. Keep your eyes shut and don't open them until I tell you, if you follow these instructions everything will be alright."

Actually it was the Head who was really worried, although his jovial smile hid it from David and Jenny.

The final morning at the Conference was boring as usual and seemed to drag on and on, it hadn't really, it had started at 10.30a.m and was all but over by 11.45a.m apart from the closing speeches.

At 12.30 p.m. everyone adjourned for lunch, this is what David had been looking forward to though Jenny still felt full from her breakfast.

Much to David's disappointment the Head wouldn't let him have very much to eat saying they would have a good tuck in later.

They went back into the Conference Area at 1.30p.m and were surprised to see so many people already there, they were no longer sitting in the designated places but appeared to be able to sit anywhere.

This seemed to surprise the Head and he frantically looked about until he recognised some of his old friends and he hurried down to join them. They were sitting 12 rows from the front in the centre section.

This was the 'Oriliance'.

Previously all the men had been wearing suits and the ladies costumes, but now most were wearing their cloaks.

David and Jenny wondered about that when a man came up to the Head with a bag, the Head thanked him and opening the bag took out their cloaks and his own.

"We had better put these on now I think." Said the Head, passing the children their cloaks, it no longer looked like a Conference nor did it feel like one.

People had started to move about a lot, groups had appeared to be settled then would get up and move to another part of the hall, and as they made their way there they would be joined by the odd person, then by a group of two or three or five or six.

Others around the hall would stand up and go and join them and so it went on.

The Head was starting to look very worried, a few people around them had got up and moved away but others had moved over and joined our group.

Jenny overheard the Head asking the Wizard on his right,

"Where are all our supporters?"

"I'm wondering that myself." He answered, "Although here comes a few more," there was nodding of heads in recognition and a large group filled some vacant seats dotted about in front and around us.

One of the newcomers was a young looking Wizard who sat directly behind Jenny who was sitting to the left of the Head-master with David on her left.

"I think we are out numbered about 2 to 1." said the man sitting to the right of the Head.

"2 to 1!! Surely not as bad as that." queried the Head as he looked around the Hall, "I hope you're wrong." He added in a very worried voice.

But before anyone else could speak the lights were dimmed and a very tall thin Wizard appeared on centre stage with one sole spotlight on him.

"Ladies and Gentleman," he paused and started thumping the stage floor with the heavy stick he was carrying. The babble of talking became fainter until there was an eerie total silence.

Jenny and David started to feel frightened.

"Ladies and Gentlemen," repeated the thin Wizard, "Fellow Wizards, I welcome you one and all to this 'Oriliance' the first we have had for many years and I call upon all those present to conduct themselves as befits a Wizard."

The Grand Wizard from South America on stage to my right will introduce the challengers, a challenge will deem to be over when one party admits defeat."

"It is now 1.45p.m and I declare the 'Oriliance 'has begun."

The tall thin Wizard left the stage and now the spotlight was on the Grand Wizard from South America who was standing close to the wings at the left side of the stage to leave as much stage space as possible for the contestants. He raised his arms and announced:

"Wizard Harry Hutchinson from Australia - challenges - Wizard Raybold Robinson of New Zealand."

The crowd remained silent, then a Wizard 2 rows down on our right stood up and declared,

"I accept the challenge." And he walked down towards the stage as another Wizard appeared from the side of the stage.

Meanwhile back at Crinkles all was peace and quiet.

Miss. Millthrop and Smithers had half thought that at noon on the dot something would start to happen, but nothing did, and when it got to 1.30p.m. They decided to have some refreshment.

However Mr. Smithers was as bad as David when it came to eating, and Miss. Millthrop was dismayed to see how fast the sandwiches were disappearing, she couldn't stand it any longer,

"Mr. Smithers, I thought I had if anything prepared too much food but at the rate you're eating those sandwiches we won't have anything left for our tea."

Smithers gave her one of his sneers, "Surely having to sit here for hours bored out of my mind you don't begrudge me one or two sandwiches, do you?"

"One or two sandwiches no, but one or two dozen! You're eating them that fast that you couldn't possibly know what's in them."

Smithers didn't reply, he stuffed one last sandwich into his mouth and stormed off down the Library carrying his chair with him. Miss. Millthrop tidied up and was trying to think of somewhere to hide the food. Smithers looked at his watch, it's not even 2.00p.m yet he thought, I've got another ten hours of this, if only I could take a book down to study but the Head said no book was to be removed from the book shelves until his return.

Meanwhile at the 'Oriliance' the Australian Wizard had put a spell on the New Zealander and he was hopping about like a kangaroo.

He was trying his best to defend himself with a spell but couldn't manage it because of all the hopping up and down.

The delegates were roaring with laughter, David was laughing his head off and Jenny giggling away, neither noticed how stony faced the Head was.

The Australian Wizard was also stoney faced, but after a while he started to laugh until eventually he was laughing so much himself that his spell started to wear off.

The New Zealander grabbed his chance and managed to cast a spell on the Australian Wizard, he caught the Ozzie by surprise when a shower of lager cans started to descend on him, fortunately, or unfortunately some would say the cans were empty.

The audience didn't know where to put themselves with laughter, the Ozzie was just about to fight back as the rain of empty cans began to ease off when down came an empty can open at one end and so large it completely covered him.

Jenny and David had to hold their sides with laughter, the Ozzie crawled out of the can and cried out that he was defeated. The audience gave him nearly two minutes of applause.

Next to be announced were two Canadian Wizards, one challenging the other over a claim that he could build or should we say Wizard up the 'World's Best Snowman'.

Back at Crinkles there wasn't much laughter in the Library, Smithers nerves were almost at breaking point as Miss. Millthrop had brought her knitting with her. Knitting, of all the things for the silly old fool to bring thought Smithers, the click, click, click, of the needles in the silent Library was like a dripping tap to Smithers.

In desperation he was now sitting in the toilet as it wasn't quite so loud in there. He was sitting with his elbows on his knees and his hands over his ears, he looked at his watch 2.10p.m. It couldn't be? It must be later than that, he listened to it, yes it definitely was ticking but he gave it a shake just the same.

I was pottering around doing a bit tidying up in my workshop when one of the pupils came racing in breathless,

"Come quick Brian," he said, "There's a fire in the potting shed it's getting quite big."

I dropped everything and dashed after the boy, some pupil must have been having a sly smoke it has happened before.

I was almost at the potting shed and could see up ahead quite a few pupils, some had formed a bucket chain to help the gardeners who were throwing buckets of water onto the fire and refilling them from the old water butt. A couple of Masters had started to connect a garden hose to the outside tap on the laundry wall, what surprised me was how large the fire was.

Then I suddenly remembered what the Head had said the other night. Something didn't feel right about this, I stopped and turning began to run back to the School one or two of the pupils who I passed looked very surprised and shouted back at me.

"Brian! Brian! Where are you going?"

I didn't reply but just kept running, but where was I running to? For want of a better destination I decided to run back to my workshop. I hadn't locked the door in my hurry to help fight the fire, now that I was back I checked out my cubby hole, everything looked okay here, or did it?

I had noticed something different but what was it? You know what it's like when you know the name of someone but can't remember it at that moment in time, and the harder you try the worse it gets.

I had subconsciously noticed something wrong, but what? The more I tried to work out what

it was the more confused I became. Right I thought, I'll go back outside in my mind's eye and I'll start from when I'd decided to do an about turn and go back to the School, I must work this out.

While I was trying to work it out Miss. Millthrop was outside the toilet in the Library,

"Smithers! Smithers! I need to use the toilet, I've been waiting for hours what on earth are you doing in there?"

Smithers looked at his watch, 2.20.p.m. he had been in there about 12 minutes, hours, where does she get hours from, he got up and opened the door,

"There it's all yours, you can stay in there for good as far as I care, as long as it stops you knitting, Oh! I've left the seat nice and warm for you."

"You're disgusting." And she slammed the door shut and put the bolt in.

"Tut, tut, temper, temper." He said, and walked away whistling to himself, he suddenly felt a whole lot better.

I had come back into the School, crossed the Main Hall then come up the stairs leading to my corridor, walked along to the door of my workshop and walked through into my den, wait a minute.....that's it! I've got it! There was a lot of dust on the ground in front of the workshop door, loft dust, that's what it is loft dust!!

I dashed outside, yes there it is, someone's up in the loft that's why they wanted me out of the way, this is the easiest and the best access of them all to the loft, but to where in the loft? Where did they want to be? Of course it's the Library.

Miss. Millthrop and Smithers won't open the door under any circumstances and that door and the bolts are really substantial, so the only alternative is to go in through the ceiling. I wasn't keen on it but knew I had to go up there myself.

Going back into my workshop I picked up and fastened on my tool belt and grabbed my most powerful torch, and my largest monkey wrench, aptly named in this case a monkey wrench for monkey business.

There was no time to hunt out the step ladder, so instead carrying out my chair and standing on it enabled me to open the loft trap door, but I couldn't find the rod to bring down the loft ladder from below, whoever was up there obviously had it with them.

Eventually I was able to bring the ladder down with a bit of a struggle and took up the large torch and monkey wrench, then I scrambled up into the loft, I stopped for a few seconds to let my eyes adjust to the darkness and to get my bearing as to which direction to go in.

Then off I went, slowly and as quietly as possible not daring to use my torch as I didn't want to pre warn them that I was also in the loft, I was assuming there maybe two people possibly more.

There was no light up ahead, they weren't using torches either.

It was absolutely pitch black and progress was so very slow, but there was nothing that could be done about that.

From my workshop to the Library is quite a long way when you're walking, but when you're travelling via the loft in the dark it seems like miles and miles away.

At the 'Oriliance' the first Canadians 'Magic Snowman' was excellent and he made it snow on stage, but the second Canadian's 'Magic Snowman' was just as good.

So the first made his grow larger and larger and the second Canadian did the same until both snowmen were absolutely huge.

The first Canadian then made his Snowman throw snowballs at the other Snowman, who then started to throw snowballs back, soon snowballs were flying everywhere, then there was roars of laughter when the two Giant Snowmen collapsed at the same time on to the two Wizards who were completely buried.

David and Jenny thought that all of this was brilliant, the stuffy conference discussions had all been forgotten, this was absolutely great fun.

At Crinkles the potting shed fire had been put out, there was quite a bit of damage but nothing serious and no-one was hurt, but why had Brian ran off everyone was asking.

I was carefully making my way under endless roof trusses and along endless roof joists until eventually I could see someone up ahead, or was it two people? Yes, it's two people.

Surely they must hear me breathing I thought it sounded that loud, but what are they doing? Of course they're listening, trying to locate the Library and now they had thanks to Millthrop and Smithers arguing.

Millthrop had come out of the toilet and had been telling Smithers what she thought of him.

"I think you're disgusting Smithers, I have never been so insulted."

"Oh you must have been many times." Gloated Smithers who was starting to enjoy himself.

"Only a sewer Rat would talk about a lady like that."

As though searching for something Smithers looked up one isle than another, "Is there a lady around here? I can't see any."

"That's it! I'm not staying here another minute to be insulted."

"But you've got to." said Smithers sarcastically, "In fact you've got to stay here another," he looked at his watch, "another 570 minutes to be exact." Definitely a victory to me thought Smithers, he was really pleased with himself having put Millthrop in her place.

Miss. Millthrop said nothing walking away dejectedly, but then a gleam came into her eye, she would knit, no, she would knit and sing. She couldn't sing and she knew it, and she only knew all the words of one song, this was getting better and better she thought.

So she made herself comfortable and started knitting and singing heartedly at the top of her voice, singing the same song over and over again. Smither retreated back into the toilet and was already deeply regretting what he had said.

Millthrops singing was drifting up through the Library ceiling providing a perfect guide to the two dark figures ahead of me, they started to move on, but they had stopped again. I could hear her singing and I knew exactly who it was and so did the two vague figures in front of me.

They appeared to have something with them, although what, was impossible to make out. I decided this was close enough and now was the time for action. Taking the powerful torch out of my tool belt I pointed it straight at them and switched it on.

The effect was incredible, suddenly where everything had been pitch black it was now under a giant flood - light.

The two figures obviously taken completely by surprise swung round and now it was my turn for a shock,

"CECILIA!! - IAN!!" I gasped.

"BRIAN!!!" - Growled Ian, "I might have known you'd be poking your nose in."

"I know what you're intending to do but it won't work, you may be able to break through the ceiling but you won't be able to break the 'Containment'." Ian glared at me.

"You know far too much for a Caretaker more than is good for you."

Below in the Library Smithers could take no more of Millthrops singing and emerged from the toilet a beaten man, his victory had been short lived. Millthrop saw him approaching and started to sing all the louder.

"Miss. Millthrop" he pleaded, "Will you please accept my apologies I was just in a bad mood." Smithers had to shout this so that he could be heard. "But will you please stop all that singing."

Millthrop stopped, and apart from the ringing noise in Smithers ears there was total silence, bliss, oh perfect bliss he thought.

"What's that?" Asked Millthrop.

"What?" Said Smithers worried in case some fresh fiendish plot of Millthrop's was about to descend on his head.

"Listen!! There's someone up there in the ceiling."

"You mean above the ceiling. They can't be up there IN the ceiling, that's impossible!"

"Oh shut up and listen."

They both stood silent, straining to hear any noise.

"Yes you're right." Said Smithers, "There are people up there but I can't make out what they're saying."

"Neither can I." Added Millthrop, "What should we do?"

"What can we do?" said Smithers turning even paler than he usually was.

I was trying to persuade Ian and Cecilia to abandon their plan, I knew just by looking at Cecilia she didn't want to be involved in this, but Ian was different.

"Why are you against Crinkles?" I asked.

"We're not, and believe it or not I have developed a soft spot for Crinkles." Said Ian, "We just want what is rightfully the property of our 'Grand Master Wizard'."

"If you stop now and join us, the Head who is a gentle forgiving man I'm sure would allow you both to stay here at Crinkles for as long as you wish."

"Let's do that Ian, let's do that." said Cecilia holding on to his arm tightly and pleading with him, "You know I love you, we could be happy here Ian." Then she started to sob.

"But that's the whole point, I don't want to stay at a place like Crinkles and turn into an old cabbage like the rest of the Masters here." said Ian in an angry voice. "Cecilia and I are to be 'Master Wizards' in a few years time amongst Wizards who are dynamic and have great plans for the future and we are going to be part of those plans."

"No Ian, NO!! Let's change our plans, let's settle here you'll grow to love it I know you will." Cecilia was holding on to him with both arms, "You know I love you Ian we could be really happy here at Crinkles together."

"Let go of me." He cried, and he broke free, it was then that I saw the axe. He swung it above his head and brought it crashing down on the floor that split wide open from the blow.

Below in the Library the whole ceiling shook and Smithers and Miss. Millthrop had flung their arms around each other in fright.

Smithers soon recovered, "They're trying to break through the ceiling." He cried.

"Do something!! Do something!!" Shrieked Millthrop. "Do something!!"

"Do what? I'm an old dinosaur librarian what can I do?" replied Smithers.

Scorn was reigning blow, after blow, after blow, onto the floor and had already smashed a large hole through the floor boards and was starting on the ceiling latting and plaster, the next blow went straight through. Smithers and Millthrop ran clear but were still covered in dust and plaster and looked like two ghosts.

"STOP!! STOP!! - IAN." Cried out Cecilia.

He seemed to have forgotten about me, there was only one thing I could think of to stop him so I aimed my Monkey Wrench at his head and threw it with all my might, but he turned to swing the axe again and it glanced off his raised arm. He stopped and turned to face me with fury in his eyes,

"DON'T!!! Ian, don't harm Brian." Cecilia screamed out. Below Smithers and Millthrop were looking up into the loft.

"Try some Magic!" Called Millthrop to Smithers, "Stop him! Try some Magic!"

"I have it won't work."

"Neither would mine." Said Millthrop, "It must be the 'Containment' that's why he couldn't use his Magic to break in, it just won't work."

Scorn just stood there looking at me, he knew I had nowhere to run, and he was fitter and stronger than me and he had an axe. I will regret for the rest of my life what I did next, I saw him starting to raise the axe again and I knew that I was to be the target.

Cecilia was sobbing her heart out and muttering Ian, Ian, don't do it, I love you, you know I do, we'll work something out.

She was wasting her time, there was no turning back now for Ian. He started to twirl the axe above his head and moved towards me, I did the only thing I could think of, I switched off the torch and leapt in the darkness to one side, at almost the same time Cecilia let out a Blood Curdling 'SCREAM'!!

Down below Smithers and Millthrop were trying to see what was happening, terrified on the one hand to go to close to the hole in the ceiling but on the other hand wanting to know what was going on.

They heard the 'Terrible Scream' from Cecilia and three seconds later Cecilia came head first through the ceiling until her body was caught in the roughly hewn hole, she hung half in the loft and half in the Library.

There was silence for what seemed like an age but was probably only seconds, then we heard Millthrop Scream! and Scream! and Scream!

"My God she's 'DEAD'," shouted Smithers, "she's DEAD!! She's DEAD!!." He kept repeating.

Scorn threw down the axe in a rage and ran stumbling in the darkness past me.

I stayed hidden with my back against the wall crouching down next to a roof truss. I don't know how long I remained there but all the time I was there Millthrop was 'Screaming' and 'Screaming'.

Smithers was trying to comfort her, but after a while his natural self took over and he told her to shut up and get a grip on herself, and try and think what they should do?

Eventually I got some composure back but I didn't feel up to trying to get Cecilia's body back up into the loft and doubted that I could anyway on my own.

The Police would have to be called off course and they wouldn't want the body moved.

Calling the Police would have to be done later, what story to tell them was anyone's guess.

I had no idea where Scorn was, but somehow felt that we would never see him again, and I also felt that any other enemies left at Crinkles would be harmless compared to him.

I switched my torch back on and made my way to the hole smashed through the floor, I could hear Millthrop crying and Smithers muttering away to himself,

"It's me Brian." I shouted down.

"Oh Brian! Brian! Cecilia's 'DEAD'!!" Sobbed Millthrop.

"Yes I know, she was accidentally killed by Scorn, (I couldn't bring myself to say Ian anymore) but he's gone now and I'm sure he won't be back."

"Get the Police Brian! Get the Police! You could be wrong he could come back."

"No we can't do that, the Police can't do anything for Cecilia and they won't catch Scorn, you must both carry out the Heads orders and stay where you are, that will do more good for everyone concerned than the Police, they can come tomorrow."

"But what about Cecilia?" shouted up Smithers.

"I can't budge her without help so I'm afraid she will have to stay there for the moment."

"Oh, NO! NO! I can't believe this," sobbed Millthrop, "I can't believe this."

"I have to go now I can't stay up here." I shouted down, Millthrop was pleading with me not to go but there was nothing more to be done up in the loft and I may be needed elsewhere."

I couldn't then and I still can't get it out of my head that Cecilia would still be alive if I hadn't switched the torch off. Of course I may have been the one lying dead.

With a numbness and sense of unreality I retraced my steps and reaching the loft hatch climbed down the ladder, and then standing on my chair pushed the ladder back up and closed the hatch.

I put my chair back in my workshop and locked the door then went down to the main School to see if everything was okay, naturally all the talk was about the potting shed fire.

Numerous pupils and masters tried to stop me to ask: Why had I ran away from the fire? Where had I been? What had I been doing? I told them all it was too long a story to tell at the moment

It was 6.30.p.m. a long day still ahead of us.

I certainly didn't envy Millthrop or Smithers the next 5 $\frac{1}{2}$ hours. Now that things had quietened down I wondered what was happening at the Conference.

I decided to have a walk around the School grounds to clear my head, we really should be calling the Police, I knew it wasn't murder Scorn didn't intend to kill Cecilia it was an accident, it would be called manslaughter.

If I called the Police now they would be all over the place, the Library would have to be unlocked and Millthrop and Smithers taken away for questioning, the place sealed off and I would also have to be questioned.

What do we tell the Police? Of course normally you would tell the Police the truth, but what would they make of the truth? They wouldn't believe a word of it and who could blame them.

If we wait until after midnight what do we tell them to explain the delay?

After midnight! Oh no!! Suddenly a terrible thought came into my mind, it wasn't 6.30.p.m. in New York they were behind us but by how many hours?

I raced back to my workshop where I had a diary with time zones in it, flicking over the pages there it was, they are 5 hours behind us, it's only 1.30.p.m in New York.

Had the Head realised this? At midnight our time it would only be 7.00p.m in New York, we couldn't take the chance,

Millthrop and Smithers would have to stay in the Library for longer than they thought, another five hours to be exact.

I decided not to tell them this until about 11.30.p.m. our time, I thought that would be soon enough to give them the bad news.

As everything was quiet in the School I decided I'd better go back to the Library and see how they were managing.

I knocked on the Library door but everything stayed silent so I knocked again a lot harder,

"It's me Brian are you okay?" I shouted through the door, there was movement from inside then Millthrop's voice whispering that low I could hardly hear.

"Brian, Cecilia's body has gone."

"WHAT!!" I cried. "When? Where to?"

"It disappeared about half an hour after you left and the hole in the ceiling has gone as well the ceiling is perfect."

"Are you sure?" I queried in disbelief.

"Of course we're sure, do you think we don't know if a ceiling has got a hole in it or not?" It was Smithers, I noticed he never mentioned Cecilia just the ceiling of his beloved Library.

"Okay, okay," I said, "We've just got to stay calm, everything's going to be alright, I'm going back up into the loft to check it out I'll pop back later."

I didn't wait for a reply I knew what I had to do, I didn't want to do it but it had to be done.

I had to go back up into that loft, so it was back to my workshop tool belt on and as I had more time I found the stepladders opened the loft hatch and up I went.

At least this time I could use my powerful torch, but I still travelled very slowly shining my torch as I went into every nook and cranny.

I can't say what I was looking for because I didn't fully know myself, but everything was undisturbed, spiders webs were everywhere and I'm normally terrified of spiders but strangely this time it didn't bother me one bit.

I finally reached the spot above the Library, or had I? I wasn't really sure, there was no sign of any damage not even the dust disturbed.

It must be further on I thought but when I checked the dust hadn't been disturbed there either.

I started to thump the floorboards with my right foot, shouting as loud as I could,

"It's me Brian, are you there Miss. Millthrop? It's me Brian." But there was no reply, I tried again still no reply well I'm obviously not above the Library.

I back tracked to where I originally thought it was and tried again, this time Millthrop replied, looking around very slowly and carefully with my torch there was nothing unusual to be seen.

No sign of Cecilia's body I was glad to say, no axe, no sign that any hole had ever been there, undisturbed dust everywhere, the only sign of any disturbance being my own footprints.

Making my way back I thought how strange it all was. It had to be Magic yet how did it work?

Scorn couldn't use Magic to break in, if he could have used Magic he wouldn't have used the axe, Millthrop and Smithers couldn't use their Magic to stop Scorn breaking through, so why did the 'Containment' allow Scorn to remove Cecilia's body? And why did it repair the damaged ceiling? Then again perhaps it was the 'Containment' that removed Cecilia's body. I suppose we will never know.

Once I had secured the loft door again I went back to the Library and gave them a full detailed report through the closed door. All three of us were baffled, if it hadn't been for the fact that Millthrop and Smithers had also seen it I would be starting to wonder if I had imagined it all.

Well the problem about contacting the Police was solved, no point in calling them now they'd think we all had a screw loose, there was no body, no axe, no hole in the ceiling and over a century of undisturbed dust to prove there never had been a hole in the ceiling, best to leave well alone.

I went down to the Main Hall for some company, Checking on the Library every couple of hours to make sure everything was okay sounded about right and in the meantime I'm here if anything else crops up.

Suddenly I felt really hungry and very thirsty so I decided to nip along and see what Cook had underway.

My timing couldn't have been better, Cook was just taking a ham and egg pie out of the oven

it looked and smelt delicious. You're not supposed to eat it straight out of the oven but when Cook offered me a slice it was gone in seconds.

"You seemed to enjoy that Brian would you like some more?" Cook asked.

Would I, you don't have to ask me twice, four cups of tea and well over half the pie later and I felt full, mind you Cook wasn't too pleased when she saw how much pie was left.

Cook had been looking at me strangely for some time.

"Brian", she said, "where have you been down a coal mine? Your face is as black as the ace of spades." For a few minutes I'd forgot about everything, simply enjoying the Ham and Egg pie and the cups of Tea, now it all came flooding back.

CHAPTER TWENTY-TWO

The Oriliance' (Part Two)

Told by Brian with information from others:

David and Jenny could not remember the last time they had laughed so much this was great fun. Now if the whole Conference had been like this that would have really been something to talk about when they got back to Crinkles.

The last challenge had been a lift and hover challenge between an American and a French Wizard, they had lifted about 8 feet from the stage and for the first couple of minutes each was able to resist the other's attempt to topple them but then they both started to topple.

They tried to regain their balance and fell forward then backwards, then sideways, everyone loved it, then the French Wizard bet the American Wizard that he couldn't balance a mere 4 feet from the ground with a top hat in each hand both containing a dozen eggs for 2 minutes.

The American laughed and accepted the challenge this was going to be so easy, only to find they were Ostrich Eggs. Neither Jenny nor David had noticed that the Head and a few other Wizards around them had not laughed once and were sitting with very solemn faces.

The stage was now in complete darkness except for the one spotlight on the Grand Wizard from South America, standing on the left of the stage he announced the end of that Challenge and that the next Challenge is from the 'Master Grand Wizard eXactamus', from the Nile Valley who wishes to announce the Challenge himself.

All laughter had stopped and a chilly silence descended on the Hall, the spotlight went out and the stage was in total darkness.

Then a grey misty light came on, the Grand Wizard from South America had left and in his place in the middle of the stage stood 'eXactamus', he was very tall, with an ashen gray face almost totally concealed, and dressed in a very dark brown robe with a hat which sat flat on the top of his head but came down the sides of his face and over his shoulders down his back and blended in to his cloak. He looked like a 'Living Mummy' Sinister and Eerie, he stood silent, then raising his right arm a long thin finger emerged from a long thin hand pointing straight at the Headmaster.

In a strange unnerving voice that made you feel extremely uneasy, (you wanted to turn away, but you couldn't take your eyes away from him, you were totally transfixed) he said, "I challenge Christian Phillpotts, Headmaster of Crinkles Academy to release their 'Containment' on the 'Wizards of Evil Book' or face the 'DESTRUCTION' of Crinkles and their supporters."

A Wizard in the front row leapt to his feet,

"'OUT OF ORDER!!' 'OUT OF ORDER!! As the President of the Wizards Council I declare this 'ORILIANCE' ABANDONED!! Switch on the Full House Lights."

The house lights started to come on one by one and the Hall began to look more cheerful.

eXactamus had said nothing in reply, but he now spread his arms out. The sleeves of his robe were huge they hung down from his wrists in a great arch towards his feet. The visual effect was unreal, he looked twice the size of a normal person. Standing with the misty grey light swirling about him like whispy smoke he appeared to be some form of prehistoric huge bat about to fly. David and Jenny sat terrified, wishing it was the Hotel or better still Crinkles they were at. One by one the Hall lights had begun to go out once again until it was in total darkness apart from the grey misty light on eXactamus.

The President of the Wizard's Council sitting in the front row jumped up once more and in a loud angry voice declared:

"I advise ALL DELEGATES here to LEAVE THE HALL IMMEDIATELY."

eXactamus still holding his arms out spoke in a chilling deep clear voice, "Everyone is to remain seated, no one will be allowed to leave, all the exits are sealed." He paused and looked down at the Wizards in the front row that included not only the President but all the members of the Executive Council. Not one of them dared to look up into his face, there was no more protesting.

eXactamus turned again to face the Headmaster "I have not heard a reply from Christian Phillpotts. Does this mean he concedes defeat?"

The Conference Hall was totally silent, then slowly the Head stood up.

"I refuse your challenge." There was a loud 'GASP' from the assembly, the Head was still standing and spoke again.

"I propose David Taylor and Jenny Moffatt to take up the challenge on my behalf and on the behalf of 'Crinkles Academy' and all that Crinkles stands for."

"Two defenders!! But what of it, send them up."

The Head turned to David and Jenny, "Go on up" He whispered, "Remember what I told you, keep your eyes closed and under no circumstances open your eyes until I tell you to. Think only of things that made you happy or makes you happy, don't be afraid, I'm here and you have lots and lots of friends both here and back at home and at Crinkles who will give you support, they won't let you down. Think happy thoughts, sing happy songs in your mind and everything will be all right."

"I don't see anyone appearing." eXactamus paused, "Does this mean that they have refused the challenge and Our Book is to be returned to us?"

"NO!! The 'Containment Book' is not yours, it belongs to Crinkles." Replied the Head.

In a strong defiant voice, then continued, "They accept your challenge and are on their way to the stage."

"David, Jenny, go now." The Head whispered and gave each of them a little hug as they passed him to get to the aisle and to make their way carefully in the dark to the stage.

"What is this!!" Boomed out eXactamus, "CHILDREN!! You send Children to do a man's work. Well so be it, take your place." He pointed to a grey circle about 8 foot in diameter on the stage to his right near to the wings.

"YES! YES! HURRY!! HURRY!! and take up your positions." David and Jenny their whole bodies shaking walked unsteadily over to the grey painted circle, which they could only just see by the dull gray spotlight on eXactamus and stood in the centre.

The Headmaster watched David and Jenny follow eXactamus's instructions to stand within the grey circle. What have I done he thought, I was sure there was no other way but now that we are actually here it feels all wrong. I should be the one standing in that circle, I only hope we have enough supporters. Without Merlin I wouldn't have dared go this far, we would all be sitting back home at Crinkles awaiting our Fate.

eXactamus again spread out his arms, "Let the challenge commence."

"What do we do Jenny?" asked David in a total panic.

"What the Head told us to do are you stupid, close your eyes and no matter what happens don't open them till the Head tells us to, start to think happy thoughts, START NOW!!!" They had both close their eyes, David started to think about playing football, Jenny about her dog Jessie.

eXactamus started to fume, and in an angry voice declared:

"So you try to block me children, you defy me, you will not meet the challenge face to face, well we shall see."

There was no more thinking time now, it had begun, the Headmaster must concentrate.

eXactamus raised Dragons, huge and ugly, breathing fire and with thrashing tails and long sharp talons they were surrounded by dozens of tiny miniature dragons with huge hypnotic eyes and evil fangs. They charged ferociously at the circle time and time again but they all failed completely. None could penetrate the unseen defensive barrier.

David was playing football and nearly scored, and Jenny was stroking Jessie whose tail was wagging like mad.

eXactamus now tried Witches, as scary as anyone could imagine. They cackled and howled like banshees shrieking at an ear piercing pitch, they tried spell after spell until they became that exhausted they could barely stand, but they had no effect. Making strange cackling and moaning noises they crawled off the stage defeated. Next appeared fearsome monsters of every shape and size, they may as well have been soft cuddly toys.

eXactamus was growing angrier and angrier, two small children defying his mighty powers.

He closed his eyes and built up his 'Evil Energy' from his Supporters at the Conference and a swirling mist appeared, it grew denser and denser and the sounds of horses and muffled voices could be heard, then it slowly began to disperse and appearing faintly at first but clearer by the second was 'Saladin' sitting on his powerful horse, and now his mighty army was appearing behind and on either side of him.

Saladin looked around at the conference delegates and then at the Children. The Head was devastated. Vicious things like Dragons and the poor powers of Witches the Head had expected and presented no problems to the children.

But to conjure up 'SALADIN' and his Army, how can I have misjudged how strong the Evil Wizards had become, I can't match this, what am I to do? He looked over his shoulder to the young looking Wizard sitting behind him, to 'MERLIN', but he was looking straight ahead.

At Crinkles everything was peaceful, Millthrop and Smithers had not been talking to each other they were still thinking about Cecilia. Millthrop kept bursting in to tears, and Smithers was starting to feel hungry but he didn't know where Millthrop had hidden the food. He was afraid to ask her where it was in case it got Millthrop annoyed and that might start her really bubbling again which he certainly couldn't handle.

Ah well he thought. This time tomorrow I can relax with the whole place to myself again.

He was thinking about this when he felt the first very light tremors, there they were again and yet again, only a little stronger. He got up and almost ran to the 'Containment Book', Millthrop was already there,

"Did you feel that?" he asked.

"Yes, what is it?"

"I don't know, how am I supposed to know?"

I was on my way to the Library making one of my regular checks, everything was peaceful and quiet about the School. I had reached the Library door and was about to knock when I felt the first tremor then the second and the stronger third.

It feels like an earthquake I thought, no surely it can't be? Not here in England.

There it was again and again, inside the Library Smithers pointed to a book at the far end of the aisle.

"Look at that book!!" Millthrop turned and just a few feet away a book was slowly starting to move out of the rack,

"There's another!!" She said, "And another, what do we do?"

"Push them back in." Said Smithers, "keep them in." As he spoke he ran down the aisle and pushed the books back but others had started to move out all over the place.

Smithers and Millthrop were now charging about all over the Library pushing books back in but for everyone they pushed back another 2 or 3 would start to move out and as though that wasn't bad enough they were becoming harder and harder to push back.

I could hear all the commotion going on inside and shouted:

"What's happening? Tell me what's happening?"

Millthrop shouted back in a panicking voice explaining their predicament, "there are books all over the floor now." She cried.

Smithers was going berserk, "My books!! My books!! My beautiful books, don't stand on them, watch what you're doing you silly woman, keep your great ugly feet off them."

I started banging on the door, "Let me in." I shouted, "Let me in."

"The Head said don't let anyone in, we aren't allowed to open the door you know that." replied Smithers.

"Don't be stupid, he didn't mean me and this is an emergency he couldn't have forseen, you need all the help you can get."

"Let him in," shouted Millthrop, "go on let him in."

Smithers in desperation to save his books decided that help was needed, and unlocked the door, I rushed in and couldn't believe my eyes it was utter chaos.

"The books!! The books!! Watch the books boy." He shouted as he relocked the door.

"LOOK!!" I yelled, "Forget these books just let them fall."

"What!! Are you mad?" Cried Smithers.

"No but you are you old fool, you can't do anything here, it's the 'Containment Book' and its immediate books we have to protect."

"He's right you know." Cried Millthrop.

"Yes he is." Acknowledged Smithers and we ran to the centre of the Library and not a minute too soon.

The 'Containment Book' was still firmly in position but the books around it were starting to try and move out, we rammed those books back in.

The far shelves in the Library were now completely empty, books were piled 3 to 4 feet deep in some places on the floor and the shelves nearer to us were emptying rapidly.

The books on the floor were starting to open up and the pages to flick over, at first just 2 or 3 books then 50 or 60 then hundreds and hundreds all with their pages flicking over, the noise was deafening.

It made you want to put your hands over your ears but of course you couldn't if you wanted to keep the 'Containment Books' in.

"I can't stand the noise much longer." shouted Millthrop.

Of course that's it, I suddenly realised the books are trying to make us cover our ears with our hands to stop us pushing them back in. I rummaged around in my pockets.

"Why have you stopped?" Yelled Smithers.

I thought I had some, yes I have! I pulled out some paper hankies and tore some in to strips then rolled them up stuffing them into my ears it was shear heaven, it didn't stop the noise completely but it dulled it to a bearable level.

I tore some more strips off rolled them up and handed them to Millthrop, she took them and popped them into her ears.

I couldn't hear her but I saw a look of delight on her face, more strips rolled up and I passed them to Smithers and even he nodded in gratitude.

It was taking all three of us working flat out to keep the main books next to the 'Containment Book' in position, even then we had lost 3 or 4 but we couldn't keep this up for hours and hours.

It was then that I noticed that a lot of the books were no longer flicking their pages over as though they knew it was a waste of time.

"Give me the door key." I told Smithers.

"What for?" he growled

"Just give me the key." He reluctantly handed it over, "I'll be straight back, keep up the good work."

Millthrops faced dropped when she realised that I was going and Smithers scowled at me.

I stumbled and fought my way over the piles of books, no point in worrying what damage I was doing to them, time was of the essence. It was fortunate the Library door opened outwards or I would have lost valuable time trying to clear enough books away to open it, as it was I lost time just clearing books away from the keyhole.

I unlocked the Library door and didn't even try to lock it behind me as there wasn't the time and in any case I would be going back in soon, I raced to where I had been working a couple of days ago.

There lay my hammer, nails and planking, I picked up the hammer and nails and stuffed them into my tool belt, was I glad I had kept it on. Now I gathered up as many planks as I could manage and was off back to the Library as fast as was possible.

I struggled with all the gear and the door but got back in and clambered my way over the books, I shouted at Smithers that he had better go and lock the door and told him the key was in the lock.

He scrambled past me and I noticed they had been losing the battle since I left, there were 20 or 30 books now on the floor near the 'Containment Book.'

"Miss. Millthrop," I cried, "grab hold of this." And I passed her one end of a piece of 3 by 1, "Hold it up level with me." She realised what I was up to and held it in place as I hammered a 3-inch nail through the plank into the book case at my end then the same at her end.

Smithers was back, he didn't say a word but I knew his heart sank when he saw me hammering these huge nails in to his beautiful mahogany book cases.

But it was working, Smithers kept on pushing as many books back as he could on his own while Millthrop helped me nail up the planks.

"I'm going back for more planks," I said, "give me the key." Off I went leaving them to frantically push in the books that were not yet boarded up.

But I had problems this time, the books knew what I was up to and were piling themselves up to try and stop me.

I managed but I knew that this would have to be my last journey, I collected as many planks as I could possibly handle and fought my way back with them. I then left Smithers with the not easy task of relocking the door.

30 minutes later the three of us sat on the floor with 50 to 60 books scattered about but most of the main ones still in position around the 'Containment Book', all held in position with 3 by 1 planks and 3 inch nails.

The rest of the Library was in a total shambles, it would take weeks and weeks to sort out, and no doubt quite a few of the books would be badly damaged.

Once we had secured the main books we tried to put some of the other books back, but it proved impossible, the books lay quiet now every shelf was empty except the main ones everything was peaceful again but the books on the floor wouldn't allow us to pick them up to put them back on the shelves.

We all sat silently as no one wanted to talk, especially Smithers who sat with his eyes closed he couldn't bear to look at the damage.

At the 'Oriliance' eXactamus called out loudly,

" 'SALADIN', command your army to defeat my enemies." And he pointed to David and Jenny.

The Head turned to Merlin:

"Merlin you must help me, I beg you, help me, I don't have the power to fight 'Saladin'. We must save the Children."

Merlin turned and looked at the Head, the Heads heart sank it was a 'Look of Contempt', he obviously feels I shouldn't have endangered the Children, I should have been more prepared, I'm lost and so are David and Jenny.

Saladin's horse reared up and he sent two of his men galloping towards the Children. David was on a toboggan run with his friends and Jenny was wrapping and putting Christmas presents around a Christmas tree which was gaily decorated with multicoloured lights, coloured baubles and Silver and Gold tinsel.

Saladin had misjudged his enemy, his first attack could not break through their defences. His two soldiers hit the invisible wall of love and returned unhurt but shaken. 'Saladin' ordered four more men to join the original two, surround the circle and all attack simultaneously, his mighty voice was urging them on.

This attack was also a complete failure, the six huge warriors didn't have the strength left to lift their damaged swords, and the circle was now surrounded by discarded broken spears. Their bodies ached from torn muscles, they couldn't understand how the two children could be clearly seen but when they tried to cut them down they may as well have been striking solid stone.

'eXactamus' and 'Saladin' were fuming, this was an affront to Saladin's army and hence to him. 'Saladin' called to his men and gathered them around him for a massive attack nothing would withstand this.

The Head was pouring out all the energy he could to try and defend David's and Jenny's invisible wall of love, but it was the wrong sort of energy it was aggressive energy so he had to stop.

'Saladin' was ready to launch his attack, he had formed his men into rows, row after row would attack, fall back and immediately be replaced by the next row, then the next, on and on until like solid stone being hit repeatedly it would crumble, so to would the invisible protective wall collapse under the repeated attacks.

Then Merlin stood up, "I can't allow this injustice to go on any longer, I call on 'KING ARTHUR' and the 'Knights of the Round Table'." There was another gasp from the delegates and there before them was King Arthur and his knights slowly starting to appear.

'Saladin' turned away from the Children and grinned, a grin which turned into a vicious cruel smile and he declared:

"At last a 'WORTHY ENEMY' who we can fight face to face, man to man, as it should be, 'Saladin' has no fight with Children."

"NO!! NO!!" Cried out eXactamus, "The Children first, 'KILL THE CHILDREN FIRST', then Arthur, THE CHILDREN FIRST!!!"

'Saladin' was not listening. He was preparing for battle with 'King Arthur'.

The Hall was pitch black, you didn't feel that you were sitting in a Conference Hall, you felt alone in outer space witnessing a scene from the past.

On your right-hand side King Arthur and his Knights were assembled, and on your left-hand side Saladin and his Army, they all appeared huge about double life size. Their horses pawed the ground and hot air came from their nostrils, you could smell the horses and feel the heat from their bodies, the conference members looked from one side to the other in total amazement.

'Saladin Roared', "Death to Arthur." And he and his men broke into a gallop.

'King Arthur called out':

"For England." and they broke into a gallop, the two groups thundered towards the stage and swung towards each other.

A huge roar went up from both sides and there was a mighty clanging as swords hit swords and swords hit shields. The horses reared up and snorted in fright, the first men from both sides were falling to the ground, some seriously or mortally wounded.

Both Saladin and Arthur were trying to fight their way through a forest of men and horses to do battle with each other. Arthur was fighting two of Saladins men one on either side of him, he raised the magnificent Excalibur and dismounted one rider with a ferocious blow which cut through his shield like a knife through butter.

Arthur turned as a mace sliced through the air only a fraction of an inch above his head.

Saladin was charging straight at Arthur from his blind side, but one of Arthur's Knights spurring his horse on galloped across the front of Saladin, but misjudged his swinging blow, his sword was only cutting through air, whilst he caught the full blow from Saladin that was intended for Arthur, it cut straight through the Knights chain mail and into his neck and he reeled to one side hanging down from the saddle of his horse as it reared up and galloped off.

Arthur unaware of how close he had been to death had slain Saladin's other warrior he had been fighting, and was now galloping to the aid of one of his Knights under attack by three of Saladin's men.

Saldin himself was now under attack by two of Arthur's Knights, whilst all around there were small battles taking place all a part of the main battle, some fighting one to one, some two against three, three against one, some had been unseated from their horses and continued the fight on foot.

The Head was directing all the powers he was receiving directly at Arthur he barely saw the actual battle as the concentration required was enormous.

Arthur had reached the lone Knight just as he had brought down one of Saladin's men but Arthur was too late to help the Knight who was falling mortally wounded by blows from both the other riders.

Arthur cut both the men down with two mighty blows from Excalibur. Saladin had seriously wounded both the knights that had surrounded him and looking up saw a clear route through the fighting men to Arthur who had his back to Saladin as Arthur was fighting four men to save an injured Knight.

Saladin spurred his horse on shrieking, "Death to Arthur." Arthur turned just in time to see the mighty sword blow descending and lifted his shield but the blow was so great that Arthur was dismounted.

Saladin galloped on unable to rein in his horse quickly enough to strike a second blow, he turned and galloped back towards Arthur who stood facing him with his shield protecting his left side and mighty Excalibur in his right hand.

He waited until Saladin was almost on top of him and he was in danger of being trampled under Saladin's horses hooves then at the very last moment he swiftly side stepped, holding his shield up he protected himself from another tremendous blow and managed a glancing blow at Saladin as he rode past which cut through the chain mail on his thigh and into the flesh.

With blood pouring from his thigh Saladin reined in his horse again and turning swiftly galloped on to renew his attack, but to Saladin's right a Knight was battling with one of Saladin's men when his horse reared and threw him into the path of Saladin whose horse stumbled over the Knight's body and Saladin found himself unseated but unhurt from the fall.

He swung swiftly round to face Arthur who was making his way towards him. They stood face to face exchanging blow after blow neither giving even an inch.

The Head suddenly lost his power, he tried to regain it but unfortunately at that very moment Saladin was bringing down a crashing blow on Arthur who being temporarily reduced in strength was forced down on to one knee.

The Head regained his power and fed it to Arthur who fought his way back up on to his feet and brought down a terrific blow on Saladin which stopped him for a couple of seconds and had forced his shield down.

King Arthur trying to take advantage of this swung Excalibur far round to his right at Shoulder height and swung the sword in a horizontal arc at incredible speed with the intention of hitting Saladin on his left side that was temporarily unprotected by his shield.

Arthur had put all his strength into the swing but half way through the swing Excalibur hit the saddle of a rider-less horse which had suddenly appeared and was passing at full gallop.

The blow was so fierce it jarred through the whole of Arthur's body, there was a tremendous cracking noise and the end of Excalibur broke away leaving a jagged end and the jarring had made Arthur drop what was left of Excalibur.

The rider-less horse lay dying, Excalibur had cut clean through the saddle and deep into the horse's side.

This was a desperate situation but worse was to come, the Heads incoming power sources were failing, Crinkles supporters were losing their energy it was almost drained , the Head had also called up and used all the energy from their supporters here at the conference.

If it had not been for Merlin they would have been defeated an hour ago and all would have been lost.

The energy of the old friends and past pupils of Crinkles had also been used up as had the energy of the parents of the present pupils, the pupils themselves and the Masters.

The Head could think of no more supporters he could call upon to draw energy for King Arthur in the fight for Good over Evil, he couldn't help David and Jenny and helping King Arthur had used up all his power.

The position of David and Jenny was just as desperate. Their protective barrier of good thoughts was almost exhausted.

When the same good thought is used time and time again it grows weaker and weaker and they had used up their whole store of good thoughts and used them over and over again.

Some as many as 6 times, those thoughts were now virtually powerless.

Arthur lay on his side trying to stave off blows with his shield which was bent and battered and still Saladin reined blows down on to him. Arthur's sword Excalibur lay broken beside him.

Surely the Evil Power Source must also be weakening by now thought the Head yet it didn't seem to be.

Groups of Evil Wizards around the hall had started chanting, "Arthur, submit, Submit, SUBMIT."

The Head dare not think what the situation was like back at the Library obviously the 'Containment' was seriously weakened, if it totally collapsed then all was lost, anything achieved here would be in vain.

If Merlin decided that Arthur's wounds were that serious he had to call a halt they were beaten. The Head looked at Merlins face but it gave nothing away, the Head felt that if it was his King he would be stopping this slaughter soon.

A Wizard in the front stood up and cried out:

"I call upon all the Wizards who are benefitting from the Wizards In Need Charity to repay Crinkles kindness in donating their 'Team Quadro' tickets to the Charity by giving power to Crinkles."

This was greeted by laughter and jeering from the Evil Wizards,

"So now you call upon the down and outs, the no hopers, the failures, the has beens." they shouted out loudly then started to jeer.

This was a mistake, the Wizards for Good at the Conference whose power had been drained found their anger rising and with it a last spurt of Magic energy. The Head felt it and it was building, not a great energy but it was there and rising, it was coming not only from inside the hall but also from outside. The Wizards in Need were responding, they might not have much to give but what little they had they were giving. Some of the Wizards at the 'Oriliance' who had been undecided who to support and had been neutral were so incensed at the jeering at Wizards who had fallen on hard times that they decided to back Crinkles. The Head directed it all at Arthur every last drop of energy he could muster.

There in front of them on the battlefield Arthur was starting to rise slowly back onto his feet.

The blows of Saladin still being deflected by Arthur's shield, he had picked up Excalibur as he rose and now stood upright with blood pouring from his shoulder, his side and his thigh.

Arthur's chain mail was ripped and in tatters, his magnificent helmet with its gold crown dinted and splattered with his blood.

His white tunic more red than white, his beautiful shield twisted and dented beyond recognition and the magnificent sword Excalibur now only half a sword with the end snapped off leaving a ragged edge where once had been a fine honed, glistening cutting edge.

Saladin huge and ferocious looked immaculate compared to Arthur, true Saladin had some minor dents in his shield and one tear in his chain mail on his right thigh that had been bleeding but in comparison he was virtually untouched and full of energy.

Arthur although back on his feet was moving too slowly and could not catch Saladin with any of his blows whereas every blow from Saladin hit their mark.

The Head could feel the last power surge starting to fade and looked at Merlin, the Head's eyes pleading for help.

'Merlin' was staring straight ahead and then he stood up:

"I Merlin, Master of Master Wizards call upon all supporters of Crinkles World Wide for one last effort, and on all good Wizards Worldwide and all Wizards who as yet have been undecided whom to support, to support Crinkles and in so doing support myself Merlin and King Arthur the like of whom we shall never see again."

"Give me one last effort, give me you're all, and give it now."

There was no jeering now from the Evil Wizards, the Evil Wizards spokesman stood up,

"I call upon ...." but before he could continue further, chants of

"SIT, SIT, SIT." started in the Hall as the Evil Wizards had already used up all their rallying calls. The Wizards for Good had started to gain confidence and no longer prepared to be subdued by the Evil Wizards.

It seemed as though the whole Hall was chanting, SIT! SIT! SIT! and the noise was so great that the Evil Wizard couldn't be heard so he was forced to sit.

Some of the Evil Wizards were looking doubtful for the first time.

However Merlin's last call meant that we had now used up all of our rallying calls.

Arthur was staggering back against the reign of blows from Saladin's great sword, he was beaten, he was about to fall again, his legs weary from the long fight could barely support him.

The Head started to feel the response to Merlin's call, the first of course from the nearest Wizards here in the Hall, incredibly from some deep, deep recess of the mind, the good Wizards in the hall were drawing out the very last of their power, there was nothing left to be called upon after this.

The Head immediately directed this to Arthur it was enough to strengthen his legs he no longer looked on the verge of collapse.

The energy was still coming in from the Hall and now joined by power from outside, from here in America, now Canada, South America, Australia, New Zealand, Japan, Africa and Asia, China, Germany, France, Holland, Spain, Greece it was flowing in so fast and so powerful the Head was struggling to receive it and pass it on to Arthur.

The Head saw Merlin watching him and Merlin gave him a slight smile which is almost the equivalent to a Knighthood in Magic Circles.

It was coming from England now, from the old friends of Crinkles again, the parents, the children at the school, the Masters, they had all found one last reserve of energy.

The Head beamed and beamed the energy at Arthur.

Arthur was no longer retreating but standing upright and firm and holding his ground, fending off blows from Saladin, parrying others and actually starting to land blows in return.

The Head still had energy coming in, his reserves were not draining away but there was not enough there to enable Arthur to attack Saladin only to hold his own.

Saladin certainly didn't look drained although he had suffered some damage in the last few minutes, actually more damage than he had dealt out.

The Head was still gathering every bit of energy he could from every corner of the World, from Finland, Portugal, Denmark even little Gibraltar and Malta.

Then he had a massive surge, this was not from someone who had given and given again this was a fresh energy source and very powerful. A Very Powerful source indeed but from where? The Head was that busy taking the power in that he had not been passing it fully on to Arthur, who was starting to fall back from a fresh onslaught from Saladin.

It's from England, the Head knew the power was from England, but what incredible power, where in England? Who in England?

A great 'Oh', from the crowded Hall brought the Heads attention back to Arthur who had stumbled and was down on one knee.

The Head directed all the energy he could at Arthur who fended off a furious blow and leapt to his feet and fought back.

Saladin and Arthur stood toe to toe reigning blows on each other.

The Head could feel more and more power pouring in to him, he was able to supply Arthur and still build his power up, then the Head had a surge so powerful he nearly blanked out himself and for a split second he saw the source, Cecilia and Ian both smiling at him.

Then the power stopped, that was it, there would be no more power from anyone.

The Head looked at Arthur standing upright and trading blow for blow with Saladin, he looked at Merlin who gave the Head a hardly noticeable nod.

The Head looked back at Arthur and poured energy in to him at such a rate that the Head started to reel and so did Arthur for a couple of seconds, then he forged forward reigning powerful blow after blow on to Saladin who was now holding his shield high for protection Arthur was driving him back and back.

Saladin tried to rally time and time again but to no avail. The Head poured in the energy no point in holding anything back it was now or never.

Arthur brought the remains of Excalibur down on to Saladin's shield with such a blow that the shield split in half and Saladin was forced to throw it away as it was now a hindrance.

Saladin now had no protection, Arthur still had his shield even though battered and badly damaged. Saladin tried one last great rush at Arthur and drove him back a couple of paces.

This is it, our last chance thought the Head and powered every last bit of energy he had at Arthur. The Head blanked out and lay slumped in his seat.

The last surge was like a thunderbolt to Arthur, who had just parried Saladin's last blow at him.

When the last huge surge arrived Arthur drove Saladin back and back and back until Saladin could parry no longer, his strength gone. With no shield to protect him and his knees giving way he could not hold his ground and he could not retreat.

He went down on one knee as Arthur had earlier but with no shield and no strength left to use his great powerful sword to parry off Arthur's blows he saw Arthur raise Excalibur broken and chipped above his head whilst holding his shield in front of him in case of a body thrust from Saladin before Arthur could land his blow.

Arthur did not know that Saladin didn't have the strength to produce such a blow, Saladin watched Excalibur descend like a guillotine from above Arthur's battered helmet with the golden crown on it, he watched Excalibur come slicing through the air and Saladin knew the battle and his life were over.

For a brief second Saladin felt Excalibur cutting through his steel helmet then he slumped to the ground. Arthur stood over him then he fell on to one knee, weary, exhausted, with many serious injuries but fortunately none fatal.

Arthur knew this was his last fight. The 'Powers of Good' would have to find a 'new champion' in the future.

The Head was still unconscious. Otherwise he would have seen the look of dismay on Merlin's face as for the first time he saw clearly Arthur's wounds.

The Hall was hushed. There was no cheering, no noise at all. Everyone knew they had witnessed an incredible battle the like of which few in the World had seen before and probably no one would ever see again.

There would never be another 'Oriliance' no one would dare risk it again.

The scene was starting to fade, the followers of Saladin were taking away the body of their leader and some of Arthur's Knights who had survived were tending to his wounds and his magnificent horse was nuzzling him.

One of the followers of Saladin had withdrawn Excalibur and wiping it clean returned what was left of it to Arthur bowing in respect as he did so. Arthur acknowledged this with a slight nod and the painful raising of his right hand in a salute.

The picture was fading more and more. Saladin's Army carrying their leader had already disappeared from view.

Barely visible now, you could just see Arthur being helped on to his horse 'Lamri' and with some of his remaining Knights on theirs they gathered in a group.

Then Arthur rode in front holding aloft the broken Excalibur with his Knights behind him, some on horseback but most on foot, a great number unable to walk without assistance they headed straight towards the Wizards.

Merlin saluted Arthur and Arthur saluted Merlin and the Head who had now recovered and was standing next to Merlin, King Arthur and his Knights were fading faster and faster and appeared as though surrounded in mist until they could be seen no more.

It was at least 15 minutes before the first whispering voices could be heard here and there in the Hall, more than 30 minutes before the first Wizards got to their feet. The doors were no longer sealed and some of the Wizards had started to leave.

Well over an hour later there was still a large number of Wizards sitting still and silent in the Conference Hall, too drained to move and trying to fully comprehend what had taken place.

However other Wizards were now in the Foyer and in various lounges and more and more talking in a normal voice no longer whispering.

David and Jenny had not seen or heard any of the great battle between King Arthur and Saladin. They had followed the Heads instructions and kept their eyes closed and thought about happy times and events.

They had been anchor points at the lowest point in the battle, their goodness holding firm had helped Arthur deal the final blow. They couldn't supply any of the energy needed by Arthur but they could and did although they weren't aware of it partially stop the full flow of Evil energy passing to Saladin.

As soon as Arthur and his Knights had left, the Head and Merlin had gone straight down to the stage to help the children, the stage was partly covered in a grey mist. David and Jenny still stood with their eyes closed. They no longer had the strange feeling of pressure to remember happiness, now the happy thoughts floated casually by whereas before they had been incredibly intense.

"You can open your eyes now David" said the Head "and so can you Jenny" and he put his arm gently around Jenny and Merlin put his around David, they opened their eyes and the Head gave them a big smile

"You both did VERY, VERY WELL." Said the Head. "We're very proud of you both."

"Did we?" Asked Jenny sleepily

"You certainly did children, by the way my name is Merlin"

The children looked in amazement, Merlin? But where is his beard? They thought, and he looks so young. "THE MERLIN?" They asked.

"Yes, 'The Merlin'" He replied.

The Head gave them another big smile and led them off the stage.

Slowly the mist cleared revealing a now completely empty stage. The stage looked so small now, yet everyone had seen not a small stage but a huge 'Battle Field'.

They all walked through the Conference Hall and on into the Foyer.

"Come on children time for us to go back to the Hotel and for you to have some well earned rest."

"And a meal Headmaster? I'm starving!!" Said David.

"Yes," said the Head smiling at David "and a Meal, a large one I think."

CHAPTER TWENTY-THREE

The Boy And The Black Knight

The Foyer of the Conference Centre was still packed will delegates the young ones didn't seem to want to go back to their hotels and were wandering about talking over the incredible events of the day.

The older delegates being so drained they could not get back to their hotels fast enough for some rest, but many were so tired that they sat snoozing in the easy chairs dotted about.

The Head, Merlin and four other older Wizards had decided to take David and Jenny to a new Hotel to avoid the crowds that would be waiting for them at their original Hotel.

Two taxis had been discretely organised and the Head asked one of the drivers if he could recommend a respectable and cosy Hotel, they accepted his recommendations and found themselves at a very old but what had been a very classy Hotel. Everyone was soon booked in and once in their rooms managed between them to summon up enough Magic to transfer some of their clothing and toiletries to the new Hotel.

David and Jenny had fallen asleep on their way across town in the cab but the Head still decided to put a sleeping spell on them to give them a really sound deep healing sleep free of any nightmares.

The Wizards all gathered in the spacious sitting room next to the children's bedrooms. It was large and cosy, a little thread bare here and there but still had an excellent charm and atmosphere, a reflection of its past grandeur. Merlin said he had urgent business to attend to but he hoped he would soon be back. The other Wizards all knew he was going to check on how badly injured King Arthur was and his Knights. The Head also offered his apologies and said he had an urgent phone call to make but would be straight back.

Ever since the 'Orriliance' had finished the Head had been wondering if everything was all right at Crinkles, and he was puzzled as to why he had seen Cecilia and Ian's smiling faces when that last huge surge of energy came.

The Head had some difficulties contacting Crinkles but eventually he got through to Miss. Millthrop.

"Oh Headmaster!!! I'm so glad to hear your voice, we've had a terrible time, a terrible time."

"Calm down Miss. Millthrop." replied the Head "Is everything alright now?"

"Well yes and no!"

"Don't worry Miss. Millthrop no one at Crinkles is in any danger whatsoever at the moment, is Brian there?"

"He's with Smithers helping in the Library."

"Could you go and get him please."

Millthrop came panting into the Library where Smithers and I had been trying to sort out some of the books and see how much damage had been done. She told me the Head was on the phone and wanted a word with me, a few minutes later I was speaking to the Head and quickly told him what had taken place. I assured him everything was being sorted and he had no need to worry, I asked if he, David and Jenny were okay and he assured me they were and looking forward to arriving back home but that wouldn't be for a few days yet.

When we had finished talking I checked my watch it was nearly 10.30p.m our time so it would be about 5.30p.m in New York. The times had been okay after all thank goodness.

I could have saved myself all that worrying, the main thing though was we'd done it, although I wasn't really sure what we had done!

Merlin was back when the Head returned to the sitting room, he looked at Merlin who smiled and nodded. Thank goodness thought the Head all is going to be well at 'Camelot'.

For some reason the sleeping spell had not put David and Jenny sound asleep in fact they felt wide awake. Jenny was calling out Headmaster and David mumbling something or other. The Head went into the bedroom with Merlin and decided he would try and persuade the children to go to sleep before he tried another sleeping spell. He had barely started his efforts to persuade the children to relax and rest when Jenny asked,

"Headmaster, could Merlin tell us a true story about 'King Arthur' and his Knights?"

"I'm afraid not children, Merlin is a very busy Wizard and he's also very tired."

Merlin was smiling,

"Oh I think I could manage a small story."

"You could!!!" Shouted David.

"Yes, but only if you promise to go straight to sleep at the end of the story."

"We will!! We will!!" Chorused Jenny and David.

"Then I will begin, this is a story of a young man, nay a young boy with the strength and determination of a young man who feels he has right on his side, a very powerful ally to have. This is the story of The 'Boy and The Black Knight'."

The boy had travelled for many days, days that had turned into weeks. He lived off the fruits of the forest, apples, berries, mushrooms, fresh spring water which he gathered in his water skin, some of the food he stored in his coarse woven bag.

He had travelled from the far North of the country and now was close to his intended destination, 'Camelot', the castle of castles, King Arthur's Castle.

In his eagerness to arrive without any further delays he decided to travel through the 'Great Wood' rather than the winding twisting road. The boy had entered the wood early in the morning and it was now a little after mid-day. He was selecting fruit from heavy laden blackberry bushes when he was startled by a strange voice from behind him.

Turning he found himself face to face with a very old lady carrying a large bundle of dry twigs on her back. She asked could a young gentlemen like himself help a tired old lady take her burden of twigs back to the little house where she lived so that she could have a cosy warm fire that evening, to keep the cold and damp out. Her house wasn't far away it wouldn't take him long.

The boy was puzzled, he had hearing as good as a Foxes yet he had not heard the old lady approaching, looking down at the ground which was covered in small twigs, nothing, not even the lightest Fawn could travel over that ground and not be heard. Further thoughts went from his mind as the old lady pleaded with him for his help.

The reason he was in the woods was to save time, not to stop and dilly dally, and yet he was not expected, he would probably be turned away when he did arrive so did it really matter if he arrived later than he intended, no it didn't.

He tured to the old lady and smiling said it would give him great pleasure to help her. She made a strange laughing cackling noise as he took the large bundle of tinder from her. Follow me, follow me, she said still laughing and cackling. They moved off the main path and onto a very small path that the boy had not noticed before, within a few minutes they arrived at a small wooden house which blended into the forest so well you could have walked past it as close as thirty paces and not realised it was there.

Come inside, come inside, urged the old lady, come inside. Her eagerness made the boy feel uneasy. How long will this tinderling last you, asked the boy?

Oh, only a day or so replied the old woman.

Then I shall go and gather more and bring it back until you have a good supply, and with the axe I see you have there I will chop up some logs for you, that would keep you warm for days without you wearing yourself out.

No!! No!! This is all I need, come inside with me and rest a while. The boy looked at her and said, I couldn't rest knowing how hard you will have to work tomorrow and the day after when this afternoon I can ease your burden.

And so for three hours the young boy worked and toiled and made journey after journey back to the little log house. He did not look closely at the old woman, if he had he would have seen her becoming angrier and angrier, more and more agitated.

She mumbled away to her 'Black Evil Eyed Cat', what am I to do? What am I to do. He wont come into the house, he's going to escape us, do something don't just sit their she shouted at the Cat raising her foot to kick it as she so often did to reduce her anger. The Cat snarled and swiftly turning ran off to hide amongst the newly cut logs. The Witch watched the boy approaching with yet more logs and rushed into the house. Reappearing almost instantly with two wooden cups, the boy grinned at her, there you are that should keep you going for a few days, I will just stack this last load of logs then I must be off. The old lady tried to look pleasant and smiled but it had the opposite effect, she looked unreal.

Rest awhile before you go, I've made us a nice refreshing drink of crushed fruits. That was very kind of you but I have my water here and that's all I ever drink.

I'll just leave a drink beside you on the chopping block you may changer your mind.

The boy didn't answer continuing with his work.

Smiling to herself the Witch silently glided back to her log house and once inside cackled away to herself with glee as she watched the back of the boy working away. She knew there was no way anyone could resist the delicious aroma from the crushed fruit and spices in the cup. Like everyone else before him he would drink it, and only one mouthful was needed for anyone to belong to her forever.

The Evil Cat hated everyone, but most of all it hated its Mistress the Witch, peeping out from the log pile it watched the Witch looking through the window of her house it saw her evil grin and grinned itself as it silently and swiftly leapt onto the chopping block and deliberately knocked over the wooden cup which landed noiselessly on a bed of pine needles at the boys feet. The Cat leapt back down and hid once more in the log pile, a couple of minutes later the boy whose back had hidden all this from the view of the Witch was surveying with satisfaction his work when he spotted the empty cup and picking it up he placed it back on the wood block.

He turned towards the log house and on seeing the old lady at the window gave her a cheerful wave and turning strode swiftly into the forest. The Witch watched him departing and once he was out of sight she dashed out of her log house and across to the large wood pile.

With glee she lifted up the empty cup, she would give the potion a few minutes to work then follow him into the wood and bring him back in her old wheelbarrow. A few minutes later the Cat watched her triumphantly heading for the tiny forest path.

The narrow path wound and twisted its way to the frequently used wide pathway through the woods. She was not surprised when she didn't find him slumped in the middle of the path, as often on becoming dizzy the poor doomed victim would stagger off and collapse in the dense undergrowth at either side of the path.

The Witch slowly and carefully checked the undergrowth and was surprised when she reached the main pathway and had not found the boy. She was becoming increasingly annoyed at herself and turning back she searched the undergrowth very slowly and very carefully but despite every effort she arrived back at her house on her own.

The Cat had never seen her so wild, she stormed into her house and the Cat could see and hear all manner of things being thrown about, then she reappeared and dancing a strange wild jig she pointed to the path leading into the forest and cursed and swore at it though she knew none of it would do any good.

Somehow the young boy had escaped her, the potion had not worked, there was not even a chance he may get lost in the forest and end up wandering back or be tempted back. He was at home in the forest as much as she was.

She would have to be patient until the next traveller came her way, the Witch went back into her log house slamming the door behind her. The 'Evil Cat' grinned with satisfaction and moved about making itself more comfortable and went into a sound contented sleep hidden in the log pile.

The boy was travelling a lot later than he had intended and was walking briskly though as usual with his eyes and ears searching for anything and everything. He faintly detected a horse and rider some distance ahead, then a loud neighing from the horse and a crashing noise at the same time, now he heard the horses galloping feet.

Without any thought for himself he broke into a run and within a few minutes surveyed the scene before him. Stretched between two trees was a stout rope and on the ground lay a Knight in Black Armour. The Knight lay unconscious, the boy tried to drag him to one side but could not move him. He looked around, he could neither hear or see anyone, although he knew it would not be long before someone arrived to see the results of their efforts.

The boy ran to the trees that had the rope tied to them and released it, he then ran a little way along the forest path and retied the rope to two other trees.

He was pleased to see that the Brigands or whoever they were had been generous with the amount of rope they had used. Taking his knife from his belt he cut through the surplus end and raced back along the forest path past the Black Knight and selected two trees and tied a second rope in position once more at roughly chest height.

The young boy ran back to the Black Knight, who still lay motionless. He tried to lift his sword but it was so heavy he could barely hold it two feet from the ground.

He could not use the sword in their defence, which left him his bow and arrows, unfortunately he was down to only six arrows.

Against armour they would be useless but against chain mail he could have some success.

The boy had barely found time to hide in the undergrowth when he heard riders approaching. He fitted an arrow to his bow and waited, three horsemen galloped along the path two out in front and one behind.

"We've got him!!!"

He heard one of the riders shout. The boy was relieved when he heard that, he had just realised they may have been innocent travellers. The first two riders galloped straight into the rope, one of them unseated crashed to the ground and like the Black Knight lay there motionless, the second rider tried to swing his horse sideways and collided with the rider behind him whose horse leaping up threw him to the ground where he also now lay motionless. The remaining rider had controlled his horse and was now preparing to make a run for it back along the path. The boy let go of the arrow with all the force he could muster, it sped at short range and full thrust into the thigh of the rider missing the bone it travelled through the other side of his leg and deep into the horses side. The horse went beserk, thrashing about wildly, careering into trees at either side with it's rider who hung limp and dazed taking a constant battering as it galloped off along the path.

In the midst of all this two other riders had approached from the other side of the path and having mistaken all this activity for some sort of battle they galloped head long to the aide of the others, straight into the second rope.

Once again a rider tumbled to the ground lying there motionless, the second rider had somehow or other dismounted, but on seeing the chaos around him was desperately trying to remount, just as he succeeded the boy let fly another arrow, straight and true it embedded in the shoulder of the remaining rider, to be followed by a second arrow in the thigh. He was screaming in agony and yelling out that he yielded, throwing his sword to the ground and falling off the terrified horse in a heap into the undergrowth.

The boy emerged from his cover, but still had a fourth arrow in his bow and his eyes darted about everywhere, his ears listening for any sound that might mean danger. He walked over to the one conscious man who lay moaning on the ground and the boy kicked the mans sword repeatedly until it was lost in the undergrowth and removing the mans knife from it's belt threw that as far as he could into the forest.

He then disarmed all the others and was greatly relieved when he saw signs of the Black Knight recovering.

A few minutes later the Black Knight was sitting with his back to a tree and his sword on the ground beside him. He was still trying to take in all that had happened.

One of the others had also started to come round but had been quickly dispatched back to the land of nod by the young boy.

The Black Knight had been asking where was everyone else, the boy explained there was no one else. The Knight couldn't understand how he had single handedly defeated four men, the boy told him five men but one had escaped, though he was in no fit state to present any problems.

The Knight suggested they should try and make their way out of the forest, he felt in no position to command or demand anything of this young warrior. The boy agreed as it would be growing dark in an hour or two. So with the help of the boy the Knight got to his feet and with the aide of a crutch made from a small branch started to make his way along the track and out of the forest.

The boy told him he would catch him up, he then removed the ropes from the trees and with his knife cut the ropes into shorter lengths. He bound the hands and feet and gagged the four horsemen and dragged them into the undergrowth. They would be safe there until later, unless of course some Wild Boar or Wolf should find them. He then tidied the track so that in the fading light it was barely noticeable that a small battle had taken place.

The Black Knight was travelling as fast as he could and listening for the approach of the young boy. It was nearly dark now and he was taken by surprise when the young boy appeared silently at his side. He was about to talk but the boy stopped him, best to stay as silent as possible until they had cleared the forest he whispered.

The Black Knight was in some considerable pain, but he didn't want the brave young boy to know that.

At last a long lazy bend in the forest path gave way to a straight path and a view to the now only just visible fields and road ahead.

Once on the road the boy waited until they had travelled a reasonable distance from the forest then he took out a small horn and blew and blew, he would stop for a few minutes then start to blow the horn again. The Black Knight was now leaning on the wooden crutch on his left side and on the boy on his right, their progress was only at a shuffling speed and it was pitch dark.

The boy blew and blew on the small horn, then at last they could see lanterns ahead.

Within a few minutes they were surrounded by half a dozen farmers with lanterns, they peered at the two of them, what a sorry sight they made. They were told to stop and sit at the roadside and others ran back to fetch a cart.

Soon more men and this time a number of women arrived with a large handcart. The Black Knight was lifted in and with the young boy walking alongside the cart was trundled towards a small group of farm buildings.

The cart was being manoeuvred into an old hay barn, but before anything further could take place a Knight arrived with six mounted pike men, word of strange horn blowing and strange goings on had reached the Castle and the Night Guard had sent out a patrol to investigate.

About an hour later and the Black Knight was on his way to the Castle in a horse drawn cart with an armed escort. The Boy was on his way back to the forest sitting alongside the driver of another horse drawn cart with its armed escort of three Knights and twelve mounted pike men. They were all surrounded by a group of farmers holding lanterns.

The boy led them straight back to the battle scene and within twenty minutes they had loaded four completely terrified bound and gagged men onto the cart. As they came out of the woods even more lantern carrying men had appeared and as far as the eye could see there were lanterns in ones and twos, fives and sixes all along the road up to the very gates of the Castle in the far distance.

The Castle itself was ablaze of light, dozens of torches had been lit along the outer walls, and the inner walls.

The internal square and the steps to the keep were thronged with people, children peeping out from every nook and cranny.

That many stories were circulating, dragons, elves in the woods, a great battle amongst the trees all completely fought in the pitch black of the forest, strange tales abounded.

No one slept much that night except the young boy and the Black Knight.

King Arthur ordered that they should not be disturbed and when they finally woke they should be allowed to eat uninterrupted. Later that day King Arthur heard the story of the battle from the young boy. Then he asked the Black Knight why he was in the woods and he told the King he was on his way to offer his services. Arthur asked how many armed men he brought with him. The Knight explained he had returned home to the far North after some two years absence and found his Mother, Father and two younger Brothers had been slaughtered along with many of his Father's old staff and retainers. That their Castle, lands and home had been stolen by Northern armed gangs in league with Scottish rougue Clansmen. He now had no family, no home, no friends and no money or any means of earning an income. He had made his way to Camelot to ask King Arthur to allow him to be one of his Knights.

Yet apparently despite being left with nothing his enemies still felt they were in some danger as long as he was still alive and had planned the ambush.

The King said apparently they were right, they are in some danger from him, as far as the young boy lending the Knight his support was concerned. Arthur told the Black Knight that he would accept him as a Knight, but unfortunately he would not be a 'Knight in Full' this was not his doing but Knights who had brought twenty or thirty armed men with them, the smallest number being six and paid for their training and upkeep as well as contributing generously to other costs would not condone Knights who had brought and contributed nothing of a financial kind to be 'Full Knights'.

He would unfortunately like many of the Kings other Knights not be invited to attend most of the social occasions, hunting parties, diplomatic visits and gatherings to discuss policy. Arthur went on to say that he would out of his own purse cover the day to day basic costs of the Black Knight including that of his fine horse which had been found nervous but unharmed also he would provide what he regretted was meagre accommodation outside the Castle, however it did have a small stable attached.

If this was agreeable then he welcomed him as a 'Knight of Camelot', and would personally be his proposer at the next meeting of the 'New Knights Initiation'. The Black Knight thanked King Arthur and assured him it was all completely acceptable to him. Indeed it was far, far, more than he could have possibly hoped for.

The King then turned to the young boy, he asked him his name and he told Arthur that he didn't know if he had a real name like other people. He didn't know his Mother or Father, he had spent all his life working for strangers for no money. Just a little food and a roof over his head at night, usually it would be a barn full of cattle or horses, which he didn't mind as they intended him no harm, he also felt completely safe, if anyone crept into the barn the animals would warn him. So he would sleep soundly and safely and in the Winter he would sleep warm because of the body heat from the animals. True, he would often be woken early morning by a cow's large tongue cleaning his face for him, he didn't mind and would pat the cow a few times and say thank you.

He went on to tell the King his nickname was 'Foxy', that's because he could out run, out hear and out see anyone. He also came from the North and had walked for weeks to find Camelot hoping someone would take him on as a page.

Arthur looked at the boy and he thought to himself this boy has proved himself brave, loyal, intelligent and skilful in one single day than most people I have known have proved in a lifetime.

The King was smiling, this was a fine boy in every way, a boy a man could be proud of to call his son, it was sad then that there was no Father, or Mother to be proud of her son.

Looking around the court there was an abundance of arrogant sons of rich Knights, they would try and make this boys life hell if he allowed him to stay.

King Arthur decided he would allow him to stay, and that he would keep a discreet eye on his wellbeing. It would have to be very discreet as no favouritism can be shown. Even a King as powerful as Arthur must maintain the Protocol, without it there cannot be a powerful Civilised King only a Barbarian leader. Although often it required large amounts of energy and frustration in the delays it caused, it was this maintenance of pecking order in the form of Pomp and Circumstance that maintained everything in the correct order, as Gravity does the Planets.

"Well young man said Arthur, if the Black Knight agrees I will appoint you his page, the cost of which I will gladly cover."

The King turned, "Black Knight what say you?"

"It is my privilege my King." He replied, bowing low "But my indebtedness to you is growing and growing and I will worry about how I will pay you back."

"Over the years I'm sure you will pay me back ten fold, of that I have no doubt, so be it then." Said King Arthur nodding to both of them.

They bowed as Arthur stood to leave the room, he had barely walked twenty feet from his throne before he was surrounded by more than thirty courtiers.

"Such is the life of Kings." Said Merlin.

Merlin smiled, "So that is how the story began of one of the 'Greatest Knights Of The Round Table' – The 'Fox'."

Merlin smiled again as he said the last words - The 'Fox'.

David and Jenny's eyes closed and they surrendered to sleep.

The Wizards were now totally exhausted and decided to put themselves into a deep Wizards trance having first put a sealing spell on the rooms just as a precaution.

It was 6.30p.m so they set waking time at 8.00a.m. Total peace descended on the rooms, which was sorely needed after such a day.

CHAPTER TWENTY FOUR

Lost in New York

David and Jenny tell the story:

At 8.00a.m on the dot the next morning the Wizards awoke. They checked on David and Jenny who were still sound asleep and decided to let them sleep on.

After freshening up and a really enjoyable breakfast they settled down comfortably for a nice long talk about past and recent events.

As Merlin said, "we have not met for many, many, years and who knows how long it may be until we meet again, for two full days they chatted stopping only to freshen up and for meals. When the evening's grew late the Wizards would put themselves into a deep Wizards trance.

The Wizards first talked about the 'Oriliance' for hours and hours then about the strange events at Crinkles Library. After some light refreshment the 'Team Quadro' match was discussed in great detail and then some of the matches from years ago. Finally it was time to talk about the old days or as all older people say the 'good old days' there was a lot of catching up to do and everyone had a very pleasant time.

It was very sad but eventually it was time to say goodbye, all promising to keep in touch and not let so much time go by before they all met up again, definitely not more than 50 years.

Future events would dictate that they would all have to meet up a lot sooner than that.

Everyone had an early breakfast and left by eight to return to their Original Hotel.

Only the Head remained at the New Hotel waiting for David and Jenny to wake up. It was about 9.00a.m when David started to stir so the Head checked the other bedroom but Jenny was still fast asleep. By 10.00a.m they were both up and complaining that they felt as though they hadn't had a drink or eaten for a week, in all they had slept for two and a half days.

David and Jenny freshened up and made their way downstairs for breakfast come lunch.

"The food's great in America." Said David, "and you get loads of it."

"If you go on eating loads of it you're going to look like a whale by the time we get back." Jenny observed that he definitely had put some weight on.

David and Jenny wanted to know if they could see some more of New York before they went home as they hadn't really seen any of it yet.

The Head said that he had a half-day bus tour planned for that afternoon and perhaps that evening they might visit China Town.

Tomorrow if they could drag themselves out of bed reasonably early they could go to the top of the Empire State Building and in the afternoon on a river cruise to see the Statue of Liberty.

"Can we go on the tram cars that go up and down the steep banks?" asked David.

Jenny glared at him, "Don't be stupid, you're talking about San Francisco, this is New York."

The Head smiled and said "Come on David finish eating and we can get away we don't want to waste any more of the day do we?"

The Head had already been in contact with the Hotel Lobby staff as to where to go for the City Tour Buses. They had now finished their meal and left the Hotel by the side entrance which was closer to the tour bus stop.

Once outside the Hotel the atmosphere of New York hit them, you felt as though you could almost touch it.

Soon they had the tour tickets and boarded the bus; sitting on the top deck so they would not miss anything. There were a couple of stops where you would be able to stretch your legs and do a little souvenir shopping at little kiosks, or buy a hamburger or ice cream.

The Head got off with them at the first stop and they all bought some small souvenirs, the tour continued and the guide on the bus pointed out various buildings and points of interest.

The second stop was at a square with grass and some trees at the centre and park benches dotted around. Ice cream, burger, and hotdog stands stood along one side with souvenir and newspaper/magazine stands on the other.

There was an assortment of coffee shops, cafes and restaurants opposite with little tables and chairs outside most of them, it was such a beautiful afternoon that they were very busy outside and almost deserted inside.

The Head decided he was too tired to get off at this stop and would just stay on the bus and rest his legs.

David as usual said he was starving despite the huge meal that he had eaten not that long ago and Jenny decided that she also wanted a hamburger they looked so delicious, so the Head gave them $5 each and reminded them that the bus was only here for twenty minutes.

David and Jenny sat on a bench eating their hamburgers as they watched the crowds and traffic go by, relaxing and soaking up the sun and hustle and bustle.

"Jenny!! Look at the size of that Cop standing on the corner over there."

David pointed across the road, the Policeman was well over 6 foot tall and built like a stone wall.

"No-one would want to mess with him." David added.

Jenny nodded, then said,

"I've been watching that man standing at the back of the bus queue I think he's a pickpocket."

"Why do you think that?" asked David.

"I notice he joins the bus queue for a couple of minutes then walks away just before a bus arrives and stands over by that building then joins a queue further down, then he reappears back at the first queue and he holds his newspaper in a funny sort of way."

"He looks like a business man to me, he's very smartly dressed." said David.

They both sat watching the man intently.

"I think you're right Jenny look he's walking towards that woman who's trying to hail a cab, he's stopped now, he's standing with his back to that building watching her and pretending to be reading his newspaper, I think he's picking the wrong people's pockets don't you?"

"Yes I agree, and I think I know whose pocket he should be trying to pick."

She looked across at the man mountain of a Policeman standing at the curb side.

"Do you think we could do it Jenny?"

"We could try, we'd have to get him to turn that corner though and that might be difficult."

"Let's try! If both of us concentrate together." said David excitedly.

"Look!" Said Jenny "A cab is pulling over and he's moving away from the wall and the lady is bending over to talk to the driver now she's opening the door, he's taken something out of her handbag."

"Yes, she's off in the cab and he's got something belonging to her, come on let's try it, quick! He's walking away from the corner where the Cop is, let's do it now Jenny."

They both sat staring across at the man and concentrating for all they were worth but he was still walking in the wrong direction, no, he'd stopped, he was turning.

"YES!!" Both David and Jenny shouted, he was now walking back towards the corner.

"Concentrate David." Said Jenny. "Concentrate!!"

"I am, I Am!!"

Getting the man to turn the corner was draining both David and Jenny of their Magic Energy however the man was turning and walking in the right direction, but now he had noticed the huge Policeman who was standing with the thumbs of each of his hands stuck down the top of his belt.

"He's trying to turn David, make him go on!!" Said Jenny with a pleading voice.

David who now looked a pale grey only nodded in reply. The man had started to turn away but now stopped and started to walk towards the Policeman.

Jenny grabbed David's hand.

"Harder!! Concentrate HARDER!!" She cried. The man was now walking very, very slowly towards the Policeman he raised his newspaper and YES!! He was trying to pick the policeman's back pocket.

The huge Policeman spun around and a hand the size of a bear's paw grabbed the pickpocket by the neck and he lifted him clear off the ground, still holding him aloft he carried him towards the front of the building and slammed him into it, then spun him around and handcuffed him in the space of a few seconds.

David and Jenny now relaxed, they sat silently for a while watching the big Policeman radio for help, and the passersby curious as to why the very respectable looking man was handcuffed.

A Police Van arrived and the man was bundled inside and it drove off.

"I wonder if the woman will get her property back?" asked Jenny.

David said, "I think I'm going to be sick."

"That's because you ate that hamburger too fast." said Jenny.

Jenny's face dropped.

"David! How long have we been here?"

"I don't know, but we'd better get back to the tour bus sharpish."

They both ran towards the buses parked at the other side of the square.

"It's still there!" Shouted David.

They quickly showed their tickets to the driver as the bus started to move off.

"Just in time gasped David." They started to make their way up to the top deck, but a lady was making her way down with her elderly mother. She smiled at Jenny and David and said,

"It's a bit too cold up there for Mum we've decided to come down."

David and Jenny had to go back down the stairs to let them pass.

"Take your time Mum these steps are steep." and the old lady did take her time, mainly David noted to please her daughter, the old lady smiled at them when she reached the bottom and they smiled back.

"At last we can get up top." Said David "I hope the Head saw us get on the bus or he'll be worried that we're lost."

They reached the top deck and looked at where they had been sitting.

"Where's the Head?" asked Jenny.

There was a lady with three children sitting where they'd previously been. They frantically scanned the entire deck.

"He's not here." said David in a worried voice.

They looked at each other then re-scanned the top deck, now realising they didn't recognise a single face and the passengers were all starting to stare at them.

"We're on the wrong bus Jenny."

"Let's check below David, perhaps he was feeling cold, he could have nodded off downstairs and not noticed us get on."

They checked below but the Head was not there either.

"What do we do now David?"

"We get off the bus and walk back, we couldn't have gone that far and it's obvious now that when we didn't arrive back in time the Head would simply get off the bus and wait for us to turn up."

Jenny nodded, "Yes you're probably right,"

They made their way to the driver and told him that they had got on the wrong tour bus and would he stop and let them off so that they could walk back to meet up with a friend.

The driver turned and looked at them in astonishment.

"Get off here! Are you sure?"

"Yes, we have to go back." David told the driver.

The bus driver shrugged his shoulders "Better you than me" he said as he pulled into the side, stopped and opened the doors.

Jenny smiled, "Thanks for stopping."

"You won't be thanking me for long, you best get the first cab you see." And with that he closed the doors and drove away.

Jenny and David looked at each other, they didn't feel too happy at the bus driver's remarks, best to set off back along the way they had come as quickly as possible. Then they realised they weren't 100 % sure which way they had come and it was starting to dawn on them that they had travelled a lot further than they had first thought.

"David." Said Jenny "It looks a bit rough around here."

"It's okay." Said David hopefully reassuringly, but Jenny was right it did look rough now that they were out of the bus, the buildings had been very smart once but they were now run down and a bit seedy. Some of the houses were boarded up and many of them that appeared occupied had groups of people sitting on steps outside looking really aimless.

"Let's look out for a cab David."

"What will we use for a fare? We've only a few dollars and an English £10 note."

"We could tell the cab driver what happened and that the Head will pay when we get back." said Jenny in a pleading voice.

"We could, but do you see any cabs about? I don't, and looking around I don't think we will, nobody here looks as though they could afford a cab."

"There may be one passing through, the bus did."

David nodded, but he was now more interested in the gang of five lads heading their way, these lads are looking for trouble thought David, do we run? But where can we run to? Do we cross the road out of their way? But that lot sitting on the steps look just as bad, no he thought, the only thing to do is bluff it out. Jenny had also noticed the gang now.

"David I think we're in trouble."

"Jenny just keep on walking, don't make any eye contact. When we are close to them smile and nod as we pass them but don't say anything and don't stop, just keep on walking."

That was good advice but as they drew very close one of the gang stepped in front of them forcing Jenny and David to stop, he stood there chewing gum and looking them up and down.

"Where do you kids think you're going man?"

"We're just walking along the street." said David. The one who had spoken was obviously their leader and tried to mimic David's English accent.

"We're just walking along the street." The others all started to laugh.

"Why do you talk so funny?"

"Because we're English." As he spoke David was trying to put himself between this trouble maker and Jenny.

"English toffs eh! We've heard about English toffs." The rest of the gang started to jeer and mockingly chanting "toffs, toffs, English toffs."

"No we're just English." David replied quietly.

"Well just English, this is our turf did I give you permission to walk along it?" He was prodding David and raising his voice as he talked, "did I? Did I? DID I?"

"No, you didn't."

"That's right, I didn't, so why are you here?"

"We're lost." said Jenny.

"You're lost eh! Poor little English you're lost, where's your 'Mammy' she must be worried." The gang was having a great time this was the best fun they'd had for ages.

"Mammy! Mammy! We're lost, we need your help." The gang roared with laughter and chorused,

"Mammy! Mammy! We're lost."

It was taking all of David's will power to stay silent.

Jenny and David obviously weren't in a position to be looking about, if they had they would have been surprised at the number of people who had started to gather on the other side of the road.

"Well lost English, this is our territory and you're trespassing so what are we going to do about it eh?"

"I don't know." Replied David.

"He doesn't know." There was more laughter, "Well I'll tell you what we're gonna do about it, you've gotta pay see, so how much you got?"

"Not a lot really." Said Jenny.

"Then you're dead meat man." The leader and the rest of the gang had surrounded them and were scowling into their faces.

"You can have this." David handed him the English £10 note.

"What's this! Toy money?"

"No it's English money."

"Its Toy money to me, Toy money, give us those watches." another member of the gang had taken the £10 note and was looking at it,

"Make her eat it." He shouted

"YEAH! Make her eat it!" Shouted the rest of the gang, the leader took the note back and with an evil grin turned to Jenny.

"Open your mouth." He grabbed her hair and pulling her head back tried to push the £10 note into her mouth.

This was too much for David, he gave the gang leader a powerful right hook that caught him square on the jaw and it took him by surprise, he staggered backwards but recovered before David and Jenny could make a bolt for it.

"Get him!!" Screamed the leader, and all five leapt at David who collapsed onto the ground. He didn't stand a chance.

Jenny looked at the gang who had started to beat up David, she seemed to swell to twice her size then burst out with a torrent of strange words, suddenly, bodies were flying in all directions.

The leader and the others staggered back from blows to their chins, then blows rained down on their noses, steel hammers seemed to hit them in the stomach, then more blows to the chin, then another and another, teeth were starting to drop out, it felt as though they were being attacked by someone with eight fists and they were.

Jenny's magic had given David eight arms and the eight arms had eight fists which were flying about like a tornado and doing the same sort of damage. He was swinging punches so fast that his arms were a blur, he stopped, and instantly his arms reduced to two.

The gang was lying scattered about in pools of blood, moaning, groaning and gasping.

Jenny and David looked about for the first time and were shocked to see the size of the crowd that had gathered, not more trouble thought Jenny I have no more Magic Energy left.

The crowd which had been keeping a respectful distance between themselves and the battle had started to slowly move closer, Oh no!! Not another bunch of idiots thought David. Then suddenly they started to applaud and cheer.

A voice in the crowd shouted out, "Well done man, well done, that'll teach them a lesson they won't forget."

Another voice cried, "I'm gonna check to see if the swine still has the watch he stole from me" and moved across to one of the gang who was lying in agony and whimpering.

"Yep, he has and I'm having it back."

Soon there were others going over the gang's clothes and searching their pockets, someone shouted,

"Shouldn't we call an ambulance?" This was greeted by a chorus of, "NO WAY"!

"Come on David." Said Jenny, "Let's get out of here." she put her arm around his shoulder and started to lead him away, he was dazed and had a bad cut above his right eye, his lip was bleeding and starting to swell so was his nose and his fists were cut and bruised.

Jenny glanced back at the crowd, well she thought that gangs finished, they'll never be able to lord it over anyone here again.

A couple of the gang were trying to get to their feet, they were completely naked as were the other gang members the crowd had taken everything, and were now booing and chanting and laughing at what had obviously been their tormenters for years.

Jenny heard a very fat old lady shouting,

"Here, you can put a pair of my old knickers on." And dangled a huge pair of knickers in the face of what had been the gang leader.

The crowd roared with laughter and started to chant,

"Put them on, put them on."

The further and faster we can get away from here the better, thought Jenny.

"Slow down Jenny! I'm all aches and pains."

"We've got to get somewhere safer!" Jenny replied. "Look David! up ahead there's grass and trees I think it's a park, come on we should be safe there."

A few minutes later they arrived at the park. "Jenny!" Said David, "I can't go any further I've got to sit down, please find us a seat."

CHAPTER TWENTY-FIVE

Central Park

When David said 'please' Jenny began to worry, he was never as polite as that so he must be really hurt. Jenny was relieved when within a few minutes she spotted an empty park bench, once they had settled down she started to ask David where his aches and pains were and how bad, had he broken anything?

David said he didn't think anything was broken, and only grunted a reply to any other questions. They sat quietly for nearly half an hour, so it came as a great relief to Jenny when he said:

"It's a huge park this Jenny, I don't know about you but I'm pretty tired and absolutely starving, how much money have we got left?" If he's thinking about food that's a good sign thought Jenny,

"I've got $1, I thought you had some money?"

"Only that £10 we had."

"We still have." said Jenny taking it out of her pocket, "I grabbed it during the fight."

"There's a hot dog stand over there do you think he might take it?"

"Let's try," suggested Jenny, "I'm pretty hungry too."

They walked over to the hot dog stand and joined a small queue, in front of them was an American boy and girl about their age casually dressed but very smart. Jenny looked down at her dress and across at David's clothes, they did both look a bit rough especially David after his fight in the street.

"NEXT." A voice boomed out.

"That's us." said Jenny.

"We'd like two hot dogs and two cokes please, but will you take this money?" David showed the £10 note to the hamburger man.

"Nope."

"But its okay, it's just that it's English money it's worth more than $14."

"Not to me it ain't."

"It is, really it's worth more than $14."

"Then go and get some other guy to give you $14 for it, NEXT!"

"But were starving." pleaded David.

"NEXT!"

David and Jenny moved away looking miserable.

The two children who had been in front of them had been listening to every word as they squeezed tomato sauce onto their hot dogs.

"I'll change your money for you." The boy said to David.

"Will you?"

"Sure, I'll give you $6 for it."

"But it's worth $14 at least and it's all we've got."

"$6 is all I've got, do you want it or not?"

"Daniel that's horrible!" It was the American girl speaking.

"No it's not! It's business, it's called supply and demand or something like that."

"It's horrible that's what it is!" She turned to David, "My name's Samantha but everyone calls me Sam, I've got enough money for 2 hot dogs and one drink and you can have the money." She started to get the money out of a pocket on her baseball jacket.

"Don't be daft sis, don't you dare give them that money we don't know who they are."

"I don't care who they are, it's my money not yours, here." She said handing the money to David.

"Thank you." Said David, "but you must take this." And he pushed the £10 note into her hand, "Otherwise I can't take your money."

"I don't believe this! I offered him $6 and you went mad, now your getting the money and only giving them $5."

"No I'm not!" Said Sam, "because I won't take the money."

"That's it! That's It!" Said Daniel.

"I'm going to buy them the hot dogs and drinks and be done with it!"

They all sat together on the grass eating the hot dogs as all the benches were full, Daniel and Sam had barely started theirs whereas Jenny and David were already finished.

"Boy you were hungry." Said Daniel

"I still am." David said.

Jenny kicked David's leg, "But we don't want any more to eat."

"You weren't going to get any more." Replied Daniel, "You're English, what are you both doing here? Are you on holiday?"

"No. We've been to a Convention."

"Been to a Convention! How old are you?"

"I'm 12 and a bit."

"So am I, and 12 year olds don't go to Conventions only old people do."

"We did! We went to a Wizards Convention." Blurted out David without thinking. Jenny gave him a hard kick.

"Wizards Convention!! Did you say Wizards Convention?" Yelled Daniel.

"No I didn't!" David was nursing his sore ankle where Jenny had kicked him twice now, as though he didn't have enough aches and pains and bruises already.

"You did! Didn't he Sam?" Without waiting for a reply he went on, "You're no Wizard."

"I didn't say I was, we are simply lost we can't find our Hotel in fact we don't know its name."

Daniel turned to Sam,

"Did you hear that?" he asked, and again without waiting for an answer started to taunt David, "A Wizard wouldn't be lost he'd just say a spell and be back at the Hotel in a shot."

"If you don't shut up I'll punch you one." said David getting to his feet.

"The state your face is in I think someone's already been punching you."

"I've already warned you." Growled David.

"David, David, stop it!" Said Jenny panicking.

"David, David, stop it." mimicked Daniel who had also stood up now.

At that David whacked him, and before Jenny or Sam could stop them they were both rolling about wrestling each other, eventually the girls managed to get them apart.

"Say you're sorry." said Jenny who was very annoyed

"Sorry to that American twit never."

"American twit am I!! I'll show you who's a twit."

"Stop it now!" Shouted Sam.

"He started it." Growled Daniel, "Talking about being a Wizard, what did that English au pair girl often say Sam?"

"Pull the other leg." said Samantha.

"Yes that's it, pull the other leg it's got bells on It." and he lifted his leg and started to shake it about. Jenny saw the look on David's face,

"Don't you dare David!" She cried out, but too late, the leg Daniel was shaking now had bells all over it. Daniel was shocked, he put his leg down and tried to remove the bells but he couldn't and now he seemed to have bells all over, he was covered from head to toe in bells.

Jenny was very annoyed. "You've turned him into a Morris dancer." But her annoyance turned to amusement and she and Sam laughed and laughed as Daniel started to dance about trying to get the bells off. The more he danced about the more the bells rang and soon a crowd of people had started to gather around them

A middle aged American couple who had been taking photographs spotted Daniel,

"Oh look darling! Look! Take my photograph with that young boy dressed so funny."

"Certainly will my little honey pot." and he clicked 3 or 4 times.

"Excellent, excellent, well give him something Ewing."

"Will do, will do, honey pot, that's for you son and thanks." And he gave Daniel $2.

Then it was a group of Japanese tourists who each bowed in turn to Daniel before taking his photograph. He got $10 from them.

Jenny noticed more and more people heading their way to see what was going on, and decided she had better do something and changed Daniel back to normal.

"Why did you do that?" Said David annoyed, "I was enjoying it."

A fairly large crowd was now milling around but couldn't for the life of them work out why everyone was over here and what it had all been about.

"Time we slipped away." said David as he caught sight of two Mounted Police coming their way.

"Hey, look at that, I made $12 in just a couple of minutes who would have thought it." But then Daniel remembered how he made the money, "What did you do to me? How did you do it? Can you do it again?"

Some days later the American couple and the Japanese group couldn't understand why they had taken a photograph of a boy just standing next to them and what had happened to the boy who had all those bells on his clothes.

David had a large grin on his face. "I told you I was a Wizard."

"Then why can't you get back to your Hotel? Why don't you Magic yourself back?"

"We can't, we've used up too much of our Magic Energy in the past few days, even putting a few bells on you has totally exhausted me again."

Jenny pulled David to one side, "David I think we should tell them a little about what has happened, it won't be that long before it's dark and we need some help."

"Okay, I will leave it up to you to decide what to tell them."

Jenny told Daniel and Sam a little about what had been happening at the Oraliance, they both looked amazed and gasped.

"This is the best day of my life!!" Said Daniel.

"It's pretty cool." Agreed Sam.

The problem now was how to help, the first thing was something more to eat, no problem there as Daniel had the $12 he had made and there was the $5 Sam still had.

"We can stop off at a burger bar, but we have to find somewhere for you to sleep tonight." said Daniel.

"It will have to be our flat." Said Sam, "We'll have to sneak them in past the doorman. If we can get them into the flat without Mam and her friend seeing them we'll be okay until morning anyway."

"Sam!" Yelled Daniel, "Have you seen the time? We aren't supposed be out this late, come on let's run."

"Wait!" Cried out David, "What about something to eat?"

"No time," shouted back Daniel, "We'll sneak you something later."

Everyone shot off, running through the park for about half a mile and then out on to a main road, waited for the green walk sign to light up crossed the road then sped along past some very elegant houses.

"We're nearly there." Panted Daniel, "You'd better let us go on ahead."

David and Jenny kept back a little so it wasn't obvious they were with Daniel and Sam who were now making their way up the steps of a large and very impressive building,

David looked at the height of the building, "Do they live there?"

"They must do." Answered Jenny, "Doesn't it look posh." and David nodded in agreement.

At the top of the steps standing outside a tinted glass lobby entrance stood a large doorman, smartly dressed in a brown coat with gold epaulettes, the coat had a dark brown collar and he was wearing a dark brown matching top hat.

"He looks like a blooming Admiral," said David, "but how on earth will we get past him?"

Daniel and Sam were nearly at the top of the steps when suddenly Sam seemed to stumble and fell back a few steps, Daniel rushed down to her side then looked up towards the doorman who started to walk down the stairs and bent down to where Sam was half lying, half sitting.

Daniel didn't turn around but started to gesture with his hand that this was their chance to get into the building without being stopped.

"David take your shoes off." hissed Jenny.

"But" David began.

"No buts do it now."

They both took their shoes off and rushed silently along the pavement up the steps and past the doorman, who had his back to them, he was still bent over Sam who was moaning slightly, they gently pushed open the door and eased through. Fortunately there was no one in the lobby, they glanced around quickly looking for somewhere to hide.

"There!" Said David pointing to a large deep padded dark brown leather settee in the corner of the lobby near one of the lifts, with a very large potted plant behind it. They dashed over and ducked down behind the settee and David peered through the leaves of the potted plant.

"What's happening?" asked Jenny whispering.

"I can't see anything, yes I can, the doorman is carrying Sam in and Daniel is following, they're coming through the doors, oh no,"

"What's wrong?" whispered Jenny, "What's wrong?"

"The doorman's looking this way he's coming over." They both ducked down then lay flat on the floor, the doorman came across and lay Sam on the settee and told Daniel to sit with his sister while he phoned their Mam's flat.

The doorman walked across to the phone at the reception desk and David and Jenny could hear him talking then the phone being put down, he came back over to Daniel and Sam and told them that their Mam was on her way down in the lift then he turned and went back outside.

"I thought we'd had it there, that was close." Whispered David.

Daniel was looking around searching for them.

"Where are you?" He whispered.

David popped his head above the top of the settee, "We're here, at the back of the settee behind the potted plant."

Daniel had been kneeling beside Sam, but now stood up and peered over the top of the settee at David and Jenny lying on the floor.

"Mam's coming down in the lift." said Daniel, "We're in flat number 80 on the 4th floor, turn left when you get out of the lift, come up in about 5 minutes they'll be putting Sam to bed, when there doing that I will let you in, the flats that large you could hide an army in it, that's the lift coming now." And Daniel went back to Sam.

The lift door opened and a man and lady rushed out and straight over to Sam and Daniel,

"'Oh Darling!!' Are you all right?"

"I only went over on my ankle Mam I don't want all this fuss."

"It's not fuss dear, we are worried about you, Bert's going to carry you upstairs and tuck you up in bed, but we'll have a look at that ankle first."

Bert lifted Sam and with her Mam and Daniel following behind they made their way to the lift,

"Press the lift button Miriam." David heard the man's voice and peeping through the leaves of the plant he saw the group standing by the lift, then the doors opened and they all stepped in, the doors closed and David and Jenny were once more on their own.

Jenny checked her watch. "They've gone and we have to follow in 5 minutes." Then Jenny saw the look on David's face.

"What's wrong David?"

"That mm..man..... that mm..man" stuttered David.

"Yes, the friend of Sam's Mother, someone called Bert, what's wrong with you why are you stuttering?"

"That mm...man is Disdorf!!"

"Disdorf! The man who sneered at us at the Convention, he's one of the Evil Wizards, the Head said that he was one of the most powerful." Jenny paused.

"That can't be possible you couldn't have seen him properly." Jenny added in a faltering voice.

"I saw him properly, and even if I didn't I'd know his voice anywhere, you never heard his voice but I did, he was the one who was giving orders to the Wizards who were with eXactamus."

"What should we do now David? Where can we go?"

"I don't know, I know we can't go up to the flat."

"We can't sit here all night either." Added Jenny.

"Can we trust Daniel and Sam?"

"Yes I think so, I think we can." Replied Jenny.

They sat quietly hidden in the corner,

"How long have they been away now Jenny?"

"10 minutes."

"10 minutes! Is that all, it feels like ages, keep down Jenny the lifts coming."

Jenny and David ducked down low behind the potted plant as the lift doors opened and two couples came out laughing and joking.

"Where should we go first?" One of the men asked the ladies.

"Oh somewhere for a cocktail I think, perhaps 'Martha's' or the 'Quilted Camel'."

They went through the lobby door and into the street their voices fading away. Over the next 10 minutes there was a lot of coming and going, one lady even sitting on the settee at the same time as David was wanting to cough, fortunately the lift came almost immediately and her companion took hold of her hands and pulled her up saying,

"Come on you can't be as tired as that." and they walked into the lift both laughing.

As quickly as the comings and goings had started they stopped, and the lobby went completely quiet. Both Jenny and David had closed their eyes and started to doze off but were woken by Daniel shaking their shoulders.

"Why are you still here? You were supposed to follow me up after 5 minutes, I've opened the flat door six times already nearly been caught twice."

"I'm down here to look for one of Sam's ribbons she's supposed to have lost, it's this one in my pocket actually, you'd better follow me back up."

"We can't." said Jenny.

"Why not?" asked Daniel

"Because your Mam's friend is Disdorf."

"Disdorf! Who's Disdorf? Mam's friend is called Bert Clark he's here on business and staying the week with us, he always stays here when he's in New York."

"Did this Bert Clark pick Sam up and carry her to the lift?" asked David.

"Yes."

"Then that's Disdorf, the one who gave instructions to the Evil Wizards at the Convention." replied David.

Daniel was confused "I don't believe it! You must be wrong."

"That's what Jenny said but I'm not."

"What can we do now?" Asked Daniel.

"We don't know, we can't think of anything." Replied Jenny.

"You can't stay here all night behind the settee, if only I could get you both across town to my Dad's. He's on holiday at the moment but I have a key, you could stay there until we sort something out."

"There is one thing I can try, I'll phone a friend of mine whose Father's a Cab driver the same as mine and see if he will pick you up and I'll give him my Dad's address and the Cab could drop you there."

Daniel fumbled around in his pockets finally producing a key.

"Let yourselves in, Dad's been away for a few days but he's due back at anytime, when he does arrive back you'll have to do all the explaining, tell him I will phone the first chance I get."

"When I talk to the cab driver I'll ask him to park outside and come up the stairs, as soon as you see him you must run for the doors, the doorman will stop the cab driver coming in and ask the name of his customer, that's your chance to nip out and run to the cab and get in."

Daniel walked over to the phone at the reception desk looking very worried, then he started to talk and a few minutes later he came back and was smiling.

"I'd forgotten Alex's dad knows mine it's all sorted, the cab will be about 20 minutes, I've got to go or Mam will want to know why I was so long. Sam and I will try and meet up with you tomorrow."

Daniel walked over to the lift and pressed the button, the lift doors opened, he turned, smiled and lifted up the blue ribbon.

"Best of luck." he whispered and was gone.

"What time is it Jenny?"

"It's 8 o'clock."

David and Jenny sat quietly thinking to themselves

"What time is it Jenny?"

"You're going to drive me mad if you start asking me the time every few minutes, it's only 4 minutes past 8.00."

"Are you sure your watch hasn't stopped?"

"It hasn't stopped, Daniel only left about 5 minutes ago."

"I'm not half hungry Jenny I wish Daniel had brought some food with him, are you sure you haven't any sweets hidden in your pockets?"

"David shut up, you're getting on my nerves I'm just as hungry as you are."

David said nothing more, just sat sulking and waiting for the time to pass and every now and then peering through the plants leaves to see what was happening.

"Keep a sharper look out David the cab should be here in a few minutes."

"Yeah okay." then he suddenly jumped up.

"He's here! Come on." and David was off heading towards the door with Jenny following.

A man had opened the lobby door and they both rushed through and down the stairs and only then realised there was no yellow cab.

Worse still the doorman was opening the door of a large black limo and getting out was one of the men Disdorf had often been talking to at the Convention.

David and Jenny recognized him instantly and they realised that he had also recognized them, but he was as surprised as they were. They swerved to his left and as they did so a yellow cab pulled up behind the black limo.

The yellow cab driver had his window down and Jenny and David ran up and shouted,

"For us?"

"Yeah, if you're the friends of Daniel." replied the driver.

"He's our friend." Said David opening the door and tumbling in followed by Jenny.

"Just take your time will ya. You don't have to wreck the cab."

"We've got to get away quickly!!" Said David in a very convincing voice, "It's 'Life or Death'!!"

"I'll get away as soon as the limo in front moves off."

"It's the limo in front we want to get away from!!" Replied David panicking.

"Oh!! '#'#'#'#'#!" Said the cab driver slamming the gears into reverse, stopping then pulling out with screeching tyres and accelerating away in a screaming first gear and just beating the traffic lights turning to red, while all the time chewing gum and repeating, "Tell me it's not going to be one of those nights." over and over again. David was looking through the back window,

"He's gone through the lights on red!!" He yelled.

"Oh!! '#'#'#'#! I don't believe this. 'IT IS' going to be one of those nights." Shouted the cab driver as he weaved in and out of the traffic. Twice more he just managed to get through traffic lights in time but each time the Black Limo followed him through on red.

He tried back alleys, hard last minute right turns, hard last minute left turns, he crossed lanes of traffic but no matter what he tried he could not shake off the Black Limo.

" What on earth have you two been up to?" He asked, "I've tried everything I know and it's no good I can't shake that bloke off, and I'm not even sure why I'm doing it."

"YOU MUST!! YOU MUST!!" Pleaded Jenny, and something in her voice made the taxi driver decide to have one more try.

"Okay, Okay," he said, "There's only one thing left I can think of, I'll switch on my cab radio and call Bertha. Hello Bertha, this is 157, this is 157 Bertha over."

"Bertha here 157, I haven't got a fare for you to pick up at the moment it's very quiet tonight."

"I don't want a fare Bertha I want a favour from you."

"Anything you want my dream guy."

"No seriously Bertha I'm in a spot of trouble here."

"Not the Cops!! Tell me it's not the 'Cops again'!!"

"No it's not the Cops, I've a big Black Buick behind me that I'm trying to shake off and can't. I've tried everything and he's still on my tail. I need a box in Bertha, I need the help of some of the guys."

"I'll call em, but I can't make em."

"If anyone can you can Bertha."

'Now then 157, that kind of talk can get a man anything."

"This is Bertha all you New York Yellas, 157 is in a spot of trouble he wants a box in on the Black Buick following him, in return he's promised to pay back all his gambling debts and treat everyone to tickets for the next Yankee Game, well that's what the man says don't blame me if he doesn't follow through."

"If you're near him, help him. Why? 'cos Big Bertha says so that's why, and one day you might need him to help you."

"Where are you 157? Now hear me all you cabbies."

"I'm in Lexington going to turn right at 42nd, then first right and first right again then back into Lex, until you guys can help me."

"Did you hear that all ya Yella cabs? Well your Bertha's going to repeat it over and over again until I get the response I need. Yes indeed! Yes indeedee!"

"Peek a boo, no more fares for you till you do!" And she went on to give out the directions repeatedly.

A couple of minutes went by and the first Yellow Cab arrived, I could see it behind the Black Limo, I told our driver and he nodded, we turned right and picked up another two next right we picked up three more next right there was another three but only one was needed.

Jenny and I watched in amazement, we now had a Yellow Cab to the right and left of us, a yellow cab was at the right and left of the Black Buick behind us and now one directly behind the black Buick and one at either side of that cab. There were nine cars now grouped together turning right and right again eight of them Yellow Cabs.

"Here's where we say goodbye to our friends." said our driver.

We had been slowing down gradually, now we suddenly accelerated away from the Black Buick while at the same time the Yellow Cabs that had been on either side of us started to move into our place so they blocked all three lanes ahead of the Black Buick and with a Yellow Cab either side and three Yellow Cabs behind it, the Buick had no choice but to go in any direction the Yellow Cabs chose.

"Beautiful!! Beautiful!! I like it, Beautiful!!" Yelled our driver as he sped away straight ahead, and the Black Buick was forced to turn right, "Thank you Bertha, this is 157 mission completed, thank you Bertha you're my favourite girl."

After all that excitement and the excitement earlier in the day David and Jenny now lay on the back seat of the cab totally exhausted with their eyes closed, neither awake or asleep but in a half way land. They could hear the cab radio and some faint conversations from time to time, but didn't sit up and take notice of anything that was happening until the cab driver called out:

"Wake up kids, we're here." The cab was pulling up outside a rather run down house in a street of equally run down houses, he stopped, turned around and grinning pointed to a yellow painted door remarkably similar to the colour of the cab,

"You've arrived." He said.

"How much do we owe you?" Jenny asked.

"All taken care of." he replied

"What about your tip?"

"All taken care of." Said the driver

"Well anyway we'd like you to have this." said Jenny handing him our £10 note.

We were out of the cab by now and closing the cab door,

"So long kids, it will be a long time before I forget tonight, if ever." Said the cab driver waving as he pulled away.

CHAPTER TWENTY-SIX

Kidnapping

David, Jenny and others tell the story.

We watched the Cab until it disappeared from view, we would never forget tonight or any of today.

Turning back to the house we started to walk up the steps to the yellow painted door, David had the key out but it opened before we could reach it and there standing in the light from the passage door was Daniel, at least what Daniel would look like in 25 years time. David and I were completely surprised to see Daniels dad, we had expected the house to be empty, but we didn't say anything.

"Hi! I'm Daniel's Dad, you must be David and Jenny, come on in." He said standing to one side to let us past and closing the door behind us. He led us to the kitchen, "I bet you're both really hungry."

"Yes." said Jenny, "I am."

"I'm absolutely starving." Replied David.

Daniel's dad set to and soon we were tucking in to some fabulous hash browns, beans, sausages, eggs and bacon with big mugs of piping hot tea.

"Thought you might like tea," said Daniels Dad, "rather like it myself, by the way my name's Mark."

We tucked in and soon finished all the food.

'Boy you two were hungry have you had enough?" Asked Mark, "Or do you want some more?"

"No that was fine thank you." Said Jenny, David didn't say anything but Mark interpreted the look on David's face and produced some Hot Waffles covered in real Maple Syrup.

They looked so delicious that Jenny couldn't resist having some herself.

"When you finish you can tell me some of your adventures." said Mark. "What you want to tell me that is, it will give your meal time to settle, then it's off to bed for both of you, I bet you need a good night's sleep."

And he was right, we talked for a while and told him how we come to meet Daniel and Samantha, then he could see that we couldn't keep our eyes open, we fell asleep immediately our heads touched our pillows.

Mark let us sleep for nearly 12 hours then made us a huge breakfast.

"Thanks for your help, it's nice of you to let us stay at your place." said Jenny.

"It's not my place Jenny that would have been the first call they made in trying to find you, this is Big Bertha's pad."

"Big Bertha's pad!!" David and Jenny said in a surprised chorus.

"Yep, Big Bertha's. I've been away for a few days, wasn't due back until tomorrow afternoon, but the way things worked out I came back last night. I went around to see if my cab was back from being repaired but it won't be ready until tomorrow. Big Bertha spotted me and explained that you two were on the way to my place, but she had been thinking about this and decided that although she didn't fully understand what was going on if a safe place was needed for a few days hers would be the best, As it happens apparently Berthas going to visit a friend for a while so her flat was going to be empty. The place is well stocked up with food and Bertha told us just to help ourselves."

"We hardly understand ourselves what's going on." Said Jenny.

"Well Big Bertha arranged for one of the guys to drop me off here and she contacted Tom who's cab you were in and gave him the new address. So here we all are at Big Berthas."

"What are we going to do now?" Asked Jenny.

"I've been thinking about that, probably best to lie low here for a day or two while I try and get in touch with Crankles."

David smiled, "You mean Crinkles."

"Yeah that's it Crinkles, your Head guy must have got in touch with them and we should be able to find out which Hotel you're staying at."

Jenny looked at David,

"We should have done that ages ago, why didn't we think of it?"

David shrugged, "I don't know, it seems so obvious now but you can't think of everything and there's been that much happening my minds totally mixed up."

"Can't we just phone them from here and tell them we're okay?" Asked Jenny.

"Could if we had a phone." Replied Mark

"There's a phone here." Said David pointing to a red phone in the corner.

"Doesn't work, Bertha sort of forgot to pay the bill I guess, I know I sometimes do, now don't you two worry I'm going to phone from a friend's, can't use the phones in the street they're always bust, anyway I wouldn't have enough money for phoning England."

"Don't you have a mobile phone?" Asked David.

"Used to have, had three nicked in four months my mate lost seven in less than a year. Only the kids have them around here, some have four or five, probably got mine, so I don't bother now. It's time for me to pick my cab up from the garage. You better not go outside, just keep out of sight and away from any of the windows. Don't answer the door if anyone knocks just stay low I'll soon be back." With that he smiled and left them on their own.

For about half an hour they sat and watched cartoons on the television then David asked Jenny if she wanted something to drink but she just shook her head and sat quietly.

"I'm just going to have a peep out of the window." Said David.

"No don't!" Cried Jenny. "You know what Daniel's Dad said someone might see you."

So David sat down and closed his eyes and was almost asleep when Jenny nudged him.

"David."

"Yes, what now?" Answered David sleepily.

"I feel something's wrong here."

"Like what?"

"I don't know, staying at Big Bertha's place just doesn't feel right"

"I'm having a coke." Said David standing up.

"Are you listening to me?" Asked Jenny annoyed. "I'm telling you I feel something's wrong David, I want to leave this place."

"How much money have you got? Because I've got nothing and we aren't going to get very far on nothing."

"I don't care if I don't have any money David I'm going." And Jenny got up to leave.

"You can't leave!" Said David, but Jenny was on her way to the front door. "I'm warning you I'm not going with you I'm staying here."

"Please yourself." said Jenny as she tried to open the front door. "David I can't get the door open, 'help me'."

"No way."

Jenny stopped trying to open the door and stood very still and silent.

"Come on back and watch the T.V." said David as he turned and walked towards the sitting room. He looked back "Come on." he said, and then he paused, shocked to see Jenny was fading away.

"Jenny! Jenny!" He cried running back to the front door but too late she was gone. "Jenny, Jenny, where are you?

Don't leave me alone." David tried the front door, Jenny had been right the door wouldn't open and he didn't have the Magic Energy left or know the spell needed to go through a door.

"Hey man!" gasped the young coloured boy who had been sitting on the steps outside the bright yellow front door. "Don't you go doing that creeping up on me, where you come from?"

"From Bertha's house." Replied Jenny.

"Bertha! Who's this Bertha?"

"The woman who lives there." Said Jenny pointing to the yellow door.

"What woman, no woman lives there." Said the boy.

"Then who does?" Asked Jenny.

"Some foreign dude."

"What does he look like?"

"Don't know, foreign like."

"Tall, short, thin, fat, think! Think!" Cried Jenny.

"Hey man! What's all this shouting at me? Why you doing that?"

"I'm sorry, I didn't mean to, only it's very important it really is!"

The boy smiled, "Well he's pretty tall and kinda thin, always wears an expensive grey suit and comes with his chauffer in a big Black Buick." The boy stopped then pointed, "That's the car just turned the corner."

Jenny dashed down the street and the coloured boy instinctively followed her.

"Where are you going?" He asked, Jenny didn't answer but darted between two cars and he followed her.

"Keep down!" She hissed, Jenny peeped over the car boot, she could see through the rear and front car windows. The black car had stopped and a tall thin man stepped out and was going up the front steps to the yellow front door. He took out a door key and he let himself in and disappeared.

"I wish I had some Magic left to stop that car." Sighed Jenny.

"Magic!" The boy looked at her strangely, "You don't need no Magic to stop that car I can do that."

"Well do it then!" Pleaded Jenny.

"What for?" Asked the boy.

"I'll explain later, just do it now before it's too late." The boy gave her another strange look but darted off running down the side of the parked cars keeping low down, he was away for a few minutes and arrived back at Jenny's side at the same time as the door of the flat opened and the man reappeared dragging David with him.

The chauffer had opened the rear door and held David as the man got in, then pushed David in beside him. There was something wrong with David thought Jenny he wasn't struggling or shouting for help he looked as though he could barely walk.

The car started to move off then stopped and reversed back to where it had been, the driver got out and stood looking down at something then he opened the boot. The young boy was smiling,

"I fixed his wheel." He said.

"What's your name?" Asked Jenny.

"My name's Josh."

"Well Josh you did a great job, by the way my name's Jenny."

"Hi Jenny, but why did you want the car stopped?"

"I'm buying time Josh, that's my friend David they've bundled into the car and I reckon he's been kidnapped."

"Kidnapped!! For loads of money?"

"Well sort of, I can't explain it all just now I'm trying to think of some sort of plan."

The chauffer was putting the boot lid down now,

"That's it," said Jenny, "I'm beaten." Jenny unknown to Josh was trying with all her might to raise some Magic but she couldn't. The 'Oriliance' had totally drained her and what she had regained during her long sleep had been used up yesterday, she had only just managed to get through the front door into the street. Jenny had no idea and didn't want to think about what might have happened if it had run out when she was only half way through the door.

The car was pulling out now and soon disappeared out of sight, she stood up and so did Josh.

"What are you going to do now tell the Cops?" Asked Josh.

"I don't know what I'm going to do," She said. "I'm not going to the Police they wouldn't understand, and they'd probably call in some social worker or something, then all that would happen is that valuable time would be wasted."

"I don't know where the Head is, I don't know where David is and I'm lost."

It had all got too much for Jenny and she started to cry.

"Hey don't cry, I ain't got no hankie." Said Josh then he grabbed her arm, "Look there's a yellow cab just pulled up."

Jenny looked up and rubbed the tears away from her eyes, it was a yellow cab and who should be getting out but Mark, she ducked down again.

"What's up now?" Asked Josh.

But Jenny didn't answer she was too busy watching Mark go up the steps put a key in the door and try to open it.

He was taking the key out and examining it, he put it back in and tried again but still it wouldn't work. Mark knocked on the door repeatedly, then getting no answer he stepped back, looked up at the windows and cupping his hands in front of his mouth called out their names.

"He's okay! He's not one of them." Said Jenny, leaping up and shouting "Mark, Mark!" He turned surprised to see her outside and ran down the steps as she raced up to him followed by Josh.

"Oh Mark, you don't know how pleased I am to see you."

"But what's going on, what are you doing outside?"

Jenny told him the full story,

"Come and sit in the Cab and let's think things over." He said.

"Can Josh come to?" Asked Jenny.

"Yeah, of course he can."

They all sat in the Cab, Jenny and Mark in the front and Josh in the back.

"We've got a right old problem on our hands now." Said Mark.

"Had you been to Bertha's house before or should I say this house before?" Asked Jenny.

"Nope, yesterday was the first time I'd been here, Bertha gave me the address and told me we should help ourselves to anything we wanted, as there was plenty of food in the fridge and freezer so just feel free she said"

"Did the key you have open the front door yesterday?"

"Actually I didn't need to use it, I went to put it in the lock and the door just swung open and I've never given it any thought since."

"We could ask Bertha what she knows about this." Suggested Jenny.

"We can't, no-one's seen Bertha since yesterday, she told me she was off for a few days to a friends but no one else seems to know anything about it, and she hasn't rang in."

"Another dead end." Said Jenny in despair.

"First things first, what was the registration number of the car?" Asked Mark, there was silence, "You didn't get it did you?"

"No, I can't believe I didn't, I just never thought, did you Josh?" Asked Jenny with hope in her voice.

Josh shook his head and everyone fell silent.

"There's been so much happening I forgot to ask you did you phone Crinkles?"

It was Mark's turn now to look stupid,

"No, I didn't."

"No!" cried out Jenny, "Why not?"

"Well I did and I didn't."

"Did and didn't?" Jenny was hopping about on the seat.

"Yeah, I must have put the number down wrong so I phoned enquiries but I couldn't remember the name properly."

"Crinkles! Crinkles!" Shouted Jenny.

"Yeah, that's it Crimples, oops sorry Crinkles"

"We'll do that now then at least I will be able to team up with the Head, but I'll have to borrow the money from you for the phone call."

"No problem." Said Mark.

The third phone box they stopped at was working and after a bit of hassle they managed to get through to Crinkles. Miss. Millthrop answered and apparently the Head had been calling almost every hour, she had his phone number and his Hotel address but what was happening? The School was in a turmoil trying to find out.

Jenny said there just wasn't time to explain everything as David had been kidnapped and she had to go as they had no more money. Jenny had only just said that when the phone cut off. Jenny put the phone down and raced back to the Cab. The second she had mentioned David being kidnapped she knew it was a mistake, but there was nothing she could do about it now.

It was a pity Jenny had mentioned David being kidnapped as no one at Crinkles could possibly do anything about it. But once word got round the School which took about 10 minutes, a lot of people there did a lot of worrying.

"I've got the address for the Head's Hotel but first I'd like to ring him, can I borrow some more money Mark?"

"Here you go Jenny that should be more than enough."

With a quick thank you Jenny dashed off back to the phone and dialled the Head. The phone started to ring.

"Oh, be in, be in, please be in." Cried Jenny to herself.

"Hello, Dr.Phillpotts."

"Headmaster!! it's me Jenny, I'm so pleased to hear your voice."

"Jenny!! Oh Jenny!! I've been so worried where are you? What happened?"

"I'm on my way over now to the Hotel, we have a Taxi here I'll explain when I see you in about, hang on." Jenny opened the phone box door and shouted across to Mark, "How long will it take us to get to the Hotel?"

"About 20 to 30 minutes."

"We'll be there in about 20 to 30 minutes I'm leaving now."

Jenny put the phone down before the Headmaster could ask any more questions and dashed back to the Cab, they sped off and 25 minutes later pulled up outside the Hotel. Jenny jumped out and Mark drove off to find somewhere to park the Cab. The Head was standing outside waiting for her and they both hugged each other with relief.

"But where is David? Still in the Taxi?" Asked the Head.

"No, he's been kidnapped!"

"KIDNAPPED!!!" cried out the Head. "You had better tell me the full story let's go straight up to our rooms."

Jenny had started to tell the Head everything that had happened since they got off the bus, then she suddenly remembered Mark and young Josh.

"Can I bring Mark and Josh up? Headmaster"

"Of course you can, in fact I'll come down with you."

The Head and Jenny went down to the Lobby but there was no sign of them, they went outside and found Mark and Josh standing in front of the Hotel.

"We didn't know your room number or your full name so we thought it best to wait out here." Said Mark.

Jenny introduced everyone and they went back up to the Heads room where he ordered some refreshments from room service.

"Well," said the Head, "I got off the bus when you didn't return and waited and waited until it was nearly dark. Then I returned to the Hotel and contacted everyone I know who was still in New York, but no one had seen either of you or heard anything. I couldn't understand what could have happened. Some friends contacted the Police and the Hospitals for me but there was no news, you had both completely disappeared."

"I was just on the verge of reporting you officially missing when you rang Jenny. But how do we find David? New York's a very big place to try and find anyone even if they aren't being hidden away."

Everyone sat looking glum, no one could come up with an idea, then the phone rang it was the Hotel Reception, a letter had been left for the Head marked extremely urgent. The Head went down to collect it and had opened it and read it in the lift coming back, he looked very worried when he came into the room.

"It's from the kidnappers, they will return David safely if we give them the book dividers."

"Book dividers!" Said Mark confused. "You kidnap somebody for book dividers?"

"It's a long story." Replied the Head.

"What are book dividers?" Asked Josh.

Jenny explained and Josh also thought it was a really stupid request.

"They are giving us until this time tomorrow to have them available for collection from Crinkles, We have to leave a reply to this note marked to be called for by Alexis at the Reception Desk."

"Great." Cried out Josh, "We see who picks it up and we follow them."

"Yes, it sounds easy." Agreed the Head "Certainly worth a try."

"What are you going to put in the reply?" Asked Jenny.

"I'm going to try and buy some time, I will tell them that I have no idea what they are talking about."

The note was written and taken by the Head to the Hotel Reception and Mark who everyone agreed was the least likely to be recognised by whoever collected the envelope hung around the lobby waiting to see who would collect it.

This was a lot easier said than done, there were three people working on the Reception Desk and often as many as 6 or 7 people gathered there.

After about half an hour Mark went over to the Reception Desk and asked was there a letter there to be collected by Alexis.

The girl checked, sorry she said there wasn't one. Mark queried this and asked her to double check. She looked again and said there was definitely no letter there, her colleague working next to her overheard the conversation and said that he had given a letter for Alexis to a lady about 10 minutes ago. She had enquired about rooms for next week and they had discussed vacancies for some time, he had given her literature and she had put the envelope into the Hotel Brochure and left.

Mark went up to report to the Head and everyone looked very dismayed.

"I'm sorry Headmaster it's my fault" said Mark "I was looking for someone walking away with a letter in their hand, it sounds stupid now but I never thought about it being hidden in a brochure."

"It's not your fault Mark, it was always what I think you call a long shot, with the Hotel Reception always being so busy it really needed more than one person. We will just have to wait till they contact us again.

"Headmaster" said Jenny "I know you have enough on your mind with David, but I'm becoming a little worried about Josh's parents."

The Headmaster nodded in reply to Jenny.

"Josh," he said, "Won't your Mam and Dad be worried about you?"

"Nah," he said, "I have no dad, he left a couple of years ago and mum's at work she won't be back until very late, she has two jobs one working in a clothing factory from 8.30a.m until 5.00p.m. then goes straight to the club where she works late."

"Do you make your own meals?" Asked Jenny.

"Nah, Mum makes them at weekends, and during the week she makes sandwiches for me and leaves money for hamburgers and that sort of stuff, I eat good man."

"What about school shouldn't you be there?"

"I don't go much."

"But you should." Scolded Jenny.

"Yeah, I know." And he gave Jenny one of his big grins.

The Head had been thinking while Jenny had been talking to Josh,

"It's unlikely I know, but I wonder if they would take David back to the flat, and it's the only lead we've got."

"It's worth a try, let's check it out." Pleaded Jenny. 10 minutes later found them sitting at a road junction waiting for the lights to change as they headed back towards Bertha's flat when Josh suddenly shouted.

"THERE'S THE BLACK LIMO!!!"

"Where?" Asked Jenny.

Josh pointed "Look there, in the outside lane on the opposite side, waiting for the lights to change same as us."

"Are you sure?" Asked Jenny.

"Yep, I recognise the chauffer."

"But Josh he's going in the opposite direction to us." said Mark. "And when the lights change we'll lose him I can't do a U turn here."

"No, but you could go through the lights and do a U turn where the traffics lighter." Said Josh.

"He'll be long gone by then." Mark replied.

"No he won't." grinned Josh. "I'll stop him." Before anyone realised what was going on he had opened the Cab door and shot across the road.

"What's he doing?" Cried Jenny.

"He's run over the road to the other side, now he's running in front of those cars and the lights are changing, strewth he's run in front of the Black Buick and he's Break Dancing!"

We were driving through the lights and looking at us was Josh grinning and dancing in front of the car, while the Black Buick's driver furiously sounded his horn.

"Oh look at this!!" Said Mark. "I don't believe it, that big truck that's coming up is going to stop us turning, I'm getting round him no matter what."

The truck driver was sounding his horn at us and winding his window down he shouted.

"Hey bud, you trying to commit suicide?" Mark ignored him and was now jostling for a position on the outside.

"It's still there," said Jenny, "It's been caught by the lights again." Our Cab was sitting two cars and a small van behind it, there was a tap on the window and the door opened and in popped Josh beaming and smiling,

"I told you I could stop him." He said smiling.

"Yes, but you could have been killed." Said the Head.

Josh shrugged his shoulders. "I did it for friends." And he gave us one of his huge grins.

We discreetly followed the Black Buick which isn't too difficult when you're in a Yellow Cab in New York, they're everywhere, thousands of them.

It finally turned down a quiet side street and we followed, when it stopped outside a small Hotel we drove straight past and stopped further down outside another small Hotel, the street was full of small Hotels on both sides of the road.

"Now what do we do?" Asked Jenny.

The problem was no one knew what to do, the chauffeur had got out of the Limo and walked into the Hotel, Mark turned to the Head.

"You stay here with Jenny and Josh as they could recognise you all and I'll have a stroll up to the Hotel and see what's what."

"Be careful." Said the Head.

"That's my middle name." Replied Mark.

Josh gave one of his big smiles and said, "I'm coming to."

Mark knew it was useless to protest and they both got out of the Cab and walked towards the Hotel where the Black Buick was parked outside. Suddenly Mark realised that Josh had disappeared, where on earth has he gone he thought looking in vain for him in all directions.

That little devil, what is he up too now. Mark was at the Hotel entrance and what a really dingy run down place it was.

He went in and walked up to the Reception where a scruffy looking bloke sat in a little office, outside on the Reception

Desk was a little bell with a homemade sign saying 'Ring for Attention'.

Mark didn't ring the bell as he was playing for time, he just had that feeling something was going to happen. Eventually the scruffy looking guy wondering why he hadn't rang the bell came out,

"What do you want? Didn't you see the bell?"

"What bell?" Mark asked.

"This bell! This bell! It's big enough isn't it?"

"Oh yes, it's big alright."

"Then why didn't you ring it?"

"Didn't see it." said Mark, the scruffy looking man was becoming annoyed.

"I'm here to pick up a fare."

"We've ordered no cab."

Just then at the far end of the corridor appeared the chauffer and another man with David who was looking very frightened, each of the men had a hand on his shoulders.

"Hey! I told you we ordered no cab so why are you still hanging about?

Mark had turned away so that David couldn't see him and the three of them had walked passed not even giving him a glance.

"Okay I must have been wrong." said Mark.

"All you drivers are the same, I'm sick of it, forever in here touting for business."

But Mark was now following David and the two men out into the street, the chauffeur had stopped, then rushed towards the car forgetting about David,

"Look at my tyres." He shouted. The second man looked down at the flat tyres, Mark had come up from behind and grabbed David shouting.

"RUN DAVID, RUN!!"

The chauffer spun round but was too far away to do anything, however the other man was able to hold onto David's arm and gripped it tightly,

"No you don't!" He cried, just then Josh appeared and kicked the man so hard in the shin that even Mark felt it, the man shouted and involuntarily let go of David to grab his ankle, before he could recover, Mark, Josh and David shot down the street with the chauffer in hot pursuit.

Mark knew they would never make it into the Cab the chauffeur was too close. Josh had shot off to the left and David and Mark dashed into a garage forecourt and dodged amongst the cars filling up with petrol, then they ran across to the side of the forecourt where there were dozens of cars lined up for sale.

Now they raced across to the car wash with the chauffer still in hot pursuit and quickly doubled back keeping very low and were now thankfully some distance from the chauffeur, they hid amongst a bunch of cars outside the filling station diner.

The chauffeur was still poking about the car wash area but once they broke cover he would be after them again, he was young and very fit, whereas Mark was already gasping for breath he couldn't have run much further and David seemed to be still in a partial Daze. They were both crouching behind a grey saloon car wondering where to go from here when a Cab pulled into the forecourt. Mark looked up, a Cab, 'that's my Cab'!! He whispered to David as it pulled over blocking the chauffeur's view.

"Come on David!" Said Mark, and still keeping very low they crept out from behind the cars opened the rear door of the Cab and swiftly tumbled in and lay on the floor along with the Head and Jenny who were also crouching down.

As the Cab moved off and drove past the pumps David peered over the back seat,

"He's searching around where we were hiding outside the diner, but he hasn't twigged that we're in the Cab." David told everyone and then ducked back down out of site. "We only just made it in time."

The Cab had now stopped to wait for a gap in the traffic, as soon as one appeared it was off like a rocket.

"What a relief, he can't catch us now. I think we can all get up." Said the Head. "And make ourselves a bit more comfortable."

The Cab was turning on to the main highway and Mark looked up from the floor at the Headmaster.

"But you're not driving."

"No," replied the Head, "I can't drive."

"I'm not driving." Said Mark with a terrified look on his face, "and David and Jenny are here that leaves only, NO!! I daren't look."

It had suddenly dawned on Mark who was driving.

"Its Josh driving isn't it!" Shouted Mark.

"He sure is man." Said Josh.

They were all sitting up now, Josh could barely see over the dashboard, and couldn't sit on the seat properly because his feet wouldn't have touched the pedals, so his bottom was just partly on the very edge of the seat. To anyone outside it would appear that here was a Yellow Cab with four passengers in the back and no driver.

Mark gulped. "Now Josh, don't panic!! Don't Panic!!!"

"I ain't panicking man, you're the guy who's panicking."

There were three lanes of traffic going in their direction, it was very, very busy and they were in the outside lane.

"Pull over Josh and I'll take over." Pleaded Mark.

"Yes pull over Josh." Said the Head, "Please."

"Can't pull over here and stop man far too dangerous, only a New York Cab driver would suggest it, anyway our turn off is coming up soon."

"But we're in the wrong lane Josh!!" Shouted Mark. "We should be in the inside lane!!"

"Yeah, I've got to move over soon."

"You can't see in the mirrors can you Josh?"

"Nope, can't see in the mirrors, but here we go." and flashing his indicator he started to turn right, he put his foot down and shot across the centre lane and straight over into a space in the inside lane barely the length of the car.

"Dam New York Cab drivers!!!" screamed the driver of the car in the middle lane who had been forced to slam his brakes on, as had the two cars and two trucks behind him.

"Did you see that!! Did you see that love!! Did you!!" His wife didn't answer she had fainted.

On the inside lane a bus, van and two trucks had to slam their brakes on to avoid hitting Josh.

Everyone was cursing and swearing, vehicles juddering, screeching tyres leaving rubber scorch marks 20 to 30 foot long on the road.

"How these guys get a license beats me, I wonder sometimes have they got one." shouted a trucker sounding his horn repeatedly.

Josh hadn't batted an eye, but the others in the back were so stunned they didn't say a word.

Josh turned onto the slip road, then left at the top and left again, after a few minutes he turned into a trading estate and stopped the Cab, he got out grinning and opened the passenger door.

"Perhaps you'd better drive now." He said to Mark.

Mark climbed out and realised his legs were shaking, while Josh climbed calmly into the back seat of the Cab. Mark sat in the driver's seat for a while trying to calm himself down.

"I hope no one got my number." He said as he finally managed to drive off.

"I was safer with the kidnappers than with you driving this Cab." Said David to Josh, but Josh just grinned.

With everyone eventually back safely at the Hotel and all in one piece, they relaxed a little.

"The first thing I must do is ring Crinkles and tell them David is safe."

After ringing Crinkles with the good news the Head organised well deserved refreshments for everyone from room service, and he made sure there was more than ample to go round as he knew David and Josh would really tuck in.

"Well." Said the Head "Let us try and work out what has been going on."

The Head was quite sure that when Disdorf's colleague saw David and Jenny outside the flat and recognised them he was as surprised at seeing them as David and Jenny were at seeing him. He instinctively decided to follow the taxi that the children had got into.

He probably phoned Disdorf on a mobile from the car and Disdorf putting two and two together had realised that this could be the cause of the strange behaviour that evening of Daniel and Samantha.

How they had met was obviously by pure chance but what an opportunity had come his way. If he could get hold of the children there was a good possibility he could get the valuable book dividers and at least rescue something from what had become a complete disaster.

"Those book dividers again." Said Josh. "How can book dividers be valuable?" He asked.

"They're very old Josh, very, very, old." Answered the Head.

"Yeah, I think it's funny people pay lots and lots of money for old stuff, I like new stuff me."

We all laughed and Josh grinned.

"Well to continue." said the Head, "Disdorf would be thinking to himself where will the children go, he knew there was some reason why you hadn't gone back to your Hotel. He didn't know of course that it was because you didn't know the name of it or where it was having swapped Hotels without you knowing, then you both slept for two and a half days."

"Two and a half days!" said Josh. "Boy you must have been tired, really tired, that must be that jet lagging or something." The Head smiled at Josh and continued,

"Well when you did wake up we had breakfast and then went straight out and I never thought to mention the name of the new Hotel. Then once outside the magic of New York took over and you never thought to ask any questions, thinking back you were both still probably a little drowsy and hadn't even realised the Hotel looked different.."

"Mind you none of this would have mattered if you had got back to the bus on time."

"Bus on time?" Said Josh.

"It's a long story Josh, too long to tell tonight." Said the Head and Josh gave another one of his cheeky grins.

Both Jenny and David started to look sheepish and down at the floor.

"Cheer up you two." said the Head. "Everything was more my fault than yours."

"Well I think," Said the Head, "That Disdorf guessed that the taxi would be taking you both to Daniel and Samantha's Dad's place."

"A few quick phone calls and no doubt a few hundred dollars and Daniel's dad Mark was told a safer place would be Bertha's, am I right?"

"You're right." Said Mark, "It was suggested that Bertha's would be a safer place and I was told where to find a key to let myself in, a key that turned out to be useless."

"Yes useless, you were never meant to be able to get into the flat with that key, only think you could, the flat of course," said the Head, "Was not Bertha's but belonging to one of Disdorf's colleagues or employees, perhaps it was the chauffeurs flat. Bertha was probably paid to go on holiday for a few days so that no one could contact her and no one would know that David and Jenny were not actually staying at Bertha's flat."

"He certainly hadn't allowed for our very good friend Josh's appearance, to Josh we all owe a great deal. Without him this successful outcome would not have been possible."

"What are friends for?" Said Josh smiling.

"Disdorf, had been forced to think very fast in order to take advantage of this unexpected opportunity." Said the Head. "What he had not realised was that Jenny still had a surprising amount of Magic Power left. As he had been that drained himself he assumed that you would be totally drained. He never dreamt either of you would be able to escape from the flat"

Josh's eyes had grown huge.

"MAGIC POWER!!! What Magic power?" Josh asked eagerly.

"That's just an expression we use in England." said Jenny. "It sort of means we are wide awake, wide awake to what's going on."

Josh looked at Jenny, he didn't grin this time but looked a little serious, he hadn't forgot how she had appeared from nowhere.

"So," continued the Head, "Disdorf was wrong footed and found he was left with only one hostage David. Mind you we were very fortunate that Josh spotted the Black Buick and recognised the chauffeur, what the outcome would have been if he hadn't doesn't bear thinking about. The help of Mark and Josh two complete strangers only a day ago in rescuing David is a debt we and Crinkle's will never be able to repay." The Head paused, he had noticed the unease in Mark and asked if he wanted to say something.

"Yeah, I'm worried Head, my two children Daniel and Samantha live with their Mum. That guy Disdorf or Bert Clark as I know him is her best friend and he always stays there when he's in New York. Daniel and Samantha must be in some danger when he's such an evil guy." The Head smiled reassuringly,

"I'm certain they're in no danger, he needs a parallel life, an apparent normal existence and he won't endanger that. If Daniel and Samantha question him at all which I don't think they will, he will persuade them that it was all largely in their imagination and a lot of what took place is exaggerated"

The head paused and noticed Mark was not really convinced, he continued.

"As there won't be any contact with us, David and Samantha would gradually except the clever explanations given by

Disdorf and look upon it as being some sort of strange adventure, on the other hand I feel it will probably never be mentioned."

"True he supported the Evil Wizards, but their powers have been almost completely destroyed, your children are definitely not important to him."

"We should have years and years of peace and quiet, but we will have to be ever watchful at Crinkles in the future. If at any time you do have worries about Daniel and Samantha then contact me immediately."

"But aren't you going to do anything to this Disdorf guy? Some revenge of some kind, make him pay in some way, kick his butt after all the trouble he's caused you?" asked Mark.

"No, Nothing." Said the Head.

"Nothing!" Repeated Josh.

"It's all over Josh. Although the idea of Mark's to kick Distorf's and a few others butts is very, very appealing, it would in fact achieve nothing other than stirring up a hornet's nest. We'll have no more trouble from Disdorf or any of his cronies, how could we, when we have you on our side Josh." Josh gave us one of his big cheeky grins and we all laughed.

"As I said before we should have years and years of peace and quiet though it would pay us and make sense to keep an eye out for anything that doesn't look or feel right. However for the moment I'm sure we'll have no more trouble."

How wrong can you be? The Head sees good in everyone, he thinks that even Evil People will change their ways. My experience of the World and Life is that Evil People change their ways if they are caught or it suits them.

Once they are clear of any punishment for past deeds, or they feel there is no advantage any longer of being reformed they pretty quickly revert back to their old ways. They do this as quietly and discretely as possible of course, no point in drawing attention to yourself.

In our case it wasn't going to be long before our old enemies reappeared, along with new ones.

"Well Mark" said the Head, "It's time for us to say goodbye and thank you for all your help, we are off back to England and Crinkles early tomorrow. It's up to you how much you tell Daniel and Samantha when you see them, if you do tell them everything they will be a little disappointed at missing all the adventures we've had together. But remember it could make the Bert Clark business a problem. It would probably be best to just say David and Jenny remembered the Hotel they were staying at and you took them back. We will keep in touch."

"Yes! We certainly will." Chorused David and Jenny.

Jenny put her arms around Mark and gave him a Kiss, David shook his hand and Mark ruffled David's hair.

"Don't go doing any of that fancy driving man if I aint there." Said Josh with a huge grin on his face.

Mark gave Josh's arm a friendly light punch then put his arm around him.

"I'm going to miss everyone." Said Mark, with a lump in his throat.

"This is for you Mark" said the Head, Handing him an envelope.

"What's this?" Asked Mark

"It's some money."

"No way am I taking it." Said Mark annoyed.

"Mark" said the Head "there is no way we can repay you for all you have done for us, this money is to cover the petrol you have used and your time when you could have had fare paying passengers, we want you to have it, you must take it, you have to earn a living and have bills to pay just like everyone else. We won't take it back"

"Okay" replied Mark, and they shook hands and patted each other on the shoulder.

We stood outside our Hotel and waved and waved till Mark's Cab with Josh's grinning face in the rear window disappeared from our view.

CHAPTER TWENTY-SEVEN

The Equalizing Room

Brian thought he knew every room, nook and cranny at Crinkles Academy, but he was wrong. Centuries ago when Crinkles as it is today was built, the original Wizards School was demolished and most of Crinkles as we know it built on the original site. A few of the original underground rooms being that substantial that it was cheaper, faster and made a stronger foundation to build on top of them rather than attempt to remove them.

All access to these rooms and corridors was lost, sealed in by the new building. All except one, the one with an Evil past – The Equalizing Room. This room had lain unused for Centuries when work started on the construction of Crinkles, and had remained unused for Centuries from the opening of Crinkles until two years ago. Since then it has been used on six occasions, this was to be the seventh.

Hundreds and Hundreds and Hundreds of years ago the original Wizards School had been very different from today's Crinkles. As well as being a School for the teaching of Magic Crafts to Young Wizards it had three other distinct functions.

Part of it was organised as a Retreat for Wizards who needed relaxation and recuperation for whatever reason. They had the freedom of the Library, the gardens and surrounding countryside and were under no pressure of any kind. Wizards came from all over the World to this retreat and stayed from a few weeks to months, the odd one even years. There was no time limit to their length of stay.

Another part of the School was set aside for Senior Wizards to be taught Advanced and Specialised Magic. These Wizards also came from around the World and would stay for weeks perhaps months. They had very little contact with anyone else at the School other than their own groups and Masters.

There was a third group of people who once again came from all over the World. They stayed from only a few days through to years, this group hade no contact with anyone being totally isolated even from each other. They were Prisoners, facing Judgment.

Facing Banishment, Internment from months to years, or Death, from a swift Death to a long painful one.

It was in this room, The Equalizing Room where the Final Judgments were made and the Judgments acted upon.

Access to this room was from outside the School and still remains to this day.

The room is some 45 feet long by 15 feet wide and has a thick wooden door at each end.

A prisoner or prisoners would be brought in through one door, they would already be chained around the ankles and arms chained behind their backs. They were now chained to the floor to await judgment. When judgment had been passed they were unchained from the floor and led away through the opposite door, they were the lucky ones. The others after judgment had been passed were tortured, sometimes mercilessly before being unchained and led out. On the floor of this room are two lines of six shackling rings.

Running down the centre of the room a rounded gulley eighteen inches wide by three inches at the deepest point, this gulley sloped towards and under the exit door. Wooden buckets full of water would have been against the walls under the candles and two or three in each corner.

The water was to wash away the blood from the stone floor and into the gulley, under the door and out of the room. Incense burners to mask the stench are still in position on the walls at either side of the candle alcoves.

Each of the side walls has six domed roofed alcoves approximately seven feet high by four feet wide by three feet deep with a wooden door at the back.

Between the large alcoves the three feet wide wall has a small alcove in the centre five feet from the floor and eighteen inches square by nine inches deep, each of which contain a large candle four inches in diameter.

When the candles are lit the light spreads clearly for about four feet, this leaves the centre of the room about seven feet in width in poor light.

Inside each of the doomed roofed alcoves is a strange self standing Robe. It has a wicker work frame from the floor to the top of the head. This frame is covered in a thick woven black wool cloth. At the back of each alcove is a wooden door that opens away from the room into a narrow passageway.

The Judgmentors would walk down the passageway to their door, unlock it using their Magic password and virtually step into the whicker framed Robe from the back. The door closing automatically once they were inside the Robe, this was the Equalizer, the male or female Judgmetors, fat, thin, tall, small, no matter what the combination once inside the whicker framed Robe they all became identical.

Standing six foot six tall in the whicker framed Robe and almost as wide as the alcove, their faces completely covered except for the tiny slits for their eyes.

Reeds insides the face masks made all the Judgmentors voices sound the same. No one knew who anyone else was, their identities remaining secret.

The only part that was flexible was the arms, when a Judgment was to be made, if it was guilty, or voting on a motion and in favour then they raised their right arm.

No arm raised meant not guilty or no to a proposed motion.

At 1 a.m on the morning of the day the Headmaster, David and Jenny were due back from America, a meeting had been called for the Judgmentors, The Evil Wizards at Crinkles to gather in the Equalizer Room.

Each had silently made their way to the old ruined Coach House that had burnt down many years ago. The damage had been extensive and as the cost of repairs was so high and the School had no need for the Coach House it had been decided to knock down the unsafe parts of the roof and walls and simply leave it as a safe ruin.

The ruin was now that overgrown by bushes it was almost hidden from view. Officially it was 'Out of Bounds' to pupils. New pupils did of course go there to explore only to find two small one medium and three large piles of old stone with some of the original mortar still attatched buried amongst bushes, mostly dense thorn bushes.

Usually about ten minutes and two or three nasty thorn scratches did the trick, and the pupil or pupils gave up any further exploring and headed back to the School.

However all was not quite what it seemed. After midnight and up to 4 a.m on a day a meeting was called, with the correct Magic words, two ferocious thorn bushes would move apart to reveal a stone wall. Further Magic words and the stonewall would reveal an opening into a passage way. Once the Evil Wizard had stepped through into the passage way the stonewall would close and the thorn bushes close in again.

From reaching the thorn bushes through to entering the passage way and everything outside returning to normal took less than fifteen seconds.

The command to attend a meeting was by an innocent look-ing discrete message on the School Notice Board. In this case it read:

Lost on about the 10th, a little book of poems, if found please hand into the School Office.

Translated this reads: Meeting on the 20th.

This is how it works, you check the notice board it's the 15th there's a note referring to the 10th. From the 10th to the 15th is five days so you add five days to the 15th equals the 20th.

If it appeared on the board on the 18th and the 15th was on the note it would be a meeting on the 21st.

Obviously other notes could be put up with dates on them but you would only be interested in the one with the secret tiny dot code at two locations.

The Judgmentor now in the passage would walk a few feet then turn right then left or left then right and walk down that passage until reaching the door leading into their alcove. Magic words known only by that person would open the door, and once inside the Robe the door would self close and lock until it was time to leave.

Each person left the school at a set time to make their way to the Equalizing Room. There was a five minute interval between each participants time. They went fully Cloaked and Hooded so that no Evil Wizard knew who another Evil Wizard was, and in the unlikely event that so early in the morning anyone else would see them they would have no idea who it was.

The only person in the School who knew all the Evil Wizards was the 'Grand Judgmentor'.

They were all gathered in the Equalizing Room wondering why the meeting had been called. Then a strange sounding voice (due to the reed voice box) said:

"Welcome everyone to our seventh meeting."

"As you know all the plans previously made have failed for various reasons, there is no time to go into detail as to why we failed, enough to say that none of us thought failure was a possibility, and we certainly thought complete failure – impossible."

The speaker gave time for his words to be digested, then continued:

"The Grand Master Wizards are having to plan a new strategy, they have left me to decide on what should be done here at Crinkles, I will give you a quick summary and my proposals in each case."

"Dr. Emanual Phillpotts, he is highly intelligent, and a superb Master Wizard, and his long friendship with 'Merlin' makes him a powerful enemy, unfortunately it would be too dangerous to eliminate him, the repercussions could bring us all down."

The speaker paused,

"In a few years time we may be able to eliminate him, but our Grand Masters want some action started as soon as possible." Once again the speaker paused, the others could hear a very dull patting noise the speaker always did this when very annoyed.

"Now we move on to that idiot Brian, the Caretaker come so called 'Handy Man'. Uneducated, no Magic Power what so ever, no match for any of us, yet he was one of the main causes for our defeat. We underestimate him, he actually has two great powers beyond our Magic to stop. He has common sense and he applies it, he's also lucky, very 'LUCKY!!', Lady Luck as they call it shines down on him. He has to go!!! And the sooner the better, we must think of something unsuspicious, for example working on roofs can be very dangerous work, very dangerous indeed."

"All those in favour of decisive action against the Caretaker, 'VOTE NOW'!!"

All the right arms instantly came out.

"Motion carried Unanimously!!!" The soft patting noise started again.

"Now we come to the children we have recruited, they are useless to us not one of them has shown any real potential and there are no signs that there will be any improvement in the future. They are only capable of creating mischief, we will continue to use them for errands and to disrupt some of the lessons to help undermine the Schools morale."

"What we need is children with the capabilities of David and Jenny on our side, of the two Jenny is the one we need, her Magic powers are exceptional and improving daily. Unfortunately I feel there is no way we could recruit her as she is too faithful to Phillpotts and the School.

That only leaves the second choice David. I feel we have no alternative but to make every effort to slowly, quietly, unobtrusively lure him into our web."

"All those in favour of making maximum effort to recruit David 'VOTE NOW'!!"

Once more all the right arms came out.

"Motion carried Unanimously!!!"

There were a few minutes of complete silence.

"Lastly I feel we need one of our cats here at Crinkles, we would have to turn it back into a kitten, no one can resist one of our cats as a kitten. It would definitely be given a home here at the School.

It was because of one of Crinkles cats, 'Humbug' I believe it's called, that the books were found in the van. It's possible that if one of our cats had been at the School it would have driven 'Humbug' away."

The speaker had started to make the patting noises again.

"The three most Disarming yet Sly, Evil cats we have are: 'Trevelion', 'Marmaduke Dance' and 'Spirous'.

If you agree that we need a cat, then vote for two out of the three when I call their names out,

'VOTE NOW'!!"

As each cats name was called those in favour put out their right arms.

The speaker announced:

"It's a draw between Trevelion and Marmaduke Dance. Let us vote again between the two cats, this time for only one cat."

The vote took place and it was announced:

"It's a draw again."

The room fell silent, then a voice identical of course to the person who had just finished speaking called out:

"Is there any reason why we can't have both cats?"

"I can't see any reason why we couldn't have the two cats." Replied the original voice. "So let us vote on having two cats."

"'VOTE NOW'!!"

All the right arms came out.

"Motion carried Unanimously!!!"

"I will arrange for the two cats to join the School as kittens, before we close the meeting does anyone wish to speak?"

There was a cold eerie silence, the minutes ticked by and no one spoke.

"As no one has anything further to add, I now declare this meeting closed, but wish to remind everyone that the School Notice Board should be checked daily from 12 noon onwards, and that when arriving for a meeting or leaving as we are about to now, enter or leave only if it is 'silent outside'. If you hear Our Crows 'croaking' don't make any attempt to enter just walk by, or if leaving stay inside until it has gone quiet.

We all have jobs to do, let us depart and make an early start."

CHAPTER TWENTY-EIGHT

Homecoming

Jenny, David and the Head were having there last delicious breakfast at the Hotel. They would soon be heading home, unfortunately none of them had seen much of New York after all, no Empire State Building, no river cruise, no Statue Of Liberty, perhaps they may come back one day, who knows.

No one could say they hadn't had an eventful time, too eventful, so much had happened they had not been able to take it all in.

It was going to be very sad leaving their new friends behind, Daniel, Samantha, their Dad Mark and especially Josh, they'd miss his cheeky grin but there were others they'd be quite happy never to see again.

Jenny and David wanted to give Josh a memento, he was coming to the Hotel to say goodbye.

It had to be something that you couldn't get in New York, this made it very difficult if not almost impossible because you can get virtually anything in New York.

After breakfast they went back to their rooms to finish packing and told the Head about the problem of a little gift for Josh. He pondered for a moment then said:

"I've got it," and he reopened one of his cases and rummaged around inside. "There!" And in his hand he held a Wand.

"It's an old and very tired Wand, a bit like me. It needs one very caring owner who will not demand any serious Magic from it, but who knows? It might just do a little Magic for Josh from time to time if he needs it, not that he will know about it of course."

Jenny and David were delighted, and so was Josh who started to cry when they gave it to him. The Head looked at Josh and we could see that he was also going to miss him.

"Josh." He said. "Could you do me a big favour?"

"Anything Head." Josh replied enthusiastically.

"Well we're off soon and we have some American money left over and we won't have time to change it and it's not much use back home, will you take it?"

"Take your money! No way man."

"You'll do us a big favour if you would."

"Are you sure I'll be doing you a favour?" Queried Josh.

"Yes I'm sure, very sure." said the Head.

"Well okay then." Replied Josh, although he still didn't seem to be convinced that he was doing the Head a favour.

The Head went out of the room and came back a little later with a thick sealed envelope which had the Hotels name and crest in the corner.

On the front he had written, 'To Josh, a great friend, a small repayment for a big debt, with all our Love from Jenny, David and the Head of Crinkles Academy, England, the Head had signed the bottom.

Dr. Christian Phillpotts.

Headmaster, Crinkles Academy, England.

Handing the envelope to Josh, he also told him there was a letter inside for his Mam, he knew Josh would give his Mam all the money. The Head rummaged around in his pockets and produced a pile of loose change.

"For you Josh." he said putting the pile of change into his hand.

"I'm rich!" Josh shouted.

"You're richer than you know Josh, you're richer than some of the richest people in the World. We've got to go now but I know Jenny and David will be thinking of you and will be writing to you soon."

"Take good care of your Mam and yourself," and the Head whispered in Josh's ear "and take good care of your Wand."

"Josh, I also have a favour to ask you. Will you do it for me?" asked Jenny.

"You bet." He replied.

"Well when David and I get back to England we will be going to school every day, will you promise me you will go to school?"

"You mean 'everyday'?"

"Yes every day."

"Not every day man, I couldn't take it."

"But if you don't." said Jenny. "You will regret it when you grow older."

"If I'd gone to school every day, I wouldn't have met up with you guys and been able to help you out."

Jenny looked at the Head and David. There was no answer to that.

"Josh." Said the Head. "Will you go to school every day without fail for one month? I think you may be surprised at how you'll feel at the end of it."

"One month!"

The look on Josh's face told us that one month in his eyes was a very long time.

"Okay." He said. "One month it is."

Jenny gave him a big hug and they both started to cry. David gave him a light good natured punch on his arm and just managed to hold back the tears.

The Head smiling patted him on the back. It was time to go down to the Hotel Reception as the cab was almost due, the Head had just settled the bill when a cab driver came over to the desk.

"Cab for a Dr.Phillpotts." He told the girl.

"That's me." Said the Head.

Gathering up our luggage we made our way outside and were soon sitting in the Yellow Cab. We all felt really sad, strange thought Jenny how fast it all finishes. One minute you're in a group of comrades and friends having faced days of danger and worry together. Then you get into a cab the door closes and that's it, it's all over.

Josh waved and waved until the Yellow Cab was out of sight, and then he ran almost all the way home.

It was Jenny's turn to have a window seat for the flight back home. She enjoyed the view after the take off and the 'Lilly White fluffy clouds' but she was still very tired and soon fell asleep.

David was bored, after the excitement of the plane taking off had passed he started watching a movie, but it was more for adults it was all talking and no action and soon he was also asleep.

The Head had to wake both of them as they approached London. Jenny loved flying over some of the famous buildings, Windsor Castle most of all.

They landed at Heathrow and made their way to the terminus to locate their luggage and had a small meal before joining the local flight back home.

Once the plane had landed they once more collected their luggage and were soon in a taxi settling down for the last part of the journey home, home to Crinkles.

So much had happened that it felt as though it was months and months since they had last seen Crinkles.

The taxi pulled off the main road and drove up to the School, they had phoned from Heathrow and again just before organising the taxi and were very surprised to see only me and Miss. Millthrop on the steps to welcome them back.

While the Head paid Ted the taxi driver we started to get our luggage out. Ted had chatted to us all the way back when all we wanted to do was sit quietly, he helped us with the luggage and gave us a big smile and said,

"It's always nice to get back home."

As he drove away Miss Millthrop and myself struggled up the steps with the suitcases into the entrance hall, as Jenny, David and the Headmaster went ahead empty handed.

"HOORAY! HOORAY! HIP, HIP, HOORAY!!" The whole School was gathered in the Main Hall clapping and cheering like 'Billy - O'.

Jenny and I both started to cry, we had cried a lot today but only a little out of sadness mostly out of happiness.

There was so much news and everyone except the Head wanted to tell their story first.

Smithers desperate to show the Head the terrible damage done to the Library and Millthrop to tell him about Cecilia and Scorn, other teachers about strange feelings and the draining of all their energy, dizziness and the desire to help or assist someone but whom and where they did not know.

Matron wanted to talk about all the pupils that had been feeling funny and very tired, and all the none stop phone calls from worried parents wondering if their children were all right as they had been feeling rather strange themselves.

The Head nodded and smiling, said:

"I'm afraid everyone will have to be a little patient for a while longer as we are so very, very tired."

The Head went to see Matron about Jenny and David having some peace and quiet, they protested strongly wanting to tell their friends all about their adventures but Matron made them go to bed.

"But we aren't tired! Not one bit!" They both cried out.

It had no effect on Matron who insisted they rested.

They lay on top of their beds in the little infirmary wide awake and fuming, but two minutes later they were sound asleep, I think the Head had something to do with that. The Matron wrapped them up under warm blankets, they slept soundly until lunchtime the following day.

The Head who had told everyone that he didn't want to be disturbed locked himself in his study, his good old comforting study, where he put himself into a light trance.

After lunch the following day the Head, Jenny and David felt fully refreshed, Jenny and David now started to tell their friends and anyone else who wanted to hear which was almost the whole School all about their 'American Adventures'.

Some of the day pupils who didn't want to miss out on the evening stories were going home later and later, saying it was detention, or extra homework that was easier to do at school. When the pupils heard about the restaurant adventure the Headmaster went up several points in their admiration. All the way from, 'A silly old dithering fool' to 'A canny old fool'.

Meanwhile the Head had organised a meeting in his study of Smithers, Miss. Millthrop and myself leaving strict orders that we were not to be disturbed.

He had arranged with Cook a lovely evening meal, he told us he didn't intend using any Magic not even to summon up food for a long, long time.

We told him the full story about poor Cecilia and Scorn. The Head didn't comment, he sat quietly and nodded at various points from time to time.

I decided I would take this opportunity to ask him about something that had puzzled me for some time. Smithers was eager to start talking about damage to the Library and I knew once he started there would be no time to get any answers from the Head. So I jumped in first.

"Headmaster there's something that has been troubling me perhaps you can help?"

"If I can I will Brian."

"We defended the Containment area, and we keep talking about the 'Containment Book'. If it's full of Evil Spells and the Good Spells to neutralise them then surely it must be a huge book or a very large set of books yet I haven't noticed either in that part of the Library."

"It's only one book Brian. It's not a small book but we do have many larger books in the Library. Somehow or other Carforth Crinkle managed to miniaturise the information contained in it, a bit like today's what I believe is called a microchip.

Neither Mr.Smithers or myself have ever tried to remove it, I personally am too afraid to try and definitely too afraid to open it up."

"That certainly goes for me too, I keep well clear of It." Added Smithers.

"Mind you." said the Head, "Mr.Smithers and myself have enough books already to go through, there's been that little time we haven't even started yet."

"Yes, there's all the replacement Containment Books in the Library's store cupboard that I haven't even glanced at yet." added Smithers.

I was looking at Miss. Millthrop who was looking down at the floor. Was she going to mention all of her Aunties books that she had? Apparently she wasn't.

I knew about them because she had asked me to help her unload her car discretely and take them up to her room where she had asked me not to mention them, and I hadn't.

Miss. Millthrop had not found the time either to read through any of them but had sorted everything into groups, she had given me four to look at as they appeared to be on joinery and D.I.Y.

There were still some questions I wanted answers to and decided to press on as the Head was in a talkative mood.

"So despite removing all those books Headmaster that were part of the 'Containment Book's' protection and removing what we all call the 'Compass Points of The World' which we decided are also there to help protect it, they left the actual 'Containment Book' behind. It couldn't have been because of the size of it so why leave it behind?"

"I can only assume Brian, that although they had been able to find out some of the secrets surrounding the protection they didn't know them all. On the other hand they may have tried to remove it and failed or been interrupted by David before sufficient books protecting it had been removed to allow an attempt to be made. Perhaps they knew they couldn't move it at that time and were content to discretely remove some of the protection, enough to enable its removal possibly during 'The Oriliance'. I can't really answer the question Brian, if I'm truthful this is all guess work."

"They still know more than we do." said Smithers. "Even with all the protection back in place for some reason they wanted Scorn and Cecilia inside the Library, what for? What were they going to do?"

"Whatever it was it needed two people, because I'm sure Scorn wouldn't have taken Cecilia with him if he could have done it on his own." added Miss. Millthrop.

"Yes I agree it must have required two people, but I've no idea why they should want to be there." said the Head.

"Another thing I can't understand Headmaster is why did all the other books in the Library turn against us? They should have been on our side."

"I think they were on the side of Crinkles, unfortunately Brian they thought you were the enemy."

"Me!! Why Me?"

"No! Not just you Brian, Mr.Smithers and Miss. Millthrop as well." replied the Head

"But why?" asked Millthrop.

"You and Mr.Smithers were stationed in the Library to protect it, but from what I wasn't sure. I just felt there would be some move against it and of course there was by Ian Scorn and Cecilia." The Head looked at us and continued.

"That move was defeated unfortunately in a very tragic way. However the Library's defence system had been activated, it somehow removed Cecilia's body or perhaps Ian Scorn did,

it certainly repaired the damaged ceiling, and I'm sure it thought you three also intended to harm or to remove the 'Containment Book'.

When it realised you were trying to keep the Containment protection books in position and not intent on removing them it backed off."

"You mean it could have done more?" gasped Miss. Millthrop.

"I think it could have done a lot more, all the other books in the library are prepared to sacrifice themselves totally to protect the 'Containment Book'. I wouldn't even try to think about what they might have done next."

Smithers, Miss. Millthrop and myself had all gone extremely pale. We looked at each other and I felt my knees shaking, we all realised now that we hadn't been fighting as we thought to save the 'Containment Book' but actually Fighting for our LIVES!

The Headmaster now went on to tell us something of the 'Oriliance' and Cecilia and Ian's crucial part in it. He finished by saying that he left it to each of us in our own way to judge Cecilia and Ian.

We had all been surprised that he kept referring to Scorn as Ian, but we thought perhaps it was a slip of the tongue until he said Ian would be hard to replace as the 'Team Quadro' Coach.

He mentioned that if it had not been for Ian, his enthusiasm and drive we would not have a 'Team Quadro' team, he also surprised us by saying that he was convinced that Ian felt the same about Cecilia as she did about him.

He also stressed yet again that it was Ian and Cecilia's help near the end of the 'Oriliance' that gave us the 'Final Victory', a Victory that would have been impossible without them. He said it went without saying that none of this must go beyond the four of us and these four walls and we all nodded our agreement.

It was at this point we had a very enjoyable meal. Cook had done us proud. After which Smithers told the Head about all the serious damage to the books in the Library, of course he would have preferred to have talked about the damaged Library books first and Cecilia and anything else second.

The Head told Smithers he would organise some reliable help the next day, and he pleased Smithers no end when he told him that he personally would come along and help for as long as Smithers thought he was needed.

As the Head said this he was glancing at Millthrop and myself, so we found ourselves a little reluctantly also offering our help.

I said I was sure I could carry out repairs to the bookshelves so that no nail holes would be seen, this pleased Smithers to such an extent that we actually saw a fleeting smile.

The Head mentioned he would like the School Concerts continued perhaps in the memory of Cecilia and that he had every confidence in Miss. Millthrops ability in that direction, in fact in any direction. This made Miss. Millthrop putty in his hands, she beamed and smiled and said she would love to have a go at a second School Concert, better you than me I thought.

"Now Brian," said the Head, "I'm relying on you to repair the fire damage and possibly improve the potting shed," and he told us he was thinking of a nice relaxing Conservatory, nothing too big but certainly not too small.

He paused for a while obviously deep in thought, then said,

"About 36 feet by 15 feet, perhaps you had better make enquiries about the price and so forth Brian. We'll also need cane furniture and lots of plants of course."

"I nearly forgot," he said, "I think we may have to replace some of the old windows, you could check that out at the same time."

I looked at the Head in amazement. We were skint. We were always skint always just one step ahead of the next bill.

"The drawing up of your requirements and getting quotations for comparison doesn't present any problems but do you realise how much all this could cost Headmaster?" I queried.

"A 36 feet by 15 feet conservatory is huge and replacing School windows wont come cheap."

The Head smiled at us, "Oh, I forgot to mention, apparently our funding is going up by a substantial amount, we are also going to receive quite a sizeable amount of money from supporters donations that have been flooding in after our 'Team Quadro' success. In fact I think there may be a Christmas bonus this year, we shall see."

We all sat absolutely dumb struck, unable to take it all in.

"I think it's time for a rather nice glass of Sherry." He added.

Drinking our Sherry we all sat quietly and rather strangely smiling at each other. Even Smithers I think was smiling, well he definitely had an expression on his face I had never seen before, so let's give him the benefit of the doubt and say it was a smile.

We were now drinking our second Sherry when Miss. Millthrop said:

"Headmaster, I feel so guilty at having pre judged Brian and falsely accusing him of so many things on so many occasions, and in front of so many people. That I would like to say here and now, I apologise Brian from the bottom of my heart, though I would understand fully if you refused my apology"

"Miss Millthrop I gladly except your apology, and in fairness to you, you didn't do anything that I wouldn't have done in your position, I do hope we will be good friends again"

"Oh Brian we certainly will."

To the Headmaster's, Smither's, and my embarrassment Millthrop put her arms around me and gave me a long kiss on the cheek, I went bright red and didn't know what to say.

The Head looked a little shocked and said, "I think I had better conjure up some tea for us all."

We then sat and chatted and joked for the rest of the evening, but now drinking tea. The Head told us that his secretary had been swamped by the number of applications to attend the School next year, so much so that some two dozen to date have been turned down as there was not a place left."

It seemed like years and years since the last time any of us had been able to relax worry free.

"Tomorrow," the Head said, "We could gather again and I could bore you with tales from America and the Conference it's entirely up to you."

We all happily accepted, we were bursting with curiosity having heard bits and pieces of stories that David and Jenny had been telling their friends.

The next day at the morning assembly the Head mentioned that Crinkles had gone through a very dramatic period but that was behind us now, and Crinkles was the stronger and the better for it.

The Head went on to say that Jenny, David, Miss. Millthrop, Mr. Smithers and last but certainly not least Brian had to have a special mention and that the School could not repay them for what they had done on its behalf.

He said that he was sure the School Staff and all the Pupils were looking forward to a very exciting future as he certainly was.

"However." he added. "I have to end on a very, very, sad note. No doubt you will all have noticed that Miss. Hudson and Mr. Scorn who I prefer to call Cecilia and Ian, as I'm sure you do also have not been at the School for the past few days.

I regret to tell you that they have left the School permanently. They will be a great miss to us all. I know they enjoyed their stay at Crinkles, and Crinkles have a lot to thank them for, but they always had intended to move on."

I looked at the assembled pupils and everyone looked surprised and very sad,

"Well." Said the Head. "You all have lessons to go to and we all have a busy day ahead. The assembly is dismissed."

The pupils started to file out and I overheard some of their conversations as they passed by.

"I wonder where they've gone?" a small boy murmured.

"I wish they'd told us they were leaving." said one pupil in a sad voice.

"We could have bought them farewell Gifts and Cards." said a group of girls.

"Do you think they left together?" asked another girl.

"Perhaps there going to get married." Suggested one of the girls, this caused a group of girls to start giggling.

Well I thought, it will certainly be many years before Cecilia and Scorn are forgotten at this School, I certainly will never forget them. 'EVER'.

The next Wizards Journal had full coverage of the 'Team Quadro' final and everyone had a copy, some pupils and Masters 2 or 3 copies and they were read from cover to cover time after time.

I had four copies, and had put three away safely as mementos for the future.

The Wizards Journal also covered the Convention, it covered all the minor matters in great detail and said it had been a remarkable and unforgettable experience for all those who had attended, but it didn't go into detail as to why it had been a 'Remarkable and Unforgettable Experience'. Everyone knew of course that it referred to the 'Oriliance' but the only mention of the 'Oriliance' was at the very end of the article which read:

An 'Oriliance' was held at the end of this year's Conference after an absence of many years, however this was a one off event and there is no intention of it being repeated next year or at any future Conferences.

Well this part of our story is almost over, we do hope you have enjoyed it. Don't forget the next time you pass a big old house that has become a School take a closer look, you never know do you? It may be Crinkles.

The School had started to settle down, a lot of the excitement had subsided and everyone was now looking forward to the start of the new 'Team Quadro' season.

Now here's a surprise, Smithers found he couldn't settle back down with his musty old books.

He still loved them, but no longer wanted to spend all his time with them, and if that wasn't a big enough surprise an even bigger one was to come. Smithers was to be the new 'Team Coach for Team Quadro. It didn't seem possible, but apparently he had been a brilliant 'Team Quadro' player in his younger days.

After a lot of effort Smithers had been able to work out the meaning of the inscriptions on the Compass Points of the World. This was to lead to incredible danger and amazing adventures that we would never have dreamt of, never mind actually take part in.

Adventures that would take us to the four corners of the World, to weird and wonderful places and yet none of the mysteries we would uncover in other places would be as important as those that we would eventually find here at old Crinkles.

They were mysteries that would appear in the future, here in the present there were still a lot of unsolved mysteries. Where is Ian Scorn? Is Cecilia actually dead?

Where did the Gold Compass Points of the World come from? Who made them and why? How did they end up at Crinkles? Are there Silver and Bronze Compass Points here as some people are suggesting and if so where? How much information is hidden away in Miss. Millthrops Aunts huge piles of papers and notes? Is her Aunt still alive?

Who were the other supporters of the Evil Wizards here at Crinkles? There must be at least two possibly four I reckon, and there still here either as pupils or Masters, perhaps both.

Was Smithers ever involved with them? I can't help it, I know it's unreasonable especially considering what we went through together but sometimes I still feel very uneasy about him.

Sometimes I rack my brain trying to find the impossible, to find some answers that will unravel some of the mysteries. I'm sure the Head knows more than he's prepared to say and often I've tried to get him to tell me more, but he either just smiles or pretends he hasn't heard me. Occasionally he holds out a little hope, saying we'll have to look into that one of these days Brian.

It was about three weeks after the Head had returned from America, it was nearly midnight and he was sitting at his desk in his study having a hot drink before going to bed.

It was a beautiful crystal clear star filled night and the Head had been looking out of his window at the Moon lit trees in the School grounds.

He loved his job, but it could be a very lonely one even though he was always surrounded by children and adults. He was the Head, and no one really relaxed when he was around they always felt they should be on their best behaviour.

He often sat alone in his study in the evenings chatting to himself. For some time now he would have a chat to the Brooms, he told them odds and ends about the School. He had told them about David and Jenny in America and about Merlin, the 'Oriliance' and King Arthur.

Of course Brooms even Magic ones don't talk, so it was always a one-sided conversation. Strange he thought, for years the 'Broom Cupboard' was never opened almost forgot about, and now it's opened every day.

He couldn't resist opening the draw in his desk that held the Broom Cupboard Key, taking the key out he then opened the study door and the familiar light escaped to freedom from his office and flowed down the corridor.

He followed it and stopping at the 'Broom Cupboard' unlocked the doors and opening them allowed the light from his study to fall on the Brooms.

"No news today I'm afraid just an ordinary sort of routine day." said the Head to the Brooms.

He ran his hand down each Broom in turn; number 1 Broom, number 2, number 3, number 4, his hand was resting on number 5, David's Broom. It was growing warmer it felt as though it was on fire, no matter how hard he tried he couldn't release his hand, his heart was thumping in his chest and he had broke out into a cold sweat. A thought occurred to him, perhaps the Broom would let him fly.

He hesitated for a few seconds then carefully unclipped the Broom and lifting it out, he closed the doors and locked the 'Broom Cupboard'. His hand no longer felt red hot as he carried the Broom along the passage, down the stairs and across the Entrance Hall, then quietly opened the front door and silently closed it behind him.

He crept out onto the front lawn and holding the Broom at 45 degrees he swung his right leg over the Broom and stood there.

His heart was beating even faster now, dare he, dare he, what if it didn't respond? Or then again what if it did? He had never been a flyer, never ever.

What have I got to lose he thought, there's no one about to see me. "Hover," he said in a quiet voice, and was thrilled when the Broom levelled to a horizontal position then slowly started to lift till it was about 5 feet off the ground.

"Please fly me over the Town and to the Sea, but not too high or too fast."

The Broom rose and flew off gently towards the Town. The Head was panicking and gripping the Broom with all his strength.

There had been someone about. David had awoken from a deep sleep with something telling him to go to the window. He got out of bed and yawning walked across to the window and looked down into the courtyard below. He smiled to himself as he watched the Headmaster starting to rise higher and higher off the ground and then flying off towards the Town, he turned away still smiling and went back to bed and was soon once more sound asleep.

The Broom was over the outskirts of the Town and bit by bit the Head had started to relax, he was starting to enjoy it, they were now flying over the Town Centre and he looked down at the rooftops, the trees, the roads, churches, shops and schools, then the Broom turned and off he went over fields, streams, rivers and hills until there was the Sea.

The Broom flew out over the Sea then turned gently back towards the beach then turned again and flew parallel with the beach over the gentle waves rolling in and shimmering like thousands of diamonds in the moonlight.

This WAS 'MAGIC', pure, pure, 'MAGIC'. The Broom turned again and flew back inland, back over the countryside. As it flew steadily over a large field the Broom started to slowly rotate through a full 360 degrees then a little further on did the same again. The Head felt like a 17 year old, what an incredible adventure, now the Broom was flying back over the Town and back to Crinkles.

When the Head landed David and everyone else at Crinkles were sound asleep. The Head quietly opened the front door crept in and closed it behind him. He paused, it was quiet and peaceful, slowly and silently with the Broom over his shoulder he made his way back to the Broom cupboard. He unlocked it, then gently wiped down the Broom with his handkerchief before he put it back in the cupboard swinging the retaining latches into place.

"Thank you." He said. "That's our little secret." The Headmaster paused, taking a long silent look at the Brooms. Then he slowly closed and locked the Broom Cupboard doors and retired to bed, a very, very, happy man.

The Rules of Team Quadro

It is played on a field just a little smaller than a football pitch. (See drawing).

The pitch is usually grass, but sometimes abroad it is sand.

At each corner on the outside of the pitch there is a pole 16 foot high and 12 inches in diameter. 90 yards apart on length and 70 yards on width.

The 4 corner posts are painted as follows, from their top to the bottom. Looking from above and going in a clockwise direction.

Bottom Right-hand Corner - RED.

Bottom Left-hand Corner - YELLOW.

Top Left-hand Corner - GREEN.

Top Right-Hand Corner - BLUE.

Each of the four teams are allocated one of the above colours by random selection supervised by the Overlooker.

At the top of each pole are 4 sets of 3 pegs. (see drawing)

The first peg on the North side is set 16 inches from the top of the pole, the second peg 16 inches centres from the first, and the third peg 16 inch centres from the second.

The South side is identical.

The East side's first peg is 32 inches from the top of the pole; the second peg is 16 inch centres from the first, and the third peg 16 inch centres from the second. The west side is identical (see drawing of Team Quadro post)

The 8ft from the last of the pegs to the ground is plain.

The 12 wooden pegs are 1 and a half inches in diameter set into the pole at an angle of 15 degrees (to stop the quoits falling

TEAM QUADRO PITCH

Flying Direction

BLUE

RED

70 CRS.

48 CRS.

90 CRS.

60 CRS.

Overlooker's
Game Start
Position.

7
DIA.
White Painted
Circle.

Poles

GREEN

YELLOW

White Painted
Flyers Starting Lines.

110 To Outer Edges of Pitch.

To Outer Edges of Pitch.

90

© E.G.DUNN.
2007.

TEAM QUADRO SCORE CARD

GAME	JUNIOR INTERNATIONAL TEAM QUADRO CHAMPIONSHIP - MILAN		

COUNTRY/TEAM	NAME	FLYING COLOUR
England. Crinkles Academy	David Taylor	Red

PERIOD NUMBER				QUARTER NUMBER			
~~1~~	~~2~~	~~3~~	4	~~1~~	~~2~~	3	~~4~~

QUOITS OFF	QUOITS ON	TIME	MINS	SECS	1/10 ths	
	✓			41	03	
	✓			38	05	
✓				37	08	
	✓			42	01	
✓				51	03	
	✓			43	07	
	✓			36	03	

SCORE MINUS	40	SCORE PLUS	50	FINAL SCORE	+10

FOULS	R=red MINOR	Y=yellow MAJOR	G=green SERIOUS	B=blue	COMMENTS
Accidental against	1Y.1G	1Y.			1Y. Major, no penalty given as red may have been part cause.
Deliberate against					
Accidental by player					
Deliberate by player					

GAME COMMENTS
Red's game shut down by other players. This was reflected in his score. Red flew well and did not retaliate. Maintained effort throughout.

RANKING OUT OF TEN	6+	DATE	March 22nd 2008

POLE WATCHERS SIGNATURE   *Graeme Armstrong*

off, although they can still be easily knocked off accidentally) and protrude for 8 inches.

There are 12 wooden quoits to a set. Each quoit is 12 inches outside diameter and 9 inches inside diameter by 1 inch thick and all quoits are painted their respective colours.

A second set of identical poles are set on the inside of the pitch 60 yards apart on length and 48 yards on width.

A Pole Watcher (equivalent to a lines man in football / part referee) is positioned approximately 8 to 10 feet above each pole and stays basically in that position throughout the whole game.

The Overlooker (equivalent to a referee in football) can fly anywhere above the game.

One player for each colour positions themselves on the starter line painted on the grass in white at the base of the poles. A painted arrow shows the direction the flyer must take.

The Outer Pole watcher signals to the Overlooker, player in position by raising his arm.

When the Overlooker has received all 4 signals, he blows his whistle to start the game.

The Flyer must start from the start line at the base of their pole and fly in the direction indicated by the arrow.

The Flyer completes two full outer circuits before taking a quoit off their outer pole. This can be any quoit there is no particular order in which they must be taken. The Flyer then heads for the inner pole of their colour, which is the start point for the inner circuits.

The Flyer must touch the inner pole before proceeding to fly the inner circuits, if they do not they must start again from their outer circuit pole.

The Flyer must complete 2 circuits of the inner poles flying in the reverse direction to the outer poles, before they try to place the quoit on one of the pegs on the inner pole. There is no special order in which the quoits have to be put on the pegs.

The game is played over four separate 'Periods', each of 20 minutes total playing time. There is a 5 minute interval between each 'Period'.

Each 20 minute 'Period' is split into 4 'Quarters', each of 5 minutes. There is a 2 minute interval between each 5 minute 'Quarter'.

Before the game starts and during the 2 minute interval between Quarters the Outer Poles are loaded with the respective coloured quoits one to each peg by the grounds men. The Inner Poles pegs having no quoits on them at the start of the game (but hopefully have of course at the end.)

There are 4 'Flyers' (players) to each team, 1 'Flyer' for each Period.

There are 4 substitute 'Flyers' per team, and can only play if the 'Flyer' they are a substitute for is injured.

A substitute 'Flyer' cannot be replaced if injured.

The Overlooker blows a whistle at the end of each Quarter and for full time at the end of each Period.

Any of the 8 Pole Watchers and the Overlooker can blow their whistles for a deliberate foul.

What is deemed as an accidental foul, the game is not stopped but the pole watcher records 10 penalty points on his chest board indicator against the person causing the foul.

Only one quoit is allowed per peg, (2 quoits on a peg is 20 points deducted from your score).

If a player in the unlikely event gets all 12 pegs on the inside pole before a 5 minute Quarter is over that Flyer's points total is doubled and they retire for the remainder of that Quarter.

If a second Flyer achieves this, they retire with 50% additional points.

Now this game is very dangerous because on the outer poles Red and Green fly anticlockwise and Blue and Yellow fly clockwise.

On the inner poles Red and Green fly clockwise and Blue and Yellow fly anticlockwise.

Flying in the wrong direction the penalty is 20 points deducted from your score and you also loose valuable time because you have to start again.

An Outside Pole Watcher watches only his Flyer on the outside circuit.

An Inside Pole Watcher watches only his Flyer on the inside circuit.

Any extra time due to injuries is played at the end of each quarter.

The points are added up for all Four Quarters, then all Four Periods are added together and the team with the most points is the winner.

Each quoit counts 10 points for your team when placed on the inner circuit pole. Any quoit dropped that reaches the ground when trying to put a quoit on the inner pole or any quoit accidentally knocked off a pole peg whether on the outer or inner pole 10 points are deducted.

A player accused of one accidental foul loses 10 points. A repeat foul loses 20 points. A third foul and the Flyer is sent off.

A Flyer accused of a deliberate foul is sent off and any points that the Flyer has gained so far are divided equally amongst the remaining teams, rounded up where necessary. For example: A Flyer sent off for a deliberate foul, and who had scored say 70 points. The points would be rounded up to the nearest number of points that can be divided by 3.

So a score of 70 points would be rounded up by 5 points to 75. 75 would then be divided by 3, so each remaining team would receive 25 points. The Flyer would also be suspended for 2 games.

Phew! What do you make of all that then? Better them than me.

TEAM QUADRO POST

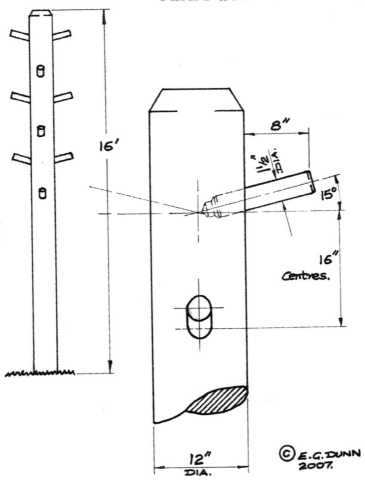

16'

8"

1½" DIA.

15°

16"
Centres.

12"
DIA.

© E.G. DUNN
2007.